SOME DIE NAMELESS

SOME DIE NAMELESS

WALLACE STROBY

MULHOLLAND
BOOKS

HODDER

First published in the United States in 2018 by Mulholland Books
An imprint of Little, Brown and Company
A division of Hachette Book Group, Inc

First published in Great Britain in 2018 by Mulholland Books
An imprint of Hodder & Stoughton
An Hachette UK company

1

A CIP catalogue record for this title is available from the British Library

Trade Paperback ISBN 978 1 473 66213 1
eBook ISBN 978 1 473 66214 8

Printed and bound by CPI Group (UK) Ltd, Croydon, CR0 4YY

Hodder & Stoughton policy is to use papers that are natural, renewable
and recyclable products and made from wood grown in sustainable forests.
The logging and manufacturing processes are expected to conform
to the environmental regulations of the country of origin.

Hodder & Stoughton Ltd
Carmelite House
50 Victoria Embankment
London EC4Y 0DZ

www.hodder.co.uk

Well is thy war begun;
Endure, be strong and strive;
But think not, O my son,
To save thy soul alive.

—A. E. Housman

For
Lt. Col. Frederick Mark Tinseth, USA, Ret.
1935–2012
and Sgt. Arnold John Tinseth II, USA

In memory of my brother
William R. Stroby
1949–2017
New Jersey Air National Guard
177th Fighter Wing

SOME DIE NAMELESS

ONE

———

THE STORM CAUGHT Devlin out on the Intracoastal just before dark. The rain was light at first, only pebbling the surface, then lashing down in staggered sheets that moved like ghosts across the water.

He steered the Pacemaker through growing swells toward the marina. Rain beat on the wheelhouse roof, coursed down the windscreen faster than the wipers could bat it away. It stopped as the boat passed beneath the Blue Heron Bridge, then picked up again harder on the other side. To the south, over the power station smokestacks of the Port of Palm Beach, lightning pulsed in the black sky.

As he neared the marina, he saw the lone figure waiting there on the dock, knew it was Bell. Devlin raised a hand to let him know he'd seen him, then eased back on the throttles. The starboard engine was running rough, out of synch with its mate. It had been fine at speed out on the salt, but now, as the rpms dropped, he could hear it starting to miss again. It would need another overhaul before long. But the Pacemaker was more than forty years old, and it was getting harder to find both spare parts and a mechanic who knew his way around the ancient Crusader engines.

He swung the boat around, reversed the engines, and began to back slowly toward his slip, looking over his shoulder as he steered.

Bell watched him come in. He wore an olive-drab field jacket, had pulled up the hood against the rain. Behind him, the pole lights on the dock were flickering into life.

Devlin's slip was at the far end of the dock. He lined up the stern, slowed the engines again, exhaust gurgling. He'd already hung the fenders off the gunwales, and now they bumped and scraped against the bulkhead on both sides as he entered the slip. He judged the distance and shut down the engines. The boat's momentum carried it in the rest of the way.

Bell got the nylon stern lines from the dock. Devlin went to the transom, caught them as they were tossed, looped them through the rear cleats, and pulled them tight.

"You're early," Devlin said. "I should have guessed."

"Permission to come aboard? Get out of this shit?"

"Granted."

Bell went out onto the short side dock. Devlin took an aluminum boat hook from the gunwale rack, used it to snag the line from the port bulkhead. He pulled on it to bring the boat closer to the dock.

A swell rocked the boat just as Bell stepped over the side. He leaped down easily, landed with knees slightly bent on the wet deck, no stumble. Still quick on his feet.

"Go on in, get below," Devlin said. "I need to secure the rest of these lines."

Bell ducked his head, went through the door and down into the low cabin. Devlin climbed out on the side of the boat with the hook, made his way forward in the rain, stepping carefully. He hooked the bowlines, made them fast to the cleats, then went back the way he'd come. Rain washed the deck, ran out through the scuppers.

He replaced the hook, went down the three steps into the cabin. Bell had already taken off his jacket, hung it from a peg on the wall below the pantry shelf, the boxes and cans there held in place with a bungee cord.

Devlin went forward into the bow, got two thick towels from the drawer below one of the bunks. He came back, tossed one to Bell, then dried his own face and hair. Bell did the same.

"You're a hard man to get ahold of, Sarge."

"Long time," Devlin said.

"It has been."

"You're looking good."

The last time he'd seen Bell had been at a private airstrip in Arizona, almost twenty years before. There were patches of gray in his hair now, but the arms and chest beneath the tight black T-shirt were still ridged with muscle. Devlin felt a pang of envy. They were the same age.

"I thought I had the right place," Bell said. "But I wasn't sure. I was expecting yachts. This is more like a floating trailer park."

"Surprised you found me."

"So am I. Seems like you didn't want to be."

Devlin took the damp towels back into the bow, hung them up. It was close and humid in the cabin. He'd worn a long-sleeved T-shirt against the sun. Now he was sweating under it.

He came back out, nodded at the dining nook with the hinged table. "Have a seat." He switched on the overhead light, then knelt by the low refrigerator, took out a bottle of Dos Equis, held it up.

"Hell, yeah," Bell said. "Come all this way."

Devlin took out a second bottle, closed the refrigerator door with his knee. He popped the caps with the aluminum opener that hung from a string on the pantry shelf. He set a bottle on the table, leaned back against the counter with his own. Rain drummed on the cabin roof.

Bell looked around. "Very retro, I dig it. This thing looks older than me."

"Close."

"How much it run you?"

"Paid five thousand in cash for it a couple years ago. A fisherman from Rhode Island was planning to scrap it. Spent another ten grand getting dry rot repaired, engines overhauled, scraping, painting. A hundred other things."

Bell rapped knuckles on the tabletop. "It's all wood?"

"All twenty-eight majestic feet of her."

"You live here? Like, all the time?"

"On the boat? Yeah. I move around a little. I'll probably take it up north again this summer. It's home, for now."

"You don't get claustrophobia? It was me, I could barely move in this bitch."

"It focuses you," Devlin said. "A place for everything, everything in its place."

"You must not have many things."

"I don't. Not anymore. But everything I need is here."

"Your hands."

"What about them?"

"You been doing some work."

Devlin looked at his palm, the calluses on the fingers, the scar where he'd cut himself on a rough piece of rebar.

"Construction," he said. "Here and there. Unskilled. I take what comes along."

"All cash, and under the table, I bet. You're staying off the grid. I admire that."

"Not well enough, apparently. You found me."

Devlin opened a counter drawer, took out the Bicycle playing card, an ace of hearts with Bell's cell number written in black ink at the bottom. He'd come home from a work site the day before, found it tucked into the hinge of the locked cabin door.

He tossed it on the table. "Good one."

"Knew you'd remember it. Figured if that didn't get you to call, nothing would."

"How'd you find me?"

"Still using your real name, so that was a start."

"Why wouldn't I be?"

"Lots of reasons I could think of. Anyway, I did a simple web search, Googled your ass. Found an address and phone number in New Jersey. Number's disconnected.

"I go there anyway, though, talk to your former neighbors in some sad-ass garden apartment complex. No one knows much about you, what you do, who you are, et cetera. But the manager tells me he thinks you keep a boat nearby. He sends me up the road to a marina, but you're not there either. Now what do I do?"

"Give up?"

"Nah. I keep pushing. But none of those white folks at that marina want to talk to me, even after I show them a badge, which, if you don't look too close, may imply I'm a licensed investigator. Still, doesn't get a brother anywhere. Jersey, man. It's full of angry white people."

A swell rolled the deck under their feet. Bell's bottle slid off the table. He caught it by the neck in midair.

"Finally I find an old man there with an eye patch, has a houseboat, used to know you."

"Reuben."

"Yeah, Reuben. Gives me a description of your boat, the name—the *Higher Tide*, whatever that means—and says he thinks you might be down in Florida, trying to beat the winter. At least that's what he heard. And all it cost me was twenty bucks."

"Florida's a big state."

"It is. But Reuben—who's my buddy now—says he's pretty sure you mentioned the East Coast, that you'd at least stop there before moving on. So I get a list of marinas in south Florida—I mean, it's gotta be south, right? No use going all that distance unless you're sure it's gonna be warm. That means south of Daytona, at least. More likely farther down."

"Makes sense."

7

"I get the numbers for those marinas—there's a lot of them—and I start cold-calling. After all, I have the name of the boat, the description. Can't be too many of those around, right? What's that name mean, anyway?"

"Nothing to me. That's what it was when I bought it. Bad luck to change a boat's name. What story did you use?"

"That I was an insurance adjuster settling a claim, trying to track you down. Had some money for you, but no fixed address or way to contact you."

"They really fall for that?"

"You'd be surprised. Hit it on the ninth call. Riviera Beach. Twenty-four hours later, here we are, drinking beer."

"Pretty slick."

"Tradecraft, baby."

"And what exactly is your trade these days?"

"Little of this, little of that. Personal security details, whatever comes along. Just like you."

"Not like me."

Devlin looked at Bell's hands. His wrists were thick, and the first two knuckles of his right hand were swollen and rounded, like stones beneath the skin.

"You getting enough work to make a living?"

"Trying," Bell said. "But it's not like the old days."

The rain had slowed. They heard the chug of a diesel engine going by on the Intracoastal. The boat moved in its wake.

"I don't mean to be rude," Devlin said. "But if you came here to play Remember When, I'm not sure I'm up for that."

"Say what you like about those days, we were pros. Doing a job and getting paid."

"Not enough."

"You ever hear from anybody from back then? How about Roarke?"

Devlin shook his head. "Not in a long time."

"He and I did a little work together after you retired," Bell said.

"A PSD in Qatar, a gig in Honduras, some other things. But I hear he's out of the game now too. You remember Villiers?"

"I think so."

"He went back to the Legion, did another five years. Don't know where he is now. Torbert caught a hot one in Sierra Leone. Diamond mine detail. He's buried over there."

"I heard. Aren't you getting a little old for this yourself?"

"Age and cunning, attitude and experience. They always win out. You interested in a proposition?"

"You can't be serious."

"I am."

"If that's the reason you came here, you wasted your trip."

"What's wrong?" Bell said. "You lose your mojo?"

"Not sure I ever had it."

"Yeah, you did. Maybe you can get it back."

"I don't think so. Not at this point."

Bell turned the bottle in his hands. "You don't even want to hear it?"

"You sure you want to tell it? Even knowing what my answer's going to be?"

"You and I, we have skills most people don't. There's not a lot of us around. Don't underestimate that, man. Celebrate it."

"I got all the celebrating out of my system years ago. Market's full of young guys, back from overseas, looking for work. I'm fifty-four. I'm done."

"Get back into it, you might feel different. We do what we're good at. You try to deny that, and what are you?"

Devlin smiled. So this was it, what it was all about, what he had suspected. And never a question what his answer would be.

"I appreciate the philosophy. And I'm flattered you came all the way down here to ask. But like I said, there's lots of young bucks looking for private gigs. And they're all quicker, smarter, and tougher than me."

"Finding a trigger puller is easy," Bell said. "Finding someone who knows when to pull it and when not, that's the difference."

"I wouldn't trust myself either way anymore. I wouldn't trust myself on much of anything. You still work for Kemper?"

Bell drank beer. "Sometimes. If the pay's right. Our arrangement isn't exclusive, though. You could say I'm more of a freelancer."

"He still in the same racket? After all this time?"

"Man, you're not up on current events, are you? You don't have a TV, radio? Read a newspaper?"

"Not often."

"You know about this thing called the internet?"

"I heard. I had a laptop once, but I sold it. Used to get online a little, but it didn't seem worth the time. Too much static, lots of people bitching at each other."

"You should hear yourself, Grandpa."

"I'll tell you what, though, just so you didn't make the trip for nothing. There's a decent seafood place up on U.S. One. I'll buy you dinner, a couple drinks. If you want, you can crash here tonight. Sleeps four in a pinch."

"You really going to leave it like that?" Bell said. He wasn't smiling. "Don't even want to hear what I have to say?"

"No, man, I don't."

"You might change your mind."

"I won't."

Bell raised his shoulders, let them fall. "What can I say?"

"Nothing." Devlin set his beer on the counter. "I have to hit the head, then we can go. You got a car here?"

"Rental. Up in the lot."

"Good. You can drive."

He pushed on the toilet stall door. It was hinged down the middle, opened inward. Inside, he shut the door, pulled the string for the light. He unzipped, urinated, and flushed, caught a glimpse of himself in the circular mirror he'd hung on the wall.

There was more gray in his hair now, no hiding it. Shadows under his eyes that never went away. And the weight he'd gained in the last year showed in his face. He touched the trail of small scars across his left temple, the bare patch in the brow there, thought again how lucky he'd been not to lose that eye.

He could hear Bell moving around out in the cabin.

"Hey," Devlin called. "How was Roarke last time you saw him?"

He pulled open the door, and a gun came through, the muzzle inches from his face.

He twisted away, slammed his shoulder into the door. The gun went off near his ear. The edge of the door caught Bell's wrist, pinned it against the frame. The gun—a small black automatic— jumped again, and the mirror exploded. A shell casing bounced off the wall and onto the floor.

Bell tried to pull his hand back. Devlin leaned his weight into the door, trapped it. He punched at the inside of the exposed wrist. Once, twice, driving it into the wall, aiming for the fragile carpal bones in the base of the hand.

Bell fired blindly. The round splintered trim from the wall, ricocheted past Devlin's head. He punched again, and this time Bell's hand opened. The gun fell to the floor. Devlin foot-swept it behind him, yanked open the door. Bell pulled away, his arm free, and Devlin stepped out, kicked him hard in the stomach.

Bell fell back, hit a vertical storage locker behind him, didn't go down. He bounced off it, used the momentum to bull forward, his hands already a blur. Devlin got his arms up to protect his face, took a shot to the lower ribs that stole his breath.

Bell crowded in with a flurry of movement, punching and kicking. Devlin tried to push him away, cover up, felt the first surge of panic. He took another blow to the ribs, swung and hit air, lost his balance. Bell roundhoused a knee into him, and Devlin went down hard onto the cabin floor, lights sparking at the edge of his vision.

He curled up to guard against another kick, but Bell stepped over him, pushed the stall door wider, looking for the gun. He bent to retrieve it, and Devlin saw his chance. He twisted on the floor, caught Bell's ankles from behind and pulled.

Bell's chin hit the rim of the toilet as he went down. He grunted, swiveled onto his back, pulled a leg free, and kicked. His heel hit Devlin's shoulder, knocked him back. Then they were grappling, the gun forgotten, Bell trying to pin him to the deck, straddle him, and finish it. Devlin slipped a punch, twisted his hips out from under Bell's weight, swung behind him, and locked an arm across his throat.

He had control now, knees on the floor, his center of gravity low, Bell in a sitting position in front of him. Bell drove an elbow back into his stomach, but it was too late; Devlin had the choke hold in place. He pulled tighter, forearm across Bell's throat, left palm behind his head, pushing it forward, cutting off the flow of blood and oxygen.

Bell reached back, clawed for his eyes. Devlin tucked his head in, tightened his grip, felt the struggles slow. Bell's hands pulled at Devlin's forearm weakly, then dropped away. Devlin held him another three seconds to make sure, then let go. Bell slumped to the floor.

Devlin tried to stand. He pushed Bell aside, stepped over him. There was a ringing in his right ear, and his face felt numb and swollen. At his feet, Bell began to gasp.

Devlin went into the stall. The gun was against the wall, behind the toilet. He picked it up. It was a Colt .25 with checkered plastic grips. Not much stopping power, but an easy kill at that range. He lowered the hammer.

Bell coughed. Devlin moved around him, a sour taste rising fast inside him. He lurched to the counter, vomited into the steel sink. He set the gun down, ran water, palmed some into his mouth, spit it out.

Bell was leaning back against the locker, watching him, chest rising and falling. Devlin showed him the gun, then sat on the top step. His ribs ached. Numbness before, pain now.

He ejected the magazine. Four rounds left, one in the chamber. He pushed it home again, rested the gun butt on his knee.

"I think this is the point," he said, "where we have a conversation."

TWO

———

THE RAIN HAD stopped. Low thunder sounded, but farther away now.

Bell rubbed the back of his neck. "You've still got some moves. Give you that." His voice was hoarse.

Devlin stood, pain in his sides, said, "Stay down." He went around behind Bell, put the muzzle of the gun against the base of his skull, patted him down with his free hand, looking for other weapons. He pulled a wallet from his back pocket, tossed it on the table. The rest of his pockets were empty. He backed away, went through Bell's jacket, came up with a pair of car keys on an electronic fob, a cellphone. He put them with the wallet.

Bell shifted on the floor. Devlin kept the gun on him.

"I guess I fucked that up," Bell said. "What happens now?"

"You tell me."

The cabin rocked as a boat went by. Bell's Dos Equis bottle had been knocked over in the struggle. It rolled across the floor, leaking foam. Devlin stopped it with his foot, picked it up, and set it in the sink. He sat back on the top step. "This isn't much gun."

"Figured it would do."

"Yeah, it probably would have. Five rounds left."

Bell grinned. "Even without the gun, I had you."

"You did."

"You want to put it down, try me again?"

"No, I don't think so."

"You gonna use it?"

"I don't know yet."

"I do. You're not. That's not how you roll."

"You sure of that?" Devlin said. "You think you know me?"

"Knew you well enough back in the day. And you know *me* well enough to know I ain't got shit to say to you."

"Maybe I should put a bullet in your leg, get the conversation started."

"Do what you feel. But there isn't gonna be a conversation."

Devlin stood. His cellphone was on the chart shelf to his left. Without looking away from Bell, he took it down, flipped it open.

"Sit there," he said. "Don't try to get up."

He backed up the steps and onto the deck. The slip on the port side was still empty. The boat that usually moored there had been gone all day. Beyond that, a cabin cruiser was buttoned up tight, no lights inside. TV noise came from a Chris-Craft four slips down. At the far end of the dock, the marina office was dark. Vapor lights illuminated the dozen or so cars and pickups in the parking lot.

The shots hadn't drawn anyone. In the confines of the cabin, they would have been little more than muffled cracks to anyone outside. It was why Bell had used a small caliber.

He went back below. If he called 911 now, the police would be there soon. He'd lose his chance to talk to Bell, try to find out why he'd come. He closed the phone, slipped it in his back pocket. Wind rocked the boat, sent a bolt of pain through his ribs.

"I didn't hear you make a call," Bell said.

"I didn't."

"What are you waiting for?"

Devlin pointed the gun at him.

"Not your style," Bell said.

"What's that?"

"Shoot an unarmed man."

"We did worse," Devlin said.

"That was then. This is a whole other situation."

"Is it? Why'd you come here?"

"Maybe I wanted to take you off. Steal your boat."

"If that were the case, all you had to do was ask. I'd have said, 'Take it.'"

He got the wallet from the table, opened it with his left hand. Inside were four fifty-dollar bills and a Georgia driver's license in Bell's name, with an Atlanta address.

"You're not gonna steal a brother's money, are you?"

He put the wallet back, picked up the phone. It was a cheap disposable. No contacts, and the only number in the call history was his. He tossed it back on the table.

"That proposition you mentioned. You were just trying to sound me out, right? See where my head was at?"

"I screwed up. I got nothing else to say. You gonna make that call?"

Devlin sat back on the step. "One thing's bothering me. We never had a beef between us. Any of us, even with all that happened. And if we did, it was a long time ago. So if you're not here for yourself, you're here for someone else. Who?"

Bell rotated his neck, winced. "Man, I think you cracked something."

"It's funny," Devlin said. "All the shit we went through together, the bad memories, I was still happy to hear from you, see you."

Bell was silent.

"You took your chances coming here too, a public place. Somebody might have seen you."

"A house would have been better, but we play the hand we're dealt, right?"

Devlin felt a sudden stab of anxiety. He thought about Karen and Brendan in Connecticut. He hadn't talked to either of them in months. Did Bell have that address? Had he been there as well?

"You shoot me right now, I wouldn't blame you," Bell said. "That's what you should do. What I'd do. But you won't, will you?"

"You want to find out?"

Bell got a leg under him, started to stand.

"Don't," Devlin said.

Bell rose, put a hand on the locker for support. "Four in the mag. One in the chamber, right? I come at you, you gonna be able to put me down before I reach you?"

"Don't do it, man. Please."

"Not much choice, is there? You think I'm going to sit here, wait for the police? Deal with that mess?"

"Don't."

Bell grinned, said, "No choice at all," and came at him.

Devlin tried to raise the gun, but suddenly there was no room between them. Bell caught his right wrist with both hands, twisted it outward, and head-butted him. It snapped Devlin's head back. Pain watered his eyes. Bell tried to pull the gun away from him, and Devlin's finger caught in the trigger. The gun cracked, and a starboard window shattered.

Devlin fell back against the steps, Bell pinning him there, the gun between them. He felt the hard muzzle against his stomach, Bell forcing the gun into him. *He's going to kill you,* Devlin thought. *Right here, right now.*

Bell's finger slipped over his on the trigger, tightened. He leaned into Devlin, his face inches away. Devlin tried to push the gun down and to the side. Their fingers tangled in the trigger guard.

The shot was muffled. Bell leaped back, bumped into the table. The gun clattered to the deck.

Devlin rolled off the steps, caught the edge of the sink, and pulled himself up, breathing hard. Bell stayed where he was. He had a hand over his stomach just above his belt.

Devlin watched him, waiting for Bell to come at him again. Bell took his hand away, looked at the blood on his palm, then at Devlin.

Devlin raised his fists, got ready. Bell walked past him, up the three steps and onto the deck. He stumbled to one side, then sat down on the port engine cover.

Devlin picked up the gun, followed him out. Bell had both hands pressed to his stomach now. His face was shiny with sweat, and the front of his pants was darkening with blood.

"Look at this shit," he said. Blood was coming through his fingers. He looked up at Devlin, as if for an explanation, a solution. He coughed and there were blood drops on his lips.

Devlin got the cell from his back pocket, fumbled with it. His fingers were slick with Bell's blood. He wiped a hand on his pants leg. It didn't help.

THREE

TWO HOURS LATER, Devlin sat in a hard plastic chair in a too-cold room with concrete walls. There was a copy machine in one corner, boxes of copy paper, an open metal supply cabinet. High on one wall was a dark-tinted plastic globe. He could see the camera lens inside.

The door opened, and a middle-aged black woman came in with a Styrofoam cup of coffee in one hand, a binder under her arm. Behind her was a big crew-cut man in a suit, talking on a cellphone. *Detectives*, Devlin thought.

The woman dropped the binder on the table with a thump. The man finished his call, put the phone in a jacket pocket.

They sat across from him. The woman gave him a frozen smile. The man looked at his watch, crossed his arms.

"I'm Lieutenant Landreth," she said. "Riviera Beach Police. This is Detective Byrne, Palm Beach County Sheriff's. He's assisting. Sorry to keep you waiting."

Devlin folded his hands on the table. They'd let him wash some of the blood off in the station men's room, but his nails were still outlined with it. His arms felt heavy, and it hurt to raise them.

"Crime Scene Unit's still at the boat," she said. "You'll need to find someplace else to stay tonight."

She opened the binder. "I have your statement about what happened between you and Aaron Bell. Anything you want to add to that?"

He shook his head.

"Let's go over it one more time, then, for the detective's benefit."

Byrne took a notebook and silver pen from an inside pocket.

Devlin told it again, the same story he'd given the responding officers. Most of it was true. Byrne took notes, Landreth only listened.

"Am I being charged?" Devlin said.

"With what?" she said.

"With anything."

She flipped through binder pages, didn't respond.

To Byrne, he said, "Have you heard anything from the hospital?"

"Bell's still in surgery. He took a round in the LLQ, just like you said."

"LLQ?"

"Lower left quadrant." Byrne touched his own stomach. "Here. Those were hollow-point rounds in that magazine. Even the smaller calibers do a lot of damage."

Bell hedging his bets, Devlin thought. *Hoping to end it quick.*

Landreth said, "So you have no idea why this Bell fellow shows up at your door, decides to take a couple shots at you?"

"No."

"He trying to rob you? You have anything valuable on board?"

"Not remotely."

"Maybe he thought you did," Byrne said. "Money. Or drugs."

Devlin looked at him. "Neither. And I'm sure you searched the boat, so you know there's nothing there."

"Could be something got tossed overboard," Byrne said. "There was time before the officers got there."

"You'll have a diver check that too, I'm sure."

"If we did, would they find anything?" Byrne said.

"No."

Byrne smiled. "Then why bother?"

"This is what doesn't click for me," she said. "You said you were in the Army with this man."

"I was."

"Then you don't see him for what, twenty years, and he shows up at your boat and tries to kill you? Doesn't give you a reason?"

"Did you question him?" Devlin said. "What did he say?"

"Not much of anything before he went into surgery," Byrne said. "He was awake and alert, but disinclined to talk to us."

Devlin felt a sudden wave of pain in his ribs, winced.

"You should go to St. Mary's, get checked out," Landreth said. "We'll have someone drive you over."

Devlin shook his head.

"Up to you," she said. "Anyway, ballistics report is preliminary, but it looks like it went the way you said. So that part checks out. We'll see what we find out about the gun."

"It wasn't mine."

"I didn't say it was. At the moment, it plays the way you told it. A struggle over the weapon, self-defense."

"More like an accident."

"Wouldn't matter either way," Byrne said. "Even if you pulled that trigger intentionally, you're immune under Florida law. Castle Doctrine. You were being assaulted in your own domicile. Self-defense or not, there's no grounds to charge you."

She cut a glance at Byrne. He met her eyes, shrugged.

"I'm free to go?" Devlin said.

"What bothers me"—she looked back at him, closed the binder—"is it feels like there's something missing from your story. So although

Detective Byrne is right in that you won't be charged—tonight, at least—this investigation isn't over."

"There's nothing missing."

She met his eyes.

Byrne's phone buzzed. He took it out, answered "Yeah," then "Hold on." He left the room.

"There's a rental car in the marina lot," she said. "Probably belongs to Bell. But we didn't find any keys on him or in your boat, just his wallet and cellphone. Any idea where they might have gone?"

"No."

"We have a call out to the rental company. They'll come and open it up for us. We'll take a look, see if we find anything tells us why he came down here."

"Sorry I can't help you more."

"So am I."

Byrne came back in, phone to his ear, said, "Thanks," and ended the call. He took his seat again.

"That was the hospital," he said. "Your friend didn't make it."

A uniformed officer drove him back to the marina. There were three police cruisers in the parking lot. Some of the other boats were lit up now, owners standing out on their decks, wondering what was going on.

The police had plugged in the boat's dockside power, turned on all the cabin lights. Two uniformed Riviera Beach officers stood on the deck with a crime scene tech, a camera around his neck. Pale blue latex gloves, inside out and stained with blood, lay where the EMTs had dropped them.

The uniform who'd driven him said, "He's here to get some personal stuff. Landreth says it's okay."

"He the owner?" the tech said.

"Yeah," the driver said. "They cut him loose."

"Go on," the tech said to Devlin. "Try not to touch anything you don't have to."

21

Devlin stepped aboard, went down into the cabin. The shell casings were still on the floor, each with a numbered yellow plastic triangle beside it. There were rust-colored spots on the deck. More blood.

The tech and one of the uniforms stood in the doorway and watched him. Behind them, the other uniforms were talking. One of them laughed.

Devlin opened the storage locker, pushed aside a pair of sun-faded orange life vests, took out an empty gym bag. He carried it into the bow, knelt, and opened the top drawer below the bunk there. He took out a pair of jeans and a T-shirt, put them in the bag.

Wind whistled through the broken window. The boat rocked gently.

"You almost done?" the tech said.

"Yeah," Devlin said. "Just a sec."

He closed the top drawer, pulled open the bottom one until it overextended and slipped off its rollers. He put three pairs of bundled socks in the bag, then shifted so his back was to the cabin door. Reaching into the space behind the drawer, he felt around until his fingers touched Bell's car keys. With his body as cover, he dropped them in the bag, then fit the drawer back into place, slid it home. He zipped up the bag and stood. "Ready."

The keys to his Ranchero hung on a peg by the sink. He got them down, went up the steps and onto the deck. The uniforms moved out of his way. The tech looked down at the bag, but no one stopped him.

He checked into a Days Inn on Blue Heron, just off I-95. In the room, he lay atop the covers, running it all through his head again. He saw the gun coming through the door, remembered the moment's pause before Bell squeezed the trigger. Long enough for Devlin to recognize the threat, react. The Bell he'd known back then wouldn't have hesitated. Was it reluctance? Or a last mercy? Bell giving him a second's advantage before the kill shot.

A tractor-trailer rolled by on the interstate, rattled his window. He'd try to reach Karen in the morning. He didn't know her new phone number. The only contact they'd had in the last year had been through her lawyer, the one she'd used for the divorce.

He closed his eyes, let sleep take him. When he woke, the luminous dial of his watch read 3 a.m.

He got both sets of keys and left the room.

He parked the Ranchero outside a shuttered swimsuit store, walked the last three blocks to the marina. The boat was dark now, but he could see police tape strung across the closed cabin door.

He moved out of the glow of the vapor lights, into the shadows alongside the empty marina office. The only sounds were the creak of lines and the scrape of bumpers, the hum of the soda machine nearby. He looked up at the security camera mounted under the eaves. The lens was cracked, and there was a bird's nest behind the mechanism. The camera probably hadn't worked in years. Bell would have seen that too, known there was no risk there.

He took out Bell's keys, thumbed the Unlock button. In one of the visitor's spots, a silver Buick flashed its parking lights.

He waited to see if the lights attracted anyone, then went to the car, used a handkerchief to open the driver's-side door. He knelt on the seat, opened the glove box. Inside was a rental contract in Bell's name with his Atlanta address. Nothing else.

He closed the glove box, went around and opened the trunk. Inside were a canvas overnight bag and a brown leather briefcase. He unzipped the bag, saw neatly folded clothes. Beneath them were a Browning 9-millimeter automatic and a carton of shells. A lot more gun than the .25, but too loud to use on the boat.

The briefcase was locked. No time to fool with it here. He took it out, used the handkerchief to shut the trunk.

He wiped down everything he'd touched, locked the car again. Walking back to the street, he slung the keys out into the water, heard them splash.

*   *   *

At the motel, he put the night latch on the door, set the briefcase on the table. Combination locks, but the latches were thin metal. He pried them open with a pocketknife.

Inside were a small spiral notebook, a leather billfold, a U.S. passport, and another cellphone, still in its packaging. The passport had Bell's photo, but the name Eldon Daniels, this time with a Wilmington, Delaware, address. It had been issued only six months before. There were no stamps on the pages.

Fixed inside the billfold was a gold badge lettered SPECIAL INVESTIGATOR. Under a flap were a half-dozen embossed business cards with the Daniels name and CORE-TECH SECURITY below it, with a logo of crossed arrows and a lightning bolt. No phone number or address.

The front pages of the notebook had been ripped out, shreds of paper still clinging to the spiral. The first intact page was filled with small, neat handwriting. A series of phone numbers and addresses, all his at one point, all struck through. Bell on his trail. At the bottom of the page, the marina address and the name of his boat.

On the second page, two street addresses, with no town listed. A single phone number, with a 215 area code. The rest of the book was blank.

He opened the passport again, looked at the photo, the face of a friend. *He came to kill you,* Devlin thought. *Don't forget that. If it had gone a different way, you'd be on a slab—or in the ocean—and Bell would be headed back to Atlanta or Wilmington or wherever, in his rental car, job done.*

He'd keep the contents, toss the briefcase into the Dumpster behind the motel. He wondered if he should have taken the Browning and the shells, against whatever else might be coming.

He thought of the boat, strung with crime scene tape. It had been his world. It wouldn't be the same now. Bell had taken that from him. He would never feel safe there again.

FOUR

HERE WAS A Philly PD car blocking the street when Tracy arrived, parked at an angle across the cobblestones. She'd heard the call go out over her mobile scanner—a 5292 on Bainbridge. She'd punched the address into her GPS, turned the Toyota around in the middle of the street.

Beyond the cruiser was a crime scene van and a detective's car she knew belonged to Dwight Malloy. This part of the block was brick rowhouses, most already gutted, some with plywood over the windows. Halfway up the street, the door to one of the rowhouses was open. Above it, a banner read ON THIS SITE: CONDOS STARTING AT $200,000, with a phone number below it.

A uniformed cop she didn't recognize was standing out on the stoop, smoking a cigarette. Crime scene tape had been stretched between two light poles and a drainpipe, blocking off the entrance.

She parked on the other side of the street, put on the lanyard with her *Observer* ID, then took a reporter's notebook and pen from the glove box. She got out, crossed the cobblestones, tucked the notebook into her back pocket.

The uniform was in short sleeves despite the morning chill and had thick, tatted-up arms. When she got closer, she turned the ID around so her picture faced outward.

"Is Detective Malloy here?" she said.

He gave her the once-over, said, "He's busy right now."

"You're new in the district, aren't you? I'm Tracy Quinn? From the *Observer*? I cover Philly PD."

He flicked the cigarette butt away, shrugged. "Can't help you."

She saw a camera flash in an uncovered second-floor window. Techs documenting the scene.

"Just tell Dwight I'm here, will you?"

"Dwight?"

Another uniform came out onto the stoop, a patrolman named Sallas. He saw her. "Hey, Trace."

"Sally, how's it going? What've you got?"

The tattooed cop said, "She's a reporter."

"No kidding."

"Is Dwight in there?" she said. "I thought I recognized his car."

"Someone call you?" Sallas said.

"Heard it on the scanner. Wasn't far away, figured I'd fall by, see what was up."

"Should have figured," he said. "Hold on, let me see what he wants."

He went back inside. The other cop stayed in front of her, the tape between them, as if worried she'd try to get by him.

Dwight came out onto the stoop. He looked tired. She lifted her chin at him.

To the tattooed cop, he said, "It's okay, Swede. I know her."

"She's a reporter."

"I know. Let her through."

Swede shrugged. "You say so." He lifted the tape. She ducked beneath.

"That was quick," Dwight said to her. "What do you do, just drive around the city all day, looking for a story?"

"That's me. Total dedication to the job."

"Might as well come in, then. It's not pretty, though."

She followed him inside. On one side of the narrow foyer, sagging stairs led up. The smell hit her almost immediately, a mix of rotten fruit and ashes. She'd smelled it before.

"Watch your step," he said.

They went up, the stairs creaking beneath them. The second floor was an open space with exposed brick walls. There were chunks missing from the plaster ceiling, white dust on the floor.

The smell was overpowering here. On the far side of the room, beneath a grimy window, lay what looked like a bundle of clothes. Two uniformed crime scene techs stood around it, one holding a heavy camera. It was Al Donovan. He'd been a photographer at the *Observer*, had taken a buyout two years before and gone to work for the city.

"Hey, Tracy," he said. "Ear to the ground, as always."

"Hi, Al. How have you been?"

He shrugged. "Why kick? No one cares."

To Dwight, she said, "How long's it been there?"

"Hard to say. It's pretty far gone. Rats have been at it."

"Hazard a guess?"

"I'll let the ME's office do that. We're off the record now, right? Only reason I'm letting you up here."

She moved closer to the body. Donovan said, "Watch where you stand."

It was a man, as far as she could tell. But the body had tightened into a fetal position, and all the skin she saw was black. The face was swollen, deformed. The jeans he wore were dark and stained, but she could see the North Face logo on the quilted jacket. Where the tail rose up in back, she saw the butt of a pistol.

"Not a gang thing," she said. "Or they would have taken the gun. Probably the jacket too."

"Good guess," Donovan said. "I always said you thought like a cop."

She moved around the body for another angle. "What is he?"

"Hispanic male is my best guess at the moment."

"Wounds?"

"None obvious, but we haven't turned him yet. You can see what we're dealing with. Lots of organic matter on the floor. It was dripping down into the room below."

"Who found him?"

"Construction crew," Dwight said. "There's a courtyard in back. Plywood was torn off the rear door. Likely how he got in."

"Was he shooting up? Any works with him?"

"None we could find."

"Lousy place to die," she said.

"It is."

"ID?"

"Looks like there's a wallet in his back pocket. We'll have a look when we turn him. ME will print him, and we'll try to get a rough Identikit sketch. You can run it online. Maybe somebody recognizes him."

"Worth a try," she said.

"Seen enough? Let's get some fresh air."

He led her back downstairs and out onto the stoop. Swede had another cigarette going. Sallas was in the cruiser, typing on the console-mounted laptop.

Dwight held the tape up, and they went under. He looked at her car. "That thing's still running?"

"So far."

He peeled off his latex gloves, and she saw he was wearing his wedding ring again. He'd gone back to her after all.

They walked toward the car, Swede watching them from the stoop. It seemed colder now.

"How are things at the paper?" Dwight said.

"Same old. Everyone's nervous, waiting for the next shoe to drop."

28

"I heard."

"Too much work, too few people. I'm staying busy."

"You never had a problem doing that," he said. "How's everything otherwise? Seeing anyone?"

She looked at him. "I need to call this in, Dwight. Let me know if you get an ID. If the techs do a sketch, e-mail it to me, and I'll see about getting it in the paper and on the site."

"I will, thanks. I was thinking, maybe we can grab a drink one of these nights, talk about some things. I still don't like the way we left it."

"I don't think that's a good idea." She took her cellphone from her belt. "I need to make that call now."

"You haven't changed much, have you?"

"Neither have you," she said.

FIVE

——

BACK AT THE office there was a Post-it note on her desk blotter that read "See me," with an *H* under it. Across the aisle, Alysha Bennett turned away from her computer and said, "He was looking for you."

"I see. Any idea why?"

"Didn't say. Not that he'd tell me anyway."

"What are the chances it's something good?"

"Slim to none," Alysha said. "News desk told me you called in a decomp. Get anything more?"

"No. Still waiting on ID and cause. Male Hispanic is all they've got so far."

"Another O.D.?"

"Who knows?"

"Any idea how long he'd been there?"

"From the smell, a while. I'll check with Rick, see if he wants me to write a short for Metro."

She tossed her notebook on her desk, walked back to Harris's office along the corridor that once housed the art department. There were empty spaces where cubicles had been dismantled, desks removed. Loose cables coming out of the floor, connected to nothing, were the only reminders of the people who'd worked there.

Harris was typing on his computer, his back to the door, when she went in. A set of golf clubs was propped in a corner.

"You wanted to see me, R.J.?"

"Yes, Tracy. A minute. Let me send this."

She took one of the chairs across from his desk. Through the window, she could see the spires of City Hall in the distance. Above them, a ghost moon hung in the afternoon sky. She thought of the views from other newsrooms she'd worked in. Newark, Raleigh. Raleigh had trees, at least, restaurants nearby. Newark had been a fortress, armed guards and a razor-wire fence around the parking lot. A downtown choked with traffic until 5 p.m., then deserted until the next morning's rush hour.

He hit a final key, turned to her. His smile showed perfect teeth. Like many women in the office, she'd found him vaguely attractive when he'd first arrived at the paper, taken over as AME of Enterprise. But that had worn off long ago.

"I've been meaning to talk to you." He got up, shut the door.

She felt the first bloom of dread. Was this it? Her seven years here ended with a Post-it note as her only warning?

She shifted in her chair. "Sorry I missed you earlier. Just got back from a crime scene. Body in a rowhouse they're renovating down on Bainbridge. I was going to tell Metro."

He sat back down, steepled his fingers. "That can wait."

Her uneasiness grew.

"These are tough times, as you know," he said. "And we have to think about the best way to utilize our resources. You agree?"

"Of course."

"And the only way we really have of gauging customer response

31

is the amount of unique hits we get online. Ultimately, that comes down to each individual writer and his or her story count."

"Readers," she said.

"What?"

"You call them 'customers,' but they're still just readers, right? They still come to us to know what's going on."

"True, but we can't ignore the realities of the situation. As you know, performance evaluations are coming up next month. These days a big part of those are story count and reader engagement. That's how we tell if we're serving our community."

Here it comes, she thought.

"Irv has asked all the AMEs to audit their staff's productivity, so we can identify any problems. We want everyone to be on the same page, going forward. And we want everyone to know what's expected of them."

"I do," she said.

He leaned back in his chair. "I'll be honest, Tracy. Your story count over the last quarter isn't where it should be, where it needs to be. And the hits... they're not exactly setting the web on fire either."

"You're talking strictly online, where all we're doing is chasing clicks. You're not counting the people who buy a physical paper every day."

"I've seen those numbers too," he said. "And they're getting smaller as we speak, subscription and single copy both. That demographic's dying off."

"I usually produce at least three stories and one enterprise a week, unless I'm working on a project that—"

He held up a hand to stop her. "I'm not here to micromanage."

"Isn't that what you're doing?"

His smile faded.

"My job—*our* job—is to consider how to best serve our readership," he said. "Whether it's online or in the paper. You're a good police reporter, Tracy. But I wonder if that's the best use of your time. I think we need to question whether we should be bothering with every North Philly shooting or drug arrest that comes down the pike."

"We let those stories go, the *Inquirer* will pick up every reader we lose."

"We don't work for the *Inquirer*," he said. "We work for the *Observer*. And the *Observer*'s goals are what I care about."

"Sometimes I wonder what those goals are."

"Right now? To stay in business. We sell ads based on hits and market share. Without those, it's not a question of what we should be covering, because we won't be covering anything at all."

"The paper's still profitable. I've seen the quarterlies." *Shut up,* she thought. *You're only making it worse.*

"This isn't a debate, Tracy. Think of it as a reminder, an encouragement."

"Consider me encouraged."

He frowned. "There's only so many ways to say this. You need to pick up the pace. I can't afford to have you sitting in court or chasing down stories all week that nobody cares about, with nothing else getting done. I'd also like to see you in the office more, so I have a better sense of what you're working on."

"We miss a lot when we don't staff the courthouse."

"That's what press releases are for. And the police are still sending us their reports, right?"

"When we ask for them. But we have to know they exist first. And the reports only tell us what they want us to know. It's what we do with them that's important, the follow-up, talking to sources. That's where the stories are."

He sat back, crossed his arms. "I'm not unaware of how a newspaper functions."

You went too far this time, she thought. She remembered what her therapist had told her at one of their first sessions. When you're upset, count to ten before you open your mouth. Especially if you're not sure what's going to come out.

She chewed the inside of her cheek. Seven. Then leaned forward, elbows on her knees. Eight. Nine.

Ten. She let out her breath. "There's always a story behind the story, R.J. And that takes time to find. Especially if someone doesn't want us to find it."

"You're forgetting I was a reporter once too," he said. "Hard as that may be for you to believe. When I was in Dallas—"

"This isn't Dallas. With all due respect, R.J., I know this city. I know how it works. I—"

The smile came back. "Are we going to play the townie card again? That's getting a little old, isn't it? My one-year anniversary is next month. The sky hasn't fallen, has it? We're all still here."

"There are a lot fewer of us."

"That's everywhere, not just at the *Observer*," he said. "We're still doing our best, fighting the good fight. There are people here doing outstanding work. Our talent pool's as deep as it's ever been."

She felt the anger coming. *Do not engage.*

"About this John Doe," she said.

"If you want, make a call on it later, see if they have an ID or cause. No need to write it."

"I was going to run it by Rick."

"You just ran it by me," he said. "I'm your supervisor. No reason to involve anyone else."

"I just thought he might—"

"Forget it. In the meantime, Ted Bryson's got a lot on his plate over the next few days. I'd like you to touch base with him, see if you can help."

She felt heat coming to her face. "What do you mean, 'help'?"

"Check in with him, see what he's got. He's following the State House renovation, and the president's coming to town again next week, so we'll need at least two advances on that. I was thinking you could live-tweet his visit and speech. That'll help increase your profile online. You can coordinate all this with Ted. I'm sure he'll value your experience."

"He's only been here three months. And I've been in this business ten years longer than he has."

"There are other criteria besides longevity," he said. "Ted was one of my key people in Dallas. I was happy to finally bring him on board here. I know he'll do great things."

"In the meantime, we're laying off people who've worked here for years. With institutional knowledge we'll never get back."

"Even more reason why we all need to be team players these days. There's no room for prima donnas."

"I've never considered myself a prima donna," she said. "I've done my job and I've worked hard."

"No one's saying you didn't. And don't think I'm not aware of your skills. Everyone knows you're good at working a source. And you did a great job with that story on the vets and their unemployment checks. We got a significant number of hits on that."

"Pension."

"What?"

"Pension checks. Not unemployment."

"You know what I mean."

"If you value my work, why are you treating me like this?"

Don't cry, she thought. *Don't let the bastard see it.*

"These things are never personal, Tracy. You should know that by now. I hate to say this, but if you don't agree with our direction, then maybe you need to reevaluate your role at this company."

There it is, she thought. *Out on the table. No veil, just threat.*

He picked up a pen, tapped it on the open planner in front of him.

"Are we done?' she said.

He set the pen down. His expression softened, a peace offering.

"Tracy, we all know reporters are territorial. It's their nature. But there's no room for turfs here anymore. We pitch in where we're needed. Understood?"

"Understood." She got up, felt unsteady on her feet.

"Ted's out today," he said. "He'll be back tomorrow. See what he needs, all right?"

He picked up his desk phone. When she was at the door, he covered the receiver with a hand, said, "And Tracy?"

She stopped, turned back to him.

"I know you may not have liked what you heard, but I'm glad we got the chance to talk. My door's always open. And story for story, you've been doing excellent work lately. I mean that."

"I live to serve," she said.

Back at her desk, she booted up her computer, scrolled through emails, deleting them as she went. Press releases, sunglasses ads that had gotten through the spam filter, a newsroom-wide message for a retirement party for someone in Sports she'd never met.

Only two emails were from readers. The first wanted an update on a story she'd written last month, about a strip-mall doctor charged with selling bogus cancer drugs made in Pakistan and smuggled into the U.S. She'd developed the story based on a tip, had gotten Health and Human Services—and eventually the FBI—involved. She'd have to make some calls, see if there had been any movement in the case.

The second email was a complaint—in all caps—that the daily horoscope hadn't run in that morning's paper.

The doctor story followed a series she'd done about veterans at a run-down residential hotel on Roosevelt Boulevard being scammed out of their checks. The two stories had kept her blissfully busy for a solid three-month stretch, working on her own, staying out of the office as much as possible, talking to sources, doing interviews. It was the happiest she'd been in years. She'd thought two strong enterprise stories back to back would earn her some breathing room with Harris, but they hadn't.

Calm down, she thought. *It's not worth getting upset. Things are what they are. Deal with it.*

When she pulled out of the lot, the Toyota's check-engine light went on. Something else. The Corolla was twelve years old and pushing 160,000 miles. But with things as they were at the paper, she couldn't risk taking out a loan for a new car.

As she drove, she heard the muffler rattle, louder than it had been that morning. Something loose under there, and getting worse. When she'd been with Brian, he'd taken care of their cars, done most of the work himself. Another thing she missed.

She beat the worst of the city traffic on the way home. The forty-mile drive to New Hope was a longer commute than she'd wanted, but it was a different world out here, farms and woods and pastures. It felt far away from the city.

She'd rented a one-bedroom fieldstone carriage house on the property of a larger estate, surrounded by woods. The three-story main house had been divided into bed-and-breakfast rooms, and there were weddings on the great lawn almost every weekend. On warm nights she'd sleep with the windows open, listening to the wind in the trees, the gurgle of the creek that ran across the front of the property.

She'd stopped at a farm market on the way, bought things for a salad, knew she wouldn't have an appetite for anything else. In the kitchen, she set the bags on the counter, dropped her cell and the lanyard with her *Observer* ID into the wicker basket there.

The smell from the rowhouse was still on her. *It's your imagination*, she thought. *Scent memory. But a shower wouldn't hurt.*

As soon as she hit the couch, she felt her energy vanish. She booted up her MacBook on the coffee table, checked her LinkedIn account. No new contacts or invitations. Scrolling through her Connections, she saw the names and profiles of others she'd worked with at the *Observer*, all laid off from the paper over the last two years, most still looking for jobs.

It had seemed like a weekly event for a while, watching people clean out their desks and carry boxes down the hall to the elevator. Those who were laid off had their computer profiles wiped and their phone extensions disconnected even before they got the news.

She clicked over to her private email box. Nothing new. At the bottom of the list were the emails she'd saved from Brian. The last ones.

She didn't blame him. There'd been too many nights and weekends apart, random and unpredictable hours that made no sense to anyone outside the business. The truth was she'd made her choice.

Powering down the laptop, she looked at her reflection in the dark screen. *Maybe it's time to finally get serious about going back to school*, she thought. *You're thirty-six. It's not too late. Or maybe it is.*

She forced herself to get up and into the bathroom. She showered, changed into jeans and sweatshirt. In the kitchen, she chopped vegetables for the salad, lost interest halfway through. She wasn't hungry after all.

She put everything in the refrigerator, opened a bottle of wine and poured a glass, took it back to the couch.

Something will come along, she thought. *Something's out there right now, waiting to happen. What was the saying? "Whatever it is you're seeking is also seeking you."*

It's on its way, even if you can't see it yet. You have to believe that. If you don't, you're done.

She found the remote under a seat cushion, turned on the TV. She drank wine, flipped through channels, couldn't concentrate. The plan for tonight: Drink the rest of the bottle. Order a pizza if you get hungry. Call in sick tomorrow, watch Netflix all day, work on your résumé. Fight the urge to call Harris and quit.

Her glass was empty. The kitchen seemed far away. For the first time in months, she wanted a cigarette.

SIX

———

WHEN THE TWO Russians came into the room, Lukas turned away from the open window and said, "You're late."

Penskoff shrugged. He wore a topcoat over a suit, had his hands in his coat pockets. Lukas assumed he was armed. The bodyguard, whom Lukas didn't know, stood behind him. He'd dressed the part—silk shirt open at the neck, leather jacket, sunglasses at night.

Tariq closed the door behind them, locked it. The bodyguard looked at him, then back at Lukas, who gestured to the battered table in the center of the room, the chairs around it.

"Finally," Penskoff said. "We do our business face-to-face. Like men."

Lukas looked back out the window. It was raining lightly, the street three floors below slick with it. They were in an old hotel in Budapest's Eighth District, far from the golden spires of the city center. Ten p.m. and the street was empty except for a gray Mercedes parked at the curb, Penskoff's driver at the wheel.

He pulled the shutters closed. He'd paid the old man at the front desk fifty dollars U.S. for the use of the suite for the evening, and no questions had been asked. It was a high-ceilinged room with a small bedroom and bathroom. Random pieces of furniture, paper peeling from the walls, water stains on the ceiling.

"You have my money?" Penskoff said.

"Cash this time, as requested." Lukas took the black canvas sports bag out from under a chair, set it on the table. He was jet-lagged and impatient. Wanted to get this done.

The bodyguard drew an automatic from a shoulder holster, went into the bedroom. Lukas looked at Tariq, who shrugged. They heard the bathroom door open, the bodyguard checking inside. He came back out, nodded at Penskoff, slid the gun back in its holster. Lukas saw it was one of the cheap Makarov knockoffs that were flooding Eastern Europe.

"We finished with the drama now, the guns?" Lukas said. "Can we sit, talk like adults?"

"*Ja zdes' radi deneg,*" Penskoff said.

"Let's speak English, Yuri," Lukas said. "Better for everybody, so there's no misunderstanding."

"You turn your back on your mother tongue?"

"My mother was born in Odessa, it's true. But my father lived in Knin his whole life, short as it was. I grew up in Virginia, went to college in Texas. So, please, no more about the motherland."

"Knin? Then he was a Serb. And so are you."

"I was once," Lukas said. "Now I'm an American."

He pulled out a chair, sat. Penskoff took one opposite. His bodyguard stood behind him. Tariq stayed at the door.

Penskoff looked back at him. "And your friend there who doesn't speak. He is also from—where you say?—Texas?"

"Tariq's a man of few words. He keeps his own counsel."

"An Arab."

"Let's stay on topic," Lukas said. He was already tired of this room, this man, his smell of stale cigarette smoke and heavy cologne.

Penskoff dug into an overcoat pocket, came out with a pack of Sobranies. "There was a time when your boss would have been here himself."

"I speak for him, Yuri. You know that. That's why he sent me. To do business, not discuss ancient history."

"He is an important man now, that I understand. He sits down with the oilmen, the politicians. He's too important to meet with an old friend."

Penskoff took out a cigarette, put the pack away. The bodyguard leaned forward with a gold lighter. Penskoff bent to the flame, puffed. The acrid smell of the tobacco filled the air.

"There's no disrespect intended, Yuri," Lukas said. "But you'll believe what you want, I guess. So let's get to it."

He pulled the bag closer, unzipped it. The bodyguard's hand went into his jacket again. Lukas looked at him, took out the thick manila envelope, set it on the table. The bodyguard let his hand drop.

Lukas said, *"Ty russkiy?"*

The bodyguard hesitated, then nodded.

"Ne pugaytes," Lukas said. "Take it easy." Tariq still watched from the door.

Penskoff looked at the envelope. "How much?"

"Open it and see."

"How much?"

"The balance. Fifty thousand."

"One hundred. That is what was agreed. What was owed."

"Those AKMs had Chinese markings, Yuri. They were supposed to be Romanian, from the Sadu plant. *That* is what was agreed."

"Yebat. What is the difference?"

"If we'd wanted AKs from China, we'd have bought them from the Chinese, at a better price. But we wanted Romanian. We *paid* for Romanian."

"You accepted the shipment. You sold it already, I am sure. You made your profit—"

"That has nothing to do with our deal."

"—and now you want to go against what was agreed."

"Fifty thousand is good money for what we're talking about," Lukas said. "I think it's fair."

Penskoff's face grew red. "*Ublyudok.*" Bastard.

Lukas looked at Tariq, then back at Penskoff. "I'll ignore that. But it brings me to the next issue. We're out of this business now. No more buying, no more shipments. This is the last time we'll meet. So take your money and go."

Lukas slid the envelope across the table toward him. Penskoff looked at him, didn't touch it. Lukas could see the anger there now, the older man trying to decide how to respond.

Lukas turned to the bodyguard. "You speak English?"

The bodyguard looked at Penskoff, who ignored him, then back at Lukas. "A little."

"What's your name?"

Penskoff put a hand atop the envelope, pushed it hard across the table. It slid off the edge and into Lukas's lap. Penskoff flicked his half-smoked cigarette onto the floor, sank his right hand deep in his overcoat pocket.

Lukas set the envelope back on the table. "All right. If that's the way it is. You don't want it, don't take it."

"He wants to fuck me? Tell him he can go fuck himself, and his errand boy too."

Lukas exhaled, sat back. "Tariq."

When the Russians turned to look behind them, Lukas took the Walther from the open bag, the suppressor already threaded into the muzzle.

The bodyguard's hand moved. Lukas shook his head, his finger on the trigger. Tariq stepped away from the door, out of the line of fire.

Penskoff looked at the Walther. "You are foolish. You are making a foolish mistake."

"I've made them before."

"There is a man downstairs, with the car. When he doesn't hear from us—"

"He's already dead," Lukas said. "I knew you wouldn't take the deal."

Penskoff looked at him for a long count. Lukas could hear his breathing. Then, slowly, he took his right hand from his pocket. It was empty. He leaned forward, reached for the envelope.

"No," Lukas said. "Negotiation's over."

Penskoff looked at the gun, drew his hand back.

To the bodyguard, Lukas said, "I'll ask you again, what's your name?"

The bodyguard looked at the gun, knowing there was no way he could reach his own in time. "Sergei."

"Okay, Sergei," Lukas said. "I want you to watch this, what's going to happen. Don't move. Don't do anything, just watch."

The piano wire caught the light. It looped around Penskoff's throat, drew tight. He tried to get his fingers under it, too late, and Tariq pulled back hard on the garrote's wooden handles.

Penskoff clawed at the wire, kicked out. His shoe thudded into the underside of the table, and the chair went over backwards. Tariq rode him down, crouching behind him, twisting the handles in opposite directions.

Sergei didn't move. Lukas kept the Walther on him.

Penskoff's heels scuffed the bare floor. His mouth opened, but no sound came out. The wire had vanished into the loose skin of his neck. His face purpled, tongue pushing out through swollen lips, eyes wide. His right heel beat a pattern on the floor.

Tariq put a knee in his back, held him that way. Lukas could smell it then, the emptying of the bowels. Tariq gave a final pull, released the handles, stepped back. Penskoff slumped to the floor.

"Sergei," Lukas said. "Have a seat."

The bodyguard's face had gone pale. Lukas nodded at a chair. Sergei pulled it out slowly, sat.

"How long have you worked for him?" Lukas said.

Sergei looked at Penskoff's body, blood beginning to pool around the head.

"Answer him," Tariq said. He was flexing his fingers to get the circulation back.

Sergei looked back at Lukas. *"Dva mesyatsa."*

"Speak English."

"Two months."

"As of about two minutes ago, you're unemployed. There's nothing to be gained by taking a stand here. You understand that, right?"

Sergei nodded.

"Lose the sunglasses. I can't talk to a man if I can't see his eyes."

Sergei took off the glasses, folded them, set them on the table. Not wanting to put them in a jacket pocket, bring his hand near the holstered gun.

"That's better," Lukas said. "Now try to follow me. Let me know if there's something you don't understand."

He nodded again. There was sweat on his upper lip.

"I could have shot him," Lukas said. "Made it easy. One in the forehead. But I didn't, because I wanted him to know what was happening to him. You understand that?"

"Da."

"English."

"Yes."

Lukas set the Walther on the table. He unclasped the manila envelope, shook out banded packs of hundred-dollar bills. He separated two of the packs, put the rest back in the envelope. "I liked the way you handled yourself. You stayed calm."

He put one pack atop the other, slid them across the table like a poker bet. Sergei looked at them.

"That's twenty thousand U.S.," Lukas said. "Starting now, you work for me. How do you like that?"

A slow smile came to Sergei's face, the tension seeming to drain out of him. "I like it."

"Go ahead, take it."

Sergei reached for the packs, then stopped, his fingers inches away. He looked at Lukas again.

"It's all right. Go on."

Sergei took the packs, put one in each jacket pocket.

"You can start earning it right now," Lukas said. "Help Tariq get that piece of shit up and into the bathroom before he bleeds through the floor."

Sergei got up, went to the body. Tariq already had Penskoff's wrists. Sergei bent and gripped his ankles, lifted. They carried him through the bedroom and into the bathroom, the wire still embedded in his neck, the garrote handles dangling.

Lukas stood, picked up the Walther, came around the table. The cigarette still smoked on the floor. He ground it out with his heel, followed them into the cramped bathroom. As he watched, they got the body up and into the claw-footed tub, dropped it facedown. Both of them were breathing hard. Tariq caught his eye in the mirror over the sink.

Sergei straightened, his back to the door, and Lukas stepped closer, raised the Walther, and shot him through the base of the skull. He dropped instantly, fell across the tub. Blood dripped down the wall tiles.

"Loyalty is dead," Lukas said.

Tariq bent, lifted Sergei's legs, tumbled him atop Penskoff in the tub, then pulled the money packs from his jacket pockets. Lukas picked up the casing, decocked the Walther, thumbed on the safety.

The banded bills went back into the envelope, the envelope into the bag. They wiped down the room with rags they'd brought with them.

When they were done, Lukas put on his jacket, tucked the Walther into his belt, the suppressor still warm. Tariq took the bag, unlocked the door, opened it and checked the hall, looked back and nodded. They went out. Lukas used a rag to pull the door shut behind them, wipe the knob.

The stairs creaked as they went down to the lobby. The familiar childhood smell of boiling cabbage drifted up through the stairwell. It turned Lukas's stomach.

The desk was empty, but he could see the old man in the small cluttered room beyond it, cooking on a hot plate. He looked up when he heard them.

In Hungarian, Lukas said, *"Gyere ide,"* and gestured. The man turned down the heat on the plate, came out wiping his hands on a towel. He had cigarette ashes on his shirt.

"Mi ez?" he said. Suspicious of them, but alert, eager, in case there was more money involved.

Lukas handed Tariq the rag, took out the Walther, slipped off the safety. The man saw it, raised his hands, and Lukas shot him twice, then came around the desk, fired once more into him as he lay on the floor.

Lukas knelt. The fifty-dollar bill he'd given the man was still folded in a shirt pocket. He took it. Leaving it would raise too many questions.

The Citroën was outside, engine running, Stenborg, their local man, behind the wheel. The Mercedes was gone.

Tariq got into the back seat with the bag, Lukas in front. They pulled away from the curb, rain spotting the windshield. Stenborg turned on the wipers.

"Just the one?" Lukas said.

Stenborg nodded. "Is done. No trouble."

Lukas took the Walther from his belt, said, "Find a spot by the river. Give me yours too."

Stenborg reached below his seat, handed him a Steyr automatic. It smelled of burned gunpowder. As they drove, Tariq looked out at the empty streets.

In his jacket pocket, Lukas's cell began to vibrate. He got it out, looked at the number. It was Farrow. He brought the phone to his ear. "What is it?"

"We have a problem. We need you back here."

"What kind of problem?"

"I'll tell you when I see you."

"You'll tell me some of it now, if you want to see me anytime soon."

Silence. Lukas said, "I'm listening."

"Someone was supposed to take care of something for us. It didn't happen. We need you to look into it. How soon can you get back?"

"We're on our way to the airport now." He looked at his watch. "Plane leaves at midnight, but I won't get back to the house until morning. I'll call you when I wake up." Tariq was watching him.

"This is a priority," Farrow said.

"I got that part. Does the old man know about it?"

"Why?"

"I'm just wondering. If something got fucked up, does he know what happened? Or are you hoping to fix it before he finds out?"

Farrow didn't answer.

"What I thought," Lukas said. "I have one more thing to do, then we're out of here."

"How did the other situation go?"

"It went. About ten minutes ago."

"You cut it close. Any problems?"

"Nothing that couldn't be handled. You can tell him our Russian friend asked about him."

"Call me as soon as you land." Farrow ended the call.

They were on a street that ran parallel to the Danube now. Dark warehouses faced the waterfront. Across the river, the brightly lit Royal Palace and Parliament Building. A world away.

Farther up, the lights of the gleaming Chain Bridge were reflected in the water. A line of taillights moved across the span.

"Up here's good," Lukas said. "Pull over."

Stenborg steered the car alongside the seawall, into the shadow of a construction crane.

"Kill the lights," Lukas said. "I don't want anyone coming along, wondering what we're doing."

Stenborg dimmed the headlights, left the engine and wipers on.

"Good," Lukas said, raised the Walther, and shot him twice above the right ear.

Even with the suppressor, the shots were loud inside the car, like pine boards breaking. A shell casing landed on the dashboard, rolled into a heat vent. Then it was quiet, except for the hum of the Citroën's engine, the swish of its wipers.

Lukas picked up the casings, got out carrying the two guns. While Tariq wiped down the car, Lukas went over to the seawall in the drizzling rain, found a spot where the crane hid him from the street. He disassembled the guns, tossed their parts and the casings out into the river, listened for the splashes.

Tariq was waiting by the car, holding the bag. They walked toward the bridge in the rain. *A beautiful city at night*, Lukas thought. *I'll have to come back here someday.*

Two blocks later, he hailed a cruising taxi, looked at his watch. They had plenty of time. Even if they were late, the Learjet would wait for them. They would be the only passengers.

SEVEN

YOU'RE A MESS," the doctor said.

Devlin sat shirtless on the treatment table. She touched the ribs on his left side with gloved fingers. The pain was deep. "Where exactly did you fall again?"

She was in her early forties, he guessed. Long black hair tied back, a single streak of silver running through it. She wore a white lab coat over sweater and jeans. He'd been to this walk-in clinic on Singer Island in the past, but had never seen her before.

"On my boat," he said. "Coming down the cabin steps. They were wet. I was a little drunk."

"You're lucky."

"I know."

Her name tag read D. STEFANO. Up close, he could smell her faint perfume, something like violets. She touched his face, the puffiness there, turned it toward the light.

"You're going to have a nice shiner. Not much we can do about that. Ice will help, or try a bag of frozen peas."

She took his wrists in her hands, gently rotated them to examine the bruises on his forearms.

"I tried to break my fall," he said.

"I can see." She released his hands. "You live on your boat?"

"Mostly."

"Alone?"

"Yes."

"You ever consider one of those Lifeline buttons?"

"'I've fallen and I can't get up'? Don't think I'm ready for that yet."

"Then you need to be more careful. Look up the accident statistics for people who live alone. Even a simple household fall can become a terminal event if there's no one else around. Not to mention a stroke or heart attack."

"I'll keep that in mind."

"No signs of concussion, so that's good. And you seem to be breathing all right. But even without seeing the X-rays, I think it's a safe bet you've got some cracked ribs."

"What do I do for that?"

"Nothing. Sleep on your back for a while. Cold compresses to bring down the swelling—the peas are good for that too. We don't tape broken ribs anymore. If the X-rays show you've got some splinters poking around in there, then that's something else. But if you did, you'd probably be in a lot more pain right now—or dead. So chances are you don't."

"Small favors."

"These scars, though." She touched the puckered circle beneath his left collarbone. "If I had to guess, I'd say this was a GSW."

"It is. From a long time ago."

"And this one on your stomach?"

"Knife. Small blade, though. Didn't go deep."

She put a thumb on his left eyebrow, pulled up the loose skin there. He blinked. She took her hand away.

"Shrapnel," he said.

"You were about three centimeters aw. eye."

She peeled off the gloves, used the foot pedal to op bin, dropped them in.

"I said you were lucky. But looking at you, I'm not sure that right word. Should I ask?"

"I was in the military."

"What branch?"

"Army Airborne, Eighty-Second."

"What was your MOS?"

"Eleven-B. Infantry. How'd you know to ask that?"

"My father was in the Army. We lived up near Fort Bragg for a while. You too, I'd guess, if you were in the Eighty-Second."

"I was at Bragg in '80 and '81. Then Germany and some other places. Korea—Panmunjom."

"You didn't get those scars in Panmunjom. Not unless an angry mama-san shot you for not paying your bar bill."

He smiled at that. "No. Not Panmunjom."

"Were you Special Forces?"

"I wasn't special anything."

"You're out now, I take it. What was your rank at discharge?"

"E-Six. Staff sergeant. Never got beyond that."

"Given your age, where would you have been in combat that got you those scars?"

"Here and there."

"Grenada?"

"Missed that one."

"Panama?"

"Missed that too."

"I get the hint. I'll stop asking questions. I probably wouldn't get much more out of you anyway, right?"

"You'd be surprised."

"I would be. You can put your shirt back on. Someone will call

when we have the X-ray results. You're going to need to come
ck, regardless."

She took a prescription pad from her coat pocket, began to write.

"I may need to go on a trip soon," he said.

"I'd rethink that, if I were you. You're going to be in a world of
hurt the next few days. It'll be worse if you're traveling."

"I'll manage."

"I'll want you back here before you go anywhere. We'll need to
go over your lab work, make sure there's no blood in your urine."

"I've had that before. I know what it looks like."

"I'm sure you do. You've had a busy fifty-four years. Let's make
sure you see fifty-five."

"To be honest, there was a time I thought I'd never see forty."

"Somehow, I don't think you're kidding."

She tore a sheet from the pad, handed it to him. "Percocet.
You're going to need it. Go easy with it if you've never taken it before. Don't drink, don't drive. Don't take more than two a day if
you can avoid it."

He looked at the printing at the top of the form. "Deandra.
That's a pretty name."

She put away the pad.

"I'll see you again in a few days, Mr. Devlin," she said. "Try to
stay alive until then."

His cell buzzed as he drove back to the marina. When he answered,
Karen said, "What do you want?"

He was surprised at the relief he felt. There was a chance Goldman, the lawyer, wouldn't have passed on the message. Or that,
even if he did, she wouldn't call back.

He steered into a Denny's lot. "I know you're not happy to hear
from me."

"An understatement."

"But I wouldn't have called if it wasn't important. We have to
talk."

"About what?" she said.

"It's probably nothing but—"

In the background, a man's voice said, "You get him?" Muffled noises as she covered the receiver, said something he couldn't make out. He waited. When she came back on, she said, "Vic wants to talk to you."

"Wait a minute. I need you to—" But she was gone.

Vic came on the line, said, "What's this all about? Why are you bothering us?"

Devlin inhaled, let out his breath. She and Vic had been married for five years, but it still hurt to be reminded of it.

"Are you still with the state police?" he said.

"Why?"

"I assume that means yes. Just hear me out, okay?"

"Go on."

"Somebody might be looking for me."

"Like who? A collection agency?"

Devlin took a slow breath, trying to tamp down his anger. "Please, just listen. It's likely nothing, but if someone *is* looking, they might try to find me through Karen. Could be they search a public records database for my name, that address comes up."

"Who's 'they'?"

"Might not be anyone. But it wouldn't hurt to keep an eye out, be careful. If you see any strangers around, get any odd phone calls, anything like that."

"You need to tell me what's going on here."

"I've told you everything I know."

"You're a piece of work. Why are you dragging your crap into our lives again? Didn't she get enough of that over the years, your drinking and your bullshit?"

Another long breath. "Maybe you're right."

"You know I am. Was that your message? Why you called Goldman?"

"It is."

"Then I got it. Anything else?"

"How's Brendan?"

Vic gave a short laugh. "You're something, you know that?" he said, and hung up.

When he got back to the marina, Bell's car was gone. He parked and walked down to his slip. It was a clear day, the sun high, and most of the boats were out. He wondered if Delburton, the marina manager, had seen him drive up. If so, he'd be down here soon, Devlin guessed, to ask him questions. Maybe ask him to leave.

The owner of the Chris-Craft four slips down was on his deck, taking cans of beer from a twelve-pack, planting them into a cooler filled with crushed ice. He was one of the few people at the marina Devlin knew. Crew-cut, with beer-belly fat over muscle, he wore a Confederate flag T-shirt with the sleeves cut off. He nodded at Devlin. "Everything all right?"

"What do you mean?" Devlin said.

"I see the law was here."

"They were."

"Anything I need to be concerned about?"

"No."

"None of my business, then," he said, and stuck another can into the ice.

Devlin stepped down onto the boat. They'd left the cabin door open, and strips of crime scene tape hung from the hinges. Flies buzzed around the dried blood on the deck and engine cover. The gloves were still there.

Down below, the casings and the yellow triangles were gone. They'd taken Bell's jacket as well.

He took the spiral notebook from his back pocket, sat at the fold-down table. He turned to the second page, got out his cell. He called the number written there, the 215 area code. On the third ring, a woman answered, crowd noise behind her, said, "Dugan's." So it was a bar or a restaurant.

54

He broke off the call, then dialed information. He got a listing for a Dugan's Tavern in Philadelphia. It was the same number. The street address matched one of those on the page.

A breeze moved the curtain over the broken window. He'd have to tape plastic sheeting over it until he could replace the glass. He got up, opened the toilet stall door. There were mirror shards on the floor, raw holes in the bulkhead where they'd gouged out the spent slugs. They would have to be patched, the trim repaired.

He went back topside, waved away flies. He would have to mop up the blood, scrub the last traces of it from the deck. The thought sapped what was left of his energy. He sat on the starboard engine cover, felt cold despite the heat of the sun. His right arm began to tremble, like an electric pulse he couldn't control. *Delayed reaction,* he thought. *A little dose of PTSD for you.* He thought about the therapy groups he'd gone to when he first got back to the States. His symptoms then had been different, but the reasons were the same.

His ribs were throbbing again. He got the Walgreens vial from his pocket, opened it, and shook out a Percocet. In the cabin, he washed it down with tap water.

Cracked ribs, he thought. *The gift that keeps on giving. Maybe a ruptured spleen and bruised kidneys as well. Pure luck he was here now, alive.*

He closed and locked the cabin door, drew the curtains to create a blessed dimness. Pain was pulsing in his sides. He went into the bow, crawled into the unmade bunk.

He thought about the notebook, the addresses there, the phone number. Places to start.

There might be a chance someone else was coming for him, he knew, to finish what Bell had started. Or he could have internal bleeding that would kill him while he slept. He was too tired to care.

EIGHT

THE GATES WERE open, so Lukas turned the Lexus into the driveway, drove up through the tunnel of oak trees to the pillared porch. There were panel trucks parked in the wide circle of driveway, landscapers at work in the big front yard.

He parked behind the trucks, got out. He'd slept fitfully on the plane, gotten another couple hours at his house outside Arlington before making the hour's drive to southern Virginia. He still felt the familiar sense of dislocation he got after long flights, the one-second remove from everything around him.

A man he didn't know was waiting for him on the porch. He wore a dark suit with an open neck, no tie. There was a white plastic receiver in his ear, and an automatic holstered on his right hip, beneath the jacket. Buzz-cut hair and wide shoulders. One of Kemper's men, running to type. Ex-cop or ex-military or both, all jacked up on testosterone and authority.

Lukas stopped at the foot of the steps.

"You're supposed to use the intercom," the guard said.

"Knew I forgot something. Gordon here?"

"Is Major Farrow expecting you?"

"Call him and find out."

The guard hard-eyed him, lifted a lapel, spoke into the button mike there. Lukas watched a squat Central American in a ball cap and sunglasses ride a mower across the lawn.

"He's coming," the guard said.

"I'll save him the trip." Lukas started up the steps. The guard moved in front of him. Lukas took a step back, smiled. "You sure you want to do this?"

"I'm going to need you to wait right there."

"You're new, right?"

The guard didn't answer.

Lukas nodded at his holster. "That a Glock 17? Looks it from here, but it could be the 22. That what he's giving you boys these days? Reliable weapon, though I'm betting you couldn't get it clear of that rig before I took it away from you."

The guard came down a step. Lukas moved back, getting ready, measuring the distance between them, and then the door opened, and Farrow was there.

"Stand down, Sergeant," he said.

Without turning, the guard said, "I told him he should have used the intercom."

"Well, he's here now, isn't he?"

"Gordon," Lukas said. "Just in time."

Farrow looked annoyed. "Come on in."

Lukas moved to step around the guard. He blocked him again. "I'll need you to raise your arms."

Lukas smiled, shook his head.

"Then you don't go in."

"Winters, it's fine," Farrow said.

"Strict policy, according to Mr. Kemper."

"Let him in, on my authority. It's all right."

Lukas waited, neither of them breaking eye contact.

"Sergeant," Farrow said.

Winters gave it another moment, then moved aside. Farrow held the door open. They went in. Winters stayed on the porch.

"What the hell were you thinking?" Farrow said. "Coming here like this?"

"Debriefing, right? I thought you'd want to hear. Last night you were anxious for me to get back."

"You were supposed to call when you landed. We would have arranged a meet. You can't just show up here anytime you want. You know better than that."

They went through the marbled foyer into the living room. A staircase ran up on each side, joined at a second-floor landing.

"Is he here?" Lukas said.

"No, he's not. And you shouldn't be either, with all these people around. It isn't good. Come on, we'll talk in the study."

They went up the right-hand stairs, and into a side room that ran the length of the house. Light poured through tall windows, lit dust motes in the air.

Growing up, this had been Lukas's favorite room. It still impressed him. Shiny hardwood floor, a big desk, wood filing cabinets, a leather couch and chairs. There were fresh flowers in a bowl on a low table in front of the fireplace. On the wall above the desk, photos of Kemper with three different presidents.

Farrow closed the door behind them. Lukas wondered again how old he was. Midsixties at least, to have done some of the things Lukas had heard about. Gray-steel flattop, deep-cut crow's-feet, but a younger man's energy, the belligerent strut of a bantam-weight.

"What's with the trucks?" Lukas said.

"Fund-raiser tonight for Senator Harlin. They're setting up out back."

"The 'Keep America Strong' guy? He still your man? Someone should tell him that catchphrase is getting old."

"I'll mention it to him."

Lukas wandered over to the desk. The top was empty except for a landline phone, a glass ashtray, and a carved rosewood box. He opened it. Cigars inside, *habanas*. He took one out, passed it under his nose, drew in the dark aroma.

"Take as many as you like," Farrow said. "We get them by the case now."

Lukas put the cigar back, closed the box. "I don't smoke."

"Right. I forgot. No smoking, no drinking."

Lukas turned back to him. "I used to play in this room, when I first got here. With my Hot Wheels. I'd set up the track right there in the middle of the floor. You remember that?"

"I remember."

"I loved those things. Now I haven't been in this room in what, almost a year?"

"Has it been that long?"

"At least. There was a time I was always welcome in this house. I knew everybody. And everybody knew me."

"Times change."

"Your man out front, he any good?"

"Winters? Army Ranger. Two tours in Afghanistan, one in Iraq. He's in charge of house security."

"I thought that was your gig."

"I've moved on."

Lukas went to the window. A wide green canvas tent had been erected on the back lawn. At the far end of it was a stage with an oversized American flag as a backdrop. Under the tent, white-shirted workers—most of them Hispanic—were setting up tables and unfolding chairs.

"How was the flight?" Farrow said. "The pilot's new. Just hired him a few weeks ago. He used to work for the Agency."

"The flight was fine. Where's the old man?"

"Up in Annapolis. He'll be back tonight for the reception. Tell me how it went over there."

Lukas turned to him. "Shouldn't we wait? Won't he want to hear this too?"

"I want to hear it first." Farrow reached into a jacket pocket, drew out a hard pack of Marlboros and a silver Zippo lighter.

"It went like we guessed," Lukas said. "I showed him the money, wanted to see which way he'd go. It was quick."

Farrow lit a cigarette, put away the pack and lighter. "He have anyone with him?"

"One man, and a driver. Dealt with."

"And our loose end over there?"

"Tied off."

"What are the chances Penskoff's people will try to come back at us?"

"From what I heard, they'll be happy he's out of the way. His time was over. He just didn't know it."

"Where's the cash?"

Lukas sat in a leather chair near the cold fireplace. "Way I look at it, that was hazard pay, with a travel surcharge."

"You kept it."

"Tariq and I split it. We earned it."

Farrow blew out smoke. "That guy makes me nervous. I never know what he's thinking. Hard to read those Arabs."

"You don't need to worry about him. He's my concern."

"Still, it bothers me. His background and all."

"We invaded his country, fucked it up forever," Lukas said. "Got most of his family killed, made him an orphan. Now he works here, for us. Ironic, right?"

"Not really. He's getting paid. Money's money. Things were rough for you too, when you were a kid. I know."

"You don't know anything about me."

"I know enough."

Lukas let that pass. "Why the rush for me to get here?"

Farrow ashed his cigarette in the fireplace. "We sent someone to do some work. It didn't happen. And now we can't find him."

"How long?"

"He was supposed to report back as soon as it was done. He hasn't. There's been no contact for almost forty-eight hours."

"He on the payroll?"

"Not officially."

"You pay him up front?"

"Half."

"Enough to make it worth running off?"

"He knew better. And he had more coming."

"What was the work?"

"Two Tangos. Stateside. He'd located them, was ready to move. That was the last we heard."

"Which means your guy spit the bit. Or one of your Tangos did him first."

"It's a possibility."

"I know him?"

"I don't think so. His name was Bell. He went way back with us, to Acheron."

"Why'd you send him instead of me?"

"He knew the targets," Farrow said. "He could get close to them. Someone else might not have been able to."

"They worked for Acheron too?"

"They did."

"Then they all worked with you."

"I was their immediate CO, yes."

There was a soft buzz. Farrow took a cellphone from his jacket pocket, looked at the screen. He silenced the ringer, put the phone back.

"How much you promise him?" Lukas said. "Turn on his buddies like that?"

"Enough. He had money issues. He was motivated."

"Offered more than money too, I'd bet. A nice cushy job somewhere in the company, right? A pension, benefits."

"Maybe."

"Which he was never going to get anyway, regardless of how things went."

Farrow took a last draw on the cigarette, flicked it into the fireplace.

"You guys kill me," Lukas said. "You and the old man both. You demand loyalty, and you undermine it every chance you get."

"It was work. A job, like any other."

"You track your guy after you sent him out? Or was he on his own?"

"We gave him a cell to use, with GPS we could follow. He switched it off about a week ago."

"You get a fix on it before that?"

"An address in Silver Spring, Maryland. An apartment he kept. It hasn't been activated since. He called me from another phone a couple days later, said he'd found both men. One was in Florida, the other in Pennsylvania."

"Pennsylvania?"

"Yeah."

"This have anything to do with that work up in Philly?"

"Does it matter?"

"To me it does. Are they connected or not?"

"Not directly, no."

"Am I supposed to figure out what that means?"

"It means no."

"You have the addresses for the other two?"

"I do," Farrow said.

"You want me to clean up this mess, it'll cost. More than last time."

"We'll work it out."

"Then my other question is why you were after them in the first place."

"That shouldn't be a factor."

"It is to me. If they're all ex-military, that's a complication. Be good to know who I'm dealing with. Bell might have told the others everything. All three might be holed up somewhere, waiting to see who comes looking for them."

"They might. That's why I called you."

"What's that supposed to mean?"

"You're a man of unique talents, Lukas. I have the feeling there's not much you can't do."

Lukas got up, went back to the window. Men were stringing red-white-and-blue bunting along the stage.

"Quite a spread," he said. "I hope the senator appreciates it."

"At ten thousand a plate, I'm sure he will. Election's only eight months away, so he'll take every dime he can get. If he stays on track and keeps his dick in his pants, he might be looking at a White House run in a couple years."

"Then he's a good friend to have."

"He will be. He has to hold on to his Senate seat first, though. Even with us backing him that might be a tough fight."

Lukas turned from the window. "Give me everything you've got on all three. I'll see what I can find out."

"Time is a factor."

"It always is. How's the other house coming along?"

"Which one?"

"The new one. On the island."

"Slow. It's the Bahamas. Nothing happens fast. And once hurricane season starts, everything slows to a crawl. We'll be lucky to get it finished this time next year."

"Maybe I'll come visit someday. Get a tan."

"I'm sure he'd like that." Farrow went to the door, opened it.

"Next time I come here," Lukas said, "I want to see him."

"I'll talk to him, see what we can work out."

Lukas faced him in the doorway. "If he thinks he can start treating me like one of his jarhead gofers—do this, do that, keep your mouth shut—we're going to have a problem."

"You know he doesn't think that way. You're special to him. And I'm sure he has plans for you."

"I'm sure too," Lukas said. "That's what I'm worried about."

NINE

———

ALFWAY UP THE hill, Tracy wanted to quit. Her legs were burning, her breath a knife in her side. Happy now she'd stopped at two glasses of wine the night before. She'd woken that morning planning to call in sick, but guilt had gotten the best of her, driven her out of the house.

She ran on, willing her legs to keep moving, and then she was over the hill, the road flattening out again. Slowing to a walk, she tried to catch her breath, pressed her palms into the small of her back. She stayed close to the guardrail, giving the few cars that passed a wide berth.

The cellphone in her waist pack buzzed, a text alert. She unzipped the pack, rooted past her keys and the two-ounce canister of pepper spray for her phone.

The text was from Harris, asking when she was coming in. *Riding my ass already,* she thought. *This won't end well.*

She considered texting him back, decided against it. She'd see him soon enough.

The phone buzzed again, an incoming call. Al Donovan's number.

"You should have stuck around," he said.

"Why?"

A pause. "You know I shouldn't be calling you, right?"

"But you did. What I miss?"

"That rowhouse body. We turned him just after you left. He did have ID. Guess what else we found."

"That's what you're going to tell me."

"A nice, shiny 9-millimeter shell casing," he said. "That decomp's a homicide."

She was on a stool at Reading Market, halfway through a bowl of jambalaya, when she saw Donovan come in the Arch Street entrance. She'd left a folded copy of the previous day's *Observer* on the seat beside her. Now she moved it to the counter, and he slid onto the stool. He wore a blue zippered jacket over his uniform, with yellow City of Philadelphia patches on the shoulders.

"Thanks for meeting me," she said. "And thanks for the call."

Grace, the counter girl, came down, brought him ice water in a red plastic glass, took his order.

"Did you write about our guy?" he said. "If so, I didn't see it."

"There was no interest up the ladder. Limited resources, so there's a lot of competition for attention these days."

"Too bad. This might change their minds." He set a small blue thumb drive on the counter between them. "That's for you."

"What is it?"

"Some information you'll be interested in. Go ahead and put it away."

She palmed the drive, slipped it in a jacket pocket.

"Our John Doe's got a name," he said. "And a rap sheet."

"The ME able to lift prints?"

"Yeah. He was in the NCIC system. Emilio Mata. Forty-five, at least that's what his sheet says. Comes up with an address too. But in D.C., not Philly."

"D.C.?"

"Yeah, long way to come to get shot, right? Gets better. There was a driver's license in his wallet. Picture matches the guy, far as we could tell, but the name on the license is Esteban Marota, and this time the address is here in Philly, over in Fairhill."

"You're losing me."

Grace brought a bowl of clam chowder, left plastic-wrapped crackers and a rolled napkin with a spoon in it. Donovan undid a shirt button, tucked in his tie, buttoned it again. He took a spoonful of chowder, blew on it.

"Nineteen years ago, Emilio Mata caught a charge in D.C.," he said. "At some point after that, he got himself a Pennsylvania driver's license under a different name. That's not easy to do."

"What was the charge?"

He opened a package of crackers, crumbled them into the chowder, and stirred it. "Weapons offense, illegal handgun. Charge dismissed."

"Why?"

"Don't know. He was on a temporary work visa from some South American banana republic. San Marcos. Not sure I know where that is." He tasted the chowder.

"Next to Venezuela," she said. "Atlantic coast, I think."

"Dwight was on the horn with their embassy today. They were very cooperative. They faxed over what they had on Mata, which was a total of one page. Say they've had no contact with him at all since the visa was issued. If he'd gotten his green card, they should have a record of it. They've got *nada*."

He spooned chowder.

"Who sponsored the visa?" she said.

"A company called Corsair Shipping. Corporate address in Delaware, but they had an operation at Penn's Landing, another at Port Elizabeth in Jersey. Both now defunct. It's all on the drive."

"Ballistics?"

"Still pending as far as any matches are concerned. Estimate is he's been dead about a month. He took two 9-millimeter rounds behind the ear. We only recovered a single casing, though, so the shooter likely picked up the other one."

"Why not both?"

"Maybe someone came along, spooked him. Could be he looked for it, couldn't find it, then just gave up and booked."

"Dwight the primary?"

"He is, for now. Working with Mendoza. He wasn't happy to see this one go into the red. I think he was hoping to write it off as an OD."

He drank water, wiped his lips with the napkin.

"I appreciate it," she said. "But why are you telling me all this?"

"I know what's going on at the paper. I figured you could use a tip on something might turn out to be a good story."

"I could. Thanks."

"Chase that down and you'll be at the *New York Times* in six months."

"The *Times* just had another round of layoffs," she said. "I doubt they're hiring."

"The *Washington Post*, then. CNN. Hell, ESPN."

"I wish. Does the *Inky* have any of this?"

"Not from me. We never had this conversation, by the way. And if asked, I'll deny it."

The jambalaya had cooled, but she finished it anyway, the taste of the spices lingering. "I owe you one."

He spooned up the last of the chowder. "I never thought I'd miss the business, but I do sometimes. It's sad to see what's happened."

"You got out at the right time, landed on your feet. That's more than most people did."

"How long have you been at the *Observer*?"

"Seven years."

"And how long since the new owners took over?"

"Year and a half. Be thankful you missed that."

"People have been bailing right and left. But you're sticking it out. Why?"

She motioned for the check. She'd had this conversation too many times, with too many people, didn't want to have it again.

Grace set the check down, and Tracy put a twenty atop it. "I'll get your lunch."

"I'll tell you why," he said. "Because you wouldn't know what to do with yourself if you left."

"Please."

"I'm serious. What would you do, get a PR job somewhere? Write press releases for Jefferson Hospital?"

"Why not?"

"Because you're too good at what you do. It's in your blood."

"Maybe I'll get a job at City Hall."

"You couldn't handle it." He untucked his tie, slid off the stool.

"What's that mean?" she said.

"It means you've got a fatal flaw that'll keep you from getting anywhere in public life."

"What?"

"Morals," he said. "You want to work for this city, you need to leave them at the door. Thanks for lunch."

The address on Marota's driver's license was an apartment above an empty bodega on North Fifth Street, on the edge of the Badlands. Salsa music blasted from a clothing store across the street.

After leaving the market, she'd driven home, not wanting to go into the office, risk getting tied up with Harris. She'd plugged the drive into her MacBook, downloaded everything for safety. On the drive were scans of the driver's license and arrest sheet, along with the single page from the San Marcos embassy. The photos on the license and sheet were grainy, but it was the same man. She'd printed them out, then headed back into the city.

There was plywood over the windows above the bodega, smoke

damage on the stucco around them. Shielding her eyes against glare, she looked through the front window. Empty shelves, some toppled over, ceiling tiles on the wet floor. Water damage from the fire above.

A wooden stairway ran up the side of the building to the second-floor door. She went up carefully, testing each step with her foot before committing her weight to it.

The door hung crooked, supported only by the upper hinge. The jamb was splintered where it had been forced. The pungent smell of smoke and damp came from within.

She pushed the door open gently, hinge creaking. Light came in around the edges of the plywood, lit up a warped floor, blackened debris. The walls were charred.

She wouldn't chance the floor in there. She took out her phone, snapped two pictures of the inside.

There was a sharp whistle below. She looked down. At the base of the stairs was a boy of about twelve, on a bicycle too big for him.

"*Hola*," she said, and started down the stairs. "*Habla usted inglés?*"

"*Sí.*"

"Do you live around here?"

He pointed up the street.

"Did you know the people that were in this apartment? Señor Marota?"

"Yes."

"Did anyone else live here with him?"

"Are you the police?" His English was flat, unaccented.

"No." She'd left her laminate in the car. "Have the police been here?"

"This morning. But no one will talk to them. Everyone is scared of *la Migra*—ICE."

"I'm not ICE. I'm a reporter."

"On TV?"

"No," she said. "A newspaper. The *Observer*. Do you ever see it?"

He shook his head.

"My name's Tracy. What's yours?"

Without a word, he swung the bike around and pedaled off. She watched him go, a vague feeling of unease settling over her.

She walked out to the curb. Next to the clothing store was a jeweler's, with lettering in the window that said CASH LOANS COM-PRAMOS ORO. On the other side, an empty storefront with a FOR RENT sign on the door.

There were other businesses on the street, apartments above them. She could knock on doors, show them the printout of Marota's license, but she knew her two years of high school Spanish wouldn't get her far.

Strike one, she thought. *But the game just started.*

In the lobby, she got that day's *Observer* from the rack at the reception desk, brought it upstairs. The paper seemed thinner every day. No Features or Business sections at all in the daily anymore. Just the A-pages up front, an abbreviated Metro section, and Sports.

Harris's office was dark, the golf clubs gone. *Dodged a bullet*, she thought.

She found Rick Carr, the Metro editor, out on the loading dock, smoking a cigarette.

"You must have been jonesing," she said. "Out here without a coat."

He took a pack of Luckies from his shirt pocket, held it out. She shook her head. "Don't tempt me. Looking for something to pitch at the five o'clock?"

"What you got?"

"A follow on my decomp from yesterday. Turns out it's likely a murder. On top of that, he's some sort of shady foreign national with at least one alias."

"Interesting. Drugs?"

"Maybe, but maybe something else. I need to make a couple phone calls, see what I can stir up, but then I'll be ready to write. I should be able to get you a version for online by six."

"Better clear this with R.J. He's your supervisor, not me."

"Which I eternally regret. Looks like he's gone for the day, though, which I think means it's up to you."

"In that case, I'll take it."

Wind blew bits of trash across the lot. A sheet of newspaper skidded across the blacktop, flattened on the tire of a delivery truck.

"I've been meaning to ask," she said. "You staying or going?"

"No comment."

"When's the deadline to turn in the paperwork?"

"May first."

"That's not much time."

"It isn't."

"And if not enough people take the buyout, we're looking at layoffs again, right?"

"More unpaid furloughs, at least. Word is they want a specific number of bodies this go-round. You see the letter we got from Corporate, encouraging us to take the buyout? 'The fate of your coworkers is in your hands.' No pressure there."

"You qualify, don't you?" she said. "You're what, fifty-five?"

"Fifty-six."

"Be a good deal for you, though, wouldn't it?" she said. "Six months' salary and health, pension. Things aren't going to get any better here."

"What would I do if I left? Nobody's hiring middle-aged guys from dying professions."

"What about that Gannett rumor?"

"That they're buying us? It goes around every six months. Maybe they are, maybe they aren't. Maybe the *Inky* will, just to put us out of business."

He took a last drag on the cigarette, dropped it on the concrete, and nudged it into a storm drain with his foot. "Might as well go back in, show our faces. Let them know we haven't quit."

"Yet," she said.

*   *   *

At her desk, she sorted through her pile of reporter's notebooks, looking for the one with the most empty pages. She got out a pen, clicked it twice, then picked up her desk phone and called a dispatcher she knew in the Philly Fire Department. Five minutes later, she was standing by the buzzing fax machine on the other side of the newsroom while the fire report she'd requested came through.

She took it back to her desk. The call had come in at 11 p.m. on February 15, a month before. A preliminary report listed the cause as arson. Traces of accelerant had been found. No injuries, and no one home at the time. An attempt to find the listed tenant had been unsuccessful.

No surprise there, she thought. *Chances are he was already dead.*

She called up a New Story template on her computer and started to write.

TEN

———

SEVEN A.M., AND there were already a half dozen men waiting outside
the bar, one in a wheelchair. A thin man in a Phillies cap sat on
the steps of the still-closed hardware store next door, reading a
newspaper.

Devlin was parked on a side street, no other cars around. Across
from the bar, the entire block was taken up by a dark factory with a
long line of broken windows.

He'd gotten into Philadelphia that morning, had driven straight
through, twenty-five hours, fueled by fast food and truck-stop coffee. On the way up, he'd detoured into Atlanta, checked out the
address on Bell's driver's license. It was a midtown parking garage.

He was feeling the miles now, the fatigue of driving, and a
constant ache in his sides. He wanted to take a Percocet, go somewhere, and sleep for a week. The cold was in his bones. The
months in Florida had spoiled him.

At seven-twenty, a red Ford 150 came past him, parked in a

fenced-in lot next to the bar. The man in the Phillies cap stood, folded his newspaper, and brushed off his pants. The one in the wheelchair backed up, swung around to face the door. The driver got out of the truck, locked it behind him with the key remote.

It was Roarke, his hair longer and grayer now. A thick beard hid the scar on the left side of his jaw. He wore a blue down vest over a red flannel shirt, the sleeves rolled up to show the thermal underneath. He limped to the front door of the bar, spoke to the men there, then took a ring of keys from the pocket of his vest, worked the locks. It all had the air of ritual, something he did every day.

He went inside, the others drifting in behind him. The man in the wheelchair rolled up to the door, waited. After a minute, Roarke came back out, got behind the chair, tilted it enough to raise the front wheels over the lip of the doorway. Then he heaved up, got the chair inside. The door closed behind them.

A neon SCHMIDTS sign came to life in the front window. Devlin waited, giving Roarke time to get settled. Imagining him inside, turning on lights while the customers waited in the dimness, then pouring the first drinks of the day.

At seven forty-five, he got out of the Ranchero, zipped up his jacket, crossed the street. There were flecks of rain in the air.

Chimes rang above the door. Inside was as he'd expected. Pressed-tin ceiling, dark wooden booths on one side, an L-shaped bar top on the other. More booths and a pool table in back. Cases of empties in the shadows against a far wall.

The skinny man was in the booth nearest the door, the newspaper spread out in front of him, a bottle of Rolling Rock and an empty shot glass at his elbow. Four men sat at the bar. The man in the wheelchair had pulled up to the short side of the L, near the service bar, where there were no stools. He had a beer bottle between his thighs, was watching the TV mounted over the bar. Local news, a weatherman in front of an animated map.

Roarke was behind the bar. He wore reading glasses, leaned with one elbow on the counter, and turned the pages of a newspaper.

He looked up at Devlin, then back at the paper, then up again. He took off the glasses, let them hang from the cord around his neck. Devlin took a stool at the far end of the bar, away from the others. They turned to look at him.

Roarke came down to where he sat, said, "Well, good mother of Christ."

Devlin smiled, said "Col," and put out his hand. Roarke caught it, squeezed. Devlin felt the power there.

"I'm thinking fifteen years," Roarke said.

"More like eighteen."

"You're the last person I expected to see here."

"In the neighborhood."

"Right," Roarke said. "And you wandered in by accident."

"Not quite. Can you talk?"

Roarke looked at him, then lifted his chin toward the back. "Grab a booth. Give me a couple minutes. I just put some coffee on. You look like you could use it."

He moved away. Devlin got off the stool, the drinkers watching him, went to one of the back booths. There were nicks in the dark surface of the tabletop, carved initials. He watched Roarke set up the men at the bar with another round. When he came back, he carried two thick ceramic mugs, a handful of creamers, and two spoons, set them down. "Sugar?"

Devlin shook his head. Roarke sat across from him.

"They're curious," Devlin said.

"Of course they are. You're a stranger in their bar."

"Who's Dugan?"

"Previous owner. I bought the place from his widow. The name's got history. Why change it?"

"Your own business. Good deal."

Roarke peeled open a creamer, poured the contents into his mug. "Your turn."

Devlin drank coffee. It was strong and hot.

"Your name came up in a conversation, so I decided to look you up," he said. "I found an address and phone number, figured it was worth a shot."

"You should have called first. Let me know you were coming."

"I wasn't sure I'd find you," Devlin said. "Or if I even had the right address."

"Now you know. Tell me about that conversation."

"I just drove up from Florida, so I might be a little foggy," Devlin said. "I'll try to make sense." He reached into his inside jacket pocket, took out the playing card and Bell's passport, set them side by side in front of Roarke.

Roarke put on his glasses, opened the passport. A smile played over his lips, then faded. "Where did you get these?"

"He came to see me. He had a driver's license on him too, in his real name, but with an address in Atlanta. It was bogus. The one on the passport probably is as well."

Roarke looked at him over the glasses.

"And that phone number"—Devlin touched the card—"was a burner. He'd just bought it."

"I don't understand."

"He had these with him when he tracked me down in Florida. Showed up out of the blue."

"Just like you."

Roarke picked up the card. "The last time I saw Bell, we were depriving some Colombian gentlemen of their laboratory facilities. I don't think you were around for that one."

"I heard about it."

"We left a few of these thereabouts. What did he want?"

"He tried to shoot me in the face."

Roarke set the card down, sat back. "Why?"

"I was hoping you could help me find out."

He told him about the fight, the gun. When he was done, Roarke looked at his mug, picked it up, put it back down without drinking. "Bell was a good man."

"He was."

"We did a lot of work together. Had each other's back."

"We did."

Devlin got the notebook from his pocket. "Look at the addresses."

Roarke took it, turned pages.

"He had that with him too," Devlin said. "The addresses and phone numbers on the first page are mine. The second page is how I found you."

Roarke put down the notebook, took off his glasses. "He tried to kill you."

"Almost did. Even without the gun."

Devlin slid up a jacket sleeve, showed the bruises on his forearm. "My ribs look the same. He gave me this too." He touched his cheekbone.

Roarke folded his arms. "And you're telling me this why?"

"I don't know why he came for me, or if someone sent him. He asked me if I'd heard from you recently. We're both in that notebook, so it could be he was coming here next. For all I knew, he'd been here already."

"He hasn't. I haven't seen him in eleven, twelve years. Not since I left Acheron."

"I hoped you might have some answers. Because right now, I don't have a clue."

"That's why you didn't call first," Roarke said. "You didn't know where I stood, what might be waiting for you."

"I was being careful. I had reason to be."

Roarke picked up the passport again, fanned through the pages. "If it's fake, it's a good one. If it's real, with a chip, it cost someone a lot of money."

"Either way, he was still in the game."

"Appears," Roarke said. He looked at the picture a final time, then closed the cover, slid the passport back across the table.

"He also had some business cards in that same name," Devlin said. "From something called Core-Tech Security."

Roarke thought for a moment, shook his head. "Never heard of it."

"Neither have I. But if someone did send him, sooner or later, they'll know it didn't go as planned."

Roarke turned his mug slowly on the table. "And whoever sent him might send someone else."

"They might."

"Are you strapped?" Roarke said.

"No."

"Trusting, aren't you? Coming in here without?"

"I didn't think I'd need it. You?"

"Something behind the bar, if the occasion arises. At home too. Bell say anything else?"

"When I asked about Kemper—about Acheron—he said I wasn't up on current events. Do you know what that meant?"

"Acheron's done, brother. Kemper branched out after that, merged with another company. It's called Unix now. Lots of military contracts, vehicles, coms, everything. He's still the CEO, but they're international. Based near D.C., I think, but offices all over. Nowhere as big an operation as some of the other firms, but I have to think he's doing all right."

"He still run mercs?"

"Depends how you define it. And who says we were mercs? We worked for a company, not a government."

"That was the fine print, yeah. But we did the same amount of damage."

"It was different then. Now it's an industry. Nine-eleven changed everything. You remember Hauser, guy we called Bullethead?"

"I think so," Devlin said.

"Little guy? German? He left Acheron in 2002, went with one of the big firms starting up then. He looked me up a few years back, wanted me to come in with him as a firearms instructor. But I couldn't leave this place. And I'd lost my taste for that work."

"What'd he offer?"

"A hundred and fifty K a year to start, training Iraqi Special Forces. I turned him down. Said I was too old, too tired, both of which were true. Three months later, he and a carful of his people were ambushed outside Baghdad. The people in the street, insurgents, whoever, dragged their bodies through the city, then hung them from a bridge."

"I heard about that. I didn't know it was him."

"All in the game, though, right? Isn't that what we used to say?"

"What game is that?"

"'Democracy for Profit.' Coming to a country near you."

"I guess it was never a game to me."

Roarke drank coffee, said, "You know, I bought this place with the severance Kemper gave me. I imagine you got about the same. Probably more with disability and all that, after what happened to you."

"Probably."

"We all took his money."

"We earned every dollar."

"We did. Maybe you more than most of us. But there isn't a morning I walk into this place that I don't think about how it was paid for, and what I had to do to earn it."

Devlin said nothing.

"What are you planning to do now?" Roarke said.

"Head up to Connecticut. My son and ex-wife live there. I want to make sure they're all right. I spoke to her on the phone, but I'd feel better seeing them in person."

Roarke stroked his beard. "You think there's an ongoing situation here?"

"I need to make sure there isn't."

Chimes rang as the front door opened. Two men in tan work jackets over hoodies came in, sat at the bar.

"I need to get out there," Roarke said. "There's a glass plant about a mile from here. Shift changes in a little while. It'll get busy then. Wait here a minute."

He got up, went back behind the bar. He exchanged greetings with the two men, put beers in front of them, took money, and rang it up on the register.

He came back to the booth with two keys on a Budweiser key chain, set them on the table.

"These are extras. My place is just a few blocks from here. Bronze one's for the street door, silver one works in both apartment locks. Go there, get some sleep. There's a spare bedroom you can use. Food in the refrigerator if you're hungry."

"That's okay. I can get a motel room."

Roarke shook his head. "I'll call one of my part-timers in later. When they get here, I'll come by. We need to talk more about this."

"What's the address?"

"You already have it," Roarke said. He tapped the notebook. "It's in there."

Devlin picked up the keys.

"Finish your coffee, then go catch some shut-eye," Roarke said. "You look like hell."

"I feel it. Thanks."

"Don't thank me yet. It's good to see you and all, but I'd be happier if you hadn't shown up." He hesitated a moment. "And I still don't know how I feel about what happened to Bell."

"He called it."

"Maybe so, but with everything we went through over the years, he didn't deserve to go like that."

"No," Devlin said. "He didn't."

ELEVEN

THE KNOCK AT the door woke him. He had an instant of panic, not knowing where he was. He pushed away the sheet that tangled his legs, sat on the edge of the bed, wiped wet palms on his thighs. He'd taken off his sneakers and socks, but slept in jeans and T-shirt. He'd been too tired to undress.

The knock came again.

"I'm awake," Devlin said. He looked at his watch. It was four in the afternoon. He'd slept almost eight hours.

From the other side of the door, Roarke said, "Something you need to see."

"Give me a minute."

The room was bare. The narrow bed, an empty dresser, nothing on the walls. The single window gave a view of gray sky, an iron bridge in the distance.

Devlin went out into the hallway, the floor cold under his feet. His mouth was dry.

"In here," Roarke called from the living room.

Devlin crossed the hall to the bathroom, took off his T-shirt, ran the faucet, and cupped cold water into his face. He dried off with a towel, looked at the mirror. His eye was yellowish but fading, the swelling gone. The bruises on his arms and sides were lighter too, but when he touched them, the pain was still there.

He put the T-shirt back on, went down the hall.

Roarke sat in a recliner in the living room, the TV tuned to a news channel, the sound low.

He held up a newspaper folded into quarters. "Bottom of the page."

Devlin took it. A two-column headline read POLICE PROBE CITY DEATH. He scanned the first paragraph.

> Police are investigating the killing of a Philadelphia man found shot dead yesterday in a vacant Bainbridge Street rowhouse undergoing renovations.

"I don't get it," he said.
"Keep reading."

> The dead man was identified through forensic evidence as Emilio Mata, a San Marcos national. However, sources close to the investigation said Mata was carrying a Pennsylvania driver's license that identified him as Esteban Marota, a city resident with a Fairhill address.

Roarke picked up the remote from an end table, muted the TV. "Remember him?"

"No," Devlin said. "Someone we knew in San Marcos?"

"He was Herrera's brother-in-law, and part of his cabinet. Minister of finance, I think. He switched sides when he saw the way the wind was blowing, sold out his compadres. Farrow put him on the

Acheron payroll, with the promise to resettle him in the States afterward if he kept feeding them intel."

"Farrow. That's a name I haven't heard in a while. How do you know all this?"

"I helped them."

Devlin sat on the couch. "Explain."

"It was right after we left San Marcos. You were still in the hospital. Farrow wanted to make good on his promise, asked if I could help Mata get sorted out over here. Acheron co-owned a shipping company that operated out of the Landing. They'd helped supply us on a couple missions, logistics and transport. Farrow got him a no-show job there, just to have something on paper. The suitcase of cash I delivered to them didn't hurt either."

"And they gave him a new ID?"

"We gave him a new ID. And yeah, Farrow handled that. A driver's license under the new name, probably some other documents. I washed my hands of it soon as I could. The guy was scum, far as I was concerned. Couldn't be trusted. I didn't want anything more to do with him."

Devlin read the rest of the story. "It says he may have been dead a month or more before they found him."

"I have no doubt he was into something got him killed. He was one of those guys who're always looking for the better deal. You turn your back on them at your peril. Last I saw of him was almost twenty years ago. Until I read that story, I didn't know he was still alive, much less still in Philly."

"Maybe somebody from San Marcos caught up with him?"

"If so, they took their time about it. More likely he fucked someone on a deal here, caught a bullet for his trouble."

"Story says it's still under investigation."

"There'll be more," Roarke said. "I know the reporter. She's pretty sharp."

Devlin looked at the byline: TRACY QUINN, DAILY OBSERVER STAFF.

"Last year, some people were scamming vets around here,"

Roarke said. "Getting them to sign over their government checks, in exchange for putting them up in Section Eight housing, an old transient hotel. Most of them were sick—one thing or another—or drinking so much they didn't know any better. Some were drinking in my bar."

"You didn't flag them?"

"It's a choice, isn't it? Whether to drink or not? I choose not to, but that's me. You see the guy in the booth today, all by himself, Phillies cap? His name's Leland. Used to be an Air Force captain. Spent five years at the Hanoi Hilton, living on rice and bugs, being tortured every day. You going to tell him he can't get drunk if he wants to?"

"I see your point."

"If they weren't drinking in my place, they'd be doing it somewhere else, running the risk of getting rolled—or worse. I look after them when I can. I didn't know about the check thing, though. If I had, I would have done something."

"What's that got to do with this reporter?"

"Somehow she got tipped to it, came down to the bar, hung around, talked to some people. At the hotel too. Took her life in her hands there. Ended up writing a front-page story, and a bunch of follow-ups. Like I said, sharp. Persistent too. Turns out the daughter of one of the victims had gone to Philly PD with the story months before, but they'd ignored it. Quinn was the one put it all together. I have her business card around somewhere."

"You helped her?"

"Yeah, introduced her to some people who might not have talked to her on their own. After the first story ran, the feds got interested. They ran a sting operation, had an undercover pose as a vet. Was a Russian guy and his wife doing it. Quinn followed the story all the way through. I think she won some award. She'll be on this one hard too. She's the type."

Devlin handed the paper back. "You think this has anything to do with Bell?"

"If there's a connection, I don't see it."

"Coincidence?"

Roarke shrugged, put the paper on the end table.

Devlin rubbed his face. "How long have you been back?"

"About an hour. I heard you in there. Still have that trouble?"

"Sometimes. Was I talking?"

"Nothing that made any sense."

"Good."

"I used to get nightmares too," Roarke said. "Not so much any-more. I went to meetings for a while, for the drinking. That helped."

"And now you own a bar."

"Yeah, I own a bar, but I don't drink. I don't need to anymore. That wasn't always the case."

"Your war stories must have made for some interesting meet-ings."

"Ever been to one?"

"No."

"You should try it. After a while, it feels like you've set down a weight you've been carrying too long. One you never needed to pick up in the first place."

"I'll give that some thought. Who's watching the bar?"

"Margaret, my night manager, came in early. She's an old-timer, worked for Dugan. I've got another bartender comes on at five, kid named Ernesto, just graduated Temple. I always keep at least two people on at night. It's safer."

"Sorry to mess up your schedule."

"I'll go in later, help them close. You're hungry too, I'd guess. There isn't much here. Cold cuts in the refrigerator. Eggs if you're feeling ambitious. We can do takeout later. Let me know what you'd prefer."

"Just something to drink right now. Water's fine."

"In the refrigerator. Help yourself."

The kitchen was small but neat, the counters clear, the stovetop spotless. A window led onto a fire escape.

There were photos on the refrigerator door. Roarke, clean-shaven in a tux, pre-scar, with Wanda on their wedding day. Another, not much later—Roarke in a guayabera shirt, Wanda in a floral-print summer dress, both of them holding tall blue drinks, flaming tiki torches in the background. Then, to the right of that, her memorial card. Killed in a car accident while he and Roarke were half a world away.

There were six Bud Light bottles on the inside rack of the refrigerator. He thought about taking one, then got a plastic bottle of water instead. He cracked the cap, took a long pull, went back into the living room.

"How is it you keep beer around?"

"I have a lady friend comes by sometimes. I keep it for her. Doesn't bother me. No appeal anymore."

On the TV was silent footage of people, dust-covered and bloody, on a wide city street, walking toward the camera with stunned faces. A plume of white smoke behind them, debris on the ground. In the distance, domes and minarets.

"Where's that?" Devlin said.

"Pick a country."

Devlin sat back on the couch. A crawl at the bottom of the screen read ALEPPO SUICIDE BOMBER KILLS 16.

"Nothing changes," Roarke said. "Just the reasons, and sometimes not even those. Why humans are still around, I don't know. That giant asteroid can't get here soon enough."

Devlin drank water. "You keep anything around from the Acheron days?"

"Like what?"

"Mementos, souvenirs, photos. Reminders."

"You got the wrong guy."

"Bell wanted to talk old times."

"And look where it got him."

"You think he had people?" Devlin said. "Wife, kids?"

"I don't know. Why?"

"Easy enough to find them, I imagine."

"And what would you say to them if you did?"

Devlin didn't answer.

"Leave it," Roarke said. "Way you laid it out, it was his play. Doesn't seem like there's much you could have done different. It went the way it went."

"We were friends. All of us."

"We were grunts. In the same unit, with the same employer, that's all. We did what we got paid to do. That was a different time, and different people. Not us at all."

"Hard to forget, though."

"We did our jobs," Roarke said. "Sometimes things happen you can't shake, no matter how much booze or junk you put into your body. But you don't have to live with them every day for the rest of your life either."

"I hope that's true."

"We're both pushing sixty," Roarke said. "What do we have to look forward to? Our first heart attack? A PSA test says we've got prostate cancer? The roller coaster peaked, Ray. We're on the downward side. Time is finite. And there's nothing we can do about it."

"And that's all there is to it?"

"You find out different," Roarke said, "let me know."

TWELVE

THE DEAD BOLT looked simple, but Tariq had been at it with the lock-pick tools for five minutes and still couldn't get the tumblers to fall right.

"Stand back," Lukas said.

"The noise."

"This place, no one will care."

Bell's Silver Spring address was a basement apartment in a pre-war building. The foyer was unlocked, and Lukas had rung the apartment buzzer, then knocked on the door. The hallway smelled of mildew and pot smoke.

Tariq drew out the pick and tension wrench, stood. "Go ahead."

Lukas took the Ruger automatic from his coat pocket, screwed in the suppressor. He stepped back, drove his heel into the door frame just above the knob. The trim splintered and sheared, and the door flew open.

He raised the Ruger one-handed, pointed it into darkness. No sound or movement inside.

They went in, moving to opposite sides so they weren't outlined in the doorway. Light wash from street lamps came through the windows high on one wall. They could see sidewalk outside, the tires of parked cars.

Lukas turned on a penlight. "Shades."

Tariq worked the miniblinds, shut out the street lighting, then pushed the door back in place until it held. Lukas fanned the penlight beam along the wall, found a switch, flipped it. Track lights went on, showed a small living room and kitchenette. A hallway led to an open door.

He held the penlight in a reverse grip, wrists crossed, the Ruger aimed straight ahead, heavy with the suppressor's added weight. Tariq took his own gun from under his jacket, held it at his side.

Lukas moved down the hall, the muzzle of the suppressor tracking the penlight's beam. There was an open door on his left, a dark bathroom. He went past it to the far doorway, aimed the light inside, saw a neatly made bed, a dresser. Street light filtered in through a single high window.

He shut off the penlight, put it away, felt around with his left hand until he found a wall switch. A ceiling-fan light went on. There was a full-length mirror in one corner of the room, a closet with a sliding door. He lowered the gun, touched the bed's top cover with a gloved finger, came away with dust.

"What are we looking for?" Tariq said behind him.

"Like last time. Notes. A journal. Laptop. Phone. Disks or thumb drives, anything he might have left behind."

Lukas opened the closet door. Clothes hanging inside, shoes on the floor. He pushed the clothes aside. Nothing behind them.

"Here," Tariq said.

On the other side of the bed, an olive-green metal footlocker was pushed against the wall. It was padlocked.

"Can you deal with that?" Lukas said.

Tariq put away his gun, knelt, and took out his tools. While he worked, Lukas put away his weapon, went to the single nightstand. Inside the drawer was a package of condoms, some loose change, an aspirin bottle, and a cellphone.

Tariq popped the lock, slipped it out of the hasp, raised the lid. Lukas showed him the phone.

"That the one Farrow gave him?" Tariq said.

"Safe bet. Looks like our guy was already off the reservation."

Lukas put the phone in a jacket pocket, knelt. Inside the foot-locker was a folded silk cargo parachute, a maroon beret, and a set of neatly pressed olive-drab camo fatigues. Beneath the fatigues was a manila clasp envelope.

He opened it, shook out a set of eight-by-ten color photos. There was a posed color portrait of a pretty black girl holding a baby. A formal shot of a young black man in uniform in front of an American flag, sergeant's stripes on his shoulder, wearing the same beret.

"Is that him?" Tariq said.

"Must be."

There were three more photos. In the first, three men in woodland-camouflage uniforms stood on a dirt road, arms around one another's shoulders. Bell, in the middle, older than in the portrait. On his right, a big man with a shadow beard, holding a can of beer in one hand, giving the finger to the camera with the other. The man on Bell's left was leaner, dark hair, not smiling. All three wore red-and-white chessboard patches on their shoulders.

"Those aren't American uniforms," Tariq said.

"They aren't. But I've seen them before."

He turned over the photo. "Field op. Osijek Aug. 1991" was written on the back in blue ink.

"What are they?" Tariq said.

"Croatian Army uniforms, but these three were professional soldiers. Private hires."

"Mercenaries."

The next picture was of the three men in a jeep, a machine gun mounted on a crossbar behind the front seats. Desert camo this time, no insignia. Bell was at the wheel, wearing mirror sunglasses, flashing a smile at the camera. Beside him was the big man, half out of his seat, a knee on the dash, arms raised, a bottle of Jack Daniel's in one hand, an M-10 machine pistol in the other. The dark-haired man was leaning on the crossbar next to the .50. There were smears of combat paint on his face, and a cigarette dangled from his mouth. His eyes were deep-set, as if he hadn't slept.

The last picture was Bell again, standing in front of a semicircle of Latino soldiers cross-legged on the ground, watching him. He wore jungle camo, held an AK-47 braced against his left hip, a banana clip in his free hand.

Lukas put the photos back in the envelope, closed the clasp.

They spent twenty minutes searching the rest of the apartment, opening drawers, dumping their contents out on the floor. The living room furniture was a thrift-store couch and coffee table, a small TV in a wall unit, a shelf with a handful of DVDs and books. Lukas opened the cases, checked the disks, tossed them aside, then shook out all the books.

A car passed on the street above, threw headlights along the edges of the shades.

"Let's get out of here," Lukas said. "This place is depressing the shit out of me."

He took the envelope with him. They went out into the hallway, and Tariq pulled the door shut as best he could. Concrete steps led up to street level.

The work car was parked a block down. It was a dark gray Crown Victoria with smoked windows and Virginia plates, the registration clean, but with a false corporate name and address. It would stand a traffic stop, but they could also walk away from it if needed, with no complications.

The street was dark and empty. They got in the car, Tariq behind the wheel. Lukas looked at his watch. It was a little after midnight.

As they pulled away, he took out the cellphone, turned it on. No call history or contacts. He punched in Farrow's number from memory, let it ring twice, then disconnected.

A few minutes later, the phone buzzed, showed a different number. Farrow being careful.

"Where did you get this phone?" Farrow said.

"In his apartment. He wasn't there. Hadn't been for a while."

"You find anything else?"

"Not much. Some pictures. The place was a hole. If you were paying this guy, I don't know what he was spending his money on."

"Hold on to this cell, it'll be easier to reach you. Where are you headed now?"

"Philadelphia. I want to see what's what before I make a move."

"Don't screw around with these guys."

"I'll play it the way I think best," Lukas said. "Like always. You talk to the old man?"

"I did."

"What he say?"

"Nothing. I told him we were on it, and there was no reason to worry. And there isn't, is there?"

"None at all," Lukas said, and ended the call. He powered down his window and tossed the phone out onto the highway.

THIRTEEN

I T ALWAYS HURT to come home.

Devlin parked the Ranchero at the curb, looked at the house, the neatly trimmed lawn, the basketball hoop on the garage.

He'd spent the night at Roarke's place, then made the three-and-a-half-hour drive up from Philly. When he'd woken that morning, Roarke was already gone. Devlin had locked the apartment behind him, dropped the spare keys through the mailbox slot in the foyer.

The house looked the same as the last time he'd seen it. *You used to live here,* he thought. *And now you don't. You had it all, and you lost it. And whose fault is that?*

His cellphone buzzed on the console. When he answered, Vic Ramos said, "Is that you out there?"

"Yes. Is she home?"

"You want to explain all this?"

"I will, let me talk to her."

"Talk to me."

"For Christ's sake," Devlin said. "Come on out. We'll talk."

He ended the call, tossed the phone on the passenger seat, got out, and stretched. A twinge of pain ran through his ribs.

The front door opened and Ramos came out, started down the driveway. Stocky and muscular, he'd be trouble in a fight, Devlin knew.

Behind him, the living room curtains opened slightly. Karen in there, looking out. Or maybe Brendan. Watching to see what would happen, but not wanting to leave the house.

Ramos stopped a few feet away, hands on his hips. "You shouldn't be here."

"Vic, let's quit the pissing contest for a minute. I'm not here to cause trouble."

"That's good. Because if you were, you'd get it."

Devlin gave that a moment. "That doesn't even make sense."

"What did you want to talk about?"

"Karen home?"

"She doesn't want to talk to you."

Devlin exhaled. "Vic, you don't need to worry about me anymore. I'm out of their lives."

"That's right."

Devlin felt the sting of that, let it go. "I drove up here just to make sure everything was okay."

"What's with the mysterious phone call? And why did you think the call wasn't enough, you had to show up in person? You in some sort of wet-brain paranoid state? I've seen that happen."

Devlin's face grew hot. He wondered if he could take him if it came down to it. Decided he couldn't. Ramos was in his forties, but had the chest and arms of a gym rat, could probably take a lot of punishment and keep coming. Ten years ago, it might have been different. Still, part of him wanted to try.

Devlin shook his head.

"Then say what it is you have to say."

94

"You know I was in the military, right? The Army?"

"What about it?"

"Karen probably told you that after that—long ago, before I met her—I did some private work. Security contractor, that kind of thing."

"So?"

"One of the people I worked with back then came looking for me recently. Not sure why. There's a chance someone else may as well. They might find this address somehow, think it was mine, come here."

"Why?"

"I don't know. It's probably nothing to worry about, I just wanted you to know what was going on, in case you heard anything."

"That sounds like a lot of—" Ramos circled a finger near his temple.

"It's not."

"You see a psych about all this?"

"Believe what you want, Vic. Blame it all on me, I don't care. But just listen to me for once. Any odd phone calls, cars driving by, strangers asking about me, anything, let me know. You have my cell now."

"You think I'm some idiot, can't keep my wife and kid safe?"

"I know you can do that. I'm just asking you to be aware. And I felt like I owed you that explanation, in person." Wanting to end it, now that he'd said his piece. He looked back at the house. The curtain was closed again.

Ramos looked off down the street, then back at him. "Long drive, huh?"

"Long enough."

Ramos gestured at the Ranchero. "I used to own one of those, when I was like seventeen. What year is it?"

" 'Sixty-nine."

"The four-speed?"

Devlin nodded.

"Still run good?"

"Most of the time."

"Listen, I don't mean to come off as a hard-ass," Ramos said. "But things are going good here. I need to protect that. And you coming here, stirring things up—for whatever reason—that don't help."

"I told you why I came."

"I'm sorry things worked out the way they did. I understand how that happens. But life moves on, right?"

"Trust me, Vic. Nobody knows that better than me."

Devlin looked back at the house. "Brendan home?"

"Nah, he's at the job. He's a good kid. A hard worker."

"I know."

"He's been saving money since he graduated. He's looking at colleges for next year, maybe."

"That's good."

"I told him if he gets that junior-college degree, right here in town, I can get him into the academy. Be a good move for him. But he has his own ideas, you know? Kids that age, what are you gonna do?"

Devlin put out his hand. After a moment, Ramos shook it.

"Anything," Devlin said. "No matter how small. Something doesn't look right, call me, let me know. Like I said, doesn't matter what it is."

"And like I said, I heard you."

"Then we'll leave it," Devlin said. He glanced back at the house, feeling the need to say goodbye to whoever was inside, not sure why.

He made two wrong turns before he found the street he was looking for. He pulled into the half-full lot of the garden and landscaping center, parked next to a station wagon. A young couple was wandering the fenced-in yard, looking at concrete fountains. Brendan walked beside them, wearing an orange canvas work apron and carrying a clipboard. Taller than the last time he'd seen him, neat beard, hair to his shoulders.

Devlin rolled down his window. The woman looked over at him, said something to Brendan. He turned then, saw him. Devlin raised a hand.

The three of them went into the office. After a few minutes, Brendan came back out alone, without the apron or clipboard, crossed the lot to him.

"Hey, chief," Devlin said. "How about lunch?"

In the truck, Brendan said, "How'd you know where I was?"

"Took a gamble. I was at the house. Vic told me you were at work. I knew you used to work there summers, holidays. Figured it was worth a try."

Brendan pushed a strand of hair from his face, looked out the window.

"Not causing you trouble, am I?" Devlin said. "Coming by like that?"

"Just surprised to see you, that's all." Still no eye contact.

"I know it's been a while," Devlin said, "but—"

"Two years this Christmas."

"I'm sorry. It's tough getting up here sometimes. And your mom's not always happy to see me."

Silence.

"If you're angry at me, that's fine," Devlin said. "You've got the right. I can't blame you."

"I'm not angry."

"Good to hear. I almost believe you. You didn't eat already, did you?"

"No."

"What are you in the mood for?"

Brendan shrugged.

"How about the pancake house over by the mall? You still go there?"

"Sometimes. Whatever."

They made the rest of the ride in silence. Inside the restaurant, Brendan was quiet, fixated on the menu.

"We can go somewhere else if you like," Devlin said.

"No, this is fine."

Devlin looked at his own menu. "They still have those chocolate chip pancakes you used to like."

Brendan didn't respond. When the waitress came, Devlin ordered first, to give him more time. She smiled at Brendan when she took his order, called him "honey."

After she was gone, Devlin said, "You're lucky. You got your mom's looks."

"I guess."

"Vic tells me you're checking out colleges finally."

"That what he said?"

"Was he wrong?"

Brendan drank from his water glass. "Vic's an asshole."

"He's in a tough position."

"Fuck him."

"Don't talk like that." Devlin felt a smile forming, stopped it.

"Where are you living now?" Brendan said.

"I moved around for a while. I'm down in Florida now. I have a boat."

"That's what Mom said. She said she hoped you'd drown."

"She didn't mean that."

"Then why is she still so mad at you?"

He thought about his answer while the waitress refilled his coffee cup. "I guess I could have been a better husband. A better father."

"You guess," Brendan said.

"You were just a kid when things went bad between your mom and me. You're not a kid anymore. You might see things differently now."

The waitress brought their sandwiches. Devlin had ordered a BLT, Brendan a grilled cheese and bacon. Devlin was sorry he'd mentioned the pancakes, knew if he hadn't, Brendan might have ordered them.

They ate without speaking. The waitress brought Brendan another Coke. When she was gone, Devlin said, "We all have our reasons. It doesn't make things right. But sometimes it makes them easier to understand."

Brendan put down his sandwich. "She said a lot of it was because of what happened to you in the Army, some of the places you went to."

"Maybe she's right. I don't know. It's hard to separate cause and effect sometimes. What's the disease, what's the symptom."

"What war were you in? She'd never tell me much."

"I'm not surprised."

"So where were you?"

Devlin looked down at his sandwich, his appetite fading. "A lot of places."

"Just like always, isn't it? You can't ever give me a straight answer."

Devlin sighed, sat back.

"I'm not a kid anymore, remember? You just said it."

"You're right," Devlin said. "I'm sorry."

"She told me you were a paratrooper."

"I was. Eighty-Second Airborne. Fort Bragg."

"Where's that?"

"North Carolina. I wanted to try to get into Special Forces, that's where they were based. You needed jump experience, and back then, most of the SF guys came from the Eighty-Second."

"Special Forces, you mean like SEALs?"

"No, that's a Navy unit. I was Army. A lot of the men in my unit wanted to go SF, but it was hard to make the cut. I didn't. I flunked out."

"How come?"

"The final test was escape-and-evasion. You jumped from a C-130 over the forest, out in the middle of nowhere, with a certain amount of time to make it to a designated area. Meanwhile, they sent other guys out to try to catch you. If you weren't where you were supposed to be at the right time, or if you got caught along the way, you flunked out."

"What happened?"

"There were fire roads all through there. Instructors would ride up and down in jeeps. If they saw you, you were out. But it was easier to run the roads than slog through the woods, especially if you were trying to make up time. So a lot of guys took the chance. They'd run on the road for a while, then cut back into the trees before they got caught."

"That what you did?"

"I tried. First couple times, I got away with it. Third time, they nailed me. Automatic fail. They drove me back to main post in a jeep. I was angry at myself. It was all I wanted, and I'd blown it."

"Did you try again?"

"No. There were other things going on at the same time. A buddy I'd known in the Eighty-Second, Roarke, told me about a private company based near D.C. that was hiring ex-military. It's common now, but wasn't back then. He'd gone to work for them when he got out of the service. I was sick of the Army, was going nowhere fast. I was young and stupid. Had all this training, wanted to use it."

"How old were you?"

"Twenty-four, twenty-five. The company offered decent pay and benefits. It seemed like the right move."

Still not knowing how much he would tell. Surprised to find he was happy to be sharing it. *This is your son,* he thought. *You hardly know him, and he hardly knows you.*

"What did you do for them?"

"Whatever was needed. Mostly training and assisting indigenous troops, in Central and South America, West Africa, places like that. We took contracts from the U.S. government too. Once we spent a month blowing up cocaine-manufacturing plants in Honduras."

"That's crazy."

"It was, sometimes. Mostly what we did was advise the locals on tactics, weapons, that sort of thing. A lot of chalk talk. They did most of the actual fighting."

"How long did you do that?"

"A few years. It paid well, so I was able to sock some money away."

"Were you in Iraq?"

"No, I was just about out of it by then. Guys I worked with went over, though. Some of them did all right."

"Why'd you quit?"

"I don't know, just tired of it. And it wasn't easy to know where you stood sometimes. In some of those places, you needed a score-card to know who was fighting who, and why."

"Where did you get hurt?"

Devlin looked down at his half-eaten sandwich, knew he was done with it. The coffee was like acid in his stomach.

"I picked up a few bangs and bumps along the way. Everybody does. Only time I got seriously hurt was in South America. That was the last real field duty I had."

"What were you doing there?"

"It was a small country next to Venezuela. They had oil fields, should have been rolling in dough, but the president and his pals in the government were stealing most of the money, hiding it in offshore accounts. A lot of people were hungry, the economy was a mess. Some of his military men wanted to launch a coup, drive him out of office. They hired the company I worked for to help train their men, provide equipment, give them a leg up in the fighting."

"You went down there?"

"We did what we could. I didn't half understand the politics at the time. And I guess we didn't really care. It was a job. The pres-ident was a die-hard left-winger, so Washington was happy to see him go. The whole thing was over in a couple months."

"Who won?"

"No one did." He slid the plate away. "They ended up trading one bad man for another."

"What happened to the president?"

"He tried to flee the country, but got caught before he crossed the border."

"They kill him?"

"They did."

"Were you there?"

"No, I'd been medevaced back to the States by then. I followed it in the news."

"What happened to you?"

"My jeep hit a mine. They were all over the place then, probably still are. For all I know, it was one of the ones we planted. Knocked me ass over head. I had some broken bones, caught some shrapnel. It could have been a lot worse."

Leaving out the rest, the roadblock, the village.

"Did you almost die?"

"Nah. They shipped me home, and I spent a few weeks in hospitals here. That's where I met your mother. She was a nurse, just out of school. I pretended to be more helpless than I was, just to get her to spend more time with me."

"Did you like it, the Army?"

"I liked the discipline, the purpose. I miss that now sometimes. Why, are you thinking about it?"

Brendan shrugged. "I don't know."

"Go to college first, then decide," Devlin said. "Get that under your belt, and it opens up a world of choices."

"You didn't."

"And I regret that."

"What happened with Mom?"

Devlin looked out at the parking lot, the traffic passing on the highway.

"Turned out I wasn't a very good civilian. I started drinking too much, and I was still having a lot of physical problems. I was just a kid when I went into the service, not much older than you. I didn't know anything about civilian life, really. I'd missed out on a lot.

When I married your mother, I was still in a bad place. I wasn't handling things well, and eventually she got tired of it. Then you came along, and, for a while, things were good. We were happy. I had everything I wanted. And then I threw it all away."

"Why?"

"Because I felt like I didn't deserve it."

Brendan picked at his sandwich. Devlin knew he had more questions, was holding back.

"Anything else you want to ask me?"

Brendan shook his head.

"We should finish up and get going," Devlin said. "I don't want to cause you any problems at work."

"What I don't get," Brendan said, "is why did it take you so long to tell me all that?"

"I don't know. Time never seemed right, I guess." Wondering if he should tell him what he'd told Vic. Decided against it. It would only worry him. He'd laid enough on him for today.

The waitress set down the check. Devlin got out his wallet. "So, college. What are you planning on studying?"

"I don't know. Business, maybe. Or something else. Not sure."

"Only problem with not knowing where you're going," Devlin said, "is eventually you get there."

"You speaking from experience?"

Devlin grinned. "Kid, I am the poster boy for cluelessness."

On the way back, Brendan said, "What are you going to do now? You going back to Florida?"

"I think so."

"I'm glad you came."

"I am too."

"Living on a boat, that must be cool."

"Not really. It's cramped. And expensive."

"If I come visit, can we go out in it? Take a trip or something?"

"Sure," Devlin said, and meant it.

FOURTEEN

I S THAT ROARKE?" Tariq said.

They were parked a half block down from the address they'd been given, a redbrick apartment building off Chestnut Street. Lukas was at the wheel. Quarter to seven in the morning and gray as dusk, no sign of the sun.

The man who'd come out the front door was big and bearded, wore a down vest over a flannel shirt, jeans, and a wallet chain. Lukas recognized him from the pictures. Older, heavier, but the same man. "That's him."

"This isn't good, working in the same city twice. It's too soon."

"I'm not crazy about it either," Lukas said. "But it is what it is."

"He have something to do with the other one?"

"Farrow says no."

"You believe him?"

Lukas didn't answer.

Roarke went to the parking area beside the building, climbed into a red pickup, and drove out of the lot, exhaust puffing white. Lukas started the engine, pulled out after him.

It was a short drive. Lukas stayed far back, just close enough to keep the truck in sight. It turned into a fenced-in parking lot beside a dark bar. There were people waiting outside, one of them in a wheelchair. Lukas drove by without slowing.

He circled the block, taking his time. When he came around again, the bar's lights were on, the sidewalk empty.

"This is good," he said.

The streets were deserted. On one side of the bar was a closed store, riot gate in place. On the other, past the chain-link fence of the parking area, was an empty lot. Across the street, an abandoned factory took up the whole block.

"We should go back to his apartment," Tariq said. "Wait for him there. We can get him alone and talk to him, find out something about the others. Maybe they're even there."

"Too risky."

"What are you thinking?"

"I'm thinking we got lucky."

He turned left down a side street of warehouses and storage units, then left again into a wide service alley that ran behind the factory. He drove slow, looked for security cameras on buildings or light poles, saw none. There was nothing worth protecting here anymore.

Halfway down the alley, at the rear of the factory, was a loading dock. A concrete ramp led down into it, the bottom filled with trash. He swung the Crown Vic around, reversed down the ramp, shut off the engine, and popped the trunk.

"What are you doing?" Tariq said. "You want to go in there now?"

"Why wait?"

"There are people in there with him."

"That's the point," Lukas said. "This way is good for us, how it'll look."

He got out, went around to the back of the car. Tariq followed him. "We even know why we're after these men?"

"Doesn't matter now, does it?" Lukas said. He flexed his fingers inside his gloves, raised the lid. "Could be some beef from way back. Who knows?"

He pushed aside the spare tire, pulled back the carpet beneath to expose the panel set flush there. When he pressed it, the lid clicked and rose up. He lifted the gear bag out of the compartment below, set it on the spare, and unzipped it.

"I still think we should wait at the apartment," Tariq said.

"You want to walk? Say the word."

"Not what I meant. I'm saying there are better ways to do this. Without other people around."

Lukas drew out the pistol-grip shotgun. The blue-steel barrel had been cut down just past the pump, the edge showing silver where it had been sawn.

"We've got him now, we know where he is. A day, two days from now, that might not be the case. We can't take the chance he rabbits. Now's the time."

He took the silenced Ruger from the bag, held it out. Tariq looked at it for a moment, then took it. He eased back the slide to check the chambered round, then tucked the gun into his belt beneath his jacket.

Lukas turned the shotgun over, loaded it with loose shells from the bag. He worked the pump to chamber a round, thumbed in another shell to replace it. It was a messy weapon, but it would look right for this.

He took two dark ski masks from the bag, gave one to Tariq. "I doubt there's cameras inside. But there might be one on the street we didn't see."

"What about the man in the wheelchair?"

"What about him?" Lukas set the shotgun atop the spare, pulled on his mask, adjusted it.

"That doesn't bother you?"

"What difference does it make?" He picked up the shotgun again.

Tariq put on his mask. Lukas took a thin blanket from the trunk, draped it over the shotgun. It was cover enough. It would be a quick walk, around the corner of the factory, straight across the street to the bar.

"You ready for this?" Lukas said. Tariq nodded.

Lukas shut the trunk lid.

"This man Roarke," Tariq said. "He used to be a bad-ass once, right? Back in the day?"

"That day's over," Lukas said. "We're the bad-asses now."

Lukas went in first. He shouldered open the door, heard chimes ring above him, let the towel drop, and brought up the shotgun. Tariq came in behind him, moving fast to his left, the Ruger out.

Behind the bar, Roarke looked up from a newspaper. Lukas pointed the shotgun at him. The man in the wheelchair saw them, but the ones at the bar had their backs to the door. Lukas counted them quickly. One man missing.

Roarke raised his hands. "Easy, now."

They heard a toilet flush. A thin man in a Phillies cap came out of a door behind the pool table. He saw them, stopped.

"Get over there," Lukas said to him. The men at the bar turned then. The television droned on above them.

The thin man looked at them, didn't move. No fear in his eyes.

"Now," Lukas said. He swung the shotgun toward him.

"It's okay, Captain," Roarke said. "All they want is the money. Everyone's gonna stay calm."

The thin man came forward.

"There's good," Lukas said. Then to Roarke, "Register."

Roarke took off his glasses, let them dangle from a cord around his neck. "Not much in there this time of day, boys. You should know that."

"Open it. Give us what you've got." He took a step closer to the bar. With the barrel cut down, range would be a factor.

"Okay. Take it easy. No one's going to give you any trouble."

"Put it on the bar." Lukas could see himself in the back mirror, a masked figure with a shotgun, Tariq to his left, covering the others.

"Hardly worth the aggravation," Roarke said. "We're talking about forty dollars here."

Lukas leveled the shotgun at his chest, finger tightening on the trigger. Roarke saw it.

"It's yours," he said. "Just watch how you handle that thing."

"Do it."

Roarke sidestepped to the register, away from the drinkers, punched buttons. The cash drawer opened with a soft *ching*. Roarke turned to face him again, and Lukas met his eyes, saw it all there, knew what was about to happen. He felt a pulse of excitement that was almost sexual, wondered if Roarke could tell he was grinning under the mask.

Roarke's hand went beneath the bar, as Lukas knew it would. It was all happening as he had visualized it, from the moment he'd first looked into Roarke's eyes. Like something from the past they were acting out again.

When Roarke came up with the gun, Lukas fired.

FIFTEEN

FOUR POLICE CARS this time, two of them parked sideways across the street outside Dugan's, blocking it in both directions. A crime scene van and Dwight's unmarked inside the cordon. All he had told her was there'd been a shooting at Dugan's. The scanner chatter had been cryptic, the dispatcher telling the responding officers to stay off the air, use their cellphones instead.

Half the block was marked off with crime scene tape. The door to Dugan's was propped open with a cinder block, two uniforms standing watch outside.

She parked across the street outside the old textile factory, hung her laminate around her neck.

The two uniforms watched as she approached. One of them went inside. A moment later, Dwight came out, went to the tape, lifted it for her.

"Thanks for the call," she said.

"You may not feel that way in a minute."

He took her aside, away from the two uniforms. It was then she caught the familiar scent coming through the open door—the rusty smell of blood, a whiff of human waste. Under it all, the tang of gunpowder.

"You knew the owner here, right?" he said. "Colin Roarke?"

"He was a source on a story I did. Did something happen to him?"

"Just so we're clear," he said. "Anything I say to you right now is off the record. Assume you're good with that. You can make whatever phone calls you need to make after we've talked."

"What happened?"

"You good with it?"

"Yeah," she said. "For now."

She tried to get a look inside, her eyes adjusting to the dimness. Camera flashes lit the scene. She saw shapes on the floor by the pool table. Closer to the bar, a wheelchair lay on its side. Another flash from a different angle, and she saw the shapes were bodies, facedown, dark patches of blood spreading out from where they lay.

"Roarke?" she said.

"He's one of them. How well did you know him?"

She tried to remember the last time she'd talked to him, couldn't.

"Not well. He was a source, that's all. Are you the primary on this one too?"

"Yeah, I was up. Mendoza's canvassing. Captain's on his way. It's going to be a clusterfuck here in a minute. If he finds out I called you, he'll have my ass."

"Then why did you?"

"Two reasons: professional courtesy. And this." He took a glassine evidence envelope from a jacket pocket, held it up with a blue-gloved hand. Her business card was inside. "Next to the register, tucked under the phone. You talk to him recently?"

"Not for months."

"Looks like you were on his mind. You sure he hasn't tried to reach out to you at all?"

"If he did, I never got the message."

More flashes inside. She saw that the mirror behind the bar had been shattered, patches of gray backing showing through.

"Robbery?" she said.

"Looks it. Register's open."

"When did it happen?"

"Haven't pinned that down yet. Couple hours ago, best guess. Two night-shifters from the Goodwin plant came in for a beer, called 911."

"Where are they now?"

"At Race Street, being interviewed."

"How many vics altogether?"

"Six. Five in the back there," he said. "Roarke behind the bar. At least we're assuming it's him, from his ID. Hard to tell. Shotgun wounds. It's not pretty."

"Two shooters?"

"At least. We'll have a better idea once we process everything. We've got Roarke's cell. We'll go through it, check his recent calls. Will I find you on there?"

"No. I already told you that."

Al Donovan came out, camera around his neck. "Hey, Tracy. Hell of a way to start the day."

"What happened in there?" she said.

He looked at Dwight, who nodded.

"Looks like they herded them in the back," Donovan said. "The one in the wheelchair must have been dragged. Made them all lie down, then took their time. Pop, pop, pop. All head shots, behind the ear or base of the skull, with a handgun, at close range. They weren't taking any chances."

"What about Roarke?"

"He probably got it first, soon as they came in the door. Shotgun blast to the chest, another to the head after he went down. Again, close range. They walked right up to him before they fired the second time."

She looked at the bar top, imagining what lay behind it.

"He had a weapon on him, a nine," Donovan said. "But it doesn't look like he got off any rounds. It's still in his hand, though."

To Dwight, she said, "This is overkill for a robbery. And from here, at least, I don't see any shell casings."

"There aren't any. At least none we've found."

"Then they took their time, picked them up."

He put the envelope away. "Come on, let's walk."

They went back out to the tape, ducked under, moved out of earshot of the uniforms.

"Any actual comment will come from the public information office, understood?" he said. "Everything we told you is on background."

"Understood. But if you're going to try to downplay what went on in there, Dwight, forget it."

"I'm not trying to downplay anything. I just wanted to talk to you before things got crazy. Since you knew one of the victims, I thought you might be able to bring something to bear on all this."

"I don't think I can."

"And you're not holding back anything I'm going to end up reading in the paper, are you?"

"Not at the moment."

"And if you think of something that might help, you'll let me know, right?"

"Of course."

"Thanks," he said. "I need to get back in there."

Once he was inside, she took out her cell, called the newsroom, got transferred twice before Rick Carr picked up. She told him where she was, what had happened.

"Six?" he said. "That's hard-core."

"It is."

"I'll send Photo out and alert everyone here. You can start dictating what you have to Alysha. She'll write it tight, get it up online, and we'll update through the day. I'm assuming A-One printwise tomorrow, of course."

She looked toward the bar. Donovan was still outside. He gave her a quick thumbs-up and went back in.

"Hang on, I'll transfer you to Alysha," Rick said. "Give her what you have so far."

More photo flashes inside. She pictured the bodies on the floor, thought about the other killings she'd covered over the years, the random, senseless shootings and stabbings. She'd lost count along the way. And now six more lives ended. And for what?

You'll drive yourself crazy asking that question, she thought. *And never find an answer.*

SIXTEEN

DEVLIN WAS HEADING south on the New Jersey Turnpike, five miles north of the Philly exits, when he saw the white state police cruiser in his rearview. It moved into the passing lane, no siren or lights, but coming fast, other cars getting out of its way.

He slowed, wondering if he'd been speeding without knowing it, had triggered a trooper's radar. In the mirror, he watched the cruiser swing in behind him. It closed the distance, and the rollers began to flash.

Devlin signaled, steered onto the narrow shoulder, braked to a stop. He shifted into neutral, switched on the hazards, left his hands on top of the wheel.

The cruiser came to a stop behind him, half off the shoulder. The late-afternoon sun glared its windshield, but he could see two silhouettes inside. They would be calling it in, running his plates, checking for warrants.

Another cruiser, lights flashing, pulled in behind the first. Traffic slowed in the passing lanes as drivers began to rubberneck, wondering what was going on, whose day had been ruined.

He waited, keeping his hands in sight. In the rearview, he saw the doors of both cruisers open. When the troopers got out, they had guns in their hands.

Devlin looked up when the two detectives came into the room. He was in a state police barracks somewhere near Atlantic City, but that was all he knew. The troopers who'd stopped him had handcuffed him at the scene, but hadn't told him anything. They'd ridden in silence to the barracks, led him into this room—just a table and four folding chairs—and left him alone, still cuffed. There was no clock on the wall, but he guessed he'd been here for more than an hour.

The two wore suits and ties, with badge holders around their necks. Philly cops. One was in his early forties, tanned and fit; the other older and heavier, sallow, carrying a green folder.

The younger one came around behind him without a word. Devlin leaned forward, let him unlock the handcuffs. The older one didn't look at him, took a seat on the other side of the table, opened the folder.

"Sorry about that, Raymond," the younger one said. "These Jersey troopers can be a little overcautious."

Devlin rolled his shoulders to uncramp them, rubbed his wrists. They were red and welted.

"I'm Detective Malloy, Philadelphia Police Department." He pocketed the cuffs. "Can I get you a cup of coffee, soda? I think there's a machine out there."

"No. Just an explanation."

Malloy took the chair opposite. Devlin flashed back to Riviera Beach, another harshly lit room.

"Aren't you supposed to introduce your partner?" he said.

The older one looked at him for the first time, unamused.

"Sorry," Malloy said. "This is Detective Mendoza."

Mendoza slid the open folder across to Malloy. He looked at it, raised a paper-clipped page to read the sheet beneath. "Couple things we were wondering about, Raymond. Maybe you can help us out."

"If I'm under arrest, shouldn't I get a Miranda warning?"

"Under arrest?" Malloy looked up from the file. "Right now, we're just talking."

"If I'm not being detained, then I'm free to leave, right?" Wanting to know what was going on, but letting them see he wasn't intimidated.

"You live in Florida?" Mendoza said.

"Part of the time."

"You have a Florida driver's license."

"I do."

"Who do you know in Pennsylvania?"

"Why?"

Malloy half smiled. "That's a simple question, Raymond. Why get nervous?"

"I'm not. Am I the target of an investigation?"

"You been through this before?" Mendoza said. "Or is that something you heard from some lawyer, told you exactly what to say?"

"I'm beginning to think I need one."

"Why? You have something to hide?"

"No. Just on general principles."

Malloy looked at the file again. No one spoke.

Silence, Devlin thought, *the most basic interrogation technique. Say nothing, hope the other person will blurt out something to fill the vacuum.* He sat back, ready to wait them out.

Without looking up from the folder, Malloy said, "You're a veteran. Allow me to thank you for your service."

"You're welcome."

"I was ROTC in high school. By the time I got done with college, though, law enforcement looked like a better idea. Twenty years later, no regrets."

"Good for you. I'll ask again: Am I under arrest?"

"You want to be?" Mendoza said.

"If the answer to my question is no," Devlin said, "then I think I'm free to go. And that's what I'm going to do unless someone starts telling me why I was pulled over and cuffed, and why I'm sitting here."

"This will only take a few minutes, Raymond," Malloy said. "Okay if I call you Raymond? Like I said, you might be able to help us here. You know a Colin Roarke?"

He looked from Malloy to Mendoza. The older man was watching him. "Yes."

"When was the last time you saw him?"

He met Malloy's eyes. "Yesterday."

"And you were at his apartment, is that right? You were staying there?"

"Last night, yes. How did you know that?"

"Security camera," Malloy said. "Outside his apartment building. We talked to the super there, pulled the tapes. He told us a vehicle he didn't recognize had been parked there overnight. We ran the plates, thought you'd be a good person to talk to, so we put out a BOLO. That's why the troopers pulled you over."

"Why did you pull the tapes? What happened?"

Malloy didn't answer.

"What were you doing there?" Mendoza said.

"Visiting. We're old friends. Did something happen? Where is he?"

"You had keys to the apartment?"

"They were spares. He gave them to me. I left them there. But no more answers until you start coming up with some yourselves."

Malloy turned to Mendoza. The older man shrugged. "Your call."

Malloy swiveled the open folder around, slid it across the table. Devlin saw photographs inside. He looked at the top one and knew then what had happened, why he was there.

*　　*　　*

They'd moved to a break room at the barracks, Devlin sitting on a folding chair, elbows on his knees, holding his Styrofoam coffee cup with both hands. Through an open door he could see a long hallway that ran down to the dispatcher's desk. They'd talked for another half hour in the interview room, then Malloy had brought him out here. Mendoza had left them alone.

Malloy was at the coffeemaker. He poured himself a cup, ripped open a packet of sugar and dumped it in, took a stirrer. He dragged an open metal folding chair across the floor, sat near Devlin.

"I'm sorry. He was your friend. This must be tough. I know it was years since you'd seen him, but still." He sipped coffee.

Devlin had told them about driving up from Florida. Nothing about what had happened with Bell. It would only complicate the situation. They could find that out on their own.

"Lou was a little brusque in there," Malloy said. "It's just his nature. Security tape shows you leaving the apartment this morning, about an hour or so after Roarke. He was gone before you woke up?"

"He was."

"So you didn't talk to him?"

"No." *Not even a chance to say goodbye,* Devlin thought. He wondered where he'd been at the time of the shootings. On the road, probably somewhere in New Jersey, heading north. Not far away.

"Your gas station and IHOP receipts match what you told us. If we wanted, we could check the tollbooth cameras on the turnpike, but there's no need for that, I don't think. It's pretty clear you were where you said you were."

"Where's my truck?"

"We had it towed to the lot here. Not safe to leave it out on the highway. Might cause an accident."

"My keys?"

"Dispatcher has them. But let me ask you, was Roarke into anything that might have put him in danger? Any enemies you knew of?"

"I thought you said it was a robbery."

"That's the assumption we're under, the most likely scenario. But it's better not to rule anything out at this stage. I like to poke around a little, talk to people who knew the victim. Could be Roarke was a target. Someone had a grudge."

"And took out five other people as well?"

"Standard narrative for this type of crime is a couple of lowlifes looking for a quick payday, with more balls than brains. They go into a place loaded for bear, panic when they see the bartender has his own piece. Maybe they're wired on something. Meth, coke, who knows. Personally, in this case I doubt it."

"Why?"

"I've got them on video."

Devlin straightened. "Inside the bar?"

"No, not inside. Factory across the street was out of business, but still had working CCTV, believe it or not. There'd been some vandalism, so the owners put in cameras, including one on the outside wall. Angle's not great, but we have a clear shot of two men going in, then coming back out again. Less than four minutes inside, by the time code. They did a lot of damage in that time. And they looked just as calm coming out as they did going in. No rush, considering what they'd just done."

"What are you saying?"

"Nothing. Odd timing, though, isn't it? You come all this way to visit an old friend, first time in years, and he gets killed in an armed robbery the next day?"

"You really trying to fit me into this somehow?"

"Not especially. I'll be straight with you. I buy most of your story. Other parts, not so much. I'm not saying you were involved in what went down, but I think you know more than you're telling. Or at least you have some ideas about it."

Devlin set his cup on the table. "Then you'd be wrong."

"Wouldn't be the first time." Malloy stirred his coffee. "We're still trying to track down next of kin. He have any family you know of?"

"He was a widower. That's all I knew. If they had kids, he never mentioned them."

"It'll be a while before they release the body. Hopefully we'll find someone before then. What will you do now?"

"Head home, I guess," Devlin said. "No reason for me to stay around up here."

"I can't stop you. You're not being detained, and you're certainly not under arrest, but I'm going to want to talk more, maybe bounce some things off you."

"I'll help if I can."

Malloy leaned forward. "Let me be clear, Raymond, so there's no mistake. This is what we call a red ball, all the way. Six homicides, innocent victims, most likely, and five of them whose only crime was needing a drink to get started for the day. That can't stand. I plan to close this, and soon."

He took a business card from his jacket pocket, held it out. Devlin took it. "My number's on there. If you're Colin's friend, you'll want to help us get the men that killed him."

Malloy stood, went to the counter, poured his coffee into the sink. "But if I think you're withholding information from me — anything at all — and I find out about it?"

Devlin waited.

"Then you're going to need that lawyer after all."

SEVENTEEN

DEVLIN WOKE BEFORE dawn. He lay in bed in the warm darkness of the motel room, and it all came flooding back over him—what had happened, where he was, the photos.

He'd checked in the night before, after leaving the trooper barracks. He needed time to think, process what had happened already, what might happen next.

After he showered and dressed, he made a cup of coffee from the portable brew pot in the room. He hadn't eaten since lunch with Brendan, but he wasn't hungry. He wanted a drink.

There was a wooden folding chair leaning against the wall in the closet. He took it outside to the second-floor walkway and shook it open, sat and sipped coffee, looking down at the parking lot. The neon sign by the entrance proudly advertised COLOR TV and IN-ROOM PHONES. The motel was one of what seemed like dozens on this stretch of South Jersey highway. The Ben Franklin Bridge was only a few hundred yards away, traffic already funneling into the city, headlights on. To the east, the coming day was a blue-pink glow on the horizon.

He coughed, his breath fogging in the cold air, drank coffee. He knew he should be feeling something more—a sense of loss, of caution, of danger. But there was only numbness.

You can't just sit and wait, he thought. There was only one way to read it. Someone had sent Bell to kill him. Then, when it had gone bad, they'd sent someone else after Roarke.

On the other side of the river, the glass-and-steel skyline of downtown Philly was catching the first light of day. The twenty-four-hour diner across the highway switched off the lights in its sign. Its parking lot was already half full. Near the entrance he could see a blue newspaper box.

He set the cup on the walkway, went down the steps and out to the highway, waited for a break in the traffic, then sprinted across. Horns beeped angrily at him.

He slid four quarters into the box's coin slot, opened the hinged front, and took out a paper. The shootings were on the front page, a bold headline over three columns. He saw the familiar byline— TRACY QUINN, DAILY OBSERVER STAFF.

There was nothing in the story he didn't already know. It was continued on an inside page, with a photo of the front of the bar, police cars on the street, the sidewalk roped off with crime scene tape. A separate story listed the victims. He saw the name Roger Leland, remembered the thin man in the Phillies cap Roarke had told him about, who'd once been an Air Force captain, then a prisoner of war.

He took the paper with him.

Tracy was at a table in the lunchroom, eating wilted Caesar salad from a Styrofoam container, when Alysha Bennett sat down across from her.

"Yum," Alysha said. "You get that from the truck?"

"Yeah, I never learn." She pushed damp lettuce around with a plastic fork. The room smelled of stale Chinese food and burnt microwave popcorn.

"Rick says I'm free for whatever you need."

"I'm hung up waiting on callbacks, but I could use some help working the phone."

"Great story today. They were talking about it at the noon meeting."

"Then I still have a job for the rest of the week at least."

Alysha nodded at the salad. "If you want to ditch that, I have some extra yogurts in the fridge. Blueberry, I think."

"Thanks. I guess I'll stick with it."

"You still run every day?"

"Allegedly. Not today."

She'd woken up early, eager to get into the office and start working the second-day story. The night before, she'd finished off the bottle of wine on an empty stomach to help her sleep. For breakfast, she'd forced down a bowl of tasteless oatmeal.

"What kind of distance you do?"

"A mile up, a mile back," Tracy said. "But the first one's uphill, so it's a killer."

"That's serious. You better watch yourself, running out there on the road, middle of nowhere."

"Safer than the city."

"You hope. Speaking of killers, where are you on the follow?"

"Major Crimes is dodging me," Tracy said. "Waiting for their press office to put together a release, I imagine. Preferably one that includes an arrest."

"Profiles on the victims?"

"That was my fallback. I'll do it regardless. But if I don't get anything else from PPD today, I'll move that to the lead story."

"You knew the owner, right?"

"Just from the stories I did last year."

"You know much about his background?"

She shook her head. "He was a veteran himself, that I knew. Army paratrooper. And a widower. No kids. I put a request in to DOD for his records. Maybe there's something interesting in there."

"You want help with the others?"

"That would be great, thanks."

"Dwight Malloy still the primary?"

"Yeah. I'm sure he's ecstatic about that."

"He won't return your calls either?"

Tracy looked up at her. "What do you mean?"

"You two still talk?"

Tracy's face grew warm. She brushed crouton crumbs from her lap, closed the container, and tucked in the tabs. "Not often. Have you dealt with him much?"

"Just a little."

"Has he hit on you yet?"

"No. Should I be insulted?"

"He'll get around to it."

"Maybe he has an issue with the whole multicultural thing."

"Wouldn't make any difference to him. You're young and hot, that's all he cares about. He's a good cop, far as it goes, but he can't help himself. He'll want you to think you're cultivating him as a source. Meanwhile, what he's trying to cultivate is something steady on the side."

"Ugh. I know it's none of my business, but—"

She stopped. Jed Wheeler, the night-desk chief, with perpetual dark circles under his eyes, walked past them to the soda machine. They waited while he fed in bills, pushed buttons. A can rumbled down the chute and thumped into the tray. He pulled it out, went back into the newsroom.

"—but you know how gossip spreads around here." Her voice lower now. "A newsroom's full of nosy people to begin with, nature of the beast."

"There was a thing," Tracy said. "It was right after Brian. It didn't last long, and it was a mistake, a big one."

"Who ended it, you or him?"

"Me. I should have known better to start with. He didn't see any problem being married, two kids, and lying to his wife about working late, or having to go out of town overnight on a case. I felt guilty all the time. Or at least more than he did."

"Like I said, not my nevermind."

"You want to call him, see what he'll give you?"

"Are you serious?"

"Why not? Maybe you'll get something I couldn't."

"Unlikely."

"Can't hurt," Tracy said. "I'm not sure what I've got now will fly at the five o'clock. Not much to update. No survivors and no witnesses, except the two workers that found the bodies. I haven't been able to talk to them yet."

She thought about the glimpses she'd gotten inside the bar, the shapes on the floor, the dark patches of blood, the wheelchair on its side.

"If you think it's worth a try," Alysha said.

"They won't dog this one. I'm betting there's a quick arrest. Last thing the mayor or commissioner wants is an unsolved multiple homicide this early in the year. It'll screw up their stats so bad they'll never recover."

She got up, wedged the Styrofoam container into an already full flip-top trash can.

"Now I feel bad," Alysha said. "Like I crossed a line."

"Not at all." Tracy took her cellphone from her belt. "Take this number."

Alysha got out her own phone. Tracy scrolled through her contacts, read a number aloud off the screen. Alysha punched it into her phone's memory.

"Got it. What is it?"

"Dwight Malloy's private line."

"That's not the cell number I have for him."

"You've got the one he uses for police business. The one I just gave you is for other pursuits."

"Will he be upset if I call him on it?"

"He will," Tracy said. "But he'll get over it."

Back at her cubicle, the desk-phone light was blinking. She dialed into her voice mail, but there was no message. Only a few seconds of silence, then a click as the line was closed.

Hang-ups irritated her, even though she knew they sometimes came from sources who'd lost their nerve at the last minute, or didn't want to leave a message. She hit the Callback button, saw the number come up on the display. The line buzzed three times, then someone picked up, didn't speak.

"This is Tracy Quinn from the *Philadelphia Daily Observer.* I think someone from this number tried to call me."

More silence, then a man said, "That was me. I was wondering if we could meet, talk."

"About what?"

"Colin Roarke."

She pulled a notebook across the desk, flipped to a fresh page, got a pen from her drawer, and clicked it open. "What about him?"

"I'd rather talk in person."

"We could work that out. Why don't you come by the office?"

"No. Somewhere else."

She wrote the phone number in the notebook, circled it. "Like where?"

"Someplace private."

"I'm willing to meet, but it'll be a public place, at least the first time," she said. "No offense, that's just the way it is. And I'll likely bring another reporter."

"Don't do that. Not yet. Hear what I have to say first."

"What's your name?"

"That's not important right now."

"Did you know Roarke?"

"I did."

"How?"

"We served together."

She wrote "Army?" on the page, underlined it. "You're a friend of his?"

"I was."

"Do you have any information about his murder? Have you talked to the police?"

He didn't answer. She drew another question mark on the page.

"I'm not from around here," he said. "And I don't know how long I'll be staying. I'm in New Jersey, just outside the city. There's a diner on, wait a minute"—she imagined him looking out a window at a street sign—"Route Thirty."

"The Ben Franklin?" she said. "Near the bridge?"

"That's it. You know it?"

"I know where it is, yeah."

"We can meet there. Say ten p.m. tonight."

"No. It'll need to be earlier than that."

"Then seven. It'll be dinnertime. A lot of people there, if that'll make you feel better."

"What's your name? How will I know you?"

"I'll know you," he said, and hung up.

She replaced the receiver, looked at it. Then she put her heels against the floor, rolled her chair out into the aisle. Alysha was talking to Rick Carr outside his office. Tracy waved to her. Alysha nodded, raised an index finger.

Tracy rolled back to her desk, double-clicked the pen, looking at what she'd written down. After a few moments, Alysha leaned in, said, "What's up?"

"I just got an anonymous call." Tracy tossed the pen on the blotter. "Someone who wants to talk to me about Colin Roarke, says they were friends."

Alysha raised an eyebrow, perched on the edge of the desk. "What else they say?"

"That's it."

"What are you going to do?"

"Meet him. Unless I change my mind."

"I should come."

"My thought too. I mentioned it. He said no, just me. This time, at least."

"I don't like the sound of that."

"It's a diner in Jersey, just over the bridge. He wants to meet at seven. It'll be busy."

"I still don't like it."

"Not sure I do either. But I don't want to scare him off until I hear what he's selling. I'll call you right afterward, in case I get something we need to write immediately."

"This guy could be some kind of nut."

"That's not the vibe I got," Tracy said. "And he specifically said he wanted to talk about Roarke."

"Who was just murdered, along with five other people. Something you should keep in mind."

"I am," Tracy said. "Believe me."

"We should tell Rick."

"Hold off. It might turn out to be nothing. If I get something worthwhile, we'll decide what to do then."

"I'm on 'til nine, making cop checks. I'll be waiting for that call, and if I don't get it..."

"I'll listen to what our mystery man has to say," Tracy said. "Then we can take it from there, see what it adds—if anything—to the story."

"And you need to watch out for your own self."

"I always do," Tracy said.

EIGHTEEN

A T SIX-TWENTY, Devlin pulled the Ranchero into the diner lot, parked in the shadows away from the pole lights, but with a view of the highway and the front door. Through the big windows he could see people at tables inside. Others were at the register, waiting to be seated.

Fifteen minutes later, a light-blue Toyota pulled in, a woman driving, no one else in the car. She parked at the other end of the lot, didn't get out. *She had the same idea*, he thought. *Get here early, watch and wait.*

A few minutes after seven, she left the car, walked up the steps to the entrance. Midthirties, wearing a thigh-length leather coat, hands in her pockets.

Inside, she spoke to the man behind the register, who shook his head. She turned to look around the room, spoke to him again. He took two oversized menus from a rack and led her away, out of Devlin's sight.

Threshold moment, he thought. *You walk through that door and talk to her, and everything changes. It'll be out of your control then, with no telling where it might lead. Or you can drive away now, forget about her, figure out on your own what to do next.*

He started the engine.

"No-show so far," Tracy said. "I'll wait a while, see if he turns up."

She was at a booth by a side window, away from the other diners, with a view of the parking lot.

"Maybe you should just come on back," Alysha said.

"I'll give it until seven-thirty, then I'm gone."

"Call me back, let me know. I'm ten minutes away if you need me."

She ended the call, left her cell on the table. Feeling uneasy now, exposed. Was he outside somewhere, waiting for her to leave so he could follow? She reached into her right-hand coat pocket, touched the cool metal of the pepper-spray canister.

Maybe you need to question your own motives, she thought. *Are you taking an unnecessary risk just to prove yourself to your bosses? To stave off what might be coming?*

She didn't hear footsteps, only felt a presence. When she looked up from her menu, a man stood there. Fifties, she guessed, tanned. Dark hair going to gray. A faint line of scars over his left eye.

"Tracy Quinn?" he said.

She nodded, and he slid into the booth across from her. "My name's Ray Devlin."

"I thought you weren't coming."

"I almost didn't. I was out there trying to decide whether to come in or not. I saw you park."

"Why didn't you beep your horn, flash your headlights or something? Let me know you were there."

"I wanted to make sure you weren't followed."

"By whom?"

"Anyone," he said.

She picked up her cell. Before she left the office, she'd entered his number into her phone. Now she scrolled down to it, hit the Call button. Two seconds later, a phone buzzed in his jacket pocket.

"Yeah," he said. "Same guy."

She ended the call. "What made up your mind?"

He looked at her.

"To come inside," she said.

"I guess I had no place else to go."

A waitress came toward them.

"Probably look better if we get something," he said. "Coffee, at least."

Tracy ordered coffee and an herbal tea. When the waitress left, she said, "You wanted to talk about Colin Roarke?"

"Yes."

"Just to be clear," she said. "I have to call my office in fifteen minutes. If they don't hear from me by then, they're sending the police here. So let's cut to the chase." Looking at him, wondering if he believed her.

"You wrote a story about a body in a vacant house."

"What about it?"

"Colin showed it to me. He knew the victim. A day later, Colin was dead."

"You think those two things are connected? Police say Dugan's was a robbery."

"That's what they say."

"But you don't?"

"I think there might be something else going on."

"Like what?"

The waitress came back, put the tea in front of Tracy without asking. She smiled at Devlin, left his coffee.

"Like what?" Tracy said again.

"I can't tell yet. Colin said he knew you, from another story you did a while ago. Said he trusted you."

"When did he tell you that?"

"The other day. I was staying with him."

"The day before he was killed?"

He nodded.

"Do the police know this?"

"Yes, they questioned me. A Detective…" Trying to remember the name.

"Malloy?" she said.

"That's it. And another one, Mendoza."

She reached into her jacket, drew out the pocket digital recorder, set it on the table. "This is just for my purposes." She switched it on. The recording light glowed green.

"No," he said, and reached for it. She moved it away before he could touch it.

"I only use it for notes," she said. "My memory's not what it used to be. You know how it is." She tried to smile, relax him. He shook his head.

"Okay," she said. "If you're more comfortable without it…" She switched off the recorder, but left it on the table, took out a notebook.

"I'm starting to think I made a mistake," he said.

Worried about losing him now, having him walk out without giving her anything. "I work better from notes."

"Can't we just talk right now? Leave that for later?"

"All right," she said. "No problem." It would have to do for now. She set the notebook aside. "You knew Roarke from the Army?"

"That and other things. I hadn't seen him in a while, but we were friends."

"What other things?" Trying to keep her tone casual. She squeezed a lemon slice into her tea.

"I need to know we're off the record here."

"You haven't told me anything worth going on the record for yet," she said. "I'm not even sure who you are."

He pulled a wallet from his back pocket, opened it, and took out a driver's license. He slid it across to her. "Just so we're on equal footing."

She looked at it, saw his picture, the name Raymond Devlin, and a Florida address.

"Okay," she said. "You're you. That still doesn't tell me anything." She would run the name when she got back to the office.

He replaced the license in his wallet, nodded at her phone. "Isn't it about time?"

"In a minute. We're not getting very far here. I'm starting to wonder if I'm the one made the mistake."

He nodded out the window. "I'm staying at that motel right across the road. It might be better to talk there privately."

"Here's fine."

The waitress reappeared. "How are we doing?"

"We're good," Tracy said. "Thanks."

She looked at the recorder, went away.

"I don't think Colin was killed in a robbery," he said. "I think he was targeted."

"Why? By who?"

"I'm not sure."

"You have any evidence to back that up?"

"Not yet. That's why I wasn't sure if talking to you was the right thing or not. At first, I didn't think it was."

"What changed your mind?"

"I still don't understand it all. But I think whoever killed Colin might be after me next."

She sat back. "Why?" *Let him tell it*, she thought. *Don't push.*

"I don't know yet. It may be because of something we were involved in years ago."

He took a business card from his wallet, handed it to her. She read it, said, "Who's Eldon Daniels?"

"His real name's Aaron Bell. He was a friend of Colin's and mine, once upon a time. Have you ever heard of that company?"

She ran her thumb over the card's embossed surface. "Core-Tech Security? No, I don't think so. What's this about?"

"I only know pieces of it myself."

"You tell any of this to Detective Malloy?"

"No. There isn't much to tell anyway. At least nothing that makes sense. You know as much as I do right now."

"Somehow, I don't think that's true."

He sipped coffee.

"How's this related to the body in the rowhouse?"

"Emilio Mata," he said. "Alias Esteban Marota. Colin knew him."

"He told you that?"

"He did. He helped him get settled here."

"From San Marcos?"

"Colin and I both did some work there years ago. That's how he knew Mata."

"What kind of work?"

He didn't answer.

"I'm not quite sure what you want here," she said. "I'm a reporter. I work for a newspaper. I write stories for that newspaper. If you're telling me there's something going on here that ties into the Dugan's homicides, and I can prove it, I'm going to write about it."

"You have resources I don't. You can find out things I can't. Maybe we can help each other."

"Maybe not. My agenda is to do my job. I'm still not sure what yours is. And this off-the-record deep-background stuff only works if I get something on the record to back it up. You want me to get involved, you're going to have to give me something worth chasing."

"The other thing," he said, "is that I have a family. An ex-wife and a son. If I'm in danger, they might be too. And I can't have that."

"Even more reason to go back to the police."

"I have nothing else to bring them right now. That's where you could help."

She felt it then, the first buzz of excitement, chasing away her uncertainty, skepticism. Wondering what was going on here, what it would take to find out.

He mistook her silence. "Are you interested or not?"

"I believe you," she said. She picked up the card. "I'm going to keep this."

"I'd be curious to know what you find out."

"I'll look into it, based on what you tell me. But I'm not a private information service. This is quid pro quo. You're going to need to come up with a lot more than you've given me. If we can help each other, fine. If not…"

"I understand. So are we off the record?"

"For the moment. And only for the moment. Going forward's a different matter. When things change, they change. And they might change quick."

She moved the recorder closer to him, pushed the Record button again. The light went green. He looked at it, making his decision.

"Off the record?" he said again.

"Right now, totally. Later on, we'll talk about it."

"I guess I'll have to settle for that for now."

"That's right," she said. "You will."

Alysha was waiting for her when she got back to the newsroom. The glass offices were dark. There were editors around the night desk, but most of the reporters' cubicles were empty.

"I thought you were going to call," Alysha said.

"Rick go home?"

"Just missed him."

Tracy sat, took out her notebook. After they'd left the diner, she'd stayed in the car and tried to write down everything she remembered from their conversation, adding it to what she already knew about Mata and San Marcos, trying to organize it all in her mind.

Alysha pulled a chair into her cubicle. "Speak it, sister."

"Everything I have is on background. But it's pretty good. I mean like really good."

"Are we writing anything tonight? 'Cause if so, I need to give the desk a heads-up."

"Not yet." She took out a pen, double-clicked it, then picked up the notebook, flipped through pages. *Start from the beginning*, she thought. *Take your time. Make the connections that are there to be made.*

"If this guy's right," she said, "it's all related. The body in the vacant, Dugan's, everything."

"Slow down."

"Okay, big picture. This is what we've got: Emilio Mata—our decomp who turned out to be a murder—is from San Marcos."

"We knew that. It was in your story."

"In the early '90s there was a coup there. The president—Eduardo Herrera—was forced out."

"I remember that."

"Herrera was a dedicated anti-American anti-imperialist, and San Marcos wasn't a domino anyone in Washington wanted to see fall. His people loved him, though—at first. Then oil prices dropped and everything went to hell, the economy tanked. Eventually there was a coup against him, led by one of his generals from the other end of the political spectrum.

"Herrera was deposed, but not before a lot of people got killed on both sides. Soldiers caught him at the Guyana border, beat him, made him beg for his life, then executed him on the spot. Filmed the whole thing. There's video of it floating around out there. It's pretty ugly."

"I think I've seen it."

"The new president, General Ramírez, started purging the country of Herrera loyalists. At least that's how it started. Then he moved on to just about anyone who disagreed with him. In this case, a lot of the opposition were students, intellectuals, priests, nuns, anybody that spoke out against the government. So the left-wing dictatorship became a right-wing dictatorship. But Ramírez was easier to deal with than his predecessor, so the U.S. looked the other way."

"And this source you met with—"

"His name's Raymond Devlin. I saw his license."

"—figures in how?"

"He and Roarke worked for a private security company based here in the States. They helped train Ramírez's men. Devlin says they tipped the balance in the fighting, paved the way for the coup. Without them, Ramírez couldn't have pulled it off. Herrera would still be in power."

"And this Mata or Marota or whatever his name is?"

"He was Herrera's brother-in-law, and a close adviser. He jumped ship, sold him out. Mata couldn't stay there, though, even after the coup, because he had too many enemies. He resettled here in the States, with a new ID."

"'Esteban Marota.'"

"You got it."

"And one of his enemies from back home tracked him down anyway?"

"Maybe," Tracy said. "Weird it took so long, though."

"Devlin and Roarke both worked for this security company?"

"And a third man, Bell. He's dead too." She took the recorder from her coat pocket. "I got it all here."

"But off the record."

"For now. But we've got our work cut out for us."

"Us?"

"I need a partner on this who knows what they're doing. Rick will clear you, won't he?"

"I don't think we can take that for granted."

"He will when he hears what we've got to tell him. We're talking seven dead men now, counting Mata. Eight, if you include Bell."

"All of which may be entirely unrelated."

"We taking bets?"

Alysha shook her head. "All I'll bet on is you're about to make our lives very complicated."

"Someday," Tracy said, "you'll thank me."

NINETEEN

LUKAS WAS SQUEEZING out his fiftieth push-up when he heard the low beep from the wall console, saw the blinking red light. It meant a car had turned into the private road that led to the house, tripped the sensors there. It would be Tariq. The road branched off from a county two-lane, ran back into the woods for a quarter mile, and ended at the house. No one came back here by accident.

He stood, arms swollen with blood, toweled off, and pulled on a sleeveless T-shirt. He slung the towel over his shoulder, picked up the Beretta 9 from the coffee table, eased off the safety. The shotgun and the Ruger had gone into the Delaware River on the drive back the day before. The Crown Vic was in the garage on the side of the house, parked next to his Lexus, and covered by a tarp.

At the front door, he saw headlights coming up the driveway. Tariq's Jeep SUV pulled up outside, triggered the floodlights in front of the house. They lit the yard bright as day.

Lukas unlocked the door, opened it. Tariq got out of the SUV carrying a brown paper bag. Lukas heard bottles clink.

Lukas held the door for him. "Money came through a little while ago. I transferred your share already."

"How much?"

Lukas took a last look into the yard. Moths flitted in the floodlights. He closed and locked the door. "Fifty K total, as promised. Twenty-five each."

Tariq had gone through into the kitchen. Lukas heard the refrigerator door open and close, then the sound of a bottle being uncapped.

He tossed the towel onto the weight bench in the corner of the room, slipped the safety back on the Beretta.

Tariq came out of the kitchen carrying a bottle of Budweiser. Lukas had let him stay here for the last six months, given him the whole top floor. But he was drinking more often now, and Lukas knew he'd have to watch him carefully for slipups, mistakes.

"Doesn't seem like much, does it?" Tariq said. "For what we did."

"It's what was agreed on." Lukas sat on the couch, set the gun back on the table.

Tariq took a chair, drank from the bottle.

"That's poison you're putting in your body," Lukas said. "What would the Prophet say?"

"What would your Jesus say about some of the things you've done?"

"I don't know. I'll ask him when I see him."

Tariq leaned over, took the remote from the table. "When I was a kid, Baghdad was full of liquor stores. Even after the invasion." He turned on the wide-screen TV. A World War II documentary. Black-and-white footage of German tanks moving across a blasted landscape.

"GIs in Camp Marlboro—the old Sumer cigarette factory—would give me money to go out and get them beer. I'd ride back and forth on my bike. That was before the curfews—and the car bombs." He took another pull at the beer.

"You want to talk?" Lukas said.

Tariq shook his head, looked at the screen.

"You don't like what happened yesterday, I get that," Lukas said. "But we've come this far, haven't we? Doing what needs to be done?"

"This was different."

"Why? Because of those others? It was their bad luck, wasn't it? Wrong place, wrong time."

Tariq didn't look at him.

"Think about it," Lukas said. "They didn't have to be there, but they were. That's fate, isn't it? Is it any different from what happened to our families? The people we lost, did they deserve it?"

"It's not the same thing."

"It's exactly the same thing. We had a job to do, and we did it. End of story."

On the table, Lukas's phone began to vibrate. He saw Farrow's number, picked up the phone.

"Are you back home?" Farrow said.

"Yeah," Lukas said. "It's done."

"I saw. You going to tell me there wasn't a better way?"

"I made a field decision."

"It was a bad one. And what do you know about field decisions anyway?"

"I'm the one taking the risks. Not you. It was my call, and I made it."

Tariq was looking over at him.

"We need to talk about that, and some other things," Farrow said. "The old man wants to see you as well."

"When?"

"Tomorrow night. At the Towers."

"Not the house?"

"What did I say?"

"I'll be there. I have something to give him too."

"What?"

"He'll see," Lukas said.

When Lukas got off the elevator, there were bodyguards waiting in the mirrored foyer. Kemper owned this hotel in Chevy Chase through a shell company, kept the penthouse for himself. From the foyer, a long carpeted hall ran down to the main room, where floor-to-ceiling windows gave a view of the lights of the city.

The guard named Bishop, with a shaven head and weightlifter's shoulders beneath his suit jacket, nodded to him. He had a lightning-bolt tattoo on the side of his neck, wore a plastic earpiece. This time Lukas raised his arms, let him pat him down.

Farrow came down the hall toward him, gestured to an open door. Lukas followed him into a room with a bank of closed-circuit TVs showing views of the apartment, the hall outside, the elevator interior, and the lobby. Two guards in blue Core-Tech uniforms with holstered guns sat at the console.

"Out," Farrow said. "Shut the door."

When they were gone, he said, "You want to tell me what you were thinking?"

"I thought we were done with that. I had to make a decision. I did. I could have wasted days, weeks, watching that guy, waiting to make a move. Instead, I saw my opportunity, and I took it."

"You made CNN, and just about every newspaper across the country, I'd imagine."

"And they all called it a robbery, right?"

"So far. But it's not just that. It's the other one too. Mata. They found his body. It was in the paper."

Lukas shrugged. "Nothing ties him to us, or anything else."

"It would have been better if he'd never been found."

"So he was. What difference will it make?"

"You seem pretty casual about all this, considering the colossal fuckup you perpetrated a couple days ago. With all that's going on now, the last thing we need is the police—or some reporter—looking into our business. Especially with Devlin still running around loose."

"One down, two to go."

"Just one now," Farrow said. "Bell's dead."

"You know that?"

"It was in the news down there. Florida. The police must have been holding it back at first. Some kind of struggle. Self-defense, from what I read online, which wasn't much. It was Devlin."

"Then it went the way I guessed. Your guy got lit up, rather than the other way around. What you get for using amateurs."

"He wasn't an amateur."

"Either way, one less thing to worry about, right?"

"You need to find Devlin and tie this off."

"Be a little suspicious, wouldn't it? All three of these guys get done in what, two weeks? What if someone makes that connection?"

"We'll have to take that chance."

"I don't get it," Lukas said. "You have a whole organization at your disposal. You could track this guy down, put him under surveillance, tap his phone, anything. And still you're coming to me."

"We can't use Unix resources for this. This is separate. It needs to be contained."

"And deniable, right?"

Lukas looked at the screens—the two guards bored in the hall, an empty elevator, three angles on people milling around the lobby.

"A hundred," he said.

"Too much."

"Not for what you're asking. There are risks involved that weren't there before. This Devlin has to know someone's coming for him next. It changes the game. And from what you said, it sounds like he still has a few moves left in him."

"The old man's not happy about all this either. I had to tell him."

"Worse comes to worst, it's all on me anyway, isn't it?" Lukas said. "It doesn't go any higher. That's what you pay me for."

Farrow nodded, looked away, then back at him. "A hundred. But only when the work's done. And no public spectacles this time. I don't want to see it on the news."

"You won't."

"Come on," Farrow said. "He's waiting for you."

They went out past the two uniformed guards and down the hall to the living room. Winters was there, standing by the windows. There were three other men in the room, none of whom Lukas knew. All the same type—short hair, thick necks, suit jackets with no ties. Two of them sat on a couch watching a basketball game on television, the sound low. They looked at him, then back at the screen. The third man sat in a chair, reading a tablet. He gave Lukas a nod.

"He's in the office," Farrow said.

They went down a side hall, stopped near a half-open door.

"You'll need to make this quick," Farrow said. "He's got an early flight tomorrow. He's in New York the rest of the week. That's why he's seeing you now. You should appreciate that."

"I do," Lukas said.

Farrow knocked lightly on the door, then opened it wider, said, "He's here."

The room was a smaller version of the study at the Virginia house, but more functional, without the warmth. A desk and chairs, couch against the wall, a filing cabinet and a safe. The single painting on the wall drew Lukas's eye. It was of a nineteenth-century sailing vessel, waves breaking over the side, nearly capsizing it. A full moon shone brightly through a gap in the clouds.

"You like it?" Kemper said. "It's yours."

He'd been at the desk, writing on a sheet of unlined paper. Now he stood, came forward. They embraced briefly, and Kemper gestured to a chair. Farrow stayed in the doorway.

"It's okay, Gordon," Kemper said. "We're fine."

"Outside if you need me," Farrow said, and closed the door.

They sat. Kemper had lost weight since the last time Lukas

had seen him. His hair was thinning, and the skin beneath his jaw sagged. But the ice-blue eyes were still sharp.

"You spoke with Gordon?" He took off a pair of rimless glasses, set them on the desktop.

"I did. We straightened some things out."

"Good."

"You look well."

"Sixty-eight. All I can do at this point is try. I heard you were at the house a few days ago. I'm sorry I wasn't there."

"My fault. I should have called first." He nodded at the door. "A lot of new faces around I don't know. And they don't know me."

"Gordon does most of the hiring, at least for private staff. I move around a lot more these days, so I need more people. He also has his own core group he likes to keep around him, and that's fine with me. Loyalty should be rewarded."

"Any of these new faces worth what you're paying them?"

Kemper smiled. "I'd hope so. Not compared to you, though, if that's what you mean."

"Quality versus quantity, right? One man on his own, properly trained and motivated, with the right skills and equipment, is better than any team. That's what you used to say."

"I did. And it's still true."

"About that thing in Philadelphia…"

Kemper raised a hand, shook his head.

"Sorry," Lukas said. "How did the party go?"

"Party?"

"For the senator."

"It went. Isabella likes to entertain, so she was happy."

"Raise a lot of money?"

"A drop in the bucket for what he'll need. More of those events to come, I'm afraid. He's nowhere near where he should be moneywise. I've lent him some of Unix's marketing people to work on his fund-raising strategy."

"One of the reasons I'm here," Lukas said. He reached into his jacket pocket, drew out the envelope full of money, set it on the desk.

"What is that?" Kemper said.

"My contribution to the senator's war chest. He needs all the help he can get, right?"

Kemper's smile faded. "You shouldn't have brought that here. There are avenues for that."

"I don't want my name on anything. I figured you could get it to him directly. There's thirty thousand there. My donation to his campaign. Gordon tells me if he's reelected, it'll be good for all of us."

"He's a man that understands his obligations, that's true. Which is more than you can say for many in his business. I'll see it gets to him."

"Make sure he knows it's from me. Tell him."

"I will. I'm sure he'll appreciate your generosity."

"I could use a good friend too."

"Can't we all," Kemper said. He opened a drawer, set the envelope inside, closed it.

Lukas looked up at the painting again. "That's new, too."

"It's called 'Storm on the Sea at Night,'" Kemper said. "It's by Aivazovsky, 1849. I got it on my last trip to Russia, in St. Petersburg. I'd had my eye on it for years."

"How much did you pay for it?"

"I'd hate to admit."

"More than a million?"

"Quite a bit more. But we've established some lucrative partnerships with Russia in the energy field over the last year, and I wanted a memento of sorts to take back with me. It was my gift to myself."

A knock at the door. It opened and Farrow came halfway in, touched his watch. Kemper nodded. Farrow looked at Lukas and went back out, left the door ajar.

Kemper turned back to the desk, tapped the paper with his glasses. "Some notes I'm making for a meeting tomorrow with the commissioner of the NYPD, and the head of their Strategic Response Group. They're interested in some nonlethal technologies we're developing. Could be quite a coup. They have almost thirty-five thousand officers. What we'd earn would be minimal compared to some of our other contracts, but the public relations value will be priceless."

"I'm sure it will go fine. It always does."

Kemper sat back, crossed his arms. "If there's anything I've learned in my sixty-eight years on earth, it's that wherever there's transition, there's conflict. It's inevitable, but it passes. There are big things ahead for us, Lukas, all of us. You're helping make that transition. Some of the faces around me may change, but never doubt that you're among family. You're like a son to me, and they all know it."

"I'll always be grateful for what you did. Finding me, bringing me over there."

"Now that things are calmer, you may want to go back home someday, visit. Croatia's a beautiful country. You might find you still have some relatives over there."

"No," Lukas said. "Everyone I knew there is dead."

Kemper folded his glasses, slipped them in a front shirt pocket.

"There are things I probably should say more often than I have. You've been invaluable to me. And I know I've put you into some unenviable positions. You've had to deal with the worst of the worst, all for my benefit, and the benefit of Unix. I haven't forgotten that."

Lukas waited, wondering where this was going.

"This NYPD deal"—Kemper touched the paper—"is the tip of the iceberg. We're also bidding on staffing for a network of private correctional facilities in the Southwest. If we get that contract—and there's no reason we shouldn't—that will be a steady source of income for years to come, decades probably." He grinned. "No one ever went broke running a prison in the United States."

"Big plans," Lukas said.

"There are other things too. Some I can talk about. Some I can't, for the moment, at least. What we've accomplished this far is nothing compared to what's in our future. The real work is still ahead of us, in a dozen different countries, not just here. And you'll share in those rewards."

"Thank you."

"Meanwhile, there are certain aspects of the business we're leaving behind. Things with too much risk, not enough return."

"I know." He thought about Budapest, the look in Penskoff's eyes when he realized what was happening. "I can do whatever you need me to do."

Kemper patted his hand, then took out his glasses again. "Back to work."

Lukas stood. "Thank you for seeing me."

Kemper nodded, but he was looking down at the paper again. Lukas felt awkward, foolish, realized the conversation was over. Kemper didn't look up when he went out, closed the door softly behind him.

Farrow was waiting in the hallway. "You satisfied? Get what you need?" Keeping his voice low.

"What I came for," Lukas said. "Yes."

"Feel better?"

"A little. Thanks for your interest."

In the foyer, the two guards waited, watching him. One of them pushed the button to call the elevator.

Farrow put a hand on Lukas's elbow. "I think we need to get some things straight."

Lukas looked down at his hand. Farrow took it away.

"I'm sure he told you about the way things are going," Farrow said. "What's coming together for us."

"Yeah, he did."

"You can't go around stirring up shit because you think you're not getting enough attention. There's too much going on now. Everybody will be taken care of. We all just need to be patient."

"I am. Tell me, those Chinese AKMs, where did they end up? Yemen? Liberia?"

"Does it matter? We're done with that side of the business anyway. Soon everything we're involved in will be one hundred percent aboveboard. We'll never have to break—or even bend—another law again."

"That's comforting to hear. Too late for our Russian friends, though."

"We do what we have to do to move forward. They were a liability."

"Like Devlin."

"Let's just say he's capable of fucking things up for all of us without even knowing it. Why you need to find him, wherever he is, take care of it. When that's done, you can get some rest, go on vacation. Spend your money."

"Thanks for the suggestion. And thank the old man for seeing me. I suppose I should be grateful for the audience."

"He loves you, Lukas. I'm not sure why, but he does. But do us both a favor—don't push it."

Lukas looked at him, wondering if there was a threat there. Winters had come out of the living room, was watching them.

"Don't worry," Lukas said. "When I start to push, you'll know it."

On the drive back, he called Tariq's cellphone.

"We need to get our things together," he said. "Be ready to move."

"What for?"

"Road trip," Lukas said.

TWENTY

ELL ME MORE about San Marcos," Tracy Quinn said.

Devlin looked down at the recorder, the glowing green light, wondered if he was ready.

They were at the table in his motel room. Noon, and the curtains were pulled back, the room flooded with sunlight. In the diner the night before, he'd given her the short version of what he and the others had done for Acheron.

"It wasn't just there," he said. "There were other places too."

"I want to fill in some gaps from what you told me. San Marcos was the last work you did for them?"

She had a notebook open on the table. Devlin could see a page of disorganized writing, sentences scrawled at different angles, words underlined and circled, multiple exclamation points.

"The last fieldwork," he said. "I was on disability for a while, then came back to some administrative duties, paperwork, mostly.

I was out of the game, though, and everyone treated me that way. I wasn't privy to any of what was going on, where anybody was being sent."

"I looked up the name you gave me, Roland Kemper, and this company, Unix Technologies. For someone with his history, there hasn't been much written about him. Until recently, he seems to have flown under the radar."

"In that industry, you pay for discretion. You don't want someone with a public face, who shows up in the papers, running the show."

"He's been quite the philanthropist at times. Hospitals, resource centers for veterans. He made a major donation to Walter Reed Medical, a couple hundred thousand. Back in the '90s, he helped fund a U.N. group that sponsored war orphans from the Balkans, brought them to the States, found families for them, set up trusts and scholarships."

"I'm not surprised. He was always generous. As much as he was earning, that probably wasn't hard. Say what you want about his dealings, he always took care of his people financially. Acheron was a good gig, until it wasn't."

"Can you give me some other names, people that worked with you?" she said.

"That wouldn't be my place, would it? And it's old news anyhow. A lot of them are dead."

"It'll be useful to have someone else corroborate what you're telling me."

"I can't help you with that. You can believe me or not. It's your choice."

"It's not a question of what I believe," she said. "It's a question of what I can prove. If I came up with some other names on my own, would you confirm or deny they worked for Acheron?"

"I might. If they were the right names."

"If you did, that would be just a starting point. I'd take it from there. No one I talked to would know how I got their names."

"You say."

"I've never burned a source in my life," she said. "You'll have to trust me."

"Is that supposed to make me feel better?"

"It's all I got."

He liked that. "Fair enough."

"When you were training foreign troops, did Acheron supply weapons to them as well?"

"Some of the groups we worked with could hardly be called troops," he said. "If you have enough money, you can always buy weapons from somebody. In most cases, the locals had no issues getting ordnance. It was learning how to use it that was the problem."

"You were mercenaries."

"Technically, a mercenary is someone who fights for a foreign government for pay. That wasn't us. We worked for an American company that contracted with other governments. We got a salary, bonuses, et cetera, but they came from Acheron, no one else."

"How much were you making?"

"Depended on the job. Where it was, what had to be done. We weren't supposed to do any actual fighting, just train whoever we were hired to train, and provide support. Basic military tactics, map reading, discipline, weapons training. Some hand-to-hand fighting. Basically, we taught whatever they needed. We had guys who'd never seen the inside of a schoolhouse in their life, couldn't read or write, and now we were showing them how to set up perimeters and ambushes, or break down a belt-fed SAW."

"What's a SAW?"

"Squad automatic weapon. Usually an M249, but basically any kind of light machine gun a squad can carry. A lot of bang for the buck, but a bear to operate."

"You were teaching men to kill."

"Mostly we were teaching them how to stay alive. There's always some rationalization goes on in war. But most times I felt we were on the right side, giving underdogs a chance against larger, better-equipped, and better-trained opponents."

"Most times?"

He saw she was waiting for his reaction, for him to take the bait. When he didn't respond, she said, "Where else were you?"

"All over. Around '91, we helped train Croatian Army troops who were fighting the Serbs in what used to be Yugoslavia. Their army at the time was new, basically just a police force. The Serbs were chewing them up at first. They needed help. That's where we came in."

"And that's what you did in San Marcos?"

He looked out the window, deciding how much he wanted to say, how to say it.

"You know much about the country?" he said. "What happened there?"

"Now I do. Most of what I read was pretty depressing."

"Herrera, the president back then, fancied himself a new Fidel. He was giving the finger to Washington, talking about throwing out U.S. oil companies, seizing their production facilities. At the same time, his people were starving, and anybody who spoke out against him ended up in prison or dead in the street."

"Then came the coup."

"Ramírez saw the time was ripe. He had part of the army behind him, but they were ill equipped and ill trained. His people reached out to Acheron, contracted for advisers. They sent Roarke, Bell, and me. We didn't know much about what was going on there politically at the time, and didn't much care. I didn't even speak Spanish."

"Just the three of you?"

"We were cadre, that's all. Instructors. The idea was we'd train a certain number of troops, who'd then pass those skills on to others. They moved us around to different units. We shared what we knew. It wasn't just fighting, though, there were other aspects as well. Gathering intel, interrogation."

"Torture?"

"I never saw any of that."

"You're not saying it didn't happen."

"After the fighting started, Ramírez's men took over an old shopping mall, used that as a detention and interrogation center. The three of us never set foot in there. I don't know what went on behind those walls."

"But you could imagine."

"I could," he said.

"Did you go along on operations?"

"Not usually, for obvious reasons. If we were killed or captured and word got out, it would look like America was involving itself in a foreign conflict, private firm or not. It would have been a mess. Would have put Acheron out of business."

"You said 'usually.' So there were times you did?"

He looked out the window again, then back at her. "Yeah, there were times."

"How long were you there?"

"Only three months. After the coup, Ramírez didn't need us anymore, and didn't want us around. Can't blame him."

"You didn't answer my earlier question. Was Acheron selling Ramírez arms?"

"Not that I saw firsthand, but I wouldn't be surprised. When we got there, a lot of the equipment his people had was Cold War era, or AK knockoffs. But after a while, the quality of what they were getting seemed to improve—Claymore mines, M-16s, better coms."

"Coms?"

"Communication setups, radios. Did I ever see money change hands, or weapons being offloaded? No. But it made no difference to me. I was happy to have them."

"This was all illegal, wasn't it?"

"Washington wanted Herrera gone, so no one was going to come down hard on us. They felt they were better off with Ramírez in place."

"You said you got hurt there. What happened?"

"I hit a mine on a road. They weren't so good at keeping track of where they were planting them back then."

"I read a lot of civilians were killed during the fighting," she said. "Murdered by both factions, especially out in the countryside. Did you see any of that?"

He gestured to the recorder. "Turn it off."

"Why?"

"Please." It had snuck up on him, and now he was seeing it again, muzzle flashes and the gray haze of gun smoke. Remembering the heavy silence that had seemed to quiet the jungle itself.

She hesitated, then said, "All right," and touched a button. The green light went out.

Here you are, he thought. *Another threshold moment. How far will you go?*

"We ended up putting together a commando unit," he said. "About twenty men we'd handpicked, led by a Sergeant Garza. They called themselves El Tigre Battalion—the Tigers. We had them conducting operations, sniping, night patrols, demolitions. Anything to chip away at Herrera's hold on the country.

"Herrera was from a village called Santa Rosa on the Rio Negro— the Black River. It's where he was born. Garza claimed he'd gotten intel from a prisoner that a company of Herrera's men were holed up there, using it as an operations base.

"Bell, Roarke, and I planned the mission. It was a predawn attack from upriver, using Zodiac boats the U.S. had supplied. There was only one main road in and out of the village, so the three of us set up a command post and roadblock. That way we could drive back any troops who tried to escape, and hold off any reinforcements they might call in from another area. We'd also be able to monitor the progress of the attack, stay in radio contact. It was a textbook operation. At least it started out that way."

"What happened?"

"The intel was wrong."

"How?"

He blinked, squinted in the light coming through the window, brighter now.

"You need to take a break?" she said.

"Yes."

"We're still off the record, you know. You have my word."

"Some other time," he said. "Not today."

She watched him for a moment, then turned a page in her notebook. He saw more scrawled writing.

"Quid pro quo," she said. "My part of the bargain. I looked up this firm Bell worked for, Core-Tech, ran some corporate database searches. It's a Delaware company, no surprise."

"What's that mean?"

"Delaware's a friendly state when it comes to setting up shell companies and tax shelters. It's easy to incorporate there, and there isn't much oversight. That's why it's a favorite for money launderers."

"Did you get an address?"

"Yes, but it won't do me any good. Probably a drop box there, nothing else. There are about seven hundred other businesses using that same corporate address. I'm trying to get some more financial documents. They're in the security business, all right, and it looks like they have a lot of contracts, here and overseas, including some dodgy countries that aren't exactly sticklers when it comes to banking regulations."

"Which means what?"

"I don't know enough to say yet. You'd need a forensic accountant on the case who knows what to look for. But if you're asking me off the top of my head, I'd say someone was doing a little money washing."

"For who?"

"That's what I don't know. And before you ask—no, I haven't found anything that links it to Unix or Kemper. Yet."

"There was no other information?"

"Just a single administrator's name." She pulled the notebook closer. "G.—the initial—Farrow. Does that mean anything to you?"

Gordon, he thought. *Still at it after all these years.*

"It does, doesn't it?" she said.

He shook his head. "No."

"Are you sure?"

"I am. Are you going to write about all this?"

"Based on a single unattributed source? I don't think my editors will go for that. That's why any other names you can give me will help."

"I think I'm done for the day."

"When can we meet again?" she said.

She was trying to stay calm and professional, he knew, not wanting to spook him, but he could see the excitement there. She'd come to this meeting prepared, had done her homework based on the little he'd told her the night before.

"I'll call you," he said.

She put away the recorder, closed her notebook, sat back. "Talking about this, does it help, or hurt?"

"What do you mean?"

"It sounds like you're still struggling with some things yourself."

"Who isn't?" he said.

After she left, he drove back into the city, slow-crawled past Dugan's, not sure why. The door was still sealed, yellow tape strung across it. Dark windows like empty eyes. He imagined what it looked like inside, blood on the floor and worse. For the first time, he felt anger.

He found an internet café in a strip mall, logged on to a computer. Unix Technologies had no website at all he could find. Core-Tech Security's site was nothing but the same corporate logo as on Bell's card—arrows and lightning bolt—and a link that said "More About Us." When he clicked on it, it sent him to a page with a cartoon of a man driving a bulldozer, and a caption that read "Under Construction! Check Back With Us Soon!"

A white pages search turned up four Gordon Farrows, one in

Ohio, one in San Francisco, another in Maine, and a fourth in Falls Church, Virginia, a D.C. suburb. He clicked through into a map program, punched in the address, saw it was a three-hour drive.

He took a discarded sheet of copy paper from the recycling bin next to a printer, wrote down the address, and headed back out to his truck.

TWENTY-ONE

TRACY CALLED ALYSHA on her way back to the office.

"How'd it go?"

"I got a lot," Tracy said. "More than I expected, but not as much as I wanted. What's the situation there, Harris around?"

"He's in a meeting. He had one of the interns looking for you a little while ago. Ted Bryson was asking too."

"They can wait. I'll be there in ten minutes. Meet me in Rick's office."

When she got to the paper, she used the back stairs. Rick was at his desk, Alysha in the chair across from him, a notebook open on her knee. Tracy closed the door behind her, took another chair. Rick's office was smaller than R.J.'s, a simple bookshelf, an untidy credenza piled with newspapers. On his desk was a plexiglass cube with a baseball signed by Steve Carlton.

"Let's hear it," he said.

"What Devlin told me is the tip of the iceberg. This is substantial, Rick. It's bigger than I thought."

"What's new we didn't have yesterday?" he said.

"An explanation of how Acheron operated, and where. Confirmation that Colin Roarke and Devlin and the third man, Bell, all worked for them."

"But all of it still off the record?"

"I'm working on that."

He looked at Alysha. "And you? Feeling the love?"

"Everything Tracy's got so far checks out. Devlin's Florida address is a P.O. box, but it's legit. We're still waiting to hear back on his military records. No criminal history I can find, and he doesn't come up anywhere else on LexisNexis. Whatever he's been doing all these years, it's been on the down-low."

"I'm a little concerned about what we're getting into here," Rick said. "We don't know what this guy's motives are, why he's decided to talk to us. We don't know much about him at all."

"My gut feeling is he's exactly who he says he is," Tracy said. "He has a friend who got killed. He wants to see someone punished for it."

"Or punish them himself. You think of that?"

"I have. But all the same, there's a much larger story here."

"You think he knows who the Dugan's shooters were?" he said.

"No. But I assume he has pieces of the puzzle we don't, that he isn't willing to give us yet. I think he will if we're patient. I didn't want to push too hard, make him skittish."

"Are we getting played?" he said.

Tracy looked at Alysha, then back at Rick. "It's always a possibility, but that doesn't make the story any less real."

He sat back, laced his fingers behind his head.

"This story goes nowhere without someone on record," he said. "You know that as well as I. A one-source story is bad enough. A one-source story where the source insists on staying anonymous is a nonstarter, regardless of what he tells you."

"I have a call in to this Unix Technologies," Alysha said. "I left a message with their HR department, trying to find out if Devlin or Roarke or Bell were ever actually listed as employees. They're saying everything has to go through their public affairs division. No one's called me back yet."

"I'll go down there if I have to," Tracy said. "Knock on their door, see what they say then."

"He didn't give you any other names, off the record or not?" Rick said.

"No, he wasn't ready for that."

"Then the question is, will he ever be?"

"Let's hope," she said. "I'm doing my best."

"I know you are." He sat up straight. "R.J. asked me to pull you off this. He says you have other obligations."

She felt her stomach tighten. "What did you tell him?"

"That I wasn't sure what you two had going yet, that I wanted to see what it was before making any decisions."

"You're equals, right?" Tracy said. "He can't overrule you."

"No, but he can go up the chain of command to Irv. Then it's out of my hands."

"Can you fend him off?"

"That's not the way things work here. These days we're all—"

"Team players," Tracy said. "I know. I heard the speech."

"But if I were to make an argument to keep you on, a lot of it would depend on what we had in front of us. The more we have, the easier it is to defend."

"Got it," she said.

He leaned forward. "Write what you have, type up your notes, send them to me. I'll talk to R.J. No promises."

"Will do," Tracy said. "Thanks, Rick."

Back at her desk, she powered up her terminal, started to go through her emails. There was one from Harris, time-stamped 11:30 a.m., that read "ARE YOU HERE?" She deleted it, then opened a New Story template, started to type. A lede had come to her in the car:

The Daily Observer's investigation of the murder of six men at a city tavern has revealed a possible connection with a shadowy private military company that has been involved in covert operations around the globe.

Good nut graf, she thought. *Now all you have to do is back it up.*

There was a tangled pair of earbuds in her pencil drawer. She straightened the cord as best she could, fit in the earpieces, plugged the other end into the recorder, and hit Play. When she heard Devlin's voice, she began to type.

Ted Bryson stuck his head over her cubicle wall, said, "Hey, Quinnster. Got a minute?" He wore a sweater vest over a shirt and tie.

She ignored him. He waved a hand back and forth above her. She paused the player, left the earbuds in, looked up at him. "What's up, Ted?"

He came around the divider, leaned against her desk. "R.J. wanted to get us together for a meeting today, talk about some upcoming stories."

"I just saw his message," she said. "But my plate's kind of full. I'm working on something for Rick. I've got calls to make, notes to transcribe."

"On what?"

"Who's asking?"

"Just curious," he said. "Normally reporters file their skedline in the system. I didn't see anything with your name on it."

"I know how the sked system works, Ted."

"Which made me wonder what you were working on that R.J. wasn't aware of when I spoke to him."

"I don't know what he is or isn't aware of," she said. "You'd have to ask him."

"I will, and I'll relay our conversation to him."

"Fine."

"I still want to sit down with you for a few minutes, go over some things. R.J. said you'd be able to make a few phone calls for me.

I'm leaving in a little while. Kid's soccer practice. You have time to talk now?"

She raised her hands off the keyboard, made typing motions.

"How about I swing back this way around six-thirty?" he said. "Will you be free then?"

"I'm sorry," she said. "Today's Tuesday? I have a spin class at the Y at seven, and it's across town."

"Spin class?"

"What, you don't believe me?"

He frowned. "All right. How about tomorrow?"

"Tomorrow's good," she said. "Let's definitely do it tomorrow."

"Right," he said, and walked away.

She switched the recorder back on. Alysha pedaled her chair across the aisle and into Tracy's cubicle.

"Careful," she said. "We're all going to be working for that guy someday."

"If any of us are still here."

"You're enjoying this, aren't you? You've been sleepwalking around here the last month like you're waiting for the ax to fall. Now you're acting like some kid fresh out of J-school just got her first byline."

"Life is short," Tracy said. "And energy is the only delight."

"You just make that up?"

"No, that was Blake."

"The country singer?"

"Close enough," Tracy said.

TWENTY-TWO

A SINGLE ROAD led in and out of the development. The guard booth out front was unmanned, the gates up. Devlin drove through, slowed to cross a speed bump. The Ranchero would stick out here, but he'd draw more attention on foot. It wasn't a neighborhood where people walked.

Side streets branched off the main road, circled around and into cul-de-sacs. The houses were all McMansions, some with stone walls in front, gated driveways. All set far enough apart to give the illusion of privacy.

It took him five minutes to find Farrow's address. It was in one of the farthest cul-de-sacs, a sprawling, three-story house with detached garage. The garage door was closed, the driveway empty. A short flight of steps led to a side door.

He parked across the street beside a high hedge, looked up at the house. No signs of activity, the windows dark. He considered going up, knocking on the front door, wondered what he'd say if Farrow answered.

You've come all this way, he thought. *Do something.*

He took one of Bell's Core-Tech cards from his wallet, wrote his cell number on the back. He got out, crossed the street, looked through the garage window. Empty. He went up the side steps, tucked the card into the screen door there. Anyone pulling into the driveway would see it.

Walking back to his truck, he saw a dark Chevy Tahoe come up the street into the cul-de-sac. He got behind the wheel, swung the Ranchero around, drove past it without slowing.

The gates were down now, though the guard booth was still empty. In his rearview, he saw the Tahoe behind him. A flashing red light began to revolve on its dashboard.

He pulled to the curb just short of the gates, shifted into neutral. The Tahoe pulled in behind him. Red light bathed the inside of the Ranchero.

He waited, watching the Tahoe in his mirror. Two men got out, came toward him, one on each side. They were dressed the same, dark suits without ties.

He rolled down the driver's-side window. A big hand appeared on the sill. The man looked in. His hair was military-cut, his jaw pitted with acne scars. "Shut it down."

The other one shone a flashlight into the truck bed.

"You fellas cops or private?" Devlin said.

"I need you to shut off your engine, and step out of the vehicle."

"On what authority?"

"Mine. You're trespassing." He pulled up on the lock stem. "Out."

"You two have badges, IDs you want to show me?"

"Shut it down."

The second man came up to the passenger-side window. The flashlight beam played across Devlin's face. He squinted, turned away.

"Last time I'll tell you," the big one said. "Out."

Devlin engaged the parking brake, switched off the ignition. The engine coughed once and died. "Coming on kind of strong for the neighborhood watch, aren't you?"

"Step out, or be dragged out. Your choice."

"You work for Core-Tech?"

The man stepped back, and Devlin saw the automatic in the hip holster beneath his jacket. "Out. Now."

Devlin opened the door, got out. The big man said, "Let me see some ID."

"You first."

The second one came around the front of the Ranchero, turned off the flashlight. He was smaller than the other one, but looked wiry, strong.

"This is private property," he said. "What are you doing here?"

"Visiting a friend."

"ID," the big one said.

The other man held up the Core-Tech card. "You leave this?"

"What if I did?"

"Okay," the big one said. "If that's the way you want it."

His right hand went beneath the jacket, past the holstered automatic and a pair of handcuffs. It came out with a stubby black stun gun.

"Hold on," Devlin said. He back-stepped, bumped into the door.

"ID. I won't ask you again." The flashing light turned the man's face red, pale, then red again.

"He's serious," the second one said.

"If it means that much to you," Devlin said. He pulled his wallet from his back pocket.

"Take out your license," the big one said.

Devlin felt something building inside him. *Screw it,* he thought. *Enough of this.*

He lobbed the wallet at the big one's face, came off the door. The man pulled his head back to avoid it, brought the stun gun up and around. Devlin stepped in close, blocked his arm from the outside, and drove the heel of his right hand into the man's nose.

It rocked him back. He took two staggering steps, more surprised than hurt. Then he grunted, came in fast with the stun gun, and Devlin sidestepped to stay outside it, hooked the man's calf with his right leg, and hit him again the same way. He went over and landed hard, the stun gun clattering on the blacktop. Devlin kicked it away.

The big man scrambled to his feet, drew his gun. Devlin moved in quick, got behind him, locked his left forearm across his throat, pulling him close and off balance. He made a choking sound, and Devlin got a hand on the gun, took it away from him.

"Right there," the second one said. He was in a shooter's stance, gun extended, feet apart.

Devlin kept the big man in front of him. The second one seemed calm, but his finger was on the trigger. *If he fires, he'll go for the head shot*, Devlin thought. *Is confident enough to think he can do it.*

Devlin held up the gun to show it was no threat, kept his arm tight around the big man's throat. He thumbed the magazine release and the clip slid out, landed on the blacktop. He knocked it away with his foot, then shoved the big man forward. He stumbled, almost fell, then turned quickly.

"Don't, Cody," the second one said. "Just step aside."

For a moment, Devlin thought the big man would come at him anyway. But something had changed in his face, a realization of how quickly Devlin had moved, turned the situation around.

"To the side, Cody," the other one said.

The big man moved away, touched his nose. Blood was spotting his shirt.

Devlin grasped the gun's slide with his left hand, pulled it back sharply. The chambered round popped out, hit the street. The second man nodded. Devlin tossed the empty gun aside.

The man lowered his weapon slowly. Devlin held his hands out to the sides, to show they were empty.

Cody sniffed, wiped at his nose, bent to pick up his gun.

"Leave it," the other one said.

Cody straightened. Devlin could see he was building up his confidence again. Devlin waited, wondering which way it would go.

The second man holstered his gun. "You almost got shot."

"I know," Devlin said.

"This range, no question."

"Weren't there better ways of handling this?"

The second man smiled. "Probably."

"Then why don't you go ahead and call Gordon now."

"The major? I already did."

"And what did he say?"

"He said he's on his way."

TWENTY-THREE

SHOULD BE pissed at you," Farrow said. "In fact, I think I am."

They sat in a finished basement, Farrow on a leather couch, Devlin in a cushioned chair. There was a small bar against the wall. On the other side of the low-ceilinged room, a wide-screen television, pool table, and a heavy metal cabinet. An open door showed a bathroom. Cody stood at the sink in there, head tilted back, a bloody handkerchief held to his nose. The second man stood by the bar, casual but close.

They'd waited on the street less than five minutes before Farrow had shown up, driving a black Ford Bronco. Now it was parked in the driveway alongside the Ranchero. The Tahoe was out front. They'd entered the house through the side door, the second man holding it open for them. He and Farrow had spoken for a moment out of Devlin's earshot before they'd come in.

Now Farrow leaned forward, tossed Bell's business card on the coffee table. "I haven't heard from him in a year, at least."

Farrow hadn't changed much since the last time Devlin had seen him. More gray in the hair, lines around the eyes, but the same attitude. On his left wrist was the silver-and-black Rolex Submariner Devlin remembered. A status symbol for airborne troops. He'd owned one just like it, had pawned it after he left Acheron.

"He had that card," Devlin said. "He worked for you."

"Used to." Farrow patted his jacket pockets, took out a hard pack of Marlboros and a Zippo lighter. "But not for a long while. He was starting to seem a little...unstable."

The man by the bar set a glass ashtray in front of him. Farrow said, "Thanks, Holly," and shook out a cigarette from the pack.

"He's dead," Devlin said.

"I heard."

"Then you know how it happened."

Farrow lit the cigarette. "We have a computer program flags the names of present or past employees if they come up online. I read the story that ran in the newspaper down there. I heard about Colin Roarke too. Hell of a thing." He snapped the lighter shut.

"You still with Kemper?"

"I run Core-Tech for him."

"Where is he?"

"Right now? New York, taking care of some business. You know him. He never stops."

"I'd like to talk with him."

"Can't do it, Ray. He's a busy man. And you coming out of nowhere like this...You might be a threat, for all I know. Bracing my people on the street—"

"They braced me. I was on my way out."

"You shouldn't have been here at all. That's enough to make me a little concerned, don't you think? This is my home."

In the bathroom, Cody said, "I think it stopped."

"Make sure you clean up in there," Farrow said. "Teresa sees blood in that sink when she gets home, there'll be trouble."

To Devlin, he said, "Teresa's my wife."

"I guessed."

"I'm sorry, Mr. Farrow," Cody said.

Farrow turned, said, "Holly, will you take him outside? I think we're fine here." He looked back at Devlin. "The sergeant and I are just going to talk old times."

"Cody, let's go," Holly said. Cody came out of the bathroom, cut a hard look at Devlin as he passed, handkerchief still at his nose, shirt stained with blood. His gun was back in its holster. They went out the side door.

"They work for Kemper too?"

Farrow drew the ashtray closer. "They work for Core-Tech, which means they work for me. Kemper has his people, I have my own. Holifield's an ex-Marine, First Recon Battalion. Good man. Cody was with the sheriff's office down here. I think I need to have a talk with him after tonight, though."

Devlin looked around. Paintings of horses on the paneled walls, Farrow's Army discharge, a framed map of Vietnam hand-painted on silk.

"Get you a drink?" Farrow said. "Got just about anything you could want back there."

"No, thanks."

"You don't drink?"

"I do, sometimes."

"Always better to ask. You never know when someone's joined AA since you last saw them."

"Not me. Not yet."

"I remember you had some hard times when you first got back to the States. How you doing with all that?"

"Fine. You know, I saw Colin too. The day before he was killed. I wanted to tell him about Bell, see if he knew anything."

"Did he?"

"No."

"Made me angry when I read about it. They catch the thugs that did it?"

"Not yet," Devlin said.

"You talk to the police?"

"I did. But there wasn't much to tell them."

Farrow ashed his cigarette. "You think there's some connection between Bell and what happened to Roarke?"

"If so, I don't know what it could be. Why do you ask?"

"I hate to bring this up, may he rest in peace, but...Bell was obviously into some shit, going back a while. Could be he had Roarke mixed up in it too. Why Bell came after you, I can't figure. But even when he was working for Core-Tech, I had concerns."

"About what?"

"He had money troubles, I knew that. He was always broke, no matter how much work we threw his way. Whether it was gambling, drugs, women...I don't know. He was freelancing for other security companies too, including a couple of our competitors. One of the reasons we let him go. Who knows what else he had going on."

"What kind of work was he doing for you?"

"Nothing major. Second or third man on some personal security details, a little courier work. To be honest, I didn't trust him anymore. His behavior was getting a little erratic. More I think about it, more I think there were drugs involved."

"He didn't look like he was on drugs when I saw him. He looked strong. He nearly killed me."

"Either way, he was screwing up too much for us to keep him. Letting him go wasn't easy, all the history we had, but it had to be done."

"You say he had debts?"

"I gathered. He had alimony and child support, I know that. And if you let those get out of hand, they'll bury you. Just ask me." He pointed at the ceiling. "Third go-round. Twenty years younger than me, but it worked out. Different experience this time, though. Older you get, the more you let certain things slide, focus on what's important."

"You have children?"

"Two daughters. One's at Vassar, the other's at Brown. Smart kids. You?"

Devlin hesitated. "A son. Just turned twenty."

"That's our immortality right there. What was it Jefferson said? 'We're soldiers so our kids can be farmers, and their kids can be artists'?"

"Something like that," Devlin said.

"We had some times, though, didn't we?"

"Emilio Mata," Devlin said. "Herrera's brother-in-law. From San Marcos."

Farrow sat back. "What about him?"

"They found his body in a vacant house in Philadelphia a few days ago. It was in the papers."

"What was he doing up there?"

"Colin said Acheron helped set Mata up in the States. Gave him a job and a new identity."

"Not on my watch. I don't know anything about that."

"He said you handled it."

"Negative."

"Why would he say that if it wasn't true?"

"No idea. Maybe he got confused. When the cops talked to you about Colin, did you tell them about Bell?"

"Didn't seem any reason to."

"What do they think happened?"

"Robbery, from the looks of it."

"Probably illegals, gangbangers, maybe. I'm surprised the police haven't caught them yet."

Devlin took Bell's card from the table, put it back in his shirt pocket.

"So what can I do for you, Raymond? You haven't said."

"Just wanted to meet, see if you knew anything that I could tell the police about Colin. They're going to want to talk to me again."

"You're helping with their investigation?"

"Not really. I think I was a suspect at first, but that blew over, fortunately. I told them if I found out anything else, I'd let them know."

"I don't think I can help you, or them. I mean, is there a chance Bell and Roarke were involved in something that got Roarke killed? Sure. But sometimes things are just the way they look. What do they call it, Occam's razor? The simplest answer is most likely to be true? We always want to construct some kind of story around things, tie them into a conspiracy. But sometimes they're just what they are. And maybe that's just what this was, a robbery."

"You could be right," Devlin said. "In fact, you probably are."

Farrow leaned forward. "Raymond, as long as you're here... this may be none of my business—and tell me if it isn't—but I'll bring it up anyway. How are you doing financially? It's been a while, your severance, disability, all that. They had to have run out a long time ago."

"I'm doing okay, thanks."

"You need a few bucks, get you by, let me know. I can make that happen. Better yet, we could set up a consulting situation, get you on the books. You wouldn't have to do much, if anything. Core-Tech will pay, and we can work it out taxwise. I'm their CEO, so who'll say different?" He grinned.

"Thanks," Devlin said. "But I don't think that'll be necessary. I appreciate the offer, though."

"Think about it. You were a good soldier, Ray, and you sacrificed a lot for the company back then. I haven't forgotten that. You need any help—with anything—just let me know."

"I will," Devlin said.

Farrow stood in the driveway, watched Devlin's Ranchero head off down the street. They'd sent Cody ahead in the Tahoe to raise the exit gate.

Drew Holifield came out the side door, stood behind him.

"You get it done?" Farrow said.

"Yeah. No issues."

Farrow turned to him. "Show me. Then I want you to look up some stories for me online, print them out. "

"Okay. Anything else bothering you?"

"That Cody. I ought to fire his ass. Guy's at least twenty years older than him."

"In all fairness, boss, he got sucker punched."

"That supposed to make it better? Call Dillon, get him over here, tell him he's on duty starting immediately. Get another man too, to stay at the house twenty-four/seven."

"You worried he'll come back?"

"Just do it," Farrow said.

When he went back in, Holifield was on a cellphone. Without taking it from his ear, he gestured at the laptop computer he'd opened on the bar. On the screen was an electronic street map, a slow-moving red dot that was Devlin's truck. The farther it went toward the edge of the screen, the more the map expanded, zoomed out to show a larger area.

Farrow took out his own cell, popped off the back panel, slipped out the SIM card. He replaced it with another from his pocket, snapped the phone back together, and activated it. He called Lukas's number. When he answered, Farrow said, "Where are you?"

"Home. Getting ready to head down where it's warm, find our friend."

"Forget that. I need you up here."

"Why?"

"Why? Because he just left my house, that's why. My fucking house."

When the call ended, Lukas set the phone on the kitchen table. Tariq sat across from him, oiling a disassembled 9-millimeter Smith & Wesson Shield on a sheet of newspaper. On the table between them was an open gear bag with another pistol-grip shotgun, boxes of shells.

"Farrow?" Tariq said.

Lukas nodded. "Change of plans."

"Why?"

"Devlin's in Virginia. He tracked Farrow down somehow, showed up at his house."

"Good for him."

"How's that?"

"Would you rather hunt a rabbit or a lion?" He began to reassemble the gun, fitting the pieces back into place.

"That some ancient Arab proverb?"

"No. But there's honor in facing a worthy opponent. He went on the offensive, rather than waiting to be found again. I respect that." He took a box of shells from the bag, opened it.

"Farrow's freaking out," Lukas said. "He sends someone to kill Devlin. A week later, the guy shows up at his door. The pressure's on. That's good for us."

"We take care of this Devlin for him, then what?"

"Then he owes us," Lukas said. "And a lot more than money."

Tariq began to feed shells into the Shield's magazine. "This is the end of it, right? Devlin's the last one? Because if he isn't, I think we need to renegotiate our contract." He slid the full magazine home.

"He is," Lukas said. "For now."

TWENTY-FOUR

HE PLACE SHE'D chosen was a coffee shop on the bottom floor of a Colonial-era house in the Society Hill neighborhood. She found Devlin waiting for her at a table near the back window, nursing a go-cup with the lid peeled back. It was late afternoon on a gray day. He'd phoned her an hour before, asked to meet.

"I'm glad you called," she said. "I was starting to worry."

He looked out the window at people passing by on the sidewalk, strolling the cobblestone streets.

"Something wrong?" she said.

"No." He turned back to her. "I'm ready to give you another name."

She got the recorder from her coat pocket, turned it on and set it on the table, then pulled out a notebook and pen.

"Actually, you gave it to me first," he said. "Gordon Farrow. He's the CEO of Core-Tech."

"When I mentioned that name, you told me you didn't know him."

"Playing it safe," he said. "Until I found out more."

"You mean you lied."

"I'm sorry."

She felt a twinge of irritation. "Then why should I believe anything you tell me?"

"I was being careful, that's all."

"He was in Acheron with you?"

"Gordon was career military. Special Forces, served in Vietnam. When he retired from the Army he was recruited into Acheron, helped get it up and running. Bell, Colin, and I all worked for him there. He'd been an officer, so it was a natural fit. He put our teams together, took care of logistics, got us where we needed to be."

"Was he in San Marcos?"

"That was one of the places, yeah. But he wasn't generally in the field with us. He was the liaison between General Ramírez's staff and Acheron. He helped plan operations, made sure they had maximum effect."

"He ran the show?"

"Tactically. But Kemper was the brains and money behind it all. That's always the way it worked. Kemper was the CEO of Acheron. Farrow was his right-hand man. Acheron was eventually folded into Unix. I'm guessing Core-Tech was Farrow's consolation prize. That's his baby. It's a straight-up security company, along with whatever else it's doing behind the scenes."

"Like laundering money for Unix?"

"Maybe."

"How do you know all this?"

"He told me."

"Farrow?" She sat up. "You talked to him? When?"

"Yesterday. He lives in Virginia."

"How'd you find him?"

"Wasn't difficult, once I had his name."

"Which I gave you." Feeling the irritation again. "What else did he have to say?"

"Bell worked for him once, didn't anymore. Said he'd left the company, gone rogue."

"You believe that?"

"No."

She opened the notebook. "Where does he live?"

He told her the address.

"He know about Roarke?" she said.

"He did."

"He have any idea who did it?"

"Not that he told me."

"And if I call him up, ask him?"

"Your guess is as good as mine," he said. "But it can't hurt to rattle his cage a little."

"You're making me worry about agendas again."

"Everything I told you is true."

"And it's all interesting," she said. "But I'm still not sure how it ties in to Dugan's."

"Someone wanted Colin and me dead. They sent Bell after me. If he'd succeeded, I think his next target was going to be Colin. He already had his address."

"That means whoever sent Bell had the resources to send someone else to kill Roarke."

"And make it look like a robbery," he said.

"Why come after you two now?"

"I don't know."

She flipped notebook pages, trying to read her own scrawled handwriting from that morning. She'd made some calls, found a project manager at a nonprofit government watchdog group who'd talked to her off the record. She'd followed that up with a call to the Associated Press bureau chief in D.C., a woman she'd worked with back in Raleigh.

"I did some more research on Kemper and Unix," she said.

"Pulled some campaign finance disclosure forms. Unix has been donating major money to a handful of politicians, both state and national. Nothing unusual about that, but their main beneficiary in the last few months has been Mitchell Harlin. You know him?"

"No."

"U.S. senator from Virginia, two-time incumbent. Unix pumped a ton of money into his super PAC, and Kemper's hosted fund-raisers for him at his house. Harlin's up for reelection this year, and Kemper's betting hard he'll keep his seat. It'll be worth a lot to him if he does."

"Why?"

"Harlin's been a fixture on the Armed Services Committee," she said. "That's his thing—'Keep America Strong,' 'Take Back America,' whatever. He helped Unix get their GSA Schedule."

"What's that?"

"A General Services Administration contract. It's a long-term, open agreement that lets Unix sell to just about any government agency. It turns on the golden faucet, gets the money flowing. It's really paid off for them, especially now. My source in D.C. says Unix is going to be up for a high-dollar contract, primarily for base security overseas. They'd prefer their contracts on a no-bid basis, of course, based on emergency need. The committee needs to approve it, which puts Harlin in the driver's seat to make that happen."

"How high?" he said.

"Way I heard it, four billion over the next three years, and that's not counting projects they've got going on here in the States. The other rumor is they plan to go public at some point in the near future, which means a big payday for everyone involved."

He looked out the window. She saw a dark car with tinted windows slow on the street for a moment, then drive on.

"San Marcos is back in the news this week," she said. "Did you see that?"

"No."

"Things are going crazy there. Infrastructure's collapsing, inflation's out of control. Lots of anger in the streets, most of it aimed at Ramírez, the president you helped install. There's a strong opposition party now for the first time since the coup, led by a doctor named Emmanuel Cruz. Ramírez had agreed to allow general elections in a couple months, then changed his mind and canceled them."

"What goes around," he said.

"They've had protests and demonstrations, a lot of violence. He's also been empowering roving bands of paramilitary thugs, the *colectivos*. They've been responsible for most of the killing there. His hold is slipping, but I don't think anyone in Washington wants to find out what happens if San Marcos goes the way of Venezuela, with food riots and kids tossing Molotov cocktails into police stations."

"Ramírez wants help?"

"Part of his military splintered off, and is backing Cruz. There's talk of another coup. Cruz left San Marcos a few days ago for Brazil. He's hiding out there, waiting for things to reach critical mass back home. He knows if he stays in San Marcos he'll be jailed, or worse."

"And when he's ready, he goes back as a hero."

"Unless Ramírez crushes his movement in the meantime. Then he's a marked man."

"You think all this has something to do with Unix?"

"That," she said, "is what I need you to help me find out."

They'd parked in a loading zone down the street, Tariq behind the wheel, engine running. Lukas had the phone Farrow had given them, loaded with the tracking software. It had led them here, the transponder signal clear and strong.

Devlin's truck was hard to miss, parked at the end of the block. Through the coffee shop window, they'd seen him at a table inside, talking with a woman. They'd circled the block twice, then come back around to where they could watch the front entrance.

"There they are," Tariq said.

Devlin and the woman came out, split up. Devlin headed toward his pickup. The woman walked in their direction, got into a blue Toyota parked ahead of them.

"Who do you think she is?" Tariq said.

"I don't know. Maybe he's banging her."

"If he's lucky. Doesn't look it, though."

"No, it doesn't."

"Then what is she?"

The woman waited for pedestrians to cross, then made a U-turn. Down the block, Devlin had gotten into his truck.

"They're headed in different directions," Tariq said.

"We can always find Devlin again. Follow the girl."

She drove past without looking at them. Tariq swung the car around, pulled out behind her.

TWENTY-FIVE

O N THE DRIVE home, she called Alysha's cell. "I got a name."

"That's a start. Whose?"

The Toyota hit a pothole that shook the car. The muffler rattle grew louder.

"Someone named Gordon Farrow." She spelled it. "Lives in Falls Church, Virginia. Affiliated with a company called Core-Tech Security. Devlin and Roarke worked with him. I should have known that already. I should have dug that up on my own."

It was growing dark. She was already out of the city and into farmland. She turned on her headlights.

"Was your boy ready to go on record?" Alysha said.

"Not yet. But we're getting there, I think. It's coming together."

"This may be a dumb question, but are you sharing any of this with Dwight Malloy?"

"Not yet. Let him read it in the paper first. We work this story right, and it could be our ticket out of here."

"Sure," Alysha said, "but to where?"

"Keep your distance," Lukas said. "And leave your lights off."

They stayed back. It was full dark now, no streetlights, thick woods on either side. A truck coming the other way flashed its high beams at them.

They came around a bend and saw the flare of the Toyota's brake lights up ahead. It made a right turn into a driveway. Tariq slowed, and Lukas saw the stone carriage house there, a bigger house farther back on the property.

"Go up a little bit, and turn around," Lukas said. "Head back to the city. I'm getting tired of all this driving around, waiting."

"What do you want to do?"

"What we came here for."

He opened the glove box, took out Farrow's phone, activated it again. The GPS map came to life, the transponder signal a glowing red dot.

Devlin had parked the Ranchero behind the motel, out of sight from the street. Now he sat on the walkway in the wooden folding chair, thought about what he'd done, what he'd set in motion. The motel sign blinked red, lit the windshields and hoods of the cars below.

He got out his cell, called Brendan's number.

When he answered, Devlin said, "Hey, champ. How's it going?"

"Dad?"

"Yeah. You're shocked, I know."

A pause, then, "What's wrong?"

"Nothing," Devlin said. "I just wanted to say hello, hear your voice." There was talking in the background. "Is it a bad time?"

"No, it's just..." Another pause. "Vic was about to take us out to get something to eat. They made me an assistant manager at work today."

183

"That's great," Devlin said. He felt foolish now. "Go on, I don't want to keep you."

"Can I call you when we're done?"

"Don't worry about it. Have a good time."

"We won't be too long…"

"No, really, it's fine. I'll try you tomorrow. And that's terrific about the promotion. I'm proud of you."

"Thanks, Dad." Louder voices behind him now. "I gotta go. Talk to you tomorrow?"

"Have fun," Devlin said, but he was already gone.

Lukas took the Beretta 9 out from under the seat, threaded in the suppressor. They were in the parking lot of a diner, watching the motel across the street. They'd tracked Devlin here, seen him come out of his room. He'd sat out on the walkway for a while, talking on a cellphone, then gone back inside. The curtain was drawn. Lukas looked up at the door, thinking it through, how he would handle it.

"You need me?" Tariq said.

Lukas shook his head. "Stay with the car. Go on over once I get inside, be ready to move."

He eased the Beretta's slide back until he saw brass, then slid the gun into the side pocket of his coat and got out of the car.

Devlin lay atop the sheets fully dressed, remote in hand, channel surfing aimlessly. He thought about finding a liquor store, getting a six-pack or a pint and bringing it back. Skip dinner, watch television, and drink until he fell asleep.

A knock came at the door. He muted the TV, got up. The knock came again.

He looked through the spy hole, got a fish-eye view of the man outside. Early thirties, black hair cropped tight to the skull.

"What is it?" Devlin said.

"Sorry to bother you. You own that blue pickup?"

"What about it?"

"Somebody backed into it, then took off. I saw them. Desk clerk told me this was your room."

"When?"

"Just a few minutes ago. Passenger-side door, but it took a pretty good hit. You want me to call the police?"

"Hold on," Devlin said. He grabbed the keys from the table, undid the night latch, and opened the door.

Lukas slammed a shoulder into Devlin's chest, drove him into the room, brought up the Beretta. The door shut behind him. He raised the gun in a two-handed grip, trying for a quick head shot. Devlin dove to the side just as he squeezed the trigger. The round hit the mirror above the dresser, shattered it.

He moved fast around the bed, and Devlin came up from the floor, sweeping a lamp off the nightstand, hurling it at him. Lukas knocked it aside with his left arm, and then Devlin was barreling toward him, head down.

Lukas sidestepped, chopped at the back of his neck with the gun. Devlin went facedown onto the carpet, and Lukas stepped over and straddled him, touched the suppressor to the back of his head. "Don't move. Don't fight me. You'll make it worse."

Devlin lay with his cheek against the carpet, breathing hard. Lukas kept the gun on him, but didn't fire. Even suppressed, the first shot had been loud. Another might draw attention.

He saw a pillow on the bed, just out of reach. It would help muffle the sound. He caught the bottom of the comforter with his left hand, yanked it toward him, the pillow coming with it. Another pull and the pillow fell to the floor. He stretched a hand toward it. Too far.

He took the gun from Devlin's head, reached for the pillow, and then Devlin was coming up fast beneath him, and Lukas felt himself being lifted. His feet left the ground, and then he was in the air, the floor rising up to meet him.

*　　*　　*

Devlin twisted the man in midthrow, drove him headfirst into the carpet. He stomped down, trying for his throat, but the shooter was already rolling away, raising the gun again. Devlin kicked at it, caught his wrist. The gun hit the wall and fell to the carpet.

They both went for it. The shooter was faster. He got his hands on the gun, rolled to his feet, spun, and fired. The round passed by Devlin's cheek, his ear, punched through the curtain and window. He grabbed the empty coffee beaker from the brew pot, flung it. It exploded against the wall near the shooter's head, showered him with glass. As the man took aim again, Devlin snatched up the desk chair and lunged with it, drove the top rail into his chest. It slammed him back into the dresser, rocked it against the wall.

The gun came up again. Devlin dropped the chair, got both hands on the man's wrist, pushed it high. He drove a knee at his groin, missed, hit his thigh, tried to wrench the gun away, couldn't. The shooter had both hands back on it, was forcing it down, angling it so the muzzle was close to Devlin's face. At that range, even if the bullet missed, the powder burn would blind him.

Devlin looked into the black hole of the suppressor. He twisted away, drove a hip into the shooter's stomach, broke his balance. He kept his grip on the man's gun hand, pulled it down, and brought his knee up hard into his elbow. The second time he did it, the gun fell to the floor. Devlin kicked it toward the bathroom.

The shooter broke his grip, swung an elbow to the side of Devlin's head that sent him stumbling back. *Get out*, he thought. *Trapped in this room you're an easy target. Stay and be shot.*

The shooter bent, reached for the gun. Devlin went for the door, pulled it open, ducked out onto the walkway. He cut to the left, kicked the folding chair over behind him, headed for the stairs.

He was almost there when he heard the crack and snap behind him, the sound of a round passing over his head. He looked over his shoulder, saw the shooter in the doorway, steadying the gun as he aimed again.

You won't make the stairs, Devlin thought. *The next bullet's in your back.*

He caught the railing with both hands, swung his hips up, felt a blow to his left shoulder. He vaulted over the railing, fell hard onto the roof of the car a few feet below, rolled off and hit the blacktop. The car alarm began to bleat, the headlights flashing.

When he looked up, the gunman was at the railing, aiming down at him. A round went through the hood of the car; another ricocheted off the pavement. Devlin scrambled behind a pickup truck, ducked low, heard a bullet hit the windshield. The next shot clanged inside the bed, set off the truck alarm.

Running footsteps. Over the truck bed, he saw the shooter hurrying down the walkway toward the opposite stairs. He heard a car door open and shut, then a squeal of tires. He raised up in time to see a gray sedan, lights off, come fast across the parking lot, bump out onto the highway. He couldn't read the license plate. Brakes screeched and horns sounded as it pulled out into traffic. He remembered the car he'd seen that afternoon outside the coffee shop.

Room doors were opening, people coming out. He touched his left shoulder, felt the wetness there, the hole in the sweatshirt. *He tagged me after all,* he thought. *Son of a bitch.*

"Slow down," Lukas said.

He was working at the Beretta, trying to disassemble it by feel. Tariq was going too fast, riding hard on the cars ahead, then jerking into the left lane, horns blaring around him.

"You get him?" Tariq said. His face was shiny with sweat.

"I don't know, but slow down, for fuck sake, you'll cause an accident."

Lukas reached over, gripped the wheel with his left hand to steady it. They rattled across the bridge, the city in front of them. Tariq slowed and Lukas took his hand away.

His elbow ached where Devlin had disarmed him. *You're lucky he didn't break it*, he thought. It should have been a clean kill, as soon as he entered the room, but Devlin had moved faster than he'd expected. There was a chance he'd hit him going over the railing, but it wouldn't have been a kill shot. He'd had the opportunity and lost it, might never get that close again.

"Turn left here," he said. Tariq steered the car into a warren of narrow streets.

"Pull up by the corner. Stop."

Tariq braked, steered to the curb. Lukas finished wiping down the gun parts with a rag. He hadn't worn gloves. That might have tipped off Devlin as soon as he saw him.

He got out, went to a storm drain, threw in the Beretta parts and the suppressor. They'd be found at some point, but it was riskier to keep the gun. He'd left shell casings at the motel, inside and out, hadn't had time to pick them up. They would match to the gun.

Back in the car, he felt a tremor in his hands. He squeezed them into fists, then opened them again, held them in front of him until they were still. "Let's go."

You were an amateur back there, he thought. *You made amateur mistakes. You can't blame this on anyone but yourself. You need to assess what happened, what you did wrong.*

Tariq pulled away from the curb. "Where to?"

"Just drive," Lukas said.

TWENTY-SIX

WHEN TRACY GOT to the UPenn emergency room, Dwight Malloy was already there. She'd been home when Devlin called her, told her what had happened. She'd driven as fast as she could back into the city.

Now Devlin sat on the edge of a treatment table in a curtained cubicle. The bloody sweatshirt they'd cut off him lay half in and half out of a plastic trash can. The ER doctor had sutured the two-inch-long wound on his shoulder, brushed the area with yellow-red disinfectant.

"What are you doing here?" Dwight said to her.

"I called her," Devlin said. "I was worried for her safety."

She looked at Dwight. "This yours?"

"EMTs reported an incoming gunshot wound. Closest trauma unit was here in Philly. I heard the call come in, recognized the name. "

"Looks worse than it is," Devlin said.

"It looks pretty bad." Her eyes were drawn to the other, older scars on his torso.

"Just a graze. I got a lidocaine shot, so I'm not feeling much back there."

"The man who shot you," Dwight said. "You sure you didn't recognize him?"

Devlin shook his head. "Just the car, and I can't even be positive about that. I couldn't see the driver."

To Tracy, Dwight said, "Tell me again where you fit into this."

Devlin looked at her, letting her decide how much she wanted to tell.

"We were following up on the Dugan's killings for a Sunday piece," she said. "Mr. Devlin here was helping us out, as a source."

"And what did you find out?" Dwight said. "Considering this is an active murder investigation?"

"I reached out to her," Devlin said. "I read her stories in the paper. I wanted to know if she had any idea who might have done the shootings."

"You wanted to talk about this case, you should have come to me," Dwight said. "I thought I made that clear in our interview."

"I was asking, not telling," Devlin said. "I didn't know anything I hadn't already told you. Still don't." Letting her off the hook.

Dwight frowned. *He's trying to figure out how all this fits together,* Tracy thought. *And he's not liking it.*

"He's telling the truth," she said. "He contacted me after he read the story in the *Observer.* We met a couple times, that's all, including this afternoon. But he didn't give us anything we didn't already have."

She watched his eyes, wondering if he bought the lie.

To Devlin, he said, "I've been on the phone with the Camden police. They won't want anything to do with this, especially if they hear it's connected to one of our cases. You think the motel has any video?"

"I wouldn't count on it."

Dwight turned to her. "I'm guessing your presence here means you're planning on writing something."

"Have to."

"And if I asked you to hold off?"

"Can't do it. Shots fired in public. Wounded man turns out to be the friend of another man who was recently murdered, also in public. This isn't going away."

"My concern," Devlin said, "is if the person who shot at me was watching us this afternoon, he may know about Ms. Quinn here as well. She might be in danger."

Dwight looked at her. "He's got a point. I know the chief in New Hope. I'll ask him to get a uniform out to your house overnight, just to be safe."

He turned back to Devlin. "You were lucky tonight."

"I know."

He gestured at Devlin's chest, the scars there.

"I'm still not sure exactly what it is you've gotten yourself into," he said. "But this might be a good time to start reevaluating your lifestyle choices."

"You okay to drive?" she said.

They were headed back to the motel in her Toyota. An ER nurse had given Devlin the top from a pair of scrubs, and his left arm was in a pale blue sling. She saw his face tighten every time they hit a bump.

"I think so," he said.

"This changes everything. You know that, right? We have to do a story." She'd called Alysha before they'd left the hospital, filled her in.

"You'll be identified in this one," Tracy said. "Police reports are public record, so there's no reason for us to keep anything back. You willing to talk about what happened, be quoted?"

"I don't think so. What will the story say?"

"'Man wounded in Camden shooting was a colleague of murdered bar owner.' Something like that."

"Makes us sound like a bunch of gangsters."

"As opposed to what?"

He didn't respond.

"Once the story's out there, other outlets will see it," she said. "Try to follow it up themselves. As I said, things change fast."

He adjusted his sling, winced. His face was pale in the dashboard light.

"Alysha got a home number for this Gordon Farrow," she said. "She'll call him, see what he has to say."

"He'll love that."

The muffler rattled loudly.

"Sounds like you need to get this thing into the shop," he said.

"There're a lot of things I need. And what I need most right now is to get a story written ASAP. Is there anything you want to add since we talked this afternoon?"

"No."

"And you didn't recognize the shooter. That on the level?"

"It was. He was young. Thirties, at most. Not someone we worked with."

"Straight up?"

"Straight up. I hope I didn't put you in a bad position with Malloy. He's a smart guy. I think he knows he wasn't getting the full story."

"My father always told me the truth is a powerful thing," she said. "Sometimes you have to be economical with it. Don't worry about Dwight. I'll deal with him."

Pulling into the motel lot, he said, "Don't stop. Go around back."

There was a Camden police car parked outside the manager's office. She saw there were lights on in his room, a square of cardboard taped over the bullet hole in the window. There were two empty parking spaces below it. Cubes of safety glass had been swept into a pile.

She drove around the building.

"It's the Ranchero over there," he said.

"The what?"

"The funny-looking blue pickup thing."

"You drove all the way up from Florida in that?"

"It's old, but it runs good. It's got a few miles left in it."

"Like its owner."

"Not sure about that part."

She pulled up behind the pickup. "Got your keys?"

"Yeah."

"You need anything from the room? You going to be able to get in and get your stuff?"

"There's nothing I need tonight. And I don't feel like dealing with anyone else right now, especially the manager."

"I'm sure he has insurance."

"Does that cover getting the room shot up, bullet holes in guests' cars?"

"Probably wasn't the first time it happened," she said. "You'll need a place to stay tonight, though."

"I'll find another motel."

"I've got a better idea." She'd thought about it on the way there. "Come back with me to my place, sleep on the couch. I'm headed back there now to work on the story. If Dwight comes through, there'll be a cruiser outside all night."

She watched for his reaction, how he would take it. Worried if she lost track of him tonight, he'd disappear on her.

"Maybe that's not such a good idea," he said. "Since someone tried to kill me tonight."

"All the more reason. It'll be safer."

"I don't want to inconvenience you."

"Seems the best solution at the moment. If you're worried about me, an officer will be there to protect you. Or I can lend you a can of pepper spray."

"No need," he said. "I have the feeling I'll be fine."

TWENTY-SEVEN

DEVLIN SAT ON her couch, tried to get comfortable. She'd given him an oversized Rutgers sweatshirt to wear, but it still rubbed against his stitches when he moved the sling. The back of his neck was sore where the gunman had hit him.

Through the front window, he could see her talking to the uniformed officer standing beside his cruiser. The Ranchero was parked under trees on the side of the house.

She'd booted up a laptop after they'd gotten there, written for a half hour, then spent another fifteen minutes on the phone with someone from her paper, talking as she typed.

Something poked his hip. He felt behind the seat cushion, found a remote control for the TV. He set it on the coffee table.

The uniform got back in the car. She came in, locked the door.

"He's here until eight in the morning," she said. "Then someone else will spell him. They'll stay as long as one of us is in the house."

"That's nice of them."

"Dwight was as good as his word. This time."

"'This time'?"

"Never mind."

She went into the kitchen. "I don't know about you, but I need a drink."

"What have you got?"

"Some not-so-great wine. About two shots' worth of Grey Goose."

"Wine's all right."

He shifted on the couch, adjusted his sling again. The dull throbbing in his shoulder seemed to go bone-deep. His arms and sides ached where he'd landed on the blacktop.

She came in with an open bottle of wine and two mismatched glasses, one with antique cars on it. She put them on the coffee table, sat in the room's only chair. "All the Waterford's in the washer. These will have to do."

"Did you send your story in?"

"Desk is reading it right now. It'll go up online soon. I'll show it to you. It'll be in tomorrow's paper as well."

"Your friend get ahold of Farrow?"

"She did. He answered, then hung up when she identified herself. When she called back, he didn't pick up."

"What's next?"

"Pay a personal visit. To the Unix office as well. They haven't responded either."

"You're stirring the nest."

"It's what we do. At least what we're supposed to do. You look like you're hurting."

"A little."

She got up, went down a hall to the bathroom. He heard the creak of a medicine cabinet opening and closing.

She came back out with two pale blue pills, set them on the table. "Try these."

"What are they?"

"They're for cramps, but they're pain relievers too."

"Cramps?"

"Not manly enough for you? Pain or not, your choice. Better to shut up and take them."

He poured wine into their glasses, set the bottle down. He took the glass with the antique cars.

"I have insomnia a lot," he said. "Don't be worried if you hear me walking around out here in the middle of the night."

"Thanks for the warning."

He took the two pills, washed them down with wine.

"You're very cool about this, aren't you?" she said.

"About what?"

"Getting shot, almost killed. Now you're acting like it was nothing."

"I wouldn't say it was nothing. But I've been through it before."

"I gathered when I saw those other scars. You get all those 'advising'?"

"Some of them."

Her cell buzzed in the wicker basket. She got up, took it into the kitchen to answer it. He couldn't hear the conversation.

After a while, she came out, dropped the phone back in the basket.

"That was the night desk. Everyone's signed off on the story. It'll be up in a little while."

"Your name's been on these stories, hasn't it?"

"Mine and Alysha's, yes."

"That means Farrow knows who both of you are."

"You think he's behind all this?"

"Maybe. Probably."

"What about Kemper?" she said.

"Doesn't make sense. Risk everything he's got—his company, his government contracts—on some street-level shootings. He's someone always measured risk against reward. A lot of risk with this, not much reward."

"That you know of."

196

"Anybody thinks I'm a threat to some worldwide conglomerate is sadly misinformed."

"Why would Farrow want you and Roarke dead?"

"I don't know that he did. He's the only one who could answer that."

She got up, took her glass to the window, looked out. "I bet our officer friend is wondering what's going on in here."

"Not if he got a good look at me."

"Meaning what?"

"Twenty years and twenty pounds ago, I might have had a chance. Maybe not even then."

"You never know."

"You and Detective Malloy seem to know each other pretty well, though. Just from reading body language, I mean."

She sat back down. "That's a long story, and not worth the telling."

"Sorry. None of my business."

She refilled their glasses. "So, which of those scars did you get in San Marcos?"

He felt his smile fade. "Is that why I'm here?"

She drank wine. "I'm sorry. My turn to apologize. Always on the job. It's a problem sometimes, turning it off."

"It's how you make your living, I guess."

"I've never been good with the work-versus-life thing, finding that balance. And we make sacrifices when we make choices. Thing is, though...what's going on at the paper now, with layoffs, buyouts, budget cuts? It's bad. But I can't think of anything else I can do, anything I'd *want* to do."

"Then there's your answer."

"I just don't want to end up one of these bitter people talking about the way things used to be. How everything was better back in the day. Nostalgia is death."

"I don't know," he said. "I think it's okay to look back. Just don't stare."

She laughed, and he felt himself start to relax again. The pain in his shoulder was gone.

"You live here on your own?" he said. "I'm not chasing anyone out?"

"Just me. I don't even have a cat. I know that's hard to believe."

"Does it bother you sometimes, living alone?"

"Occasionally, but I get over it. How about you?"

"It suits me," he said. "Sometimes I think it's not so healthy, though. You end up living inside your own head too much."

"You're right about that."

"You've never been married?"

"No. Came close once. Engaged."

"What happened?"

"He was a good guy, a public defender. We tried to make it work, but we had different priorities. When he got offered a partnership at a firm outside San Diego, it was an easy call to make. For him, at least."

"He ask you to go with him?"

"He did not. I couldn't blame him."

"That what you meant by sacrifices?"

"One of them," she said.

"He still out there?"

"He is. Married, with a kid."

"Could have been you."

"Maybe. Sometimes I like to think so. But probably not."

"I'm prying. I'll stop. Sorry."

"Nothing to apologize for."

He sipped his wine, touched the sweatshirt. "This where you went?"

"Yes, New Brunswick."

"What for?"

"You mean why did I go there, or what did I study?"

"The second."

"Journalism and mass media. I minored in art history."

"That must be useful."

"Yeah. You ever need someone to tell you the difference between a Velázquez and a Vermeer, I'm your girl."

"For someone who studied art, your walls are bare."

"I've only lived here seven years. I'll get around to it soon."

He caught himself yawning. His eyes felt watery.

"You look whipped," she said. She got up, went into a hall
closet, came out with a pillow and a folded comforter. "These'll
have to do."

"They'll be fine."

She set them on the arm of the couch. "I'll be getting an early
start tomorrow. They'll want me in the office ASAP, get working on
the follows. Other outlets will be on the story now, and I have no
intention of getting beat. They'll be looking for you too."

"They will?"

"Yeah, they'll want to talk to you. But you're not going to talk to
them."

"Why not?"

"Because there's only one reporter you can trust with this story."

"Is that right?"

"It is," she said.

He was falling again. Vaulting the rail, gunshots behind him. But
there was nowhere to land this time, only a deeper darkness, a cold
void with no bottom.

He woke, kicked out, felt his heel hit something hard. He sat up
fast. Pale moonlight came through the front windows, showed the
outlines of the room, the empty chair, the dark television. Through
the window, he could see the cruiser parked outside.

He pushed the comforter away. Moving hurt. He got his watch
from the coffee table, looked at the dial. Three a.m.

"You okay?"

She was standing in the half-darkness of the hallway, watching
him. She wore a terrycloth robe over sweats, was barefoot.

He put the watch down, saw what he'd kicked was the arm of the couch. "Was I making noise?"

"You could say that."

"Sorry."

His mouth was dry, his throat sore. The wine bottle on the table was empty.

"How are you feeling?" she said.

"Like someone used me for a piñata. Do you have any water?"

She went into the kitchen. He wiped sweat from his face, felt the burn of the stitches when he moved.

She came back, set a bottle of water on the coffee table.

"Thanks." He cracked the lid, drank.

She settled into the chair across from him, left the light off.

"Have you ever had any counseling? For PTSD, anything like that?"

"I did, a while ago. I guess it didn't take."

"You should look into it again. As a vet, you probably qualify for free treatment through the VA."

"I'm done with that, I think."

"It might be good to talk to someone, get some of that stuff out. Like you said, it's not healthy to live inside your own head too much."

He looked at her, wondering if this was the time to tell it.

"Do you have any more of those woman pills?"

She got up, went into the bathroom, came back out with a single tablet. "Last one. But go ahead, I have a scrip."

He took it from her, put it on his tongue, and sipped water.

She sat back down. "I'm a good listener if you need one. Part of the job."

"Sometimes we ask about things we think we want to know. Then, later on, we wish we hadn't."

"Try me."

She was watching him, her face in shadow. *If you're going to do it*, he thought, *then do it.*

"I told you about the village on the river, our mission there."

"You said your intel was wrong, but you didn't say why. Did you mean there were no government troops there after all?"

He drank more water. "I guess I owe you the rest of that story, if you want to hear it."

"I do."

"You may not feel that way afterward."

"I'll take the chance."

"Like I said, Colin and Bell and I had set up a roadblock. We had some fifty-five-gallon drums out in the road, with concertina wire strung between them, a couple Claymores on the shoulders. We were in a technical—a heavy-duty pickup with a .50-caliber M2 mounted in the back. I was on the gun, Bell was manning the radio.

"The sergeant I told you about, Garza, led the raid. Even from where we were, you could hear gunfire, see smoke in the distance. Every once in a while we'd hear a hand grenade go off—a very specific sound. Bell was trying to raise Garza on the radio, get a sit rep, but he wasn't responding. We had no idea what was going on there.

"Then we heard a motor up ahead, saw this beat-up pickup truck coming down the road out of the jungle, straight toward us. It was going too fast, bouncing all over the place. We didn't know if it was Herrera's men, a suicide bomber, or what. Colin fired his AK in the air, but the truck kept coming."

He drank water, looked down at the floor, then back at her. *You've come this far,* he thought. *Tell it all.*

"The windshield was cracked and dusty, so I couldn't see much behind it. I racked the .50-caliber, and the driver started beeping his horn, which struck me as strange at the time. Like we were just going to move aside, let him through."

"Did you see any weapons?"

"No, but sometimes if you wait for that, it's too late. As the truck got closer, the driver kept craning his head out the window, shouting something I couldn't understand."

201

"He didn't stop?"

"He slowed a little. Colin tried to wave him off, but it didn't work. The truck was about fifty yards away when I opened up."

"You fired on them?"

"It was a stress reaction. Fight or flight, right? Have you ever seen a .50-caliber round?"

She shook her head.

He held his thumb and index finger a few inches apart. "It's a big chunk of steel and lead and copper. Will go right through a concrete wall. My first burst vaporized the windshield. The driver tried to swerve at the last minute, cut the wheel hard to the left, ended up broadside to us, about ten yards away. I stitched the passenger side from the front fender to the back bumper. It was like my thumbs were frozen on the trigger.

"Some of the rounds must have hit the engine, stopped it dead. It seemed to get real quiet then, I remember, though that may just have been my imagination—my ears were still ringing."

Stop stalling, he thought. *Get through this part quickly. Get it said.*

In the silence, he could hear a clock tick faintly in another room.

"Colin went up to the truck with his AK, looked inside, then lowered his rifle and just stood there. That's when I knew."

His mouth was dry again. He sipped more water.

"Who was in the truck?" she said.

"I went over just as Colin opened the passenger-side door. There were three people inside, the driver, a woman, and a little boy she was carrying in her lap, maybe four or five years old. The boy had a bloody bandage on his leg. I knew then what had happened. They were civilians, had fled the fighting in the village. What the driver was yelling was '*Niño*' and 'Hospital.' If I'd waited another few seconds, I would have understood. I would have seen who was inside the truck. But I didn't wait."

"Christ," she said softly.

"I warned you. Sure you want to hear the rest?"

"Yes."

"Guess was they were trying for the hospital, about five miles away. They would have made it too, if we hadn't been there, blocking their way. On their road. In their country."

"What did you do then?"

"Nothing. I was just numb. We couldn't do anything for them. All three were dead. We just stood around. Nobody said anything."

Seeing it all again, the smell coming back to him—gunpowder and gasoline and death.

"What was going on in the village?" she said.

"Still nothing on the radio, so we knew something was wrong. We went on in. Bell drove the technical, Colin manned the .50. I sat up front. I felt cold all over, and my hands were numb."

"You were in shock."

"Some of what happened after, I remember vividly. Some is just a blur, still. We headed down into the village. It was quiet now. No more shooting.

"The village wasn't much. Concrete shacks, prefab aluminum roofs and walls. A lot of the homes were shot up or burnt out. Garza was sitting in front of one of the shacks, drinking a beer and smoking a cigar, an M-16 across his lap. Four men were kneeling in the street in front of him, with their hands tied behind them. No uniforms. They were civilians, as far as I could tell. The rest of the unit was watching us, to see how we'd react.

"The other vehicles in the village were all shot to pieces. I'm not sure how the people in the pickup had gotten away. It looked like Garza and his men had gone from door to door, dragged everyone out, then torched the houses."

"What about Herrera's troops?"

"There were none there. There never had been."

He listened to the clock tick. *Finish it*, he thought.

"There was a drainage trench behind the houses that ran down to the river. We smelled it before we saw it. There were about fifty bodies in there, mainly women and kids. A few men, but mostly kids. Some of the women were naked. Everyone was dead.

"I asked Garza about the prisoners. He said they were soldiers, Herrera's men, that they'd taken off their uniforms when they knew an attack was coming. I said we'd bring them back with us for interrogation. I knew if we didn't, he'd kill them.

"He wouldn't hand them over. Told us to mind our own business, that we were *gringos* who took *dinero de sangre*—blood money—and we'd done what we were paid for. He said this was between his people, that we didn't understand. They held weapons on us—men we'd trained, carrying American-made rifles.

"I told Garza we wanted the prisoners, wouldn't leave without them. He smiled then, got up, said if we really wanted them, we could have them. I knew what was coming. Maybe if I'd moved faster I could have stopped it. But I didn't. He raised his M-16, and shot them all in the back, right there in front of us, one after the other."

He heard her slight intake of breath.

"I drew my sidearm, a .45, was going to shoot him. Colin stopped me. If I had, the others would have killed us all right there, then probably blamed it on Herrera's men. There'd be no one around to say different. Thinking back on it, I wish I'd shot him anyway. I should have died there. Needed to."

"What happened then?"

"There wasn't much we could do. Bell was back in the tech, trying to get us to leave. Garza was grinning, watching us back down. We drove out of the village. Bell was angry at me, said I'd almost gotten us all killed. He said Garza was right. We'd done what we were paid for. It wasn't our war."

"But these were men you'd trained, armed."

"Yes."

"You facilitated what they did."

He picked up the bottle, drank the rest of the water.

"How do you feel about that?" she said.

"How do you think I felt? Later on, we found out what happened. It was Herrera's home village, so it was personal. No troops had ever been there. The point of the raid was to send a message. It was a symbolic gesture."

"What about the people in the pickup?"

"We didn't know what to do. They had no ID, and any relatives back in the village were likely dead as well. I couldn't leave them out there for the animals, the elements. I got an e-tool and dug a grave in a field there by the roadside. Buried them next to each other."

The pill was starting to kick in, fatigue taking over again.

"Did Farrow know about the village? What was going to happen?"

"He said he didn't, and I had no reason to doubt him. Two days later, it was all over. Herrera tried to leave the country, didn't make it. Ramírez and his people took over. Mission accomplished."

"You came back to the States then?"

"We were scheduled to leave by boat. I was on my own in a jeep, on the way to the rendezvous point, when I hit the mine. The next thing I remember is being in the back of a truck, with Colin driving. He fixed me up as best he could, then got me medevaced. Saved my life. A day later I was at a hospital in Tampa. I had two broken legs, a broken wrist, shrapnel in my back and in my face." He touched his left eyebrow.

"When I was well enough to travel, they transferred me to another hospital up north. Acheron paid for everything."

"Did you keep track of what happened in San Marcos after that?"

"I did."

"So you know about the purges, the crackdowns?"

"Yes," he said.

"Estimates are Ramírez killed more than five thousand of his own people over the last decade, imprisoned thousands more."

"I know."

"Do you ever wonder if he could have come to power without your help?"

"Every day," he said.

Silence between them.

"Nice story, right?" he said.

She said nothing.

"You're the first person I ever told that to," he said. "The whole thing, I mean. No one else knew it all, besides Colin, Bell, and Farrow. Not my wife, not my priest, not even the therapist I saw when I came back. And if the next thing you ask me is if you can use any of that in a story, the answer is no. Not yet, at least."

"I'm sorry about all this," she said. "What you had to go through."

"We helped light the fire. Then we got burned. There's no one else to blame."

She sat back. He tried to read her expression in the dimness. Wondered if she was frightened of him now.

"I'll find another place to stay tomorrow," he said. "Get my things from the motel. I'm sure your friend Dwight will want to talk to me again."

"You can bet on that."

"That pill's starting to work. I think I might be ready to try to sleep again."

She got up. "Get some rest. We've got a lot ahead of us."

She went back to her bedroom. He stretched out on the couch, looked up at the dark ceiling. He wasn't sure how he felt, if it had been right to tell as much as he had. *Either way*, he thought, *it's done.*

Her sleep was thin, fragmented. Bits of dreams woke her every few minutes. Awake, she thought about what Devlin had told her. *You wanted to know*, she thought. *And now you do.*

The nightstand clock read 4 a.m. when she got up, went barefoot down the hall to the living room. Devlin was snoring softly, but every few seconds an arm or leg would jerk almost imperceptibly.

Who is this man sleeping in your house? she thought. *How is it he came into your life? What else has he done that he can't talk about, can't face? And do you even want to know?*

She watched him for a while, lying there in the moonlight. *You've given me your nightmares,* she thought. Then she turned, and went back down the hallway to her bed.

When she woke in the morning, he was gone.

TWENTY-EIGHT

LUKAS WOKE TO the steady beep of the driveway alarm, saw the light blink on the bedroom wall console. He rolled off the bed, took the Sig Sauer automatic from atop the nightstand. Morning light came through the windows.

He dressed in jeans and T-shirt, walked barefoot into the living room, the gun at his side. At the front door, he looked out, saw Farrow's Bronco pull up into the yard, Holifield at the wheel.

He heard a noise behind him, turned to see Tariq on the stairs, fully dressed, a gun in his hand.

"Gordon," Lukas said. He slipped the Sig into his belt, let the fall of his shirt cover it. He unlocked the door, went out, the ground cold under his feet.

Holifield stepped down from the Bronco. Farrow got out on the passenger side. He wore a pale green flight jacket and sunglasses.

"What are you doing here?" Lukas said.

"You don't check your messages?" Farrow said.

"We were on the road until late. I turned my phone off."

"We need to talk."

Farrow looked past him, at Tariq on the stairs. "Alone."

He nodded toward the woods beyond the garage.

"Hold on," Lukas said. He went back inside, said "It's okay" to Tariq. He slipped on sneakers, got a jacket from the closet.

Farrow had started down a trail that led deeper into the trees. Lukas followed him. Holifield stayed beside the Bronco, thumb hitched into his belt, just forward of the gun holstered there.

They came to a clearing, birds singing around them. Farrow turned to him.

"When were you going to tell me what happened?"

"There were complications. It didn't go like it was supposed to. I'll make it good."

"A reporter called my house last night."

"About what?"

"I didn't wait to find out. I hung up and called my lawyer. She was from the same paper that's been writing these stories every other goddamn day. Have you seen them?"

"No, why?"

"They've got all the pieces. It's just a matter of time before they start putting them together. Doesn't take a genius to see where they're headed with this. Right up our ass."

"A newspaper? Forget it. You're giving them too much credit."

"This reporter had my name, my home phone. She's probably got my address, is on her way there now."

"How'd she get your name and number?"

"No idea how she got the number. But I can imagine where she got my name."

"Devlin," Lukas said.

"He's a problem that should have been solved a while ago and wasn't. Now he's an even bigger one—for both of us."

"I said I'll make it good."

"I have to see the old man today, give him a sit rep. But first

I wanted to talk to you, hear your piss-poor excuse for what happened, and how you're going to fix it."

"You want me to come with you? Talk to him?"

"Are you crazy? He won't want you anywhere near him, hot as you are right now."

Lukas felt a flush of anger. "No one's happy with the way things went."

"You understand what's at stake here, the possible repercussions? A reporter called the Unix office as well. Bad enough they used my name in the paper. If they try to bring the old man into this? No telling what happens then. This thing's sprawling, and it's gotta stop."

"Devlin's the key," Lukas said. "Anything a reporter is getting is coming from him. Take him out of the equation, and they've got nothing. It's the same with the cops. Without Devlin, there's no case, no story."

"And considering you had a shot at him and blew it, how is it you think you'll get close to him next time?"

"There's always a way."

"Maybe those reporters need to go as well."

"Take out a reporter working on a story? That's the last thing you want. Who do you think the police will suspect first?"

"It could look like an accident."

"You're not thinking clearly. You want to try something that stupid with your own people, go ahead. But don't ask me to be involved."

"Sometimes," Farrow said, "in extreme situations, we have to take chances we normally wouldn't. Maybe this is one of those times."

"Can't the old man put pressure on someone local, throw some money around, get the story killed?"

"It's not that easy. And I told you, there can't be any link to Unix. His position is this is our fuckup. We need to fix it. He's right. And we will."

"I'll deal with it."

"One other thing." Farrow took a folded piece of yellow legal paper from his jacket pocket, held it out.

"What's this?" Lukas said. He opened it. Written on the sheet in pencil was an address in Connecticut.

"It's where Devlin used to live," Farrow said. "His ex-wife still does. You lose the scent, she might know where he is."

"That's a reach, isn't it?"

"He won't go back to Florida. We found him there once. And it seems like he wants to cause as much damage up here as he can. One way or another, you need to stop him."

"What happened yesterday was a random shooting," Lukas said. "No one was killed. Happens up there every day. That story will die quick unless they tie it to something else. And without Devlin, that won't happen."

"That's a big risk you're taking."

"Everything's a risk," Lukas said.

TWENTY-NINE

TRACY HAD JUST gotten in, was on the way to her cubicle, when she saw Alysha standing in the conference room, waving rapidly at her through the glass. Rick Carr was at the table in there, along with Irv Siegel, the executive editor, and Susan Van Ness, the nervous twentysomething who ran Digital.

Tracy went to her desk, unlocked the top drawer, grabbed what she hoped was her most recent notebook, and started for the conference room.

"Tracy!"

She turned. Harris was coming up behind her. "I've been looking for you."

"Hey, R.J. What's up?"

He moved in close to her. She didn't step back.

"You never responded to my emails. And don't say you didn't see them."

"I didn't."

"Unacceptable. You work for me, in my department, under my supervision. I thought we were clear on that."

She looked back over her shoulder at the conference room. "Sorry, this other story…"

"Ted tells me you wouldn't meet with him either."

"Didn't get a chance."

"No excuse. What did we talk about in my office the other day, about being a team player?"

Rick had gotten up, opened the door to the conference room. He pointed at Tracy, then inside.

"Speaking of teamwork," she said to Harris, "I think they're waiting for us."

Siegel sat back, said, "Now that we're all here."

He was in his sixties, his hair and beard wiry and gray. He wore reading glasses, had loosened his tie. There was a folded copy of the morning's paper at one elbow, an electronic tablet at the other.

It was the first time she'd been in a meeting with him. He'd come to Philadelphia after stints in Cincinnati and St. Louis. At both those papers, he'd overseen large-scale staff and budget cuts. She'd never spoken with him directly before, had no idea what he thought of her or her work.

"Sorry," she said. She looked at Rick, who was tapping a pencil on a legal pad. "You're in early."

He gave that a small smile. "Thanks to you."

She sat next to Alysha, looked up at the framed front pages on the wall—9/11, the Phillies winning the 2008 World Series, the MOVE bombing from 1985.

"First of all," Siegel said, "I understand we have some ongoing safety concerns."

"New Hope police were at my house last night," Tracy said. "They'll be back tonight as well. It's probably not necessary."

"I'd rather they be there than not. If I need to make a phone call on that, let me know. Or we could put you up in a hotel for a few days. Your choice."

"Thanks, but I think I'd rather stay at home."

He looked at Alysha. "Bennett, that goes for you too. I'd feel better knowing you're both safe until we have some resolution here, preferably in the form of an arrest."

"If you're offering me a free hotel room for a couple nights, I won't say no."

"We'll set that up." He looked around the table. "Who wants to go first?"

Harris had taken a seat across from Tracy. "I just want to go on record to say I didn't know anything about this. Whatever story Tracy's working on, it was with someone else's okay."

He looked at Rick, who was doodling on a corner of the pad.

"Noted," Siegel said. He turned to Tracy. "I've read our stories, and Rick's filled me in on what we know so far. Tie all this together for me."

She told it all straight through, from the body in the Bainbridge Street house and the shootings at Dugan's to her meetings with Devlin, what he'd told her.

"You're confident this Roarke was targeted," Siegel said.

"Yes."

"And our source is this man"—he pulled the tablet closer to him, tilted it against the glare—"Raymond Devlin, who got shot yesterday, across the bridge."

"He is," she said.

"And he thinks Roarke's death is connected to work the three of them used to do?"

"He does."

"And what exactly was that?"

"Security contracting, military training, maybe arms dealing," she said. "They went all over the world, but the last time the three were together was in San Marcos, during the coup. They were

214

there to help destabilize the Herrera regime, give the opposition troops an advantage."

"I saw something on the wire about San Marcos this morning," Rick said.

"Ramírez, the president they helped put in power, is losing his grip," she said. "He's canceled elections and dissolved their congress. He also put thousands of protesters in prison via military courts. Human Rights Watch is investigating allegations of widespread torture."

"How much of what Devlin told you is on record?"

"Not enough," she said. "But the more we dig, the deeper the story gets. What he has told us, about Acheron and Unix, matches up with our reporting. How connected Unix is politically—and how far-reaching its influence is—we still don't know."

"It sounds like there's a lot of things you don't know," Harris said.

Alysha cut him a glance. Tracy ignored him.

"Roland Kemper, who runs Unix, is a big-money political supporter," she said. "He's been a major contributor to Senator Harlin's reelection campaign, that we know for sure. We have the records to prove it."

"We're still trying to put together a complete list of who else benefited, now and in the past," Alysha said. "That'll tell us more."

"Where are the other outlets on this?" Siegel said.

"The *Inky* and Philly.com picked it up," Tracy said. "But all they've got is what was in our story. Nothing new."

"But they'll be trying to find Devlin."

"They will."

"Any way we can keep him under wraps?"

She thought about last night, the man stirring in his sleep on her couch, the story he'd told her.

"We can try," she said.

Siegel said, "Rick, what do you think?"

He tapped the pad. "I think it's our story. We broke it, and we need to hold on to it, work it as hard as we can. The real question is how it all relates to this Unix—if it does. Someone needs to do a deep data dive on all these companies, if we haven't already."

"On it," Alysha said. "I asked Sylvie in the library to help. They're running some searches for us."

"It sounds like we're well on our way to having a solid story," Siegel said. His look took in both Tracy and Alysha. "But we're not there yet. As far as these larger issues, I don't see the smoking gun. Figuratively, I mean."

"There is one," Tracy said. "We just haven't found it yet."

"Get me someone else who worked for Acheron or Unix, off the record or not, but better on," he said. "And I think we need to shake Mr. Kemper's tree a little."

"I have calls in," Alysha said. "And I'm trying to find a private line. I'm not expecting much. I think we'll need to go down there, stake them out."

"Let's stay on it," he said. "Susan, any questions?"

She pushed her glasses up higher on her face. "Has there been any thought as to how we can monetize this content?"

Tracy looked at Rick. He was doodling again.

"We're figuring that out," Tracy said. She'd expected the question. "We'll shoot you our stories as soon as they're ready, and any art that's available as well."

"We have video? Video is key if we want the max number of hits."

"I'll look into that," Tracy said. "I understand there's some surveillance footage from outside Dugan's. If they release it to us, you can put it up online."

"One thing to keep in mind as we go forward," Siegel said. "As Rick says, this is our story, and if anything new breaks, we need to get it first. But we also need to get it right. I don't want to have to walk back something we've written because we jumped the gun, went with it before it was ready."

"Understood," Tracy said. Alysha nodded.

"Good," Siegel said. "Which leaves me with only one other question for you all."

"What's that?" Tracy said.

"What do you need?"

After the meeting broke, Siegel headed back to his office. Harris left the conference room without a word.

"Okay," Rick said. He stood, the pad under his arm. "You heard the man. Let's get at it."

He held the door for them. Phones were ringing on the empty desks they passed. When Tracy reached her cubicle, she put out her fist. Alysha gave it a bump.

"You heard the man," Alysha said.

"I did."

Waiting for her computer to boot up, Tracy saw movement in the hallway, looked up over the cubicle wall. Harris was walking toward the elevators, golf bag over his shoulder.

Dwight Malloy had called ahead, and when Devlin got to the motel, his duffel bag was at the front desk. The manager, a Chinese-American with a nasal New York accent, told him he was responsible for all damage to the property, that it would be charged to his credit card, no arguments, no negotiations. Devlin just nodded, thanked him, and carried the bag out to the Ranchero.

He tossed it into the truck bed, then popped the hood, looked around the engine, the firewalls. He unscrewed the air filter cover, lifted out the filter. The manager watched him through the window.

When he was done with the engine, he crawled under the chassis. It took him five minutes to find it—a magnetized black box about two inches long and an inch wide, attached to the frame beneath the passenger side, spotted with mud. He had to tug hard to get it free.

He crawled out, wiped dried mud from the transponder. It was in a spot that had been easy to reach. It would have been the work of seconds to kneel, reach under, and fasten it there.

He replaced the air filter and cover, closed the hood, got in, and started the engine. The manager was still watching him.

Devlin took out his cell, started to punch in Malloy's number, then stopped. He could bring the transponder to them, have them find the manufacturer, chase down whoever it had been sold to. But it would likely be an answer he already knew.

Time to start turning this around, he thought. He was tired of being hunted, a target.

He pulled the Ranchero out onto the highway, made a right before he got to the bridge. An access road led down to the riverfront. Industrial docks here, long out of use. He parked the Ranchero near a warehouse, walked out onto a weathered concrete apron. He could smell the water. Traffic trundled by on the bridge above him.

He tossed the transponder out as far as he could, watched it arc and fall, splash and disappear.

He got back in the Ranchero, drove out of the lot. Gray clouds were gathering. It looked like rain.

THIRTY

WHEN THEY GOT to the gate, Holifield leaned out the window and punched in the security code Farrow had given him. The light beside the keyboard stayed red.

"Doesn't work," he said.

"For Christ's sake," Farrow said. "Try it again." *They changed the code*, he thought. *Another sign of the old man's paranoia.*

Holifield was reaching again when the gate lock clicked, triggered from inside the house. They waited as the gates clanged, opened inward. Holifield drove through.

When they were halfway up the drive, Winters stepped out of the trees, put a hand up for them to stop. Holifield braked. Winters came up on the Bronco's passenger side, pointed at the rear door. Farrow looked at him, confused. Winters tapped a knuckle on his window, pointed to the door again.

"Go ahead," Farrow said. Holifield hit the switch to unlock the door. Winters opened it, got in.

"What are you doing?" Farrow said.

"Just gonna ride up with you, that's all."

"Why?"

"No reason." He turned and looked into the cargo area, then faced forward again.

"The fuck?" Farrow said.

Holifield was watching him in the rearview. "We have an issue here, Slick?"

"No issue," Winters said. "Go on up." The gates swung closed behind them.

When they reached the circular end of the driveway, Winters said, "Park over there," and pointed at a spot away from the house. Holifield pulled up. Winters said, "You stay," and opened his door.

"This is bullshit," Farrow said, but Winters had already gotten out, shut the door behind him.

"What do you want to do, boss?" Holifield said.

"Wait here. I'll see what's going on."

He got out, followed Winters toward the house. Bishop, the guard from the hotel, came down from the porch to meet them, took what looked like a small black walkie-talkie from his coat pocket, turned a dial. Red LED lights glowed on the front. A bug detector. Without a word, he waved the antenna in front of Farrow, then down his sides, switched it off, and stepped away. Winters quickly patted him down from behind.

"What is this, Val?" Farrow said.

"You can go in now."

Farrow walked fast up onto the porch. In the foyer, the guard named Reece was talking into a button mike on the lapel of his suit jacket. He nodded at Farrow as he went past.

Kemper was in the first-floor music room, standing by the white-and-gold grand piano. He was looking out a window into the back-yard, hands clasped behind him. Farrow saw the stage was still there, the oversized flag above it. Bunting across the front read KEEP AMERICA STRONG.

"That was embarrassing," Farrow said. "All the years I've worked for you..."

Kemper turned to him, stepped away from the window. "I'm sorry, Gordon. This thing has me rattled."

"I told you, we're working on it."

"Calls to Unix. Calls to you. Stories in the newspapers. I'm not used to this type of attention. I don't like it. It's a danger to our business, our goals. And it's a danger to us personally as well."

"I'm taking care of it."

"You see our young friend today?"

"I did. He thinks he can keep it contained."

"Do you?"

"Maybe. I'm not so sure."

Kemper nodded, went to the piano, idly plinked notes. "Not what I wanted to hear."

He traced a finger down the keys. "I never learned to play. Always wanted to, but other things took precedence. Isabella plays beautifully. Have you heard her?"

Farrow shook his head.

Kemper closed the keyboard cover. "I sent her to Houston today, where her mother lives, in a house I bought for her. The mother, I mean. Woman's had a rough time of it. Alcoholic husband, a drug-addict son. I paid for the kid's rehab. Twice. Isabella deserved better parents. But we don't get to pick our birth families, do we?"

"We don't."

"She was Miss Texas one year, did you know that? Not that long ago, either. I sent her away today, and I don't like to do that. I like to have her close, to know she's in the house, even if I can't see her."

He brushed a speck of dust from the top of the piano.

"We've been talking about children again, even met with a doctor in D.C. That's a dream I've had for many years, as you know. This time it might finally happen. First-time father at my age, hard to believe, right?"

"Why did you send her away?"

Kemper faced him. "Because, Gordon, I don't know what's going on here yet. And nobody who works for me is giving me the answers I want."

"We're on it, Roland. We just need some more time."

"Senator Harlin has a speaking engagement here tomorrow night. Or I should say 'had.' I canceled it."

"Why?"

"The same reason. An event like this, I don't want to risk reporters showing up, trying to get in, asking questions, bothering the guests outside the gates. Or worse yet, protesters. Winters and his men would deal with them, but it might look bad if there are cameras there. So I told Mitchell I wanted more time to prepare, said we'd reschedule soon. And we will. When all this is settled."

"It will be."

"Mitchell knows little about our other activities, and I'm sure he'd like to keep it that way. He's not the sharpest knife in the drawer on his best days. But if he gets dragged into an investigation—especially a criminal one—there's no telling which way he'll jump. His loyalty can't be trusted, unless there's money attached. If we lose his sponsorship in Washington, we lose a valuable asset."

Farrow heard footsteps behind him, turned. Winters stood in the doorway.

"It's okay, Val," Kemper said. Winters nodded and went off.

"I hired that fucking guy," Farrow said.

"And he was an excellent choice. Loyal to a fault. But you always were a shrewd judge of character, Gordon. That's what made you a fine officer."

This son of a bitch is about to fire me, Farrow thought. *After all I've done for him, everything I've had to swallow over the years.*

He straightened his shoulders. "What are you trying to say, Roland?"

Kemper walked back to the window.

"You've been a great aide to me," he said. "A good friend too, when I needed it. But sometimes I wonder if you see the totality of things in the same way I do."

"What do you mean?"

"We started with almost nothing, you and I. And look at all we've built. I don't think either of us wants to watch it fall apart."

"Nothing's falling apart."

Kemper turned back to him. "I'm bringing Unix into another arena altogether, Gordon. This deal we're pursuing with the senator, with the committee, it's worth more than you can possibly imagine. Four billion to start. *Billion.* And there are other projects in the works that will bring us almost as much over time."

Farrow took out his cigarettes, fumbled getting one from the box.

"Please," Kemper said. "Not in here."

He replaced the cigarette, closed the pack.

"This kind of deal," Kemper said. "It's historic. There's no other word for it. If it goes through—and in the current political climate I'm confident it will—our great-great-grandchildren will never have to work a day in their lives. How many people can say that, that they can give a gift like that to the ages?"

"I wouldn't know about that. I was an Army brat. We moved from post to post, and they were all the same. What I've got, I earned. Nobody ever handed me anything."

"One of the reasons I hired you. You are steadfast, Gordon. You do what has to be done, sometimes at great personal risk."

"You trying to cut me loose, Roland? If so, come out and say it."

"No one's cutting anybody loose. I need you even more now, in fact. Our friend in the south wants to speed up the timetable, have boots on the ground within the month."

"How come?"

"He feels his situation's deteriorating. He wants to get ahead of events before it's too late. It'll be a larger team this time, I think, with more actual fieldwork involved. Any actions we take there will need to be decisive. I'm sure our friends in Washington will approve, even if not publicly. I've asked Val to choose the best of his men, the ones with the most combat experience. You'll lead the team, of course." He smiled. "Are you ready for a new adventure?"

Go to San Marcos with Winters and you're never coming back, Farrow thought. *He sees you as a risk now too, just another weak link in the chain.*

"Sure," he said.

"Before we do that, though, we have to deal with our domestic matter. A disgruntled ex-employee can cause a lot of trouble for us, especially one who saw as much as he did, knows as much of our history."

"I understand." *And for that, you still need me,* he thought. *For now.*

"I just want you to be clear on the enormity of all this," Kemper said. "What's at stake. And to know you're taking the appropriate steps to remedy the situation."

"I am."

"And you have enough personnel, I assume, to do what needs to be done? Between Lukas and your own men?"

"I do, but Lukas is another matter."

"Why?"

"I think he's lost his fastball. And some of his decision making has been..."

"Questionable?"

"Yeah."

"It happens," Kemper said. "Sometimes we recover from it, get back on an even keel. Sometimes we don't. At that point, the options are limited."

"What exactly are you saying?"

Kemper looked out the window again. A breeze rippled the flag.

"I'm saying do what you need to do. However you see fit."

Farrow let that sink in. "Are you giving the order?"

Kemper didn't turn.

"I'm going away for a few weeks," he said. "To the island. Check on how construction's proceeding, ride herd on the contractors if need be. Feels like it might be a good time to make myself scarce around here for a while, until things are sorted out."

"You want me to call the airstrip, have them prep the plane?"

"Tell the pilots to file a flight plan for Treasure Cay tonight, round trip. They'll be coming back empty after they drop us. Then call whoever you have to at the airport there to make sure the helicopter's gassed up and waiting when we arrive. I assume the helipad at the house is finished?" He turned back to Farrow.

"It should be. I'll find out."

"That new pilot, what's his name? The one who worked at Langley?"

"Chambers."

"Call him. He'll be coming with me. I'll need someone to fly the chopper once we're there."

"You want me to head down first, scout it out?"

"Not necessary," Kemper said. "You'll have your hands full here."

Right, Farrow thought. *You go hide. Leave me to clean up the mess.*

"Is that it?" he said.

"If anything else occurs to me, I'll have Winters call you."

"You do that," Farrow said, then turned and left.

He ignored Winters and Reece when he passed them in the foyer, walked out to the Bronco. He was on his own now.

Farrow got in, and Holifield started the engine. They headed back down the driveway.

"I need two good men for some work tonight," Farrow said. "Contractors, off the books. Ask Dillon if he knows someone can be trusted, won't fuck it up."

"Tell me what you need, boss. We can get it done."

"No," Farrow said. "Trust me. What happens next, you don't want to be anywhere near."

THIRTY-ONE

D RIVING HOME, TRACY tuned the radio to KYW 1060, the all-news station, wondering if they'd picked up the update she and Alysha had filed. For the first time, they'd named Kemper, Farrow, and Harlin in the same story. No one at Unix headquarters or Harlin's office had returned their calls, but she knew the effect the story would have. It was the first domino. The others would start falling soon.

Rain began to spot the windshield. She switched on the wipers, took out her cell. No new calls or messages. She set it on the passenger seat. If there were still no callbacks tomorrow, she'd have to drive down to Virginia, start knocking on doors.

The check-engine light blinked on, the muffler rattled. A gust of wind pushed the car slightly. There was little traffic in either direction, nothing but woods and road in her headlights.

She had to watch for deer here, had a near-miss the previous fall. Coming home after a late shift, she'd caught a glimpse of glowing eyes behind the guardrail, and a big buck had vaulted over it onto the road. She'd stood on the brakes, the Toyota slewing to the side, and braced for an impact that never came. The deer had vanished as quickly as it appeared. A half hour later, she was still shaking.

The rain began to come down harder. Static crackled on the radio. She wished she'd had a last cup of coffee before leaving the office, just enough of a bump to send her home alert.

From nowhere, a dark shape filled the rearview, loomed over the car. She saw her taillights reflected in a steel push bar.

The impact jolted her forward against the shoulder harness, just as she heard the taillights shatter. *You've been hit*, she thought, and then the Toyota was slammed forward again. Something scraped and fell away from the back of the car with a tearing sound.

She gripped the wheel, floored the gas pedal, fear sweeping through her. The engine whined and hesitated, the transmission lurching as it failed to engage. High beams flashed on behind her, lit the inside of the car.

The next impact shook her in her seat, hammered the car forward. She heard the steel bar crunch into the Toyota's trunk. She twisted to look behind her, was blinded by the high beams.

When she turned back, the road curved away, woods ahead. She slammed the brake, already knowing she wouldn't make the turn, the vehicle behind her pushing hard.

The guardrail rose up in front of her.

When she came to, the deflated airbag was in her lap, the chemical smell of it filling her nostrils. She didn't know how long she'd been out. The engine was running, steam hissing out from under the buckled hood. A horizontal crack ran across the bottom of the windshield. The wipers were still going, pushing away the rain.

One headlight was out. The other showed woods. The Toyota had gone off the road and down the steep slope, had come to rest wedged between two trees. It was canted to one side, the driver's side higher.

She felt strangely calm. *You're okay*, she thought. *You're alive. Now you just have to call for help.*

One thing at a time. She switched off the ignition. The engine sputtered and died, the wipers stopped in place. The dashboard display glowed, but the check-engine light was out.

There was pain in her forehead and knee. She felt her face, but there was no blood there. *All right*, she thought. *All right. You can walk away from this.*

Where was her phone? She felt the seat where it had been, saw it on the passenger-side floor. She bent for it, couldn't reach it, the shoulder harness holding her back. Fumbling with the buckle, she unsnapped it, then fell into the passenger seat, her legs wedged under the wheel. *Not too graceful*, she thought. She hitched her knees, felt for the door latch, tugged. The door creaked, protested, and swung open abruptly. She tumbled out onto the wet ground.

She lay on her back, feeling the rain, then rolled onto her hands and knees, tried to stand. Her feet slid out from under her. She reached for the door to catch herself, sat down hard in the wet grass, her back against the car. Water coursed around her, sluicing from the roadway. Below her, the slope led into thicker woods, the trees there close together.

Okay, she thought. *That wasn't so swift. Try again.*

Dizzy, she reached for the open door, gripped the armrest, tried to pull herself up.

"Hey, lady, are you okay?"

She looked up, saw the man standing on the shoulder about fifteen feet above her. An SUV had pulled over, engine running, hazards blinking. She could see the rain in its headlights. There was a gap in the guardrail where her car had gone through.

She raised a hand to him, heard a car door open and close. A second man joined the first. Two silhouettes up there, looking down at her.

She reached for her phone on the floor, fell short, and slipped to her knees in the mud.

"Hold on, there, ma'am. Don't be moving around so much. We're coming."

A bright flashlight beam shone down into the car. She knelt there, resting, then gripped the door again, pulled herself up.

Leaning against the tilted roof for support, she watched the two men pick their way carefully down the slope, the flashlight beam bouncing. It steadied on her face as they got nearer.

"It's okay," she said. She raised her hand again. "I'm all right."

"You will be," the first man said, and then the front passenger-side window popped and starred. She looked at it, wondering what had happened. Then she heard another snap and cough, and something struck the roof of the Toyota, whined off past her ear.

They're shooting at you, she thought. *Why would they do that?*

The driver's-side window cracked and collapsed. She pushed away from the car. Another shot holed the rear window. Her feet lost traction on the slick grass and she fell onto her back, rolled, and slid farther down the slope. She came to a stop where the ground leveled off at the edge of the woods. Palms in the mud, she pushed the ground away, stood.

The two men were at the Toyota. They shone the flashlight into the car, then on the grass around it. She held her breath. The light beam crept down the slope, panned across the ground in front of her, then up her legs and onto her face.

She turned into the trees and ran.

THIRTY-TWO

SHE WENT FROM tree to tree, pushing off one for the momentum to reach the next. It was starting to rain harder. Fear was a solid thing inside her.

About thirty feet in, she stopped, looked back. They were standing at the bottom of the slope, still short of the forest, talking. She couldn't make out the words.

The flashlight beam pierced the woods, swept along the ground about five feet from her. When it moved farther away, she chanced it, turned and went deeper into the woods, hoping the rain would cover the noise. Her jacket sleeve caught a branch that whipped back at her, stung her face just above her right eye, made her cry out.

The light tracked toward her fast. A snap and cough, and bark flew from the tree to her right. She pushed away the branch, kept moving. Another crack. They were using some sort of silencer, the shots not sounding like gunfire at all.

Don't move in a straight line, she told herself. You'll make an easier target.

She could hear them behind her now. They'd been reluctant to come into the woods at first, but now they were pushing through the underbrush. She moved behind another tree, her back against it, tried to catch her breath. There was a mad fluttering in her stomach. She thought she could hear her own heartbeat.

She felt her pockets, angry she'd left the phone in the car. The can of pepper spray was still in her right-hand pocket. It had been there since the night she'd first met Devlin. It was no use to her now.

A shot kicked bark off a tree about ten feet to her left. They had no target, were trying to panic her, get her to run, show herself. Did they both have guns, or just one of them? Was one the spotter, the other the shooter?

Rain pattered in the branches above her. The flashlight beam moved toward her, then away, strayed far to her left. She turned and began making her way through the woods again, tree by tree. Her foot caught on something and she pitched forward, hit the ground.

The flashlight beam snapped toward her, and two shots sounded almost as one. She heard bullets pass through the trees above her. She rolled behind the log that had tripped her, looked back toward them. They were coming closer, but taking their time, being careful.

Behind her, there was a faint glow on the other side of the woods. There might be a house there, or a street. She was too scared to move, too scared to stay where she was.

A shot kicked up mud to her right.

"Shit," one of them said. "Jam."

She knew what that meant. *Now*, she thought. *Do it. Move.*

She got to her feet, ran toward the glow, staying low. A branch raked across her face. She leaped over another log, kept running.

"There she goes," one of them said. A louder shot behind her, echoing in the woods, no silencer this time. Two guns.

Almost at the edge of the woods now, the light bright through the trees. Suddenly, the ground sloped away below her. She was moving too fast to stop. She fell forward, landed in mud, slid down a few feet to where the ground was flat again.

She lay there, stunned from the impact. She was in a backyard. A pole light lit up an expanse of bare dirt, a row of small single-story houses. All the windows were dark. *Condos or apartments*, she thought. *Never finished. Empty. No one there to help you.*

Another loud shot behind her. As if on cue, the rain picked up, sheeting past the pole light. She heard one of them cursing. They were coming through the woods. When they reached the top of the slope, they'd see her. She wondered if she'd hear the shot that killed her.

You can't stay here, she thought. *You have to move. Now.*

She got her feet under her, ran to the first door, twisted the knob. Locked. She moved to the second. This time the knob turned, and she swung inside, pushed the door shut behind her. Two locks, one on the knob, the other a dead bolt higher up. She worked them both, heard them click.

She backed away from the door. The top half of it was four panes of glass. Light came through, lit a stretch of wet linoleum floor. An unfinished kitchen. There was a wide countertop, but an empty space where the sink would go, a window above it. The floor was slick, and a steady drip came from the ceiling.

Beyond the kitchen, a short hallway led to another empty room. A living room, likely, with a front door.

She stayed out of the light, leaned against the counter. The rain on the window made liquid shadow patterns on the floor. Her forehead stung. She touched the skin above her right eye, felt blood where the branch had hit her.

She'd counted seven units, seven doors. Had they seen which one she'd gone in? One of the men would go around front, she guessed, watch the doors there, in case she made a run for it that way. *Stay here*, she thought. *Keep away from the windows. If you're lucky, you can hide here until they give up.*

Voices in the backyard, closer than she expected. She held her breath, tried to hear what they were saying above the rain. Were these the men who'd tried to kill Devlin? *They're hunting you now,* she thought. *And they're right outside that door.*

A rattling noise on the other side of the wall. They were trying the door of the first unit. She heard glass break, then someone moving around inside. They'd be coming in here next.

An hour ago you were safe and warm, with friends, in a place you belonged, she thought. *And now this is the way you die. Scared and alone and cold.*

She took the pepper-spray can from her pocket, gripped it tight. If she could, she'd try to get one of them before they killed her.

The flashlight beam came through the door glass, lit up the wall beyond. It moved closer, grew brighter. To reach the living room, she'd have to run through the light and past the window, offer a target. The doorknob rattled.

One of the lower panes shattered, made her jump. Glass fell to the floor. A gloved hand came through, deftly unlocked the dead bolt, then reached down, felt around for the knob. She heard the click as it was unlocked. The hand withdrew, and the knob began to turn. The door opened slowly, the hinges creaking.

The man had long dark hair, combed back and plastered down by the rain. A scar bisected his lower lip. He opened the door halfway, pointed the gun inside. It was in his left hand, the flashlight in his right. He eased his head in, paused, listening.

She acted without thinking, threw herself against the door. The edge of it caught him across the face, pinned his head against the jamb. The flashlight fell to the floor inside, rolled. She raised the pepper-spray can, held it an inch from his eyes, and thumbed the trigger button. Thick red mist sprayed out. He screamed, and she fired another burst into his open mouth, held the button down.

The gun went off, loud in the enclosed space. He pulled his head back, freeing it, and she slammed the door on his left wrist.

233

The gun fell. She kicked at it, sent it spinning across the wet floor.

Glass broke behind her. Front door. She turned to see a figure come through the darkness of the other room, fill the doorway there. There was a pop, and something hit the wall near her head.

The gun, she thought. *Get the gun.*

She dropped the pepper spray, dove for the gun on the floor. She got ahold of it, fumbled as she brought it up, her finger finding the trigger.

The gun went off before she could aim, the muzzle flash lighting up the kitchen. She fired again, the trigger not seeming to need any pressure at all, felt the recoil up to her shoulders. The man threw himself through the doorway and back into the other room. She fired a third time, saw the bullet plow wood from the doorway trim.

She slipped on the slick linoleum, fell, then got up again, pulled the back door open. The man there was on his knees in the mud, gagging and coughing, hands over his face. She went past him, running. Her momentum carried her up the slope. She slipped once, got her footing again, and then she was in the trees.

She tossed the gun, not wanting to look behind her, kept going. Branches slashed at her. Then she was out of the trees, and at the car, its one headlight still shining, dimmer now.

The interior light was still on, the seats littered with bits of safety glass. She saw her phone, grabbed it, started up to the road. There was yelling behind her, back through the woods, one of them blundering through the trees.

The SUV's engine was running, the hazards and wipers clicking as if in rhythm. She saw the steel push bar on the front grille, what they'd used to ram her, send her off the road.

She tried the driver's-side door. Unlocked. The keys were in the ignition.

More shouting behind her. She climbed up behind the wheel, pulled the door shut, and hit the armrest button, heard the door locks snap. Then she shifted into drive, cranked the wheel to the left, and pulled off the shoulder, spraying gravel behind her.

In the rearview, she saw a figure come up over the guardrail. There was the blur of a muzzle flash, and a bullet pinged the back hatch of the SUV.

She hit the gas. Her eyes stung, tears coursing down her cheeks. Some of the spray must have blown back at her.

She powered down the window, put a cupped hand out into the rain until she had a palmful of it, then wiped at her eyes. It eased the burning, but the tears wouldn't stop.

THIRTY-THREE

ANOTHER NIGHT IN a hospital, Devlin thought. This time he sat in the waiting room, watching the closed door to the emergency unit, hoping someone would come out and talk to him.

There were a half dozen others in the room, looking up at a TV mounted high on the wall, the sound low. A Hispanic woman held a toddler who was crying quietly. Rain washed down the big windows of the emergency-room entrance.

The security door opened and Dwight Malloy came out, looked around and saw him, crooked a finger. Devlin got up. Malloy spoke to the guard at the desk, then held the door open. Devlin went through.

"In here," Malloy said. He pointed to an unoccupied treatment room, drew the curtain shut behind them.

"How is she?" Devlin said.

"Scared. A little scratched up, but she'll be okay. She's tough."

"I know."

"She said she called you. She tell you what happened?"

"Some of it. She was upset, but trying to keep her cool. Doing a good job of it, I thought. There were two men involved?"

"We have them. New Hope police found them walking down the road in the rain. One was still messed up from getting a faceful of pepper spray."

"Good for her."

"Both have long sheets, and one has an outstanding warrant. Bad guys, but not exactly criminal geniuses. She ran them both ragged. We recovered two handguns at the scene. The SUV they were driving was stolen. We're charging them with attempted murder, aggravated battery, auto theft, B&E, vandalism, and anything else we can come up with."

"Are they talking?"

"No, they lawyered up," Malloy said. "Joseph John Avril and Theodore Lewis Statt. Those names mean anything to you?"

Devlin shook his head. "No. Never heard of them before."

"Sure of that?"

"I am."

"Unlikely they'll admit her," Malloy said. "They'll probably send her home in a little while. I'll make sure she gets there. New Hope police will be at her house again tonight. In the meantime, we'll see what we get out of those two clowns we picked up."

"Find out who's paying their lawyer, that's your answer right there."

"I doubt it'll be that simple. If I'd hired them, and they screwed up like that, I'd leave their asses in jail."

"Can I see her?"

"For just a few minutes, yeah. My partner's in there, as well as another reporter from her paper. I think one of her editors is on his way too. What she needs now mostly is to rest, decompress. Getting shot at, running for your life, can be pretty traumatic. But you know all about that, don't you?"

*   *   *

The curtain was pulled back in the treatment room. Tracy Quinn was sitting up in bed, wearing a hospital gown and slowly eating a cup of chocolate ice cream with a plastic spoon. There was a butterfly bandage above her right eye, and her hair was matted and wet. He felt a swell of anger.

Malloy came in behind him. Mendoza stood to one side, along with a young, light-skinned black woman.

Quinn sat up straighter, said, "Hey."

"Hey yourself," Devlin said. "Last time we were here, it was the other way around."

"Now I know how you felt."

She pointed her spoon at the other woman. "Alysha Bennett. Raymond Devlin."

Bennett glared at him. He nodded to her.

"I felt like I needed to call," Quinn said. "Warn you. I didn't know where they might be headed next."

"Nowhere, after the way you handled them."

She looked down at the ice cream, and he saw the tears come. No one spoke. Bennett put an arm around her shoulders, squeezed briefly, then let go. She turned to Devlin.

"Can I talk to you a minute?"

Malloy moved out of their way. Devlin followed her out into the corridor, and away from the treatment room.

She turned to face him, and he saw the anger there.

"No more bullshit," she said. "And no more of this 'off the record' noise. My girl in there almost got killed behind this mess. I'm still not sure just who or what you are, but you need to step up. You're part of this. She trusted you."

"I've told her everything I know."

"I'm writing a story about what happened tonight. And we'll be writing another one every day, until all this is out in the open."

"Good."

"So you need to talk to me."

He looked at his watch. It was a little after ten.

"Am I keeping you?" she said.

"Tracy has my number. I'll do what I can to help you."

"When?" she said, but he was already moving down the hall toward the red exit sign. He pushed open the fire door and went out into the rain.

"I don't like this," Tariq said.

They cruised slowly past the house, Lukas at the wheel of the Lexus. The address was a darkened ranch house on a block of identical homes. They'd left the Crown Vic in Virginia. It was too hot now, after what had happened at the motel. Too much of a chance Devlin or someone else had gotten the plate number.

"We're running out of options," Lukas said. "If you have a better idea, say it."

The transponder signal from Devlin's truck had gone dead that morning. It might have been a malfunction, but more likely Devlin had found it, destroyed it. Another advantage lost.

He U-turned down the street, came back. It was a neighborhood of well-cared-for homes, garages, wide lawns and driveways. A wet fog had drifted in, cast auras around the streetlights.

Lukas pulled to the curb, shut off the lights and engine. The house was a half block ahead, on the opposite side of the street.

It had been a four-and-a-half-hour drive, and now it was after midnight. Lukas had decided this was the way to do it, quick and bold. Find the ex-wife, get her to tell them where Devlin was, maybe take her with them if they had to. There was always the chance they'd find Devlin here, his truck in the driveway. But that would mean luck was with them, and he knew they couldn't count on that anymore.

"Nice neighborhood," Tariq said. "A long way from Sadr City. I used to dream about America. I always imagined it looked like this."

Lukas took gloves from his coat pocket, pulled them on.

"If we take her, then what?" Tariq said.

"Stash her someplace, get in touch with Devlin. Make him come to us."

"Then we'll have to kill them both, won't we?"

Lukas could see a light fixture mounted above the garage door, next to a basketball hoop. Motion detector. There would be others on the house as well.

"More civilians," Tariq said.

"Fortunes of war."

"I'm just wondering if it's worth the risk."

"As long as he's walking around, Devlin's a threat to all of us. No way around that. We take care of him, we get our money, and then we can do whatever we want. You can go back to Sadr City, spread your wealth around."

"Maybe I will."

Lukas pointed at the attached garage. "The window on the side. We'll see if it's wired. If not, we'll go in through there, try the door that leads into the house. You work the locks, and we're in."

"And if the window's alarmed?"

"We find another way. A basement door, maybe. There's always something. People are never as careful as they think they are."

Tariq looked at the house, didn't speak.

"If you're not up for this," Lukas said, "you can wait here."

"No. Let's get it done."

Lukas reached beneath his seat, took out the Sig tucked into the springs there. It was loaded with 9-millimeter subsonics. Along with the suppressor, they would cut the noise of a gunshot in half.

Tariq was pulling on his gloves. They hadn't brought masks, would have to go in without them, take their chances.

Tariq took the Shield automatic from his waistband. "You should have asked for more money."

"Next time," Lukas said.

Together, they got out of the Lexus, and crossed the street to the dark and silent house.

*   *   *

Tracy looked up from her MacBook, said, "It's getting crowded in here."

She was at the kitchen table, Alysha across from her, talking to Rick Carr on her cell. Dwight Malloy sat at the table with them, drinking instant coffee he'd made himself. Four uniformed officers, two from New Hope and two from Philadelphia, milled around the living room, talking, their belt radios squawking every few minutes.

At the hospital, they'd wanted to keep her overnight for observation, but she'd refused. Dwight had driven her home, a ride filled with awkward silences and empty small talk. She'd showered and changed when she got there, but still felt cold. There were deep bruises on her shoulder and side from the seat belt harness, and her whole body was stiff and sore.

Alysha's story was on her screen. Rick had sent it to Tracy for a final read before posting it online. It felt odd seeing herself quoted as a source.

"I should have you down at Race Street making a statement right now," Dwight said. "Only reason I don't is so you can meet your deadline. I hope you appreciate that."

"I do."

She hit the Send icon, watched the story vanish from her screen, sat back, and let out her breath.

Alysha ended her call. "You hanging in there?"

"I'm all right. Just tired."

"This type of thing sneaks up on you," Dwight said. "You think you're fine, but you're running on nervous energy. Then suddenly you're out of gas."

"Story should be live soon," Alysha said. "Rick's going to stick around for a while. We can update if we want, just need to call him."

"Long day for him," Tracy said.

"You too. He says you stay home tomorrow. They'll call you if they need you. I'll pick up the follow, and stay in touch. Irv's going to give me a couple more bodies to help chase some things down. Full-court press on this one, Ms. Quinn. And it's all your fault."

To Dwight, Tracy said, "What will happen to those two men?"

"Are you asking as a victim or a reporter?"

"Both."

"They'll be arraigned tomorrow, out here. They're from out of state, so bail doesn't seem likely. No sign of a lawyer yet, either."

"What about my car?"

"Police wrecker winched it out. It's at Hammond Brothers in New Hope. But I suspect your insurance company's going to total it when they see it."

"Good."

"You're taking all this very calmly," he said. "With a sense of humor, even. That's good to see. But Trace, trust me, from personal experience. When something like this catches up with you, it hits—and hits hard. And it stays with you for a good long time."

Later, when she was alone in the house, she tried Devlin's phone again. It went straight to voice mail. It was the third time she'd called him since she'd gotten home. She felt a growing sense of alarm. Where had he gone? What was he planning on doing?

She tried to sleep, woke after half an hour, the sound of gunshots in her head. Dwight had been right, she knew. She'd interviewed people who'd gone through this type of trauma, survived violent attacks. It never left you. It tainted everything that came after it.

Rain lashed at the windows. She looked out at the cruiser in the yard, checked the front door locks again, made sure all the windows were latched.

She tried Devlin's line again. There was no answer.

THIRTY-FOUR

——————

EVLIN CAME OUT of the trees, looked down at Farrow's house. He'd parked the Ranchero a half mile away, made his way up a wooded hill behind the development, estimating distances while he climbed. It had taken him less than three hours to drive down here, with little traffic on 95. The sky was clear. He'd left the rain behind.

The house was dark, except for a lighted window in the side door that led to the basement room. Farrow's Bronco was in the driveway, parked nose out. The Tahoe was in front of the house.

How many men inside? At least two from the Tahoe, maybe more if Farrow had decided to beef up the detail since his last visit.

He started down the hill. When he reached the driveway, he stayed close to the Bronco, saw the red light blinking on the dash. There were shadows here, between the garage and the house, enough to hide in. Three steps led up to the side door. He could hear voices behind it.

*   *   *

Farrow looked at the cellphone on the bar top, waiting for it to ring.

Drew Holifield and the man named Dillon were shooting pool quietly, the only sound the click of the balls, the scratching of cues being chalked. A third man, Ryan, the youngest of them, sat on the couch, leaning forward, elbows on his knees, tapping his foot on the floor, nervous.

The toilet flushed, and Cody came out of the bathroom, wiping his hands on a paper towel. To Farrow, he said, "Still nothing?"

"Did you hear the phone ring?"

"Sorry, boss. Just asking."

Farrow took a bottle of Johnnie Walker Black from the bar rack, poured two fingers into a cut-glass tumbler. He realized now he'd made a mistake, entrusted important work to men he didn't know. He'd moved too fast, without enough preparation.

He'd paid the two men five grand each, with five more to come, and given them a burner phone to call him when it was done. Now he had to resist the urge to try the number. There was always the chance the police had caught them and taken the phone.

The snub-nosed S&W .38 with mother-of-pearl grips was where he'd left it, on the shelf behind the bar. He opened the cylinder, checked the loads, then closed it again. The men heard it, looked at him. He tucked the gun into his belt. It made him feel better.

He drank, looked at his Rolex. It was almost two. He was conscious of the emptiness of the house above him. He'd sent his own wife to her sister's in Phoenix that afternoon. There was too much danger now, from too many sides.

Dillon chalked his stick, said, "Joe and Theo are good men. They won't fuck this up."

"Then why haven't I heard from them?" Farrow said.

"You will. Something must have come up. Whatever it is, they're pros, they can handle it. They won't let you down."

"They'd better not." He took a pack of Marlboros from the bar top, shook one out. Dillon turned back to the table, leaned over to make a shot.

Outside, a car alarm began to blare.

Devlin stepped away from the Bronco, its headlights flashing, the alarm sounding. The sole of his boot had left a dirty footprint on the driver's door. He moved back into the shadows.

The side door opened and a man came out, looked down at the Bronco. He was young, twenties, maybe, hair cut so close that scalp showed. There was a Glock holstered on his right hip.

When he came down the stairs, Devlin let him go past, then stepped behind him, kicked the back of his knee, and locked an arm around his throat to hold him up. He pulled the gun from the kid's holster, touched the muzzle to his temple. "Inside."

He pushed the kid forward, hooked one hand in the back of his collar. They started up the steps, and then Cody was in the doorway, holding a gun.

Devlin aimed the Glock at him over the kid's shoulder. "Back up."

Cody didn't move. Devlin could hear the kid breathing fast.

"Three seconds," Devlin said.

Behind him, the alarm stopped.

"Two seconds."

Cody backed into the room. Devlin guided the kid up the steps and through the doorway. Farrow stood behind the bar to his left. On the other side of the room, two men were at the pool table, sticks in their hands. One of them was the guard Farrow had called Holly. The other was older, his dark hair slicked back.

Devlin moved inside, keeping the kid in front, kicked the door shut behind him. Cody took a step back. Devlin kept the Glock centered on his chest.

"Put your weapon down," Devlin said. "There on the couch."

He didn't move. Devlin watched him. He'd disarmed him once

before, knew there might be a grudge there that could override his common sense.

"Do it, Cody," Farrow said.

Cody lowered the gun, set it on the arm of the couch.

"Move back," Devlin said. "Farther."

To the other men, he said, "Guns on the table."

This was the dangerous part, he knew. Five men, and at least two of them still armed. Unlikely he could tag them both if they drew at the same time.

Farrow was watching him, a lit cigarette dangling from his lips. Holly still held the pool cue in his left hand, its butt on the floor. The other one set his stick on the table, had the presence of mind to free his hands. He wore no jacket, had an automatic holstered on his left hip, butt forward for a cross draw with his right hand. He was the one to watch.

"It's okay, Dillon," Farrow said. "Do what he says."

Dillon's eyes narrowed. Devlin aimed the Glock at his chest.

"Go on," Farrow said. "You too, Holly. I don't think Raymond's planning on shooting anyone in here tonight." He looked at Devlin. "Am I right, Sergeant?"

Dillon reached across and drew his gun from its holster, set it on the table, but within reach. Holly put his beside it. He still held the pool cue.

Devlin let go of the kid, shoved him hard. Cody stepped back, and the kid fell in front of him, then got to his feet "I'm sorry, Mr. Farrow," he said, out of breath. "I didn't see him out there. I—"

"Shut up," Farrow said. He set his cigarette in a glass ashtray on the bar top.

Devlin took Cody's gun from the couch arm, put it in his jacket pocket. To the kid, he said, "What's your name?"

"Ryan."

"Ryan, I want you to collect those weapons, and put them on the bar over here. Do it slowly, and without walking in front of me." Trying to show more confidence than he felt.

Ryan looked at Farrow, who said, "Go ahead."

Cody raised his hands, uneasy. He knew if any shooting started, he'd be in the cross fire.

Ryan went to the pool table, picked up the two guns. Devlin kept the Glock on him. He came back, set them on the bar.

"Now reach under Cody's jacket, and take out that pair of handcuffs there."

The kid looked at him, then Cody, uncertain what to do. Cody lifted the tail of his jacket, exposing the empty holster, the snap case with handcuffs, and the stun gun.

"Get that too," Devlin said.

The kid unsnapped the case, took out the cuffs, then the stun gun.

"On the bar," Devlin said. "Then take the handcuffs and put them on those two gentlemen over there. Left hand to left hand."

"Fuck that," Holly said.

Devlin pointed the gun at him.

"We really need all this drama, Raymond?" Farrow said.

"No drama. As long as they do what I say."

They all looked at Farrow. He nodded. "Sooner we get this over with, the better."

Holly set his pool cue on the table. Devlin heard the clink of balls knocked aside. The kid ratcheted a cuff around his wrist. Dillon held his left arm up over the table. *He's going along to bide his time*, Devlin thought, *waiting until he sees an opening.*

"If I guess right, Holly has another set on his belt as well," Devlin said. "Go ahead and take those out."

The kid reached under Holly's jacket, came out with the second pair.

"Now you and Cody, same thing," Devlin said. "Left to left."

The kid did as he was told.

"Now step away," Devlin said. He twisted to point the Glock at Farrow. "Come out from there."

"I'm armed," Farrow said.

"Come around."

Farrow stepped out from behind the bar, hands at his sides. Devlin saw the gun in his waistband. "On the bar."

"Right." He used two fingers to draw out a snub-nosed revolver by its grip, set it with the other guns. "Didn't expect to see you again so soon, Ray."

The Glock felt heavy. His palm was slick against the grip. He had to keep control of the situation, knew it could go bad quick.

He looked at the other men.

"You four." He nodded toward the open bathroom door. "In there."

"No way," Holly said.

Devlin moved the Glock to cover him. *They're waiting to see what I'll do,* he thought. *How I'll handle it.*

To Farrow, he said, "Is your family home?"

"Why?"

"I guess that's a no," Devlin said, raised the Glock, and fired once into the low ceiling. Cody back-stepped fast, dragging the kid with him. The others didn't move.

Bits of acoustic tile drifted down. Devlin's right ear rang.

"Was that necessary?" Farrow said. Some of his cool gone now.

Devlin pointed the gun at the others again. "Bathroom."

They stayed where they were. Farrow said, "Go ahead. I'll deal with this."

Cody and Ryan went in first. Dillon next, watching Devlin the whole time. Holly was last.

"Shut it," Devlin said. "I see that knob turn before I tell you to come out, I'll start firing through that door."

Dillon reached past Holly, pulled the door closed.

Farrow exhaled. "What is it you want, Raymond?"

Devlin aimed the Glock at him. "You shouldn't have gone after the woman."

"What woman?" He reached for a pack of cigarettes on the bar top. The one in the ashtray had gone out. "You mind?"

He took out a cigarette, put the pack back down, and got out his lighter. He lit the cigarette, gestured at the gun. "You want to be careful with that. Those Glock triggers can be touchy."

"Might solve a lot of problems if I just put a bullet in you now."

"Why would you want to do that?" He turned his head, exhaled smoke.

Devlin nodded at the cellphone on the bar. "Are you waiting for a call?"

"Not especially."

"Did you send them after her?"

"After who?"

"The reporter. The one who wrote about Acheron. About you."

Devlin watched for his reaction. His expression didn't change.

"Did something happen to her?"

"Something did. But she's fine. The cops have the two men who attacked her. I'm sure you'll be hearing about that."

"Why? I had nothing to do with it. I have a problem with reporters, I call a lawyer. That's what I pay them for."

"Then who sent them? Kemper?"

"I'm still not sure what you're talking about. But if I had to guess, I'd say yes."

"Step over there by the couch."

When he did, Devlin moved behind the bar. He could hear the men talking in the bathroom, their voices low.

"You the one put the tracker on me?" Devlin said.

"You blame me?" Farrow said. "You're a bit of a loose cannon these days, Sergeant. I felt inclined to protect myself."

Devlin took Cody's gun from his pocket, set it with the others. He put down the Glock he'd taken from the kid, fieldstripped the other three automatics. The firing pins and magazines went into a jacket pocket, the rest of the parts into a wastebasket. He dropped the stun gun on the floor, stamped down on it twice, cracked the plastic.

"Chances are one of my neighbors heard that shot," Farrow said.

"Police could be on their way. That'll be tough for you to explain, won't it?"

"You'll think of something." He put Farrow's .38 in his other jacket pocket, picked up the Glock again.

"I'm starting to think you came here without a plan," Farrow said. "That you're making this up as you go along. And you've got no idea how it ends."

"Who tried to kill me?"

"I heard about that. I don't know."

"Not good enough, Gordon. Not by a long shot."

"I'm a businessman. Would I risk everything I have on a stupid move like that, hire someone to pop off at you in public, other people around?"

"You tracked me."

"That was in my own best interest, don't you think?"

"Is that how they found me?"

"Kind of trail you're leaving, it wouldn't be hard. But it wasn't me. Now, can we sit down, have a civilized conversation? I can't handle all this standing anymore. I'll tell you what I know, but I need to sit."

Devlin nodded at the couch, came out from around the bar. Farrow sat. "Grab that ashtray."

Devlin took it from the bar, set it on the coffee table, stepped back. He held the Glock at his side.

Farrow pulled the tray closer, ashed his cigarette. "You know who Lukas Dragovic is?"

"No."

"He works for the old man. Not for Unix, more of a private thing. He's a Serb, grew up here in the States, but he comes from a town called Knin, part of what used to be Krajina, a Serb republic inside Croatia."

"So?"

"In '95 the Croat Army swept through there, shelled the city, killed a lot of people, mostly civilians, drove the rest out. Then they burned all the houses, to make sure no one came back. They were settling scores, doing the same things the Serbs had done to them elsewhere, and worse.

"Roland saw some news footage of refugees leaving the city, a long line of them on a dirt road, mostly kids and old people. There was one boy, eight, maybe nine, all cut up, covered with dust, carrying a stuffed bear. Had that thousand-yard stare already, you know? Old man saw this kid, and it got to him for some reason. Maybe he felt guilty about the role we'd played over there, I don't know. He sent me to find him.

"It took a while. Town was shot to shit, bodies everywhere. You couldn't get away from the smell. Finally tracked him down to an orphanage they'd set up outside the city. Kid's whole family bought it in the attack. He was so shell-shocked, he couldn't even remember their names. But he still had that bear."

"You brought him here?"

"Roland chartered a plane for us. He'd started funding some aid organizations for orphans and refugees on both sides of the fighting. He sponsored a group of them himself, brought them over, found homes for them. But Lukas was always his favorite. He took him under his wing, practically raised him. Paid for his education, gave him a job."

"Doing what?"

"Whatever needs doing. Knowing the old man, he probably saw something he could take advantage of. Nine years old, that kid was already hard-core."

"What's that mean?"

"No emotions, at least that I ever saw. Roland had him in a boarding school here in Virginia when he was a teenager. Kid was catching a lot of grief there—weird name, foreign accent. You can imagine. Apparently, he was getting bullied by some upperclassmen. They had a hazing thing where they'd grab the smaller, younger kids, toss them into an old scummy pond behind the school. Just kid shit, you know. For laughs.

"One day Lukas got word he was next. You gotta remember, this kid's like thirteen, looks ten. Easy prey. Sure enough, that night they come busting into his room, try to drag him out of bed. But this kid—gotta give him credit—had taken a combination lock from the gym, put it in a sock, and tied it off, had it with him in the bed. He started whaling on them. Got the first boy, the ringleader, good. Fractured his skull. Lucky he didn't kill him. Sent the other ones running.

"Anyway, Roland had to pay a lot of money to smooth it over. Kid got kicked out, of course, but Roland had the charges dropped, paid off anyone he needed to. He found another boarding school took his money and didn't ask any questions. He paid for it all. College too.

"The kid's smart, have to give him that. Pull a trigger on you without blinking, though. All the shit he saw growing up, no surprise he came out the way he did. Still, he isn't like you or me. We did what we had to do and got paid. This kid loves his work. If Roland sent someone after you, it was probably him."

"He kill Colin?"

"He did."

"For what reason?"

"Risk reduction."

Devlin felt his patience slipping away. "Talk sense."

Farrow leaned forward, put out his cigarette.

"You still don't get it, do you? What was going on in San Marcos, what we did there."

"I was there. I saw."

"You saw some of it. Just another job, right? Help the locals along. But Roland was selling them weapons too, and that shit was straight up illegal, as far as Uncle Sam was concerned. They blind-eyed some of it—they wanted Herrera gone too—but at one point there was a shipment of Stinger missiles involved, and that got everybody nervous. Washington was worried they'd end up in the hands of the cartels, or Shining Path or somebody worse."

"I never saw any Stingers."

"We kept you guys away from all that. That was a separate deal. Once Ramírez took over, he offered to sell them back to the U.S.—at two hundred grand a pop, still in their crates. Everybody made out on that one. Trouble was, once he was in power, he wasn't so good at staying there. He still needed us."

"For what?"

"People were in the streets almost as soon as he took office. Everything he'd spent would be wasted if he couldn't keep his own people under control. So we helped target some of the opposition, take them out. Kept the ship of state running smoothly, raking in that oil and gas money. He had cash to spend, and Roland was happy to take it."

"I didn't know this."

"You were out of the picture by then, stateside with broken legs and a faceful of shrapnel. Bell and Roarke went back, though."

"To do what?"

"Those grassroots resistance movements fall apart if you put enough pressure on them right away. The trick is not to wait, let their momentum build. Kill a couple students, priests, show them you're serious, and the rest fall in line. Once they realize it's not a game, their revolutionary fervor tends to fade."

"Were you in charge of that too?"

"It was my job. I'm not proud of it, the part I played. But it was the mission at hand."

"Is that what you tell yourself?"

"Raymond, I am the most self-aware motherfucker you will ever meet. I knew *exactly* what I was doing. We put Ramírez in power, and kept him in power. Which made some people very happy, and some people very rich. But you want to know what the most ironic part was?"

"What?"

"We were selling to Herrera's people too, at first. Then Ramírez came to us with the better deal."

"That's what it's always about, isn't it?" Devlin said. "The better deal."

"What do you think? Hell, after you left, we did shit you never even knew about. Somalia, Libya, the Ukraine, a dozen other places. San Marcos was just another war."

"To make a buck."

"That's why all wars are fought, Raymond. If you think different, you're being naive."

"Why come after me and Colin? Why now?"

"Hand me those smokes?"

"Later."

"You want to hear what I have to say, or not?"

Devlin took the pack from the bar, tossed it onto the table. Farrow took out another cigarette, lit it.

"I wasn't totally forthright with you last time we spoke, Raymond. I wasn't sure where you were coming from, who you might be working for." He blew out smoke.

"You're talking about Mata?"

"We set him up here, and for a long time he was smart enough to keep his mouth shut. Then a few months ago, when things in San Marcos start jumping off again, he decided to make some noise, saying he had a story to tell about what happened over there, and unless we ponied up some cash, he was going to tell it. He wanted five hundred thousand, you believe that? He got a message to me finally, which is the stupidest thing he could have done. You can guess what the old man's response was."

"He sent Lukas."

"Yeah. Can't feel sorry for Emilio. Got what he deserved finally, the treacherous fuck. The body being found, though, that was just bad luck."

"That's why he wanted Mata dead. Why Colin? Why me?"

"You guys knew too much, saw too much. What happened in that village, especially. Mata said he had documents, photos, to prove what Acheron had done there. He had your names too. For all we knew, you and Roarke were in on it with him."

"We weren't."

"I didn't think so. And that's what I told Roland. He said he couldn't take the chance, there were too many things going on that would be endangered. Unix has contracts coming up worth billions. If any of this came out, what happened back then, it could torpedo the whole thing, keep the company from eventually going public. You know him, the way he thinks. If anything, he's more paranoid now than ever." He blew out smoke.

"Were there documents?"

"Lukas didn't find anything at Mata's place. He torched it anyway, just in case. Odds are Mata was bluffing. Didn't matter, though. Had to be done. You see what's going on over there now?"

"Ramírez is in trouble again," Devlin said.

"It's been brewing for a while. When you're all stick, no carrot, things fall apart. He and Roland made a deal to send another team over in a couple weeks, help him get his shit squared away again, before it's too late."

"Kill some more students? Priests?"

"From the news, I'd say Ramírez is getting a head start on that already."

Devlin felt light-headed. He sat in the chair, the gun in his lap, thinking it all through.

"It was a waste," he said finally. "All of it. There was no need."

"Tell that to the old man."

"None of us would have talked."

"He needed to be sure. Bell was supposed to deal with you, then Roarke. But that never happened, because you dealt with him first."

"So you sent this Lukas to finish the job."

"Not me. Roland. His idea. I was never on board with it. We were a team, after all. But I understand his logic. Maybe one of you sees the news, has a sudden attack of conscience, calls up the

New York Times or whatever. It would be the end of him, the end of Unix. The end of everything. Far as he was concerned, the three of you were an unsustainable risk."

"You saw as much as we did. More, even."

"He's needed me up until now. But I don't fit in with his current political aspirations. I'm a grunt, like you, a reminder of what he wants to forget."

"You took his money all these years," Devlin said. "You could have gone to someone, talked, blown the whole thing wide open. You could have warned us."

"Could I? That's easy to say now. You weren't in my position. We all do what we have to do. When you're in, you're in. There's no good guys and bad guys in war. Everyone's a bad guy soon enough. Innocent people get hurt. You know that more than anybody."

"Where's Kemper now?"

"He left the States. He's on his way to the island."

"What island?"

"Doesn't have a name. Piece of property he owns in the eastern Bahamas, off Green Turtle Cay in the Abacos. Not much of an island, really. It's only about seven acres, mostly rock. The house he's building there isn't even done, but I guess he thought it'd be a good place to lay low for a while, wait for this thing to blow over."

"It won't."

"Don't be so sure. He's got a lot of friends and deep pockets, and he's been doing this for a long time. But the first thing he'll try to do is tie things up here. That means you and me. That's where Lukas comes in."

Devlin looked at the bathroom door. The men inside had gone silent. He took out the .38, held it for a moment, then tossed it onto the couch. He waited to see what Farrow would do.

"That a last gesture to a comrade in arms?" Farrow said. "Or are you hoping I'll reach for it?"

"Maybe both."

Farrow leaned forward, put out the cigarette.

"I'll know soon if what you've told me is true," Devlin said. "If not, we'll see each other again."

He tucked the Glock in his belt. He wanted a weapon with him now.

When he was at the door, Farrow said, "Raymond, can I make an observation?"

Devlin turned back to him.

"You're not a killer, Ray. Not like the rest of us. You never were. Be thankful for that."

THIRTY-FIVE

HERE WAS NO alarm on the garage window. Tariq had played the penlight beam along its inside edges, looking for wires or contact blocks. Then he'd used a small screwdriver to rock the window out enough to slip the latch. Together they lifted the window out of its frame, the metal damp from the fog, and set it in the grass.

Lukas shone his own penlight inside. Two vehicles, an SUV and a compact, which meant the woman wasn't alone. No dog bowls, no cages. A refrigerator, recycling buckets, and a bundle of newspapers bound with twine. He fanned the light over the far wall, saw the door that led into the house.

Tariq went in first, Lukas boosting him, the window just wide enough. Lukas followed, swung his legs inside, touched down on the concrete floor. They waited, listening for any sound from beyond the connecting door.

Tariq took out his lock-pick tools, moved to the door, and knelt on the single step there, went to work on the dead bolt. Lukas stood behind him, shining the penlight over his shoulder. A series of scrapes and clicks, and then Tariq twisted the tension wrench, and the lock came open.

Lukas could feel the adrenaline now, pulsing inside him. They listened at the door. After a few moments, Lukas nodded, and Tariq tried the knob. It turned easily.

Lukas switched off the light, took the Sig from his belt, threaded in the suppressor. Tariq stepped back, put the tools away, drew his own gun.

Lukas opened the door slowly. They were looking at a dark kitchen, tile floor, a granite countertop. Red lights glowed on appliances on the opposite wall. A sliding glass door with vertical blinds led to a rear deck.

Lukas gestured to Tariq to wait, then stepped quietly into the kitchen.

"Right fucking there, pal. Do not move."

Ceiling lights flashed on. Lukas turned toward the voice, and there was a man in the hallway off the kitchen, dark-haired and muscular, wearing gym shorts and a gray T-shirt. He was pointing an automatic at Lukas's chest. Behind him in the hallway were a woman in a bathrobe and a teenage boy in T-shirt and sweatpants.

"Put the gun on the floor, and kick it over here," the man said. "Then get on your knees."

Lukas raised his hands, holding the Sig high. "I think I've got the wrong house."

"Yeah, you've got the wrong house, all right. Do what I said. Now."

In his peripheral vision, Lukas saw the connecting doorway was empty. Tariq had backed into the shadows there.

"Karen, the two of you go back to Brendan's room," the man said. "Call 911."

"Be careful," she said.

"Go!"

Lukas took a step back, conscious of the glass door behind him.

"I'm putting the gun down. Just relax. I think there's a misunderstanding here."

"No misunderstanding," the man said. "Put it down or I shoot you where you stand."

The woman and the boy had gone into a room off the hallway, shut the door. Lukas lowered the Sig slowly, set it on the floor in front of him.

"Kick it over here."

He put his foot on the Sig, slid it across the tile and into the hallway. It landed near the man's feet. Lukas could see Tariq just outside the door now, crouched forward, the Shield in both hands. He was listening, trying to place exactly where the man was before he broke cover.

"I thought this house was empty," Lukas said, trying to keep the man distracted, talking. "I didn't know there was anybody living here."

"On your knees. I won't tell you again."

"I can explain this," Lukas said. "I don't think you—"

Tariq swung out of the doorway and into the kitchen, the gun up. The man shifted his aim and shot him through the throat.

Blood spotted Lukas's jacket. Tariq fell back, and Lukas closed the distance just as the man swung the gun toward him and fired again. The round went past him and through the sliding glass door. In the bedroom, the woman screamed.

Lukas slapped his right hand on top of the gun, swept his left elbow into the man's throat, overbalanced him. He kicked out his legs, took him down. The woman and the boy were back in the hallway now, the woman screaming again.

From the corner of his eye, Lukas saw the boy going for the Sig. He stripped the gun from the man's hand, swept the barrel hard against his forehead, turned and aimed as the boy bent toward the Sig. The woman screamed "No!" and Lukas fired into the floor near the gun, blew up a divot of splintered wood. The boy sprang back, and the woman wrapped her arms around him, dragged him away.

Lukas held the gun on them. The man sat up, a hand to his forehead, blood there.

Lukas picked up the Sig, backed into the kitchen. At his feet, Tariq lay gasping and choking, blood pumping from his wound.

The woman and the boy were frozen. The man was looking up at Lukas, hand still held to his face. Lukas raised the Sig, sighted down the suppressor at him.

Tariq gave a wet rattle and went silent. Lukas steadied the Sig. The man watched him, waiting for the bullet.

If you kill him, you'll have to kill all of them, Lukas thought. *There's no other way.*

He shifted the muzzle of the suppressor to the boy and the woman. They hadn't moved. *Do it,* he thought. *Do it now.*

He could hear a siren in the distance. He lowered the Sig, then turned and fired three times through the vertical blinds and into the sliding door. The glass gave way and cascaded out onto the deck.

Lukas looked back at the man, the woman and boy behind him. Then he turned, pushed through the blinds and onto the deck. A motion sensor clicked on, bathed him in light.

He leaped off the deck, landed in the side yard. He flung the man's gun into bushes, ran toward the front of the house and the street beyond. Just as he reached the Lexus, a police cruiser with flashing rollers came down the street, caught him in its headlights. He raised the Sig, fired three times, saw the rounds hit the cruiser's windshield. The driver jerked the wheel to the left, and the cruiser jumped the curb and came to rest on a lawn.

He got in the Lexus, tossed the Sig on the passenger seat, started the engine. There were more flashing lights ahead. He gunned the engine, swung around the rear end of the cruiser. At a side street, he cut a hard left that made the tires squeal, then a right, then another left, all through residential streets, headlights off.

More sirens now, but as he drove they seemed farther away. He tried to calm himself, slow his breathing. At the intersection ahead was a main street he recognized, the way they'd come. He slowed then, turned on the headlights, looked in the rearview. There was no one following.

He headed south.

Dawn was a faint light on the horizon when he got back to the house. He needed to stay organized, clearheaded. If someone had gotten the plate number on the Lexus, it might be traced back here. The house and the work car were full of evidence, fingerprints, DNA.

Too much had happened in the previous weeks, they'd drawn too much attention. Mata's body, the bar shootings, the attack on Devlin. At some point, someone would put it all together. There was nothing to be done about any of that now. The house was fucked.

You should have killed them all, he thought, *left no witnesses.* But he'd met the eyes of the woman and the boy, and couldn't pull the trigger. *Maybe there are some things you won't do after all.*

Too late now. Too late to think about anything besides what came next.

He filled a duffel with clothes. The Sig went into the weapons bag. He carried both out to the Lexus, stowed them in the trunk.

Tariq's Jeep SUV was parked in the garage alongside the Crown Vic. He got both sets of keys, powered down the windows in each vehicle.

There was a six-gallon red plastic gas can under the workbench, almost full. He splashed the interior of the work car with gas, popped open the fuel door, and unscrewed the cap, then did the same with the SUV.

The can was still half full when he carried it into the house. He started upstairs, poured gas in each room, then in a trail down the stairs. He emptied the last of it in the living room, doused the couch, the carpet. The harsh fumes made his eyes water.

He took a last look around. He would miss the house. It had

been his only real home for the last five years, a place where he could do as he pleased, live as he wanted, with no one to answer to. And, like all his homes, he knew it would never last.

There was a roadside emergency kit in the Lexus trunk, with three striker flares. He took out two, shut the lid. In the garage, he took the cap off a flare, struck it twice. It flashed and sparked. He tossed it onto the front seat of the Crown Vic. Flames filled the interior, the sudden wave of heat driving him back, singeing his eyebrows. Thick black smoke bloomed up, flattened and spread against the ceiling. The SUV caught almost immediately.

Back in the house, he struck the second flare, tossed it onto the gas-soaked couch. The upholstery burst into flame. Fire raced across the floor.

He left the front door open, got into the Lexus, started the engine, backed away. Smoke began to pour out the door. He wheeled around, headed down the driveway. In the rearview, he saw flames rising up from the house and garage, smoke billowing, hiding the stars. Halfway to the county road, he heard the flat thump as one of the gas tanks ignited. When he looked back a last time, the sky to the west glowed like a false dawn.

Alone again, as you always were, he thought. *As you were meant to be.*

THIRTY-SIX

D EVLIN'S PHONE WOKE him. He heard the buzz, saw the screen glow in the motel-room darkness. He got the phone from the night-stand, saw Brendan's number and the time—3 a.m. He felt a surge of alarm, kicked off the covers, sat up.

When he answered, it was Vic Ramos on the line.

"There's some people here want to talk to you," he said.

Devlin spent twenty minutes on the phone, first with two state cops, then with an Agent Healy from the New Haven FBI field of-fice. He told her about the shooting at the motel, gave her Dwight Malloy's name. He didn't mention Dragovic, Farrow, or any of the rest of it.

When Ramos came back on the line, Devlin said, "How are they? I can be up there by morning." He was in a motel outside D.C., had gone there after leaving Farrow's house.

"I don't think we need any more help from you. You've done enough damage."

"I'm sorry about this."

"You should be. I don't know what it is you're involved in that caused this, but you'll pay for it. I told Healy about your coming up here last week, what you said. They're going to want to talk to you more. This isn't over."

"I gave her my number. Can I talk to Karen?"

"No."

"How's Brendan?"

"How do you think he is? They're both wrecked."

"Can you put him on the phone?"

"Forget it."

Devlin paced the room, a hollow feeling in his stomach.

"I didn't start this," he said. "But maybe I can finish it."

"What's that mean?"

"It means take care of Karen and Brendan, whatever happens."

"You think you need to tell me that?"

"I want them to know I love them. And that I'm sorry. For everything."

"A little late for that, isn't it? If it's up to me, you'll never talk to either of them again."

"Tell them, Vic," he said, and ended the call.

It was dusk when Lukas drove up to the lighted guard booth, powered down his window. The guard inside wore a Core-Tech uniform, was reading a magazine. He slid open his door halfway, was about to speak when Lukas rested the Sig's suppressor on the windowsill and fired twice. The guard fell backward off his stool, went down.

Lukas got out, pushed open the booth door. The guard lay on the floor, not moving. Lukas put another round into him, then hit the switch to open the gate. When it rose, he got back in the Lexus and drove through.

He parked down the street from Farrow's house, got out. The house was dark, the driveway and garage empty. He'd been here only once before, but remembered the layout. He kicked in the side door, went in with the gun up, finger on the trigger.

The room was dark except for the light spill from the open bathroom. He stepped inside and away from the door, listening, sensed he was alone. The smell of cigarette smoke hung in the air. Farrow hadn't been gone long.

He went up a short flight of stairs into a kitchen, then searched the rest of the house. It was empty.

THIRTY-SEVEN

O**N HER WAY** up to the newsroom, Tracy grabbed a paper from reception. She'd read the final versions of the stories online, wanted to see how they'd been played in the print edition. Alysha's mainbar took up most of the front page above the fold. A five-column headline read OBSERVER REPORTER ATTACKED. Then under it, TWO HELD IN ASSAULT LINKED TO INVESTIGATION. There were mug shots of both men and, embedded in the copy, a thumbnail photo of herself. It was the same one that was on her laminate.

Rick Carr was talking to Alysha at her desk. He saw her coming and frowned.

Tracy held up the paper. "Nice to see it the old-fashioned way. Headlines could be better, though. Where we at on the follow?"

"I thought we agreed you were staying home today," he said.

"I was going stir-crazy. Thought maybe if I came in I could help."

Tired as she was, she hadn't slept more than an hour at a time.

She was dragging now, but the idea of staying in the house depressed her. She needed to be around people. She needed to work.

"How do you feel?" Alysha said.

"Ready to rock." She'd taken two ibuprofen, but her knees still ached, and her left shoulder and side were sore to the touch. She'd put a fresh bandage over her eye.

Rick took a chair from an empty desk, rolled it over for her to sit.

"Thanks," Tracy said. "How are we doing?"

Alysha looked at Rick, then back at her. "No breaks yet. The senator's people got back to me. 'No comment' at this time, but they're promising something later today. I'm sure they're putting together a judiciously worded press release as we speak. You talk to Devlin?"

Tracy shook her head. "Tried. Can't reach him. Haven't seen him since the hospital. Anything new on the two men they arrested?"

"Still in custody in New Hope. No bail," Rick said. "One of them had a warrant out of Kentucky for agg assault. We're following up on them as well."

"What's the plan?" Tracy said.

"Russ Jones from Metro is on his way down to Unix headquarters in Virginia," Alysha said. "He'll see if he can shake something loose from Kemper or his people. He'll try Farrow's house in Falls Church as well. I'll drive down tomorrow to help."

"What do you need me to do?"

"We've got it covered," Rick said. "We don't need you here today. Go home. Rest."

"I've got a better idea," she said. It had come to her on the cab ride there. "Since I can't be involved in our main stories, objectivity-wise, how about I write a first-person sidebar on what it's like to be run off the road and shot at?"

"You serious?" he said.

"If you don't want it, I'll pitch it to the *Inquirer*."

"Funny." He looked at Alysha, who shrugged.

"All right," he said. "Write a skedline, and I'll add it to the budget. Get me a draft by the five o'clock meeting. Call Photo too, have them get a couple shots of you at your desk to run with it. Figure twenty inches for the print version."

"I'll need thirty, at least."

"Make it twenty-five."

"Got it."

"It's all yours," he said. "Drive it away."

At her desk, she tried Devlin again from her cell. She was waiting for his voice-mail message when the line picked up.

"Where have you been?" she said. "I've been trying to reach you for hours."

"I got your messages."

She heard background noise, traffic.

"Where are you going?" she said. "Are you running out on us?"

"I'm not running out on anything. You did your part. Now I have to do mine."

"What are you talking about?"

"Something I need to deal with. Something that should have been handled a long time ago."

"Don't get cryptic on me."

"These people you think you're after," he said. "They'll never stop. They have no reason to. And they can buy their way out of anything. You need to understand that."

"What are you talking about? What are you doing?"

"Look after yourself," he said, and ended the call.

She tried him back, and this time it went to voice mail. She threw the phone on her desk.

THIRTY-EIGHT

HE GATE TO Kemper's driveway was open. Farrow turned the Bronco in. Holifield sat beside him, an Uzi across his lap, covered by a jacket. The other three men were in the Tahoe, following close. They'd drawn weapons from the gun cabinet before rolling out.

It was coming to an end, he knew. He'd lit a fuse by giving Lukas's name to Devlin, lit another by sending Lukas after Devlin's family. Risk on all sides, but maybe the way to solve both problems. Now he had to protect himself, cover his own ass.

He'd booked a flight to Thailand via San Francisco that night. Once he was there, he'd figure out what to tell Teresa and the girls. He had enough money squirreled away in offshore accounts to keep him going for a while. Holifield and the others would have to fend for themselves.

They drove up through the oaks. As they neared the house, he saw there were no lights on inside, no vehicles out front.

"Place is empty," Holifield said.

"Can't be sure of that. Keep your eyes open."

"What are we here for anyway?"

"I need to know if there's anything here ties any of us to this mess."

"Like what?"

"Files, records, whatever. The old man might have left something behind just to fuck me. I can't take the chance."

"Why bring us along?"

Farrow looked at him. "You work for me. I need another reason?"

"Just want to know what we're getting involved in here."

"He might have left someone to watch the place. If so, I want leverage in case there's a problem."

"We're the leverage."

"That's right."

Farrow drove up to the porch. The Tahoe pulled in behind him.

He looked up at the house. "I ought to burn this fucking place down. All I put into it."

"That the way things are now?" Holifield said.

"That's the way they are." He took the .38 from his belt, opened the door. "Let's go see what he left us."

Lukas drove past the open gate, went up a quarter mile, and pulled into the empty lot of a golf course. The moon was only a glow behind the clouds.

He pulled on his gloves, got out. The Sig was in his waistband, an extra twelve-round magazine in his jacket pocket.

He started back down the road, staying close to the thick hedge that bordered the course. Soon he came to the head-high stone wall that marked the edge of Kemper's property. He got his arms over the top of it, pulled himself up, rolled his hips across, and dropped down on the other side. He landed in a rosebush, had to disentangle himself, pull thorns from his jacket.

He stayed clear of the driveway, the cameras and sensors there, made his way up through the trees. There were lights on in the house. Farrow's Bronco and a dark SUV were parked in front. No other vehicles.

He waited in the shadows of the trees, looked at the house. He thought about the times he'd spent there as a boy, overwhelmed by the new life he'd been handed, the second chance he'd been given. He'd been happy then, for the first time he could remember. It was a world away from the life he'd known before. A lifetime away from what he'd become.

"You tell me what you're looking for," Holifield said. "I might be able to help."

Farrow shook his head, distracted. He was going through filing cabinet drawers, then dumping them out on the study floor. Papers, folders. He sorted through files and contracts, looking for his name or mentions of Core-Tech.

He'd brought a pry bar with him to force the cabinet locks. There would be other files at the Unix office, he knew, but anything sensitive or incriminating would be here, where the old man could keep it close.

Holifield sat in a leather chair near the fireplace, watching him, the Uzi on the low table, next to a bowl of dead flowers.

Farrow kicked the last of the files aside, went to the big desk. The two safes he knew about elsewhere in the house had been open and empty. Roland wasn't coming back anytime soon, if ever. He'd played it as best he could, but still the old man had outmaneuvered him. He was never out ahead.

He sat in the desk chair, the .38 digging into his waist. The top drawer on the right was open. In it were a daily planner, a gold pen set, and a cigar trimmer. The deep bottom drawer was locked. He forced the claw end of the pry bar into the top edge, pulled up until the wood cracked. The lock broke, and the drawer slid open. Inside was a single maroon photo album.

*　　*　　*

A man stood in the floodlights on the front porch. Lukas had never seen him before. He was young, with close-cut hair, an automatic holstered on his hip.

Lukas took out the Sig, knelt behind a tree. Wind moved the branches above him. He waited.

After a few minutes, the man came off the porch, walked toward the side of the house, stepped up close to the hedges there. Lukas heard him urinating. He moved silently across the driveway and came up behind him, put a hand on his shoulder, and pushed the suppressor into his spine.

"Just be cool," Lukas said low. "Don't move. Don't reach."

The man froze. Lukas pushed him into the hedge, facing the house. With his free hand, he plucked the gun from its holster, tossed it away. He leaned in, put his mouth near the man's ear.

"What's going on here has nothing to do with you," he said. "Don't take a risk you don't need to. How many men inside?"

No response. Lukas screwed the suppressor into his back.

"No one will hear it if I shoot you. You'll die without a sound right here, facedown in your own piss. That's the way they'll find you. Again, how many men inside?"

"Four. I mean, three. Besides me."

"Farrow in there?"

"Yes."

"Kemper? Winters?"

"I don't know who they are."

They haven't told this one anything, Lukas thought. *Only what he has to do.*

"The ones inside," Lukas said. "Where are they? Be specific."

"Cody's in the backyard. Dillon and Drew Holifield are in the house with Mr. Farrow."

"Just the three of them and Farrow, you're sure?"

"Yes."

Lukas pushed him deeper into the hedge, and fired twice.

He started around the side of the house, staying in the shadows close to the wall. Low mist lay like a carpet across the grass. He crept up to the rear of the house, stopped. He visualized the patio there, the yard just beyond, the French doors that led into the dining room.

Just a few feet away, he could hear a man's labored breathing.

Farrow opened the album on his knee.

"What's that?" Holifield said. He wandered over.

The first photos were professionally shot portraits of Roland and his most recent wife, then older pictures, like the ones on the wall. Roland shaking hands with politicians, businessmen. Three pages after that were empty, with faint yellow blocks where photos had been. *Portraits of the first two wives*, he thought. *Now paid off and written out.*

Holifield opened the cigar box on the desk. "Can I snag a couple of these?"

"Go ahead."

He took out a *habana*, smelled it. Farrow tossed the clipper on the desk.

He flipped pages. On the last one, an oversized color photo of a group of children around a Christmas tree. He recognized this room, decorated for the holidays. Stockings hung from the fireplace mantel. The star at the top of the tree almost touched the ceiling. Presents were laid out on a velvet blanket. The kids in the photo ranged in age from five to about ten. And in the middle of the group, unsmiling, dark hair cut short, Lukas Dragovic.

When Lukas looked around the corner of the house, there was a man standing just outside the French doors. He was big, thick with muscle, and Lukas could see acne scars on his neck and jaw. He carried a short-barreled silver-and-black pump shotgun, a police model.

The tent was gone, but the bare stage was still up. The top-left corner of the big flag had come loose, was snapping loudly in the mounting wind.

Lukas stepped around the side of the house, brought up the Sig, said, "Cody." The man turned, and Lukas head-shot him once, watched him fall.

He stepped around the body, tried the French doors. They were unlocked. He went through into the empty dining room. The hallway ahead was clear. He heard voices from upstairs, knew they were coming from the study.

"Anything interesting?" Holifield said.

Farrow shook his head, closed the album. The .38 was digging into him again. He moved it to the small of his back, beneath his jacket.

He looked at the files strewn on the floor. Coming here had been a waste of time. Part of him wanted to set it all alight, leave the fire to spread. But there would be no sense in that either. There was nothing to do now but head home, start packing.

This place, this part of your life, is done, he thought. *Accept it. Time to move on.*

Lukas was almost at the living room when a man stepped out into the hallway in front of him. He saw the gun on his left hip, butt out, raised the Sig. The man's right hand went for the gun, and Lukas shot him through the wrist, then again in the chest. The gun was still in its holster when he hit the floor. Lukas stepped over him, headed for the stairway.

He ejected the Sig's magazine, fed in the fresh one. He wanted a full clip before going upstairs.

He stopped at the bottom step. It was quiet up in the study. Had they heard the shots?

When the voices began again, he started up the stairs.

275

*   *   *

"You hear that?" Farrow said.

"What? I didn't hear anything."

"Downstairs."

"It's that flag out back you heard," Holifield said. "Wind's gonna take the whole thing down soon." He clipped the end of a cigar. "Light?"

Farrow put his Zippo on the desktop. Holifield took it, lit the cigar, puffed until he got it going. "Thanks."

He handed the lighter back. Farrow reached for it, then looked past him, saw Lukas there in the doorway, a gun in his hand.

Too easy, Lukas thought. There was Farrow, sitting at the old man's desk, looking at him. Holifield, one of his men, in front of it, with his back to the door. No one else in the room.

Holifield turned, lit cigar in hand, saw him, then looked toward the fireplace. Lukas followed his gaze, saw the machine gun on the table there. He aimed and fired in one smooth movement. The round hit Holifield in the shoulder, knocked him into the desk, and Lukas put two more into his chest before he hit the floor.

Farrow pushed away fast from the desk, stood, the chair tipping over behind him. Lukas swung the Sig toward him. The cigar had landed, smoking, on the desktop.

Farrow looked at him, then out into the hall.

"They're all dead," Lukas said.

Farrow looked back at him. "You are a son of a bitch, aren't you?" Keeping his cool.

"Thought I might find you here," Lukas said. "Where's the old man?"

"Gone."

Lukas came farther into the room. "Guess I shouldn't be surprised. There's an old proverb: 'When the tree falls, the monkeys scatter.'"

276

"That right?"

"Tariq's dead."

"I'm sorry to hear that."

"You set us up."

"I gave you an address, that's all."

"Was it even the right one?"

Farrow reached into a jacket pocket. Lukas tightened his finger on the trigger.

The hand came back out with a pack of Marlboros. He held them up. Lukas nodded.

Farrow thumbed the pack open. There was only one cigarette left.

"Does Devlin know who I am?" Lukas said.

"He does now." He took out the cigarette, crushed the pack, and tossed it on the desk. "But he's the least of your worries."

"Why?"

"The old man's decided both of us are expendable. That's why he left us behind. One of the last things he did was give me the okay to take you out."

"I don't believe that."

"Believe what you want." He speared his lips with the cigarette. "He's cutting ties with anybody who can hurt him. He'll send Winters—or somebody else—to deal with us. Damage control is his genius."

"You and me, we're in the same boat?"

"He fucked us both. His plans for his future don't include either of us. The only thing to do now is what he's doing. Limit our exposure, look after ourselves."

He picked up the Zippo from where it had landed on the desktop, lit the cigarette, snapped the lighter closed. His hands were steady.

"You sent me after Devlin's family. Did the old man know about that?"

"Would it matter if he did?"

"It would to me."

"He doesn't want to know how things get done. He just wants them to happen. That's what he paid me for."

"What are you going to do now?"

"Get far away, monitor the situation." He took a deep drag on the cigarette. "If they take the old man down, I don't want to be anywhere near him. Afterward's a different story."

"Maybe you'll run Unix then," Lukas said.

"Maybe." He blew out smoke, nodded at the Sig. "I saved your life, you know. You owe me that. Got you out of that shithole country, brought you here. If I hadn't, where would you be now?"

"Maybe I'd be better off if I'd stayed there."

"You think you're gonna prove your loyalty to him by taking me out? Buy your way back in with my scalp? It won't work. You were useful to him once. Now you're not. The same with me."

"I'll have to think about that."

Farrow squared his shoulders. "You're not as tough as you think you are, kid. I've done things you can't even fucking imagine. So don't give me that dead-eyed hard-guy bullshit. I was taking lives thirty years before you were born, face-to-face, eyeball to eyeball. You got the stones to pull that trigger, do it."

Lukas watched him. Any fear there was gone now.

"We were soldiers," Farrow said. "We don't get to complain if we lose. The way things worked out is the way they worked out. None of that shit's personal."

"This is."

"Then pull that trigger."

Lukas blinked sweat from his eyes. He saw Farrow's gaze shift, toward the door behind him.

One moment, the doorway was empty. A second later, Farrow saw Dillon there, shirt blotched with blood, using the jamb for support, holding a gun. Lukas saw him, turned, and both of them fired. Dillon went down.

Farrow reached behind, smoothly drew the .38.

Lukas swung back toward him, and Farrow fired, saw the round hit the wall over his head. He cursed, dropped his aim, fired again, but Lukas was already spinning away, back through the open door.

Farrow crouched behind the desk. He swung the .38's cylinder open. Three rounds left. He snapped it shut.

The room reeked of gunpowder. He felt a fierceness sweep through him. *Now we're down to it,* he thought. *No more talk, no more lies. Down to the element. What was real.*

Lukas kept his back against the wall. The other man lay dead at his feet in the doorway.

He looked down the stairs at the empty living room. *You can just leave,* he thought. *Walk out. There's nothing to be gained here, nothing to be won.*

"Hey, motherfucker," Farrow said. "You run out on me?"

Lukas stayed just outside the doorway, listening. Would Farrow try for the Uzi? If so, he'd have to cross the room. Lukas would hear it, could hit him before he reached it.

"You hear me, kid? What are you gonna do?"

He wiped sweat from his eyes, looked down the stairs again. He could be down there, out of sight, before Farrow even knew. All he had to do was walk away.

Farrow took a last drag on the cigarette, flicked it away. He could hear Lukas breathing out in the hallway.

He cocked the .38. *Enough hiding,* he thought. *You got three hot ones in here. Three chances to stay alive. Make 'em count.*

"You still there?" he said. "You got the balls to do this face-to-face?"

The breathing sounded closer now. He heard the creak of a footstep inside the room.

He swung up from behind the desk, the gun in both hands, and there was Lukas, ten feet away.

They fired at the same time. Farrow heard a bullet go past him, stood his ground, squeezing the trigger of the .38, the hammer rising and dropping, the big room filling with the sound of gunshots. He felt rounds hit him, drive him back, heard the .38 click on an empty chamber. Then he was on his back on the hardwood floor, looking up at the high ceiling.

Lukas moved to stand over him, aiming down. Farrow tried to speak, but his mouth was full of blood. He looked into the muzzle of the suppressor.

Lukas fired twice. Brass hit the floor, rolled, and was silent. The only sound was the snapping of the flag outside.

There was a bar of heat along his left side. He unzipped the jacket, peeled it back. One of Farrow's shots had creased him just above the hip. The others had gone wild. His sweater was torn, the material dark with blood. Adrenaline was keeping the pain away, he knew. He would feel it later.

He went back downstairs, his footsteps echoing in the empty house, then out the front door and into the wind.

By the time Lukas found a motel, his left pants leg was soaked through to the knee. The wound had stopped bleeding after a while, was already scabbing over, dry and rough to the touch.

At a twenty-four-hour drugstore, he'd gotten what he'd needed. Tried to keep the pain out of his face while he paid the clerk, hoped he didn't see the blood.

He peeled off his clothes in the motel bathroom, looked at the wound. It was a dark red line an inch above his left hip bone, where the bullet had scored the flesh. Under the shower, it started to bleed again. Pink water swirled in the drain.

He dried off, poured alcohol on his side. The pain made him gasp. He took the tweezers he'd bought, stood sideways in front of the bathroom mirror, and extracted the strands of fiber he could see in the wound. When he was done, he doused it all with alcohol again, put two gauze patches across the wound, and fastened them in place with surgical tape. The cotton immediately began to darken.

He reloaded the Sig from the box of shells in the gear bag, then got his phone, called the number he had for Kemper. Five rings, then nothing. He hung up.

He lay naked atop the bed, drifting with eyes half closed, the Sig beside him, when the phone buzzed. He brought it to his ear.

"What's your location?" Winters said.

"Does it matter? Let me talk to him."

"Not gonna happen."

"He'll want to hear what I have to say. I had an issue with the major."

"And?"

"It was dealt with. I need to know where I stand."

"Keep this phone," Winters said, and broke the connection.

Fifteen minutes later, it buzzed again.

"He wants to talk to you," Winters said. "Down here."

"He knows the situation? That I'm exposed?"

"That's why he wants you here. Where are you?"

Lukas didn't answer.

"Play it your way," Winters said. "There's a Learjet registered to the company leaving Richmond International tomorrow at noon. You need to be on it."

"To where?"

"You'll see when you get there," Winters said, and ended the call.

THIRTY-NINE

EVLIN LEFT RIVIERA Beach at dawn. He'd gotten into Florida at eleven the night before, slept a few hours, then gassed up the boat and steered out of the inlet, heading south by southeast.

It was a straight sixty-mile run to the Bahamas. He'd made it once before, so he plotted the same course again, the charts spread out on the galley table.

The wind was light as he crossed the Gulf Stream, the sky clear, and he made a good six knots as he bore south on open water, the engines running smoothly.

Four hours later, he cleared Customs and Immigration at West End, then topped off the tanks and headed south again. It was another hundred miles to Green Turtle Cay, but he took it slower now. Running between the islands, he had to watch for shallows, had learned to gauge water depth by its color. Brown meant rock or coral just below the surface. Lighter brown could be shoals or sandbars. Green where the water was deeper. Dark blue as it grew deeper still.

He reached Green Turtle at dusk, tied up at a marina. There were darkening clouds to the east. He refueled, wanting to keep the tanks full in case he had to leave quickly. He ate sandwiches on board, stood on deck, and watched the squall blow in. When the rain started, he went below, closed the hatch and door.

As the boat rocked lightly in the swells, he went into the bow, pulled out the bottom drawer, retrieved the leather shaving kit he'd hidden there. Inside was the Glock he'd taken from Farrow's man, along with the extra magazines.

He ejected the magazine, cleared the chamber, worked the slide, and then dry-fired once to test the trigger tension. He seated the magazine again, jacked a round into the chamber, lowered the hammer.

And just what will you do with it? he thought. *When the time comes, will you be able to use it, do what needs to be done?*

He put the gun away again, fit the kit back into the space behind the drawer, slid it closed. Then he crawled into the bunk, listened to the rain on the cabin roof, let the sound lull him to sleep.

Lukas looked out over the blue water, watched a gull dive-bomb the surface, fly off with a fish in its bill. The bow of the speedboat rose and fell, spray flecking the windscreen.

The Lear had landed at the airport at Treasure Cay, and he'd taken the ferry over to Green Turtle, where Winters and Bishop had met him in a Land Rover. They'd driven to a private dock where a third man waited with the boat. All three were dressed the same, loose tropical shirts over jeans.

Lukas sat on the rear bench, the duffel at his feet. Inside were clothes and first aid supplies. The gear bag with the guns was in the Lexus, in the airport's long-term lot.

From his seat alongside the driver, Winters turned to look back at Lukas. "Saw a tiger shark out here yesterday." Speaking loud over the engine noise. "Big fucker. Ten feet, at least." Lukas could see the butt of the gun holstered beneath his shirt.

Next to Lukas, Bishop swallowed, closed his eyes, opened them again, and looked at the horizon. *Seasick*, Lukas thought.

The boat bounced along, picking up speed, the inboard engine churning up the water behind them. Lukas flexed his left arm. His side was stiffening. He'd have to change the dressing again soon.

They passed a buoy bobbing in the water, a black box fixed to its side. There was another a few hundred feet away.

"Sensors," Winters said. "All around the island. No one gets close without us knowing it."

The wind felt good. Lukas pulled his sweat-slick shirt away from his chest, let the air cool his skin. When he lifted the tail of his shirt, he saw the gauze was dark again.

Winters pointed to it. "Farrow give you that?"

He didn't answer.

"Landscapers showed up this morning, found the mess you left. Fortunately they called the Unix office before anyone else. Call got routed to me. I never liked Gordon much myself. But he had a long history with the company, I'm told."

Winters faced forward again. Now Lukas could see the island, a blot on the horizon that grew larger as they neared it. There was a dock out front, with another, bigger, boat moored alongside it. A wooden stairway ran up the rock face, with a landing every fifteen feet or so. At the top, a peaked roof emerged from thick foliage and palm trees. The north and south sides of the island were sheer cliff.

They neared the dock. Lukas could see NO TRESPASSING signs on the pier, and a gate that led to the stairway. He turned and looked back toward Green Turtle, almost out of sight now.

The driver slowed, and the blue of the water lightened as it grew more shallow. Lukas could see coral below the surface, darting fish.

Bishop was first out of the boat. He looked relieved. Lukas threw his duffel onto the dock and followed him. Winters came up last. The driver stayed at the wheel.

Lukas looked up at the stairway, the rock face, the house at the top. "Let's go," Winters said behind him. "Time to see the wizard."

The two heavy entrance doors were dark wood with leaded glass. The guard in front of them wore camouflage pants and a black T-shirt, had an M-16 slung in front, muzzle down. He nodded to Winters and Lukas as they passed.

Inside was a wide, marble-floored area. Corridors on each side, a staircase in the center. Lukas followed Winters up to a room that took up the entire second floor. The east wall was a triptych of floor-to-ceiling windows. Kemper stood at the center panel, looking out. When he heard their footsteps, he turned and smiled.

"Lukas, you're a welcome sight. I was worried."

Lukas let himself be embraced. Kemper looked older than he'd ever seen him, with deep worry lines around the eyes. *All this is weighing on him*, Lukas thought, *aging him*.

"Downstairs if you need me," Winters said.

"Thank you," Kemper said. "Take that to his room, Val, will you please?"

Lukas looked at Winters, held out the duffel. He could see the resentment there. Winters took the duffel, went back down the stairs.

"The accommodations aren't much," Kemper said. "No real furniture yet. Hope you won't mind roughing it for a few days, until we're better equipped."

Lukas looked around. There were sawhorses scattered about, piles of block and tile on tarps to protect the parquet floor.

"It'll be a while before it's finished," Kemper said. "But I thought you might be safer here with us for now. I've been concerned about you, with all that's going on. Now I see my concerns were warranted."

"I was concerned too, if I'd be welcome here."

"Of course you are. Why would you not be?"

Lukas walked up to the windows. From here there was a view

of the entire east side of the island. A flagstone verandah was one level beneath, with two stairways branching off it. One ran down to a helipad built out over the water, the other to a boathouse farther below. A black two-seater helicopter was parked on the helipad, next to a prefab hangar. An air sock fluttered on a pole.

"Impressive," Lukas said.

"This is going to be the music room," Kemper said. "We'll put the piano here, by the windows. We'll be able to watch the sunrise. I think Isabella will love it here."

"I'm sure she will."

Kemper touched his elbow. "Let me show you around outside."

They went down a set of stairs, and out a sliding glass door onto the verandah. At the front of it was an observation deck supported by steel beams sunk into the rock. Kemper walked out to the railing. Lukas followed. Far below, the water changed from a light blue around the island to a darker hue beyond.

"I'm not much for boats anymore," Kemper said. "Never was, really. The local environmentalists aren't happy when I use the chopper. They say it disturbs the wildlife. With what I'm spending down here, though, I'll do as I please."

"Don't you always?"

Kemper smiled. "You like it here?"

"It's beautiful. Will it ever be finished?"

"Hopefully soon, now that I'm here to keep an eye on the contractors. The ones who were dogging it will be sorry when it comes time to get paid. That's when we renegotiate, whether they want to or not."

"That won't make you very popular."

"I'm paying well, so I deserve to get what I'm paying for. They haven't even mounted any of the house security cameras yet. They say the electrician I sent down from Lauderdale last month botched the wiring. I have a Unix team coming in next week to finish the installation. All that's working right now are the wireless sensors on the buoys. That's our first line of security."

"I guess you don't get many visitors."

"The locals know not to come out here for the most part. One did a few months back when I was here, tried to tie up down by the boathouse at night. Probably hoping he could climb up to where the construction was, steal some copper piping or scrap metal. He'd tripped the sensors, so we were watching him the entire time, though he didn't know it. Winters put a few rounds over his head with a rifle. That turned him around quick."

Lukas heard the growl of an engine, watched the speedboat come around the side of the island. The driver slowed near the boathouse, reversed, then backed and filled into the slip inside, cut the engine.

"I was building this place for when I retired," Kemper said. "I think that time is coming soon."

"What about all your projects, contracts?"

"They'll go through. What's happened in the last two weeks is an inconvenience, nothing more. It will pass. I still have plenty of friends in the States with their hands out. I've been funding some of them for years. Time they earned their keep."

"And Senator Harlin?"

"Him most of all. He knows he needs us on board. Or rather, he needs to be on board with us."

"You sound confident."

"If there are repercussions, we'll ride them out, stall and deflect as necessary. This will all be forgotten by Election Day. It'll be a distant memory by the time our major contracts are finalized. We have one last foreign venture coming up soon. Winters is organizing it. Then we'll shut down that part of the operation for good."

Lukas rested his elbows on the railing, looked out at the water.

"What happened at the house," Kemper said. "Was that just you?"

"Yes."

"What about your Arab friend?"

"He's gone."

Kemper looked at him. "How do you mean that?"

"Gone," Lukas said.

"I'm sorry."

"The way it fell."

"I always knew Gordon was working on his own thing. He was ambitious enough. Already planning for a future when I wasn't around, when he ran Unix. But he thought too highly of himself. He was a soldier, not a businessman."

"Then you're fine with the way it went down?"

"I've got my people—through an intermediary—floating another narrative for what happened at the house. Gordon was a disgruntled and criminal employee, there to rob the place in my absence, thought I had money hidden in the house. There was a falling-out between him and his fellow thieves. Winters sent some people over to adjust the evidence to reflect that. It's a solid story. One you needn't be part of at all."

"We still have another issue," Lukas said. "Devlin."

"Forget about him. He's not worth the effort. He can't touch us, and there's no one left to support any story he might tell. We can stonewall any investigation. At some point down the road, if he's still a problem, we'll address it then. Maybe offer him some stock after we go public."

"And if that doesn't work?"

"Then we'll deal with him however we have to. We still have a few teeth left, don't we?"

The sky was growing darker, dusk coming on.

"You must be hungry and tired," Kemper said. "We'll rustle up something from the kitchen for you, then you can rest. Life here is a little spartan for the time being, I'm afraid. Cots and air mattresses. We should have some furniture next week."

"I'll be fine." He felt the last forty-eight hours catching up with him, weighing him down.

Kemper put an arm around his shoulder, squeezed. "This is our future, Lukas. Here. Now. Don't worry about anything that happened before. We ran into trouble, some issues from the past that came back to haunt us. But we faced them down. They're over. And you know something?"

"What?" Lukas said.

"We won."

FORTY

EVLIN WOKE LATE the next morning, took a taxi into the town, such as it was. He walked around until he found what he was looking for—a downscale bar on the water, away from the marinas and hotels. Pickup trucks and Mini Mokes in the dirt lot. On the dock beside the bar, a shirtless black man wearing a Giants cap was cleaning fish on a wooden table, tossing the guts out into the water. Gulls squawked above him.

Not yet noon, and the bar was already crowded, the TV on the wall showing a soccer match. There were about a dozen men inside, in what seemed like every shade of skin color, but with the same rough look about them, one Devlin recognized. They were men who made their living on the water.

He got a Kalik Gold at the bar. The bartender—a black man in his sixties with snow-white hair—was happy to take his U.S. dollars. Devlin asked if he knew a man who would hire out his boat for a sightseeing trip.

"The hotels, they have plenty guides," the bartender said. "Anything you want, fishing, sightseeing, diving. You ask at the desk, they fix you up."

"I'm looking for something a little more unofficial," Devlin said. "The smaller the boat, the better. And someone who doesn't mind going out at night."

The bartender looked at him for a long moment, then nodded to the open back deck, where there were a half dozen spool tables with wooden chairs. "You go sit. Maybe I ask around."

Devlin carried his beer out of the dimness of the bar and into the harsh sunlight. He wore a T-shirt and shorts with sandals, but was already sweating. He took a table at the far end of the deck.

A dog, some sort of shepherd mix, came trotting out of the bar, sniffed him.

"I got nothing for you, buddy," Devlin said. The dog looked up at him, tongue hanging. Devlin put out his left hand, let him smell it. The dog gave it a tentative lick, then sniffed the air again, got up, and went back into the bar. There was something cooking inside, the scent of wood smoke drifting out.

Devlin looked out over the railing. Casuarina trees and poisonwood grew right up to the pebbled shore, in the shadow of the untrimmed palm trees. Blue water stretched out to the hazy horizon.

He was almost finished with the beer, feeling slightly lightheaded, when a man came out of the bar carrying a Kalik. He was skinny and tall, wore painter's pants, a polo shirt marred with bleach spots, and a khaki baseball cap that read MERCURY MARINE on the front. Sunglasses hung from a lanyard around his neck.

He pointed to the seat across from Devlin, waited for him to nod before he sat. Up close, Devlin could see he was in his midthirties, but with wind-etched lines in his face and a deep tan. "How's it going?" the man said.

Three words was all it took. "You're American," Devlin said.

The man extended his hand. "Chase."

Devlin shook it. "Ray Devlin. Chase a first name or last?"

"Only one you'll need. But if you insist on a last name, make it Manhattan."

"Got it."

"Spencer said you were looking for a sightseeing guide, possibly at night?"

"Sound like something you might be interested in?"

He set the beer on the table, lifted his cap and pushed back thinning blond hair, pulled it back down again. "Depends."

"You know these waters well?"

"Been guiding here nine years, so well enough."

Devlin took the folded chart from his back pocket, opened it on the table. He pointed to the red mark he'd made based on Farrow's description.

Chase turned the chart around, pulled it closer to him.

"You know an island, right about there?" Devlin said.

"Hardly an island. Mainly just a house on a piece of rock. Not even finished yet, though they've been shipping materials over there for about a year. Some American with money to burn is the word going around."

"Anyone there now?"

"I see boats go back and forth once in a while. A chopper went over a couple days ago. There's a helipad there, on the Atlantic side."

"Could you get me there, on that island, at night?"

"Why?"

Devlin didn't answer.

"You know the people that live there?" Chase said.

"The man who built it, yeah."

"You can't just ask for an invitation? They're particular about their privacy. A friend of mine got a little too close a while back, and someone at the house took a couple potshots at him."

"Hit him?"

"No, but I assume they could have if they'd wanted to."

Chase scratched his elbow, and Devlin saw the mottled flesh on the outside of his left forearm, blotchy patches of pink and white hairless skin that stood out against his tan.

On a hunch, he said, "You get that overseas?"

Chase turned his arm to look at the skin there, as if he'd forgotten about it. "Yeah, Anbar Province, '04."

"What unit?"

"Second Battalion, Fourth Marines."

"The Magnificent Bastards."

"You know your stuff."

"How'd it happen?" Devlin said.

"Hit an IED on the airport road near Ramadi. Humvee got blown to shit. I was the only one walked away."

"I'm sorry," Devlin said.

"You ever serve? You look like you might have."

"Eighty-Second Airborne. Long time ago. Nothing like what you went through."

"I was lucky. I got sent home with a fucked-up arm and hip, but that's it. Lot of guys I knew over there never made it back. And some who did had bad things happen to them after they got home. A few by their own hand."

"Where was home?"

"Bar Harbor, Maine."

"So you know boats."

"Since I was a kid. Wasn't much work when I got back there, though, and I'd had enough of that weather. So once I healed up, I decided to fuck off down here for a while. It was supposed to be temporary, first stop in a longer journey. But here I still be, so go figure."

"You married? Kids?"

"Negative."

"Any family back home?"

"Not anymore. So no reason to go back."

"There enough work down here?"

"If you know the right people," Chase said. "It helps if you have a fast boat, and can keep your mouth shut."

The dog came back out, went to Chase, and rubbed against his leg. He scratched behind its ears.

Without looking at Devlin, he said, "What are we talking about here?"

"I want to get on that island. I'm looking for someone to take me out there, drop me off. That's all. They don't have to stick around."

"And how will you get back?"

"I'll work that out later."

"Seems to me you've only got half a plan. Or a half-assed plan."

"Part of the deal is they also forget it ever happened, if anyone asks afterward. Other than that, they'll have no connection to me whatsoever, nothing that could tie them in."

"Deniability."

"Safest way."

"I hear you."

"How much?" Devlin said.

The dog grew bored, snuffed around the deck, then padded back inside.

Chase took off his cap, resettled it. "You sure you don't need someone to come with you, watch your back?"

"Absolutely not. I need a ride out there. That's it."

"Well, with gas and mileage, the risk involved...say five hundred U.S.?"

"Say three hundred U.S."

"Cash?"

"Of course."

"Well, in that case, say four hundred. And better make it in advance."

Devlin put out his hand. Chase took a moment, then shook it. "When do you want to take this trip?"

"Tonight," Devlin said.

*　　*　　*

Lukas walked the grounds, trying to get a feel for the layout. The sun was high. He'd slept heavily the night before, woken late, but was dogged with a tiredness he couldn't shake.

He'd counted six guards on the island, including Winters and Bishop. Some of them he'd seen before. All were armed.

Most of the palm trees around the house showed blight, with large swaths of branches brown and dying. Weeds sprouted through the flagstones on the verandah. On the north side of the property was an empty swimming pool, its walls decorated with a mural of elaborately drawn mermaids and sea creatures. Rainwater had gathered at the bottom, where the drain was clogged with dead vegetation and palm fronds. Flies buzzed around it.

Back in the house, he got a bottle of water from the big steel refrigerator in the bare kitchen. Bishop and a guard called Kane were playing poker at a butcher-block table, money in front of them. Bishop looked at Lukas, nodded, went back to his cards.

Kemper was out on the observation deck, talking on a cellphone. A cast-iron table and chairs had been set up on the verandah, along with a propane grill. Lukas went out the sliding glass door, took a seat. Shadows were lengthening as the sun dipped behind the house. On the pad below, a man was wiping down the helicopter's canopy.

Kemper finished his call, nodded to Lukas, came over, and took the chair beside him. He set the phone on the table. "Isabella. She wants to know when she can come down here. I think she misses me."

Lukas nodded at the man below. "He looks familiar."

"That's Chambers, my pilot. He's one of my Lear captains. That's likely where you know him from. I'm keeping him here now to care for the chopper, take me wherever I need to go."

"Won't all these guys get bored?"

"Not for long," Kemper said. "Don't say anything to anyone yet, but I'm making arrangements to bring some women in from Nassau. That'll keep them quiet, for a while at least. I'll rotate some of them back to the States, if they insist. In the meantime, they're being well compensated for taking an extended Caribbean vacation."

"You trust them?"

"I'm paying them."

"You trust me?"

Kemper looked at him. "Why would you ask that?"

"I'm a liability to you, aren't I? Like Farrow was."

"Not at all. If I thought you were, you wouldn't be here."

Kemper took a dark *habana* from a shirt pocket, sliced off the end with a trimmer. He got a lighter from another pocket, worked the wheel, but the wind kept blowing out the flame. Lukas leaned over, took the lighter. Kemper cupped the cigar against the wind as Lukas got a flame. The cigar tip flared.

"Thank you," Kemper said. "I could never smoke around Isabella, so it's a relief now to have one whenever I want."

Lukas watched whitecaps dot the water below.

"We'll cook steaks out here tonight," Kemper said. "We have enough supplies laid in for a couple weeks. Then I'll send someone over to Green Turtle or Treasure Cay, get what we need. You're welcome to stay as long as you like, of course. But I need to ask, is there anything I should be aware of that might connect you to what happened at the house?"

"No. I was careful."

"We'll give it some time regardless, keep you out of the way here. But after things calm down, I may need you to go back to the States to handle some business."

"Whatever you need."

"Real business. Not like what you've done in the past. There won't be a need for that type of activity anymore. Have you met all the men?"

"Most of them. I recognized faces."

"Solid, to a one. Gordon had an excellent eye when it came to hiring."

It was almost dark. Behind and above them, lights flickered inside the three big windows, then went on, cast shadows on the flagstones.

Kemper exhaled fragrant blue smoke.

"All things have their time," he said. "Men too. In his time, Gordon was the man I needed. We built Acheron together. That was the start, the bedrock for all that came afterward. But it's more like scaffolding. You need it to get the work done, but afterward you pull it down."

"That's a cold way to put it."

"Acheron had its day, then its day was over. The same with Core-Tech. Gordon couldn't see that, resented it even. You solved a problem I was eventually going to have to deal with myself."

Lukas closed his eyes, felt the breeze. *This is where Farrow imagined he'd be someday,* he thought. *Sitting outside with the old man on a tropical island, shooting the shit. Knowing he'd finally arrived, gotten what he'd worked for.*

"How long do you intend to stay here?" Lukas said.

"I'm not sure. I've applied for Bahamian citizenship. I'll spread around some cash, build a couple schools, a new wing on a hospital. They love rich Americans. No reason I can't run Unix from here. You can be my eyes and ears back in the States. I'll need that now."

A shadow appeared on the flagstone a few feet away. Lukas turned and looked up to see Winters standing in the center window, watching them. After a moment, he turned and walked away.

They sat that way without speaking, watching the night grow darker, the sky fill with stars.

"This is our reward," Kemper said. "For everything we've had to do, whether we wanted to or not."

Lukas looked at him. Kemper's face was lost in shadow.

"You and I both, we've come a long way," Kemper said.

"We have."

"This is what we've earned. Enjoy it."

"I will," Lukas said.

297

FORTY-ONE

TRACY LISTENED TO Devlin's line buzz for the seventh time, then click over to voice mail. There was no outgoing message, just a tone, then dead air.

Alysha looked across the conference-room table at her. Tracy shook her head, disconnected the call.

"He didn't punk out on us, did he?" Alysha said.

"I don't know. I hope not." She set down the phone, picked up a pen, double-clicked it.

The table was covered with piles of paper and folders. Everything they knew or could pull about Roland Kemper, Unix Technologies, Core-Tech, and Acheron. In front of Tracy were Freedom of Information Act requests that would go out in the morning to the departments of Justice, Defense, and Homeland Security, asking for any and all files related to Kemper and his companies. She knew it might be months before they saw any documents back—and those likely heavily redacted.

"It's what, two days since you've heard from him?"

"Almost. I don't like it any more than you do."

Alysha took a sheet of paper from a folder open in front of her, scanned it. "Hello. Here's something interesting."

"What?"

"I know how rich people love their tax-shelter vacation homes, so I asked Sylvie to see if she could find any other residences that might be in Kemper's name."

"She turn up anything?"

"Not beyond his Virginia address. But she cross-referenced Unix as well and found this." She handed the paper across.

Tracy took it. It was a list of companies and addresses.

"Am I supposed to know what this is?"

"Tax filings tied to international sales of certain restricted security systems. That's a list of contracts from the previous fiscal year in which both Unix's and Core-Tech's names come up as vendors. Check out the final listing."

"Isabella Properties? In the Bahamas?"

Alysha waited.

"I don't get it," Tracy said.

"Where have we heard that name before?"

It hit her then. "Kemper's wife."

"Bingo. Can't be coincidence, right?"

"Can't be."

"And that business address? It's a private island."

"His own island? What's that cost?"

"Nice place to run to if you're trying to avoid annoying reporters."

Tracy sat back, looked at her. "You think Devlin knows about it?"

Alysha shrugged. "If you knew about it, and you were holding a big enough grudge…"

Tracy's phone buzzed. It was Russ Jones in Virginia. She opened the line, put it on speaker. "Hey, Russ. It's Tracy. Alysha's here with me. Any luck?"

"Yes and no."

"What's that mean?"

"That Gordon Farrow we're searching for?"

She looked at Alysha. "What about him?"

"We can stop looking."

Devlin sat on the deck, watched the sun sink, dyeing the water blood red. Then he went below, dressed in dark jeans and T-shirt, black sneakers and nylon jacket. He lay back on the bunk, closed his eyes, and drifted into a thin sleep.

He woke just before 8 p.m., the time they'd agreed on. He got out the Glock, checked it again. Two extra magazines went into his jeans pockets. From a drawer in the counter, he took out the envelope with the six hundred dollars in traveling money he'd drawn from ATMs in Florida the day before. He counted out four hundred in twenties, put them in another envelope.

The Glock didn't fit in the jacket pocket, so he tucked it tight into the waistband of his jeans, switched off the cabin lights, and went on deck.

Chase was standing on the pier. He wore a black sweatshirt with the hood down, dark pants.

"This baby belongs in a museum," he said. "Sweet lines, though. Gasser or diesel?"

"Gas." Devlin zipped up the jacket to cover the gun.

"A pair of the old Crusader engines, right? Chargers or Challengers?"

"Chargers. V8s."

Devlin could hear music and laughter coming from other boats. He stepped up on the gunwale, and Chase caught his hand, helped him onto the dock. "You ready?"

"I am," Devlin said.

Chase had an old Chevy pickup parked in the marina lot. As they drove, Devlin took out the envelope from an inside jacket pocket. "All twenties, if that's all right."

He untucked the flap so Chase could see the bills there.

"Good enough," Chase said. "Why don't you go ahead and stow that away there."

Devlin closed the envelope, put it in the glove box, shut it.

"I'm not sure what you're getting me into," Chase said. "But I guess I'm along for the ride."

"That's all it is, a ride. You drop me, and then you go home."

"Roger that," Chase said.

They drove to the other side of the island, where Chase kept his boat, a nineteen-foot Bayliner inboard runabout, red and black. It was fiberglass, with a low profile on the water, light enough to move fast on the open sea.

They walked out on the old dock, the boards loose and uneven beneath their feet. A handful of small wooden fishing boats were moored here. One was all but sunken, only the tip of the bow and the roof of the wheelhouse showing above the surface.

The clouds had parted, and the half moon was bright, lit the surface of the water. They stepped down onto the boat.

"Come have a look," Chase said. He took a folded piece of paper from his hoodie pocket, opened it on the dashboard above the controls. He switched on a penlight, said, "Hold this."

Devlin took it, shone the beam on the paper. It was a rough map, drawn in pencil, of a kidney-shaped island.

"I asked around, got an idea of what this place looks like from all sides," Chase said.

"Was that smart?"

"People I trust. I wanted to know as much as possible before we go out there. I figure it was worth the risk. Now here"—he touched a straight line extending from the island—"is the only real dock. It's on the west side, the way we'll approach. It goes out about thirty yards. They usually keep a boat moored there, a forty-foot Cantius cruiser. That's the main vessel they use to go back and forth when they need supplies.

"Over here on the east side—the Atlantic side—there's a place where they store another boat, a Sea Ray, that's smaller and faster. A twenty-footer, from what I've seen of it. It's kept in the boathouse most of the time. The helipad is higher up—here—and the house itself has big windows that look out on it all. Great view. Though I guess they paid enough for it."

"How about coming in that way?"

"Won't work. There's no real dock there, just the boathouse, and you have to watch the tides. There's a reef on that side that'll knock the bottom out of a boat if you don't see it in time. And there's no beach to speak of at all there. If you tried to swim in, you'd get pounded into the rocks. The north and south sides are steep cliff, so forget about going in that way. The only place to land a boat is out front."

"How do they get up to the house from there?"

"A wooden staircase runs up from the dock, with a couple landings along the way. That's the only route in from the front. There's a gate at the end of the dock, though, and I assume they lock it. I don't know what you're going to do about that."

"Are there walkways on the east side?"

"Two sets of stairs, one from the boathouse, one from the helipad. They both run up to a big porch-verandah-type thing there, right below the windows."

"How do they get their power?"

"There's a propane-fueled stationary generator in a concrete blockhouse here"—he touched the map—"on the south side of the property. Everything runs off that."

"So if someone interfered with the generator, they could shut down power to the whole place."

"Maybe, if they didn't get shot first. And I'd say there was a good chance of getting shot first, all the men they have up there."

"Any sense how many?"

"From what I've heard, six or seven, at least. Now, this moon is going to be good for me, but not so good for you. We'll be going in at midtide, so it'll be easier for me to navigate, bright as it is. But it also means you'll be easier to spot once I drop you off."

"We go straight in to the dock? That's a lot of exposure."

"Thought about that too. It's not ideal, but we can make it work. We'll run dark the whole way, no lights. There are pole lights on the dock we can fix on. Depending on which way the wind's going, I'll cut the engine halfway across. Then we use those."

He pointed to the inside of the gunwale, where two fiberglass oars were racked. "Commando raid, right? *Cockleshell Heroes.* Ever see that movie?"

Devlin shook his head.

"We row the rest of the way in, hope the current's not too bad. We'll pull right up to the dock, just short of their cruiser if it's there. It rides high, so it'll give us some cover. I'll let you out, then push off, row back out past the channel, and start the engine again. They might hear it when I do, so be aware of that. Sound travels far out here at night."

"Got it."

"Can I make a suggestion?"

"Go ahead."

"I have no interest in getting involved in whatever you're doing over there. Not my business. But I hate the idea of dropping you off, and you not being able to get back in a hurry if you need to. And there's probably a good chance of that, right?"

Devlin didn't answer.

"Here's my idea. You give me an estimate of how much time you need to do whatever it is you have to do. I come back then, still running dark, pick you up. You gotta be there when I do, though, because I won't be able to hang around long without being seen. Then, when I get you back to Green Turtle, we can talk about how much more money you owe me."

Devlin shook his head. "I don't want you more involved than you are."

"I said my piece."

"You did."

He folded the map, put it back in his pocket. Devlin clicked off the light.

"Then let's get to it," Chase said.

The lights of the island grew brighter as they neared. The runabout bumped along, the bow flinging spray. Chase had already throttled back, and Devlin knew they must be nearing the halfway point.

"Glasses in that chart drawer," Chase said.

Devlin opened the compartment under the dash. Inside were a pair of binoculars and a .45 automatic.

"What's this?" he said.

"Souvenir."

"Is it licensed?"

"Down here? No way. I keep it for sentimental reasons—and sharks."

"Wouldn't a rifle be more practical?"

"Yeah. Probably."

Devlin raised the binoculars. He could see the dock clearly now. There were three pole lights along its length. A sign at the end of the pier read PRIVATE DOCK! NO MOORING! NO TRESPASSING! in bright white paint. The pilings were out of the water with the ebbing tide, and he could see wide strips of rubber fastened to them.

The big cruiser was moored on the dock's starboard side as he faced it. He scanned the dock again, saw the metal gate at the end. Beyond was the stairway. At the top of the island, through palm trees, he could see the lighted windows of the house.

"Stay out of the water if you can," Chase said. "Sharks feed around here at night. There's barracuda too, but they probably won't bother you."

"I don't plan on doing any swimming."

They passed a buoy on their starboard side.

"Here we go," Chase said, and killed the engine. The night went quiet. Devlin put away the binoculars, looked at his watch. Ten p.m.

"Time to muscle it," Chase said. He pulled up his hood.

All at once, Devlin was aware of the vastness of the empty sea around them, wondered what waited under its moonlit surface. What might wait for him ahead, beyond the lights.

Water slapped gently against the hull. Chase unracked the oars, took a position on the port side. Devlin went to the starboard gunwale, bent, and dipped his oar into the water. From here in, there would be no more talking.

It took them a few minutes to find their rhythm, but soon they were gliding across the smooth, flat surface. They rowed slowly, the oars making little noise as they bit into the water, propelled them forward. Devlin's shoulder was a dull ache. The Glock was cold against his skin.

The island loomed. His stomach clenched, and he felt a sudden urge to turn back. Knew if he did, it would never end. There would always be danger. For Quinn and for himself. For Karen and Brendan as well. The fear would live there, in the back of his mind, along with the guilt for bringing something into their lives they didn't deserve. He had to face the threat, end it. It was the only way.

Almost there. He had a memory flash of being in a C-130 over Sicily Drop Zone at Fort Bragg, his first night jump. Standing in full combat gear, static line hooked, cold wind rushing in through the open hatch. Watching the light above the door, waiting for it to turn from red to green.

The dock was suddenly close. Chase flattened his oar in the water to slow their momentum. Devlin did the same. They rode in silently. Chase took in his oar, set it gingerly on the deck, got a boat hook from the gunwale rack.

The pier smelled of seaweed and creosote. Devlin set his oar next to Chase's, crossed to the port side to get ready. The cruiser was in front of them, and Devlin thought they might hit it, but Chase used the hook to snag one of the heavy rubber strips, check their motion. He held the boat steady, turned to Devlin and nodded.

Green light. Devlin took a deep breath, let it out slow. He stepped up onto the gunwale, ready to climb onto the dock.

"Good luck," Chase whispered, and then his head snapped back, and something warm and wet spattered Devlin's face. He heard a far-off crack, and Chase fell heavily onto the deck. The hook dropped into the water.

More cracks. The windscreen disintegrated. The boat slid out from under Devlin's feet, and he leaped for the dock, fell short. He hit the water, went under.

Darkness closed over him. He felt the sharp edge of panic. Then his feet hit sand. He bent his legs, pushed up hard and broke the surface, dragged in air. He was beneath the dock, the support beams just above his head. He lunged for them, got an arm around one of the X-braces, kept himself from going under again.

Chase's boat was drifting from the dock. More rounds hit it. The same flat cracks from somewhere above, a rifle with a suppressor. The impact of the bullets pushed the boat backward.

The shooting stopped. He pulled himself up onto the X-brace, hooked his legs onto the next one to take his weight, his back just clearing the water. Light came through the slats above him. He heard shouting, the clang of the gate opening, then heavy running footsteps on the dock. Shadows passed over him.

He tightened his grip on the cross brace with both arms, pulled himself higher, his muscles cramping. He began to shake.

To his left, he saw a man lean over with a boat hook. After two tries, he snagged the empty windscreen frame, pulled the Bayliner closer to the dock.

"Tie it up," another man said. "We don't want it floating off."

"Is he dead?"

"That's what you're gonna find out. Get down there."

A man clambered down into the boat. It bobbed under his weight. Devlin clung to the beam. If the man turned this way, he would see him.

"Well?" the one on the dock said.

"Oh yeah, he's dead, all right. See that head wound?"

"Check his pockets."

"I didn't sign up for this, Bishop. This is some cold-blooded shit."

"Check his pockets."

After a few moments, the man in the boat said, "Nothing. Just this."

"What is it?"

"Some kind of map. What do we do with him?"

"Leave him where he is," Bishop said. "Until we see what they want."

The man climbed out of the boat, back onto the dock. "They're not paying me enough for this."

Devlin was shaking uncontrollably now. He closed his eyes, concentrated on holding on to the X-brace, his face pressed against the oily wood. Pain shot through his left arm. The muscles there began to spasm.

The men moved off down the dock. Devlin heard the gate open and close, then footsteps on wooden stairs.

He let go.

"Quality shots," Lukas said. "Good grouping."

Winters lowered the M110, said, "Thanks."

They were on the second landing, watching the men on the pier below. The rifle had a night scope mounted in front of the regular tactical scope, with a shroud over where they joined, to keep out light. Winters had rested the long cylinder of the suppressor on the railing when he took aim.

"You sure there was only one?" Lukas said. Wondering if it was Devlin on the boat, if he had somehow tracked him all the way here.

"Yeah," Winters said. "I had the scope on him as soon as he reached the dock."

"Wouldn't it have been better, take him alive, find out what he wanted out here?"

"Mr. Kemper's orders," Winters said. "No one gets near the place without authorization. Especially someone coming over here this time of night, no lights on. This is private property. He's a trespasser. Why take a chance?"

The old man's scared, Lukas thought. *More scared than he'd let on.*

"What'll they do with the body?" he said.

"That's easy down here. Just dump it over the side. Let the sharks take care of it."

"And the boat?"

"Haul it out in the ocean and sink it. No one will know he was ever here."

"And that's it?"

"That's it," Winters said. "He should have read the signs."

FORTY-TWO

DEVLIN BROKE THE surface, paddled toward the base of the pier until he felt sand beneath him. He crawled out of the water and into the tight space where the pier met rock. He lay there shaking, trying to catch his breath.

Thumping footsteps on the stairs above, then the creak of the gate opening. Men came out onto the dock, more of them than before. Their shadows moved across him.

He touched his belt. The Glock was gone.

Lukas shone the flashlight down at the man lying in the boat.

Beside him, Kemper said, "You know him?"

"No." The man's face was distorted from the bullet wound to his forehead. But it wasn't Devlin.

"Anything in his pockets?" Lukas said. Above them, bugs circled the pole light.

The man named Reece held out a folded piece of paper. "Just this."

Lukas took it, opened it, tucked the flashlight under his arm. It was a roughly drawn map of the island, spotted with blood. He showed Kemper.

"What do you think he was doing here?" Kemper said.

"Now we'll never know," Lukas said. He looked at Winters, who was standing behind them, the M110 slung muzzle down.

"I was acting on your instructions, Mr. Kemper," Winters said.

"You were. You did well."

Lukas turned back to Reece. "No ID on him, wallet, anything?"

"Just that paper. We haven't searched the boat yet."

"Coming out here like this, no engine, no lights, no identification," Kemper said. "I think we can take it for granted he meant me harm."

"What should we do with him?" Bishop said.

Lukas turned off the flashlight, folded the paper, and put it in his pocket.

"Bring the Sea Ray around," Kemper said. "Hook this thing up and tow it out past the reefs."

Bishop said, "What about the body?"

"Leave it there," Kemper said. "Put some more rounds in his stomach, so he doesn't swell up and come to the surface anytime soon. Sharks will do the rest. Get the boat out a few miles, open the cocks, shoot more holes in the hull if you have to. Just make sure it goes down. I don't want to see any trace of this mess in the morning."

He turned to Lukas.

"Come up with me," he said. "We have to talk."

Devlin lay back against the rock, listened to the men above him, inches from his head. Shadows shifted across his face. He heard the gate close, then feet on the steps, the sound receding as they climbed. He was alone again.

He thought about the .45 in Chase's chart drawer. They'd be watching the dock now, and there was little chance he could reach the Bayliner without being spotted. Once in the lights, he'd be an easy target. But he couldn't stay here either, risk being seen when they came back for the boat.

Water lapped against the pilings. He tried to remember Chase's description of the island, picture the map. If the house was at the third landing, then it was what, forty feet above him, fifty?

He could try to make it to the boat, and get killed in the process. Or he could go straight at them, climb up to the house, figure out what to do when he got there. If he did.

There was a gap between the rock and the back of the stairway big enough to squeeze through. More space behind it. The rock face here wasn't as steep as on the other sides on the island. It was more a gradual slope, dotted with scrub and vegetation.

A cloud crossed the moon. He sank fingers into thick wet sand, rubbed some on his face and neck. If he could stay quiet enough while he climbed, he might be able to reach the top without being seen.

He pushed his way through the gap, slid behind the stairs, looked up. As the stairway rose, it stood farther out from the rock, to make up for the slope of the land. There should be more than enough room for him.

He climbed.

"What do you think this means?" Kemper said.

He'd turned off the second-floor lights, as if not wanting to present a target to anyone outside. Now he stood by the windows, looking out into darkness.

"I don't know," Lukas said. He could see both their reflections in the glass. Below them, the verandah was brightly lit.

"I feel like I'm in someone's crosshairs, and I don't like it."

He turned to Lukas. "Do you think that man followed you here?"

"No chance."

"Then who was it?"

"He came alone, so he wasn't law. Maybe it was just another thief, come over to see what he could steal."

"Do you really believe that?"

Lukas didn't answer.

"There are too many things in the balance right now," Kemper said. "I can't afford any more risk. Tell Winters I want at least two men on shifts outside, all night long."

Lukas saw lights go on in the boathouse below, then heard engine noise, muffled by the glass. They watched the Sea Ray pull out, running lights on, then pick up speed and head off around the island.

"Tell me," Kemper said after a while. "Did Gordon say anything? At the end?"

"Not much. Something about loyalty."

"He was a wise man in his way. A brave one too. When you found him, at my house, did he know what you were there for?"

"I suppose he did."

Lightning flashed out in the darkness, a distant pulse.

"I'm tired," Kemper said. "And feeling very old tonight."

Kemper turned to him, opened his arms. Lukas stepped forward into the embrace.

Devlin stopped to rest at the second landing. He braced his back against the rock, feet pressed against the inside of the walkway to take the strain off his legs. His wet clothes were drying in the warm air, his sneakers tightening on his feet. His ribs ached, but his breathing was under control, his head clear.

He could hear generator noise not far above him. The smell of cigarette smoke drifted down. They'd have a guard in the front yard, someone to watch the stairway and the pier below.

He heard the buzz of an engine, looked down to see a boat coming around the south side of the island, its navigation lights on, heading for the pier.

He looked above him. Ten more feet, maybe fifteen, would

bring him to the front of the house. He'd stop just below to look and listen, then try to make his way up through the foliage and trees in the side yard, away from the guard. He could use the sound of the generator as a guide, circle around to the blockhouse. He'd have to be careful in the darkness. He remembered what Chase had told him about the north and south sides, the sheer cliffs and the drop.

Chase. Devlin wondered what he would do when he got back to Green Turtle. He could ask at the bar, find someone who knew him, try to track down whatever family he might have left somewhere. Decide what he would tell them.

You're being optimistic, he thought. *You probably won't make it back yourself.*

The thought of Chase, what had happened to him, brought the anger back. *Keep going,* he thought. *Settle this one way or another.*

He turned back toward the rock, reached for a handhold, dug his toes into the sloping ground, and climbed toward the lights above.

FORTY-THREE

LUKAS'S ROOM WAS on the lower level, facing east. There was an air mattress on the hardwood floor, sheets that smelled faintly of mildew.

He switched off the overhead light. There was no lock on the door, just a round hole where the dead bolt would eventually go. Dim light showed through from the hallway beyond.

A sliding glass door led onto a small balcony. He went out and watched flashes of light on the horizon, heard a distant low boom. Standing at the railing, he had a view of the rocks far below, the illuminated boathouse. To his left, the helipad and the verandah. Winters, Kane, and Bishop were out on the observation deck, talking.

He heard the rumble of an engine, saw the Sea Ray coming back around, towing the runabout. As he watched, the two boats headed out to sea and vanished in the darkness, the engine noise fading. He remembered what Winters had said, how easy it was to get rid of a body here.

A breeze blew in. He dragged the mattress across the floor and out of the moonlight, bundled the sheets atop it. Then he raised his jeans leg, reached into his sock, and drew out the steak knife he'd palmed at dinner. It was wood-handled, with a serrated blade. Not much of a weapon, but all he had for now.

He sat in the corner behind the hall door, put the knife on the floor beside him, pulled up his legs, and waited.

The guard on the front patio had an M-16 slung over his shoulder, an automatic on his hip. A cigarette hung from his lips.

Devlin had skirted the patio, come up below a stand of palm trees and casuarina on the south side of the house, away from the lights. Just past the trees was the concrete blockhouse, the generator in there rattling away. A stone path led from the blockhouse to a side door in the main building, about thirty feet away. That door was a smaller version of the ones in front, heavy wood with leaded glass. There was a security light over the blockhouse, but the trees just a few feet away were in darkness.

The guard took a last puff of the cigarette, flicked it away, and yawned.

Devlin moved quietly into the trees. He wasn't tired anymore. Adrenaline drove him forward.

The guard wandered to the landing at the top of the staircase, looked down. Devlin could hear engine noise below. They were towing Chase's boat away.

He left the trees, moving fast, then crouched against the side of the blockhouse, still in shadow. The guard didn't turn.

He could feel the vibration of the generator through the wall. There was a window just above him. He raised himself up, looked inside. Light came through the front windows, showed cables and circuit breakers, a sprinkler system along the ceiling. The generator resembled an oversized air-conditioning unit, with pipes that ran out through the opposite wall.

The window was new, still had the manufacturer's sticker. He put his fingertips against the glass, pushed up. It rocked in its frame, but didn't open.

The guard turned away from the landing. Devlin eased back into the trees, held his breath.

When he began to fall asleep, Lukas stretched out on the floor and did twenty slow push-ups. The rush of blood and oxygen cleared his head, woke him. His side stung, but the bandages were still in place, the wound dry.

He heard the rising sound of an engine outside, went to the balcony. The Sea Ray was returning, faster now, no longer weighed down by the runabout. It slowed outside the boathouse, swung around, and backed in through the open doors. The engine cut off.

Two men left the boathouse, started up the walkway. The only sounds were the muffled generator noise, and faint thunder in the distance.

He went back to his corner, sat, watched moonlight creep across the floor.

He was drifting again when he heard footsteps in the hall. Light and slow, weight evenly distributed, a conscious effort not to be heard.

He took a breath, stood, his back to the wall, knife in hand, and waited for the door to open.

When the guard turned his back and lit another cigarette, Devlin moved quick and silent out of the trees. He locked a forearm across his throat, took him down.

They landed in a heap, the M-16 pinned beneath them. The guard snapped his head back into Devlin's face, jacked an elbow into his stomach. The blow took his breath away, broke his hold. The guard tried to rise, buck him off, bring up the rifle. Devlin got an arm across his throat again, pulled back hard, tightened the choke hold until the guard went limp.

He had to move fast. He disentangled the rifle, caught the ankles of the guard's heavy boots, dragged him facedown into the trees, left him on a bed of casuarina needles. He retrieved the rifle to get it out of the light.

The guard stirred, gasped. Devlin drew the automatic from his holster, pushed the muzzle into his side so he could feel it.

"Be smart and you'll live through this." Devlin kept his voice low. "Do you understand me?"

The guard took a breath, nodded.

With his free hand, Devlin patted the deep pockets of the guard's fatigue pants, found a buck knife and an extra magazine for the pistol.

He kept a knee on the man's back, set the automatic aside, picked up the rifle. The magazine was combat-taped to a spare one, upside down for quick reloading. He released the magazine, peeled off the tape. It was flat black and nonreflective, about ten inches' worth. Some of the adhesive would be gone, but it would work well enough.

He pressed the tape over the guard's mouth, smoothed it down. The guard's eyes widened, and he started to struggle again. Devlin picked up the automatic, put the muzzle to the nape of his neck. "What did I say?"

The guard went still. With his left hand, Devlin began to pull at the lace of the man's boot. It wouldn't come loose, so he took the knife, eased the blade open with a thumb until it locked in place. He sliced through one of the thick laces, pulled it free from its grommets, used it to tie the guard's wrists together behind him. Then he cut the lace off the other boot, bound his ankles. He closed the knife, pocketed it, picked up the automatic again. He leaned close to the guard's ear.

"This is the safest place for you. Stay here, and you'll be fine. You manage to get free, get up, and start moving around, you'll get your head shot off. You understand?"

The guard looked to the side, breathing heavy.

"Show me you understand."

He nodded.

Devlin stood, put the automatic in his belt, picked up the rifle. He'd need a diversion. No telling how many men were posted on the grounds, how long it would take until they realized one of their own was missing.

He brushed sand off one of the M-16 magazines, blew into it to clear the mechanism. He fit it into the rifle's receiver, slapped it home. The spare mag went into a back pocket.

The guard had twisted on the ground, was looking up at him. Devlin worked the bolt to chamber a round, went up to the block-house window, and drove the butt through the glass.

It shattered, collapsed inside. He turned the gun around, fit the butt against his shoulder, aimed at the generator, and squeezed the trigger.

Bishop came through the door first. He moved in fast, raised an automatic, and fired twice at the dark shape of the mattress. Lukas heard the sharp snaps of suppressed rounds.

He threw himself against the door, slammed it into the second man, lunged with the knife just as Bishop turned toward him.

Too dark to pick a target, so Lukas aimed for the face, felt the knife strike flesh and hard bone. Bishop screamed, and Lukas caught the gun with both hands, twisted it from his grip. The knife hit the floor. He shoved Bishop out of the way, turned and fired three times through the closed door, heard a gasp on the other side. The rounds left splintered holes in the wood.

He swung the gun back toward Bishop, now silhouetted against the moon, fired twice into his center mass. He stumbled back and fell out onto the balcony.

Gun smoke drifted in the cylinders of light that came through the door. There was a whimpering on the other side.

Lukas pulled the door open. Kane lay on the floor there, crawling backward. He was bleeding heavily from the side of his neck, trying to stem the flow with one hand. The other held a silenced pistol. He raised it weakly and fired once, unaimed. The round hit the door jamb.

Lukas kicked the gun from his hand, sent it skittering down the hall, left him there to bleed.

The butt of the M-16 punched back into Devlin's shoulder. Sparks flew from the generator as the rounds ripped into its side. He squeezed off another short burst, and yellow and blue flames leaped out, triggered the sprinkler system. Water hissed down. The flames died as smoke and steam filled the blockhouse. He stepped away from the window, waited for someone to come running.

Lukas was halfway up the marble staircase when he heard the gunfire. The lights flickered once and went out.

He raised the gun, waited, then went up the rest of the way and onto the second floor. It was awash in moonlight. He moved away from the windows. He had the high ground here. No one could come at him without being seen.

Gun up, he waited in the darkness.

A man came out the door into the dark side yard, an automatic down at his side, said, "Kirk, where are you?"

He saw Devlin, stopped short. Devlin raised the M-16, fired a burst over his head. The man leaped back into the open doorway, quick-crawled inside, slammed the door shut behind him. Devlin let him go, then fired another round through the top of the heavy glass panel. It would keep him inside, his head down.

Devlin circled toward the back of the house, using the palm trees as cover. To the east, the sky was beginning to lighten.

More gunfire outside. Lukas wondered who was shooting, and at what.

He saw shadowy movement on the far side of the dark room, raised the gun, and fired. The round broke glass somewhere. He heard voices below, running feet. He pointed the gun down the staircase, waiting for a target to present itself. His side ached, and the dressing beneath his T-shirt was wet, the wound bleeding again.

He sensed movement at the base of the stairs, fired, heard a round ricochet off marble.

"Hey," a voice said.

He spun, and Winters stepped out of the shadows on the other side of the room, the M110 up at his shoulder.

Lukas fired, felt a hammer blow to his chest. He tried to raise the gun, felt another blow, this one to his shoulder, went over and down.

The room seemed to spin around him. He couldn't breathe.

Winters came toward him, trying to line up a clear shot. Lukas fired upward, saw him flinch. Another round from the M110 gouged the floor near his face. He gripped his right wrist with his left hand to steady the gun, kept firing until the automatic's slide locked back empty.

Winters dropped the rifle, took two drunken steps, and fell backwards down the marble stairs.

Lukas tossed the gun away, tried to stand, couldn't. He touched his chest, felt the blood-soaked T-shirt, tried to process it all calmly. *He hit you at least twice, but you're still breathing. You need to compress the wounds, stop the bleeding, get some kind of dressing on them.*

Then, from outside and below, came the roar of the helicopter's engine.

Devlin came out onto a patch of ground just above the verandah, saw the two stairways and the helipad below. He heard the crack of gunfire inside the house, saw muzzle flashes in the windows above him. A cluster of shots, then silence.

Engine noise below. The helicopter was starting up. It coughed exhaust, and the rotors began to spin. He could see the silhouette of the pilot inside. The rotors picked up speed, raising dust from the pad, and the helicopter began to tremble, ready to lift off. To the east, the sky was a paler blue. Dawn coming fast.

A sliding glass door opened on the verandah, and two men came out, started down the steps to the helipad. It was Kemper and the guard from the side door, the one Devlin had driven back into the house.

He brought the rifle to his shoulder, aimed it down at the stairs ahead of them, leading them slightly, slid his finger over the trigger.

FORTY-FOUR

LUKAS CRAWLED ACROSS the floor, pulled the M110 to him. It was slick with Winters's blood.

He dragged himself to the wall. He was weak, dizzy. *You've lost a lot of blood*, he thought. *You may not have much time. You need to finish this.*

He braced his back against the wall, forced himself to stand. He coughed, tasted blood, spit it out.

Through the windows, he saw Kemper and Reece on the stairway to the helipad. Kemper slow, Reece trying to hurry him along and shield him at the same time. They reached the pad, stooped to avoid the spinning rotors.

The M110 had a second magazine taped to the first. He reversed them, fed in the full clip, worked the bolt, and stepped back from the center window. He raised the rifle and fired four times. Glass exploded out onto the verandah, rained down on the flagstones. What was left of the window collapsed in its frame. A cool breeze blew in around him.

He unclipped the night scope and shroud, tossed them away. He wouldn't need them.

Devlin watched the two men going down the stairway. He tracked them with the M-16's front sight. *Easy to do it,* he thought. *Squeeze the trigger, end any threat the old man might present to him or anyone else in the future. Pay him back for all he'd done. For Bell, for Colin. For San Marcos. For all of it.*

He aimed at the helicopter, his finger tight on the trigger. The two men reached the pad, ducked under the rotors' blur. The guard got Kemper up into the right side of the cockpit, leaned in to help secure his seat harness. Then he backed away, staying low, gave the pilot the thumbs-up. It was a two-seater. He knew there'd be no room for him.

Devlin let the front sight drift over the pilot, Kemper beside him. Easy shots.

He steadied the rifle, held the sight on them. Then he eased his finger off the trigger. He wasn't killing anyone. Not today, at least.

A crash of glass, and one of the windows above the verandah splintered and fell apart. There was a man standing there, framed in the empty window, aiming a rifle.

The helicopter began to rise.

Lukas inhaled, tucked the rifle butt into his shoulder, looked through the scope. He watched the helicopter hovering, its skids a few feet off the pad. He centered the crosshairs on the cockpit, let his breath out slow, and squeezed the trigger. The gun kicked back, and concrete dust puffed off the helipad. Reece threw himself to the ground, elbow-crawled toward the hangar.

Lukas adjusted his aim, fixed the crosshairs again, squeezed the trigger once, twice, three times, the gun thumping into his shoulder. The helicopter seemed to falter in its ascent for a moment, then put its nose down and sped out over the water. He watched it go.

*   *   *

Devlin saw the helicopter climb, sunlight glinting off its canopy. From above him came the sharp cracks of the rifle. The helicopter picked up speed as it headed out to sea, toward the rising sun, its shadow trailing across the surface of the water. It climbed higher, then began to lose altitude and bank to port. The pilot tried to right it, get the nose up. Devlin pictured him in there, fighting with the controls.

The helicopter made a long, slow, graceful arc, and hit the water at a forty-five-degree angle. Spray exploded around it, the rotors chopping into the water. One broke off and flew away, skipping over the surface. The helicopter flipped onto its back, skids up, and began to sink nose first. The silver tail rose up above the waves, the rotor there slowing, then stopping.

The tail seemed to hang there, straight up out of the water, all that was visible now. Sun flashed off the metalwork. Then it slipped below the waves and was gone.

Lukas lowered the M110, watched the helicopter go under, the glint of the sun on its tail as it sank.

The rifle was heavy now. He let it slip from his hand to the floor. Then he sat down amid the broken glass and spent casings.

The room was filled with red sunlight. The breeze coming through the empty window frame had warmed. He turned toward it, closed his eyes, felt the sun on his face.

Devlin went in through the side door. There was a narrow hallway here, stairs. He went up with the M-16 at his shoulder, finger on the trigger, came out into a big empty room.

A man sat on the floor near the window, a scoped rifle across his knees. The T-shirt he wore was soaked through with blood. His eyes were closed. More blood on the floor, a trail of it that led to a marble staircase. Another body halfway down.

Devlin aimed at the man by the window, moved closer, saw it was the one who'd attacked him at the motel, who'd murdered Roarke and the others. Who'd gone after his family.

The man opened his eyes. Devlin kept the front sight locked on him. "Are you Lukas?"

The man gave a weak smile, shifted slightly, but didn't try to raise the rifle. Wind moaned through the window frame.

"You," he said. "I should have known." He coughed, and there was blood on his lips.

"Put the weapon down," Devlin said. "Slide it away."

Lukas's hand went to the rifle's pistol grip, his finger into the trigger guard. Devlin took a step closer. Glass crunched under his sneakers. "Put it down."

Lukas coughed again, wet and deep. His finger curled over the trigger. "If you were going to shoot me, you'd have done it already. I don't think you are."

"Don't..."

"Too bad," Lukas said. He reversed the rifle, put the muzzle under his jaw, and pulled the trigger.

FORTY-FIVE

EVLIN STEPPED BACK, lowered the M-16.

"Is he dead?"

He turned, swung the rifle back up. A man was standing at the top of the marble stairs, his hands raised. The guard who'd gotten Kemper into the helicopter.

"Don't move," Devlin said.

"Believe me, I'm not."

Devlin nodded at the pistol on his hip. The man drew it out by its butt, set it on the floor. He looked at Lukas. "He dead?"

Devlin recognized the voice. It was the man who'd complained about having to board Chase's boat, search the body.

"He is." Wind rolled the shell casings on the floor.

The man cocked his head toward the shattered window. "They didn't make it."

"I saw."

"You think he hit the engine or the pilot?"

"I don't know. Maybe both," Devlin said. He felt tired, leaden.

"You don't need to worry about me. I'm hired help. This is just a job."

"What's your name?"

"Reece."

"Are there any more of your people around, Reece?"

"I don't think so. I think they're all dead."

"You all worked for Kemper?"

"We did."

Devlin pressed the magazine release, shook the rifle once. The clip fell to the floor. He pulled back the bolt, ejected the chambered round, then took the closed buck knife from his pocket.

"One of your buddies is in the trees by the side of the blockhouse. Tied up. You better go cut him loose." He tossed the knife.

Reece caught it, looked at him. "Who are you, anyway?"

"I'm one of you. At least I was."

Reece backed away, gave Devlin a last look, then went down the side stairs.

Devlin dropped the rifle. The room was full of light, and the sounds of wind and water.

Devlin drove the Sea Ray. Reece and the other guard, whose name was Kirkland, sat on the rear bench seat, sharing a joint Reece had produced from a cigarette pack. Kirkland was shivering, wrapped in a blanket from the house. He looked at Devlin with something between anger and fear. But the fight had gone out of him.

"I wonder if we'll still get paid this month," Reece said.

Devlin looked at him. "If you want, I'll take you back there. You can hang around, find out."

"I'll take a pass on that." He held out the joint. Devlin shook his head.

There were other boats out, the water calm and flat. Devlin kept his speed down, steered to the southwest, Green Turtle Cay in sight. Reece had shown him on a chart how to find Kemper's private landing, said he had the keys for a Land Rover parked there.

Kirkland said, "What will happen to them? Back there."

"Someone will find them," Devlin said. "Sooner or later."

He thought about Chase, what they were leaving behind. Reece had told him about Farrow, what Lukas had done. *So much death*, Devlin thought, *and for no good reason.*

"What about us?" Reece said. "What do you think we should do?"

"Make yourself scarce," Devlin said. "Get out of these islands as soon as you can, however you can. Cover your tracks. It'll take them a while to work out what happened. There's a good chance they never will."

He'd wiped down the M-16 and its magazine before leaving the house. His prints were nowhere else. As soon as they'd left the boathouse, he'd dropped Kirkland's automatic and the extra magazines into the water. He didn't need a gun anymore, didn't want one.

Reece took a last draw on the joint, pinched it out.

"I think I need a new profession," he said. "Something safer. And indoors."

Devlin drove on, the sun at his back.

He had them drop him a half mile from the marina, walked the rest of the way.

The *Higher Tide* was as he'd left it. No police on board. No customs officials or Bahamian constables demanding to know where he'd been, what he'd done.

He unlocked the hatch and door, opened them to air out the cabin. He knew he should leave as soon as possible, head back to the States. But the fatigue was on him hard now.

He went below and crawled into the forward bunk. If anyone came for him, they could find him here.

In seconds, he was asleep.

*   *   *

When he woke, the cabin was filled with moonlight. He got up, threw water on his face in the sink, then went on deck.

The marina was 1 a.m. quiet. He could hear faint music and television noise coming from some of the boats, but the pier was empty.

He unplugged and stowed the power hookup, cast off the lines, started the engines. Reversing out of the slip, he turned on his running lights. Once in the seaway, he steered northwest, opened the throttle, and felt the engines respond. Soon, the lights of the island were out of sight. High above, the moon was the color of bone.

FORTY-SIX

AFTER SHE DRESSED, Tracy made coffee, brought the mug outside. It was 9 a.m., the grass still damp, a low fog in the woods.

The uniform in the New Hope cruiser was talking on a cellphone. He looked at her, and she waved to let him know everything was all right. He went back to his call.

The rental Honda the insurance company had given her was parked alongside the house. She leaned against the fender, got out her cell, checked her messages for the fourth time that morning. No missed calls. She scrolled down to Devlin's number. Her thumb lingered over Redial.

The phone buzzed alive. She almost dropped it, spilled coffee as she fumbled it to her ear.

"You sleeping in?" Alysha said.

"Just getting organized. Heading out soon."

"Be ready to work. Things are hopping."

"What?"

"Word from D.C. is at least three senators are going to call for a select committee to investigate Unix and its government contracts. Maybe a special prosecutor as well. Twenty minutes ago, a fax came through from Harlin's office. He's suspending his reelection campaign. My bet, he resigns by the weekend."

"Let me guess. To spend more time with his family."

"His words exactly. You'd think they'd have come up with a better go-to cliché by now."

"Dominoes," Tracy said.

"Falling fast."

"Anything new from Virginia?"

"Eric says still no sign of Kemper, and he's not the only one looking. Said the house was crawling with law—state and federal. He couldn't get past the gate. Any word from Devlin?"

"Not yet."

"Farrow and four of his men turn up dead, and our guy's in the wind. I wish I were as confident as you those two things are unrelated."

"Doesn't feel right. Something else was going on there. I don't think he was involved."

"Think or hope?"

"Both." Wishing she felt as sure as she sounded.

"Rick says if he doesn't turn up, one of us needs to go down there and look for him."

"In Florida?"

"Yeah. I told him in that case, it should be you. Any other angles you can think of we should be chasing?"

"I gave Dwight Malloy the Bahamas address we found. I felt like we owed him something. Or at least I did. He said he'd pass it on."

"My guess is the feds will send someone down there. Why do I feel none of this is going to end well?"

"Your unerring reporter's instincts. Tell Rick I'm on my way."

In the car, her phone buzzed again, a number she didn't recognize. She put the call on speaker.

331

"Hello? Is this Tracy Quinn?" A young woman's voice.

"It is."

"Hi, Tracy. This is Samantha Battle from Action Ten News? Great stories this week. We're doing a spot on our five-thirty, following up on Unix Technologies, and how it's connected—if it's connected—to those shootings in town a while back."

"You should be talking to Alysha Bennett," Tracy said. "She's the main reporter on the story now. You can reach her at the *Observer*."

"I've tried. She wasn't very cooperative."

"Keep trying," Tracy said. "But I don't think I can help you."

"Actually, what we're most interested in is your own story, of how you were attacked. What you wrote is just so compelling. I'm sure our viewers would love to know more. Could you come down to the station today, talk about it on camera? It would be great exposure for you."

"Not interested. But thanks."

"We can take care of transportation and any—"

"No, really. Thanks, though."

"Can I ask why?"

"I just don't think I'm up for it."

"Why are you print people so hard to get along with?"

"Excuse me?"

"We're all on the same team, aren't we? Why do you always act like you're better than us? No wonder newspapers are failing."

Tracy had to laugh. "Samantha," she said. "You have no idea."

By 10 a.m., the *Higher Tide* was back in its slip. Devlin was exhausted, but too wired to sleep. He activated his phone, saw six missed calls, five from Tracy Quinn. The sixth was a local exchange, a number he didn't know.

He got Quinn's number on screen, hit Callback. She picked up on the first ring.

"You're alive," she said.

"More or less."

He could hear voices around her, ringing phones.

"When you go missing like that," she said, "you get people worried. Especially me."

"Sorry. Decided to take a little trip. Didn't know I needed permission."

"A trip? In the middle of all this? This broke big, in case you didn't see. Just about every media outlet in the country's been calling us. Has anyone tried to contact you?"

"Not yet. But I think I'm done being a source for anyone for a while."

"This thing's nowhere near over."

"Maybe it is, for me."

"You don't get away that easy," she said. "I've still got a cop parked outside my house at night."

"Can't hurt."

"Are you in Florida?"

"Why?"

"Don't disappear on us again. You need to stay in touch."

"I will. You know how to reach me."

"And don't do anything foolish."

"Too late for that," he said.

After they disconnected, he clicked through to his last voice mail. It was from Dr. Stefano at the walk-in clinic on Singer Island, asking him how he was, reminding him to come into the office to go over his X-ray results and blood work. He touched his shoulder. Soon he'd have another scar to show her.

He got the Percocets from the galley drawer, popped one with a palmful of water. It felt like a deep ache had settled into his whole body.

He went down into the bow bunk, stretched out. As he started to drift, he thought again about the doctor. What was her first name? Deandra. He remembered her perfume. Something like violets.

FORTY-SEVEN

W HEN SHE FOUND Devlin, he was on the deck of his boat, shaking ice into a cooler. Two days since she'd spoken with him, her calls going right to voice mail. She'd caught an early flight from Philly to West Palm that morning, picked up a rental car, and driven to Riviera Beach.

"You should answer your phone," she said.

He squinted up at her on the dock, shook in the rest of the ice, closed the cooler lid. "Sorry."

"Surprised to see me?"

"Not really." He brushed ice from his hands. "How'd you find me?"

"I'm a reporter, remember? You said you'd stay in touch. I took you at your word."

"What can I do for you?"

"We're still looking for Roland Kemper."

"Can't help you with that."

"They found four bodies on an island he owned in the Bahamas. But not his. Has the FBI contacted you?"

"No, why?"

"They're assisting the Bahamian police. If you haven't heard from them yet, you will."

"It'll be a short conversation. I have nothing to tell them."

"Anything you want to tell me?"

"Like I said on the phone, I think I'm done with all that."

A woman came out from the cabin. "Ray, where's the—" She stopped when she saw Tracy. "Oh, I'm sorry. Hello."

The woman was a little older than her. Long black hair with a streak of silver. She wore shorts and a halter top.

"Hi," Tracy said.

"Tracy, this is Deandra. She's a doctor. Deandra, this is Tracy. She's a reporter."

"A reporter," the woman said. "That must be interesting."

"Every minute of the day," Tracy said. "You going on a trip?"

"Just a run down to the Keys," he said. "Sorry I couldn't help you more."

"You know I don't give up that easily, right?"

"I do."

"We're still working on this story. And you're still part of it."

"Maybe," he said. "But not today."

"I have your cell number. And if you change it, I'll find your new one."

"I don't doubt you will."

Tracy looked at the woman, then back at Devlin, and said, "Safe travels."

"You too," he said, and then she turned and walked back to her car.

Devlin watched her go, knowing everything she'd said was true, that he hadn't seen the last of her.

"What was that all about?" Deandra said.

"Nothing to do with me," he said. "Not anymore."

*   *   *

Tracy got back in her rental. *All this way for nothing*, she thought. Maybe she'd try to get down to the Bahamas, do as much reporting from there as she could. She needed to regroup, think it through.

On the console, her cellphone began to buzz. When she answered, a woman said, "Is this Tracy Quinn?"

"Who's this?"

"My name's Amanda Dutton. I'm from the *Washington Post*, and I—"

"I don't think I can help you," Tracy said. "And anyway, the person you want to speak with is Alysha Bennett. You can reach her at—"

"No, actually it's you I'd like to talk to."

"Why?"

"Sorry, I should have been more clear. I'm the *Post*'s senior editor for Recruitment and Development. We'd like you to come in, meet with a few of our editors, maybe talk about some job opportunities."

"Job opportunities?"

"Yes, we've been following your work in the *Observer.* I can't promise anything, but we'd like to talk at least, see if you might be a good fit here. If you're interested, that is."

Tracy said nothing.

"Hello? You still there?"

"Yes."

"Thought I'd lost you for a moment."

"No," Tracy said. "I'm still here."

"Can we schedule a visit for sometime next week? What day would be good for you?"

"Any day," Tracy said. She felt herself smiling. "Any day at all."

Devlin steered the Pacemaker out of the inlet, headed south. Deandra sat on a deck chair, her eyes closed, face turned toward the sun.

The port engine started to miss. He gave it a little more throttle and the noise faded. The sky was cloudless, the water calm.

He thought about Bell, waiting on the dock for him, the day it had all begun. Roarke at the bar, the look in his eyes when Devlin had first walked in. Chase on the boat as they headed out to the island, moving silently over the night sea. All of them gone now.

"Everything okay?" she said.

He turned to look at her. She was watching him.

"Something crossed your face," she said. "Like you were someplace else for a while. Someplace bad."

He shook his head. "No, I'm right here. Where I want to be."

She sat back, closed her eyes again. "This is nice."

"Yes," he said. "It is."

ACKNOWLEDGMENTS

Many thanks to Josh Kendall, Nicky Guerreiro, Reagan Arthur, and everyone else at Mulholland Books/Little, Brown for helping me bring this one home. Thanks also to my agents, Robin Rue and Joel Gotler, for their patience and support.

ABOUT THE AUTHOR

Wallace Stroby is an award-winning journalist and the author of seven previous novels, four of which feature Crissa Stone, the professional thief dubbed "crime fiction's best bad girl ever." His first novel, *The Barbed-Wire Kiss*, was a Barry Award finalist for best debut novel. A native of Long Branch, New Jersey, he's a lifelong resident of the Jersey Shore. Visit his website at wallacestroby.com and follow him on Twitter @wallacestroby.

You've turned the last page.

But it doesn't have to end there . . .

If you're looking for more first-class, action-packed, nail-biting suspense, follow us on Twitter @**MulhollandUK** for:

- News
- Competitions
- Regular updates about our books and authors
- Insider info into the world of crime and thrillers
- Behind-the-scenes access to Mulholland Books

And much more!

There are many more twists to come.

MULHOLLAND:
You never know what's
coming around the curve.